IN THE GREAT QUIET

IN THE GREAT QUIET

A Novel

LAURA VOGT

LAKE UNION
PUBLISHING

Published by Lake Union Publishing, Seattle
www.apub.com

Material from *Land in Her Own Name: Women as Homesteaders in North Dakota* by H. Elaine Lindgren used by permission of North Dakota State Press. John Joseph Mathews material from *Wah'kon-tah: The Osage and the White Man's Road* (University of Oklahoma Press, 1981) used with permission by the Mathews family. John Lewis Solomon quote via original public domain letter, dated 1879.

EU product safety contact:
Amazon Media EU S. à r.l.
38, avenue John F. Kennedy, L-1855 Luxembourg
amazonpublishing-gpsr@amazon.com

ISBN-13: 9781662535307 (paperback)
ISBN-13: 9781662535314 (digital)

Cover design by Richard Ljoenes Design LLC
Cover image: © Mary Wethey / ArcAngel Images; © Em Levesque, © hanshan97, © YRABOTA / Shutterstock

Printed in the United States of America

for the women

my grandmothers
the women of my Hays family

HISTORICAL NOTE

Where the Indian passed in dignity, disturbing nothing and leaving Nature as he found her; with nothing to record his passage, except a footprint or a broken twig, the white man plundered and wasted and shouted; frightening the silences with his great, braying laughter and his cursing.

—John Joseph Mathews, Osage writer and historian

When I landed on the soil, I looked on the ground, and I says, this is free ground. Then I looked on the heavens, and I says them is free and beautiful heavens. Then I looked within my heart, and I says to myself I wonder why I was never free before?

—John Solomon Lewis, Black homesteader

Oh, I was anxious to go. I don't know but I just had a feeling I wanted to get away from my former home and go out in this world. All I had was a desire to go and I did.

It was not so easy.

—Christine Larson Tollefson, female homesteader

History, even though people might tell you otherwise, is an unstable, amorphous science. It's perspectives, theories, even dreams.

My background is in the history of mentalities, a specific approach to cultural history that uncovers how those of the past looked upon their world. I love to dig into *how* people saw their environments. I'm especially drawn to microhistories and chasing down the meaning of odd moments, little glimpses into the past that contradict the version of history I have in my head. Above are three different voices, three different perspectives of the Oklahoma land rushes of the 1890s. For some women pioneers, such as Christine Larson Tollefson, homesteading was an extravagant gift. If they could just be brave enough, could just race fast enough—they could have land, of their very own, at a time when women had little autonomy. *In the Great Quiet* is the story of my ancestor, my great-great-grandmother Minnie Hoopes, and her journey into the unknown. Though this narrative is rooted in my own heritage, I must make it clear: Hers was one point of view and, often, a broken one. The land rushes are grounded in so much darkness.

Colonization is built upon brutality toward the Indigenous. The history of frontier settlement and the forced removal of Native tribes is full of lies and distortions, displacement and unspeakable violence. The fundamental concept of westward expansion is shocking and atrocious. While researching, I was continually gutted reading accounts of the horrors inflicted upon Indigenous people. Minnie's story is positioned from another lens—a sometimes problematic one—but her vantage point, nonetheless. The displacement and violence enacted on Native populations must not be overlooked.

In my research of homesteading women, I most enjoyed reading primary documents, such as journals and interviews. There are many rich accounts of pioneer women full of gratitude and hope, along with terror for life alone on the frontier. These stories, ripe with vivid emotion and wide-ranging adventure, all the iconic expansiveness and hazards of the Wild West, are where I situate this narrative of my family.

The tale you'll read is fiction. But a true woman of our past, Minnie Hoopes, lives again in these pages. She was my grandmother's grandmother, and this is her story as I've dreamt it.

Welcome on in, reader. I've a story for you.

AUTUMN

September to November 1893

Caldwell, Kansas

Boundary Line of Oklahoma Territory

September 16, 1893

almost high noon

It begins with the earth.

She says,

Once, they listened for my voice. With the crash of dawn over the horizon, they'd press their palms against my skin, wet me with their tears. A swipe of soil across the brow, a crumble of my body in their palms, my cinnamon-red hue as sacred as blood. Once, I was cherished. But that was longago.

Today, I scream, and you do not hear.

Today, I'm brittle and fragmented and so thirsty I spit out coughs of despair and ash. You call it dust storm, drought, famine. Today, your storytellers speak of a hunt. I feel your wheels scrape into my skin, wagons collapsing my throat, hoofbeats stomping along my spine. Then—alone in the wild distances something begins. Across my body, women speak. Memories intertwine, forward and backward, across eons, the reality of one ancestor blending with the truth of another: a new history of women arriving.

Once, the prairie was quiet and I was alone. But that was longago.

Time continues to turn, around and around I spin. Today, I will tell you such tales. Of women who drove cattle dressed as men and women who swallowed thunderbolts as newborns. Women determined, women lost. Women seemingly ordinary, women larger than life. Some women recorded in the annals of history, others told as fireside lore.

Settle in, listen. I have stories to tell.

CHAPTER ONE

Sometimes I wondered if I was too comfortable with the dark passageways within me. If I knew those secret, unlit spaces too well. But shadows don't bother me overmuch. And sakes alive, no one was honest with themselves anyhow, everyone creating their own aliases. The Kid, Wild Bill, Bitter Creek, Rose of Cimarron. I didn't have a summer name yet—but perhaps by sundown.

I jerked my wrist, checked my watch. Ten minutes till high noon.

The crowd was the colors of black, smoke, fire. The prairie gingerroot, ash, clay. Fifteen thousand souls vibrating in their skin, bodies sweat slicked with anticipation. In moments, gunshots would blast, and the race would begin.

I wrought Cricket's reins and leaned forward in my saddle. Soon we'd gallop into the unknown frontier—I'd flee past and grasp something new. One hundred and fifteen thousand pioneers had registered for forty-two thousand homesteads, at least that's the tale that went round twilight bonfires. Wretched grum odds. It was told this race tempted the darkest of humanity, those with the most greed, with the most chilling stories, and come nightfall, half would drag north again, dismissed back to their haunted, hungry lives, their daisy-printed skirts trawling behind them in the red dirt. Today the quickest, the harshest, the most lawless would win. But today, women had a chance.

How much longer? Seven minutes.

The cowboy beside me gnawed tobacco, hips slouched in his saddle, stallion's shoulders bony. I didn't believe his nonchalance: His fists twitched with anxiety. Blistering sunbeams struck through the clouds of dust to burnish the wooden handle of his Winchester. Like me, he'd tied his supplies about his racehorse: a tin pail clanging against a frying pan, a Colt revolver strapped beside a sack of oats, a white claim flag snapping in the wind. I paid little mind to what his flag said. But mine was stamped, in red the hue of paintbrush wildflowers, with my name: Minnie Hoopes.

The cowboy spit. Curled his lip at me.

I winked back.

"Where's your husband, doll?"

"Buried that mouthy feller in the ground. Dug the hole myself," I said.

He sneered and looked away.

Wasn't true. I'd never had a husband nor murdered him, but I didn't have patience for such an attitude. Cowboys like him bullied women like me, those who sought their own homestead, those unmarried or widowed, divorced or deserted. And, on that matter, I wouldn't be marrying anytime soon. As I'd then forfeit my land to my husband.

Maybe the cowboy was a bank robber or horse thief. Or perhaps a cattleman looking to gobble up some land to sell before the summer roundup. And he was one of *thousands*. I'd never seen anything like this swarming crowd of coal and umber before. There were blacksmiths and bankers, gospel preachers and tight-jawed widows, formerly enslaved folks and even one dapper gentleman wobbling over the cracked earth on a bicycle. And of course—criminals of every kind.

It'd been a fiery, impatient summer. Water had run dry a while ago. Supplies had dwindled. We were hot, thirsty, barbaric. A drought and an economic depression, the Panic of 1893, swept across our country. And true enough, panic hovered over the crowd like a fog. But as for me, I'd experienced desolation. There was no way in all-fired creation I'd go back to Kansas. What actually terrified me, those nights under the starlit sky waiting for the Strip to open, was myself. What *wouldn't* I do to grasp my own future?

Storytellers prophesied that today began a new age. An era unlike any before: desperate, wrathy, full of havoc and ruin. Plain speaking? Today would be an all-overish disaster. And yet, in the mayhem, I didn't observe disorder and brutality. I saw possibility. I'd always relished the annihilation of control. I'm not saying I approved, just saying what was.

I glanced at my wristwatch. Five minutes.

Behind me, thousands of covered wagons clamored with unruly children, chattering chickens, moaning cows. A mother sat on the bench of her prairie schooner, a fabricated smile static below her crisp poke bonnet, a basket of fruit clutched between her hands, a bawling toddler gripping her skirts. Around me crowded a flock of buckboard wagons and buggies. Before me, a smudge of roughened cowboys and criminals cloaked in black vests and Stetsons, leaning forward over their racehorses. They stretched for miles along the boundary line, their jackets a long smear of graphite across the muted soil. Soldiers maintained the line, hands resting on their rifles. And beyond, our prairie.

The expanse sloped to an unending horizon. A vast sweep of bone-colored pastureland strewn with craggy grasses and clumps of red soil; the meadow shades of gold and saffron and crumbled redwood. The earth, bursting with stories. The land, rumbling with sound.

I sipped from my canteen. The tea leaves failed to mask the foul-awful, salty taste of the water. In a buggy beside me, my older brother Willie patted his brocade waistcoat, searching for a smoke or the time, his other hand clasping the horses' reins. He caught my gaze, and his face split in a wide grin full of teeth and mischief and premonition. On the bench beside him, my eldest brother, Ezra, glowered at the boundless universe before us, his whip clenched in his fist. Willie gossiped with the folks next to us, making pals along the way, as he always did. Those sweltering weeks camping before the territory opened, I'd hauled barrels of water from the creek to sell for twenty cents a ladle, while Willie had charmed a circle round town, collecting friends and whiskey. And Ezra, well, he'd scowled at the skyline and yelled at the sun to get moving.

My brothers sought broad ranges suitable for crops and cattle, hopefully miles and epochs away from my own claim. Rather than a barren patch of grassland, I'd scouted rolling fields, nestled up to a wandering creek and flanked by a wildwood. Weeks ago, we'd raced across the Strip, training our horses and determining our route. Beneath the prismatic summer sun, I'd pressed my black ankle boots into the dry clay and eaten from a bramble of sand plums. I'd found an isolated space, perfect to breed my horses. I yearned, desperately, for somewhere faraway, with clear water trickling by.

Wind lashed hair across my face. Minutes now.

And then the hollers and shuffling vanished—even the horses held their breath. It was a quiet distinct from anything I'd known before. The hush eerie and unsettling and somehow full: heavy with hope and longing. I slipped my fingers along Cricket's buckskin withers, hummed a reassurance to him.

The crowd tugged toward the prairie, awaiting the distant boom of the cannon. I untied the bow clasped round my throat and dragged the navy gingham of my bonnet across my face, swiping off layers of dust and sweat. I shoved my hat in a pocket and swallowed, breathless.

One minute.

A wail sounded behind me, some babe unaware of the gravity of this moment. The cry shot shivers down my neck. The roar of the wind ebbed, abandoning us to silence. A pause. I felt on the edge of my own story, tottering between known and unknown. I gulped soil-flecked air, leaned forward, gripped Cricket's black mane, my heart thrashing against my bones.

Boom.

A thunder of hooves, a riot of gunfire, the cannon's echo haunting the length of my spine. I kicked Cricket, and we shot forward.

The crowd roared with hollers and whoops as we galloped downhill. Dust surged in a thick red vapor. The sound unfamiliar, a combustion of flesh and cloth, sweat and expectation, like the reverberation of thunderclouds.

Buckboards jolted and coughed. Wagons crumpled, wooden limbs strewn about the dirt.

A stallion reared, legs kicking at the dust cloud, panicked. The rider held on, face ashen, veins bulging on his forehead. Then he was thrown backward, tossed to roll about the prairie, surely now trampled to death. Before me, another horse collapsed.

I jerked Cricket's reins, avoided the calamity.

Behind me, my brothers' buggy shattered across the terrain—but they still followed. Those on racehorses shot ahead, the schooners fell behind, and a mist of carmine and brown swelled between. The wind tasted of dirt and minerals, of the deep mysteries lost in the underneath. Below, the ground throbbed with hoofbeats. The earth pulsed, as if we shook a heartbeat back into the dying land.

A spoked wheel busted in the gorge of a buffalo wallow: The buckboard rattled, then crashed. I gripped Cricket with my thighs and leaned into the swelling clouds of earth. Nothing seemed solid. Just sound and motion. Everything a nebulous whirl, carbon and ash and copper and the white of claim flags flashing like starlight, the dust blurring this moment to something like a delusion. This race etched itself over my past, redefining all that came before. I recognized it would become a pivot of my life, separating after from before.

Round the fires, folks whispered of what horrors might come on this day, of what some might stoop to in pursuit of their greed. Robbery, assault, murder. In this territory, my natural lawlessness would have value. This was a day where you needed to lose control, to be comfortable with those hidden corridors of your flesh, to explore your own darkness. I didn't know my limits nor what I could live with.

What I knew? I wouldn't be going back north, and I had no idea what I'd do to stay. I'd never much respected rules. And that was what scared me. Not prophecies of blood or ruin, but my thirst for so much, for everything, for something of my own.

CHAPTER TWO

I plucked at my split riding habit, the skirts sunk in the creek, the white hem now a sodden smear of amber clay. Sure enough, the race had hardly begun before my brothers' buggy crashed.

Willie crouched beside the half-submerged wheel, his ostentatious fringed chaps soaking in the mud, his fingers clawing at an imperceptible fracture in a spoke. His grip slipped across the sludge. He was already half drunk, the day long from over.

"Well now, I'll just rip this spoke off, hammer another on, and we'll be a'going." Willie pushed back his flop of hair and knocked his hat into the muck. "Damnation."

Ezra shoveled mud away from the wheel, his tweed waistcoat straining across his stocky frame. As always, Ezra said nothing.

"That'll take too long." I puffed out some air.

After the cannon boom, rushers had spread in all directions, covered wagons lagging, racehorses dashing away. The roar dimmed, and I could hear isolated sounds now: the echo of distant gunfire, some pa berating his child, the clink of a metal cup in a barrel. Nesters waded past through the gully and climbed the rise. If we didn't get out of this creek bottom, them bastards would steal my land.

Before me, the spindle of an oak chair sank in the mire—my brothers' buckboard overflowed with unnecessary supplies. If we'd just tied our provisions about our horses and left the cursed buggy in Kansas, like I'd argued all summer, we wouldn't be stalled. I'd almost ditched my brothers last week to join Annetta Daisy and her community of women. Bonfire lore went that in the run of '89, with revolver shoved in her waistband and stake in hand, Daisy leapt from a train, staked claim, and reboarded before the train passed on by. Supposedly, she'd held on to her homestead despite a gun battle. And rumors went that she'd help any woman file and stake claim: they just needed a six-shooter and a horse. But I hadn't left my brothers. Supposed I wasn't up for friendship. So here I was, stuck in a swamp.

Willie sighed and stood, hands pressed to his back. "It's a doozy, the broken wheel."

"It's not broken, just stuck in this abyss." I yanked a shovel free of its ties and cleaved the blade through the clouded water. "Just dig, alright?"

A cowboy swung off his black mustang and thrust out his hand for my tool. Mud splashed the front of my skirt. Sunlight slashed behind his hat—golden skin, roughened from sunlight and dust, stretched across a square jaw.

"What in thunder you doing?" I swatted at a cloud of gnats. "Go on—get after your own land."

"Minnie," Ezra warned.

I rolled my eyes and kept working.

"You reckon you'll survive all on your own?" The cowboy's voice was rich and deep.

"I can take care of my own damn self," I said.

He stood there, considering me. His face held no expression, just crisp, green eyes.

I pressed back the tendrils of hair fuzzing from my twist. "Look here, cattlehand, I don't have time for this." I gestured between us. This wasn't the occasion to battle for the biggest toad in the puddle. I'd duel cowboys when land was at stake.

The cowboy tipped his hat. "Ma'am," he drawled.

He vaulted onto his mustang, and his thighs turned the beast upstream. I plucked my sweat-soaked blouse away from my collarbone, then spun back to the buggy. Willie hovered, jaw slack, his spade drooped at his side.

"Blazes, Willie—why aren't you digging?"

In a crate on their buckboard, the white wings of chickens flapped. "That feller," Willie said, "him there—"

"What?"

"That's the Lawman."

I faltered, sludge sloshing around my calves. That cowboy was the notorious, cold-blooded gunfighter, the one gossiped about fireside? No one knew what he'd done, but he'd spooked the Dalton Gang. Whispers said he'd betrayed them. Or something else gruesome and deranged. Apparently the Lawman crafted his own law, doing whatever he felt suitable, no matter how diabolical.

"You know, the renegade Bitter Creek and the rest of the Wild Bunch avoid." Willie snorted. "Don't get us shot before we even get a spread."

The outlaw scaled the rise, the muscles in his shoulders tensing and adjusting beneath his charcoal vest. Well, I reckoned that was what an outlaw looked like. The type of human who'd slit your throat or burn you alive just to steal your land.

"Lawman," I hollered.

He rotated, his bearing easy, subdued.

"Don't take 'em rolling hills by Crooked Creek," I called. "It's mine."

A vein beat on his jaw, but he paused. Why wasn't he frazzled like the rest of us? His energy was slow and controlled, like a warm, oozy summer mudslide. Well, I supposed if you were cozy with bloodshed or robbery or whatever anarchy this untamed land tempted, well then, there wasn't need to rush.

His voice carved across the brook. "You do realize this is a race?"

I blew at my hair, flicked my hands for him to move on.

"Ride quick." He galloped up the hill, his mustang's glossy, black mane frothing in the wind.

The outlaw was right: I must hurry. Fixing the rig wasn't working. My brothers started quarreling about how to fix the buggy, and I was stuck, digging into the mud, waiting on their decision, while gunfighters and widows grasped all the claims. Growing up, my younger sister Magnolia and I had always planned to homestead. Long years racing through tunnels of wheatgrass or lazing about springtime wildflowers, watching clouds scatter on by, dreaming up what could be. We just knew someday we'd strap our supplies about our horses and go. My parents had chased their yearning for wide spaces and adventure, leaving family and decorum back East and finding a homestead on the Kansas plains. Pa, with his unbreakable pioneer gumption, and Ma as gardener, caretaker, shepherd. She wouldn't define herself as a tenacious explorer—but that was the woman I'd watched.

I'd learned that while a woman couldn't own much, if she had enough grit, enough determination, she could homestead. Four years ago, during the sworling excitement of the first land run, I just knew—I must go. And now, here I was, headed into the unknown. Finally ready to stake my own claim, waiting on my foolhardy brothers. My fingernails dug into the shovel's wooden handle, the metal tip submerged in the mucky creek. Beyond the rise, the wide sky arched. The color a watery, purpled brown like saltmarsh asters, a plume of smoke bubbling against the burnished horizon. Another prairie fire.

During the long nights waiting for the Strip to open, the smoke of a thousand campfires smudged the sky. My brothers and I strung up canvas tents below a sweet gum tree, where spiny balls scattered the ground and exasperated my back through my saddle blanket. I'd wake and wander into the open, toss my blanket cross riddled dirt, and watch the stars slip round the firmament, those faraway sparks crisp, then fuzzy and indeterminate.

Memories of home flickered in and out like starlight, crisp moments, then fuzzy and faraway. Bygone places. The swampy creek, where quicksand grasped my knobby childhood ankles, gilded leaves floating down in autumn, the cloudlike tufts of yarrow in springtime. The faroff pasture beyond the thicket where fireflies buzzed through summer grasses, hazy cottonwood seeds floating on by. The live oak bough that swooped over the yellow milkweed, where Magnolia and I would sprawl, reading aloud tales of Calamity Jane and Belle Starr till dark shifted over the meadow, something lavender and indistinct hanging about the air. When we couldn't quite see day any longer, we'd wrench up our skirts about our calves and race home for supper.

As we camped along the border of the Strip, the night sky seemed quiet and faraway, the childhood memories clogging up my thoughts idyllic and fanciful. In the end, Magnolia hadn't come along to homestead. She'd married instead. Under the starlight, I sifted through my memories and couldn't determine anymore what had been real. The stars sharpened white, then blurred to gray. When I thought into my future, I saw a world altogether different from what I'd once imagined. There was the vast prairie, my calico skirts snapping in the wind, summertime flowers blooming in the evergreen shadows, and a far-ranging quiet. It was better this way, to start a new life alone.

In the swampy rivulet, my brothers still arguing, the scent of burning woven into the atmosphere, I knew it was time to leave. "Your plan is dumber than a sack of hammers." I tossed the shovel at Willie and vaulted onto Cricket. "I'm leaving."

"It's barbaric out there." Willie's grip on the shovel slipped. "You, by yourself—"

"Alone, on my own homestead?" I said. "You know I'll handle whatever comes my way."

Willie groaned and rubbed his face, his palm dripping translucent brown creek water onto his mustache. "You're fixin' to catch yourself an alias, like Little Britches or the Bandit Queen."

"Mayhem Minnie?" I gulped water from a canteen. "I'll snatch my land. You two, yours. Meet at the land office at sundown."

Ezra wiped a fleck of soil on his pocket watch with his handkerchief. "Shouldn't be off on your own, anyhow. Women, owning property."

"Just watch me." I clicked to Cricket and turned upstream, done wasting time.

A gust of wind slapped my face, cold where silt coated my skin, and as I climbed the rise, I felt bygone days drop away.

CHAPTER THREE

As Cricket galloped, a red froth blurred the space between his ankles and the earth. The sunburnt expanse of bluestem grasses stretched and stretched until prairie faded away. I saw not a soul, yet I felt the press of bodies, rushers scrambling throughout the land. Cricket vaulted over a dry creek bottom, then leapt over a knee-high line of flame. We were close to the claim I'd scouted—half a mile, perhaps.

It was hushed, alone in the wide unknown.

My life before chattered with voices. In the stillness, remembrances of moments bursting with noise settled over me. Growing up, it'd been the three of us dashing across the prairie: Magnolia and me and our neighbor Lark, a boy born the month after me. Lark, always with some new shenanigan; Magnolia with her eager goodness; and, off yonder, the muted tones of my parents and brothers. That first autumn day, after Magnolia's birth parents had passed on from the grippe, I'd sat on the bough of an elm and waited for my orphaned cousin. My scraped, six-year-old knees pulled against my chest. Lark leaned against the trunk below, his boots crossed at the ankles, the mahogany leather worn and unlacing from the soles. He pushed off the tree and rocked forward, then back onto his wooden heels, tiny puffs of dust clouding, his energy never containable.

Our buggy rolled up the path. Black lace shadowed Ma's face, mourning for her sister and brother-in-law. Pa halted the wagon, and Ma lifted Magnolia, her toddler face blanched, petal-pink dress dingy and torn along the hem. I'd expected a baby, eyelids swollen and red, but the line of Magnolia's profile was elegant, her demeanor almost serene.

"Her hair's so shiny." I picked at a scab on my elbow, scowled at Magnolia's glossy, blond ringlets.

Lark bumped back against the bole and pulled apart the length of an oat stalk. Ma lowered Magnolia to the grass and clasped her tiny hand, leading her uphill. Ma palmed the sway of her own back, realigning her posture.

"Why isn't she crying?" I asked.

Lark tossed the stems away and grinned up at me, his smile quick and lopsided. "I've some burr acorns we can shove beneath her quilt."

I scooted to the edge of the branch, readying to hop down, when Magnolia tripped and collapsed into nettle. She pushed herself up, eyes wide, face white—but she didn't cry. The sugarberry canopy above her swayed, scattering shadows and light across the grass, and a bucketful of yellow leaves cascaded down. My heart tumbled in my chest, and I just knew: I'd forever care for Magnolia with everything that was within me.

"No."

"Alright," Lark said, "suppose we could—"

"Look at her." Ma scooped Magnolia up and slipped inside our home, Magnolia's tiny pink fingers clutching Ma's sleeve. "She's so delicate."

Lark rocked back onto his heels. "Yeah, she's a baby."

I swung from the branch. "We protect her. No matter what."

Lark shoved at his tawny hair. "Sure enough."

"Promise. None of our usual nonsense and horsefeathers." I swept bark fragments off my hands with a loud clap. "She's ours now."

I'd held out my palm for our secret handshake. He took my hand, and ever after it'd been Lark and Magnolia and me exploring our little realm, dreaming of what could be beyond. But then they'd both chosen to stay back in Kansas. Now it was only me, headed into the frontier.

A copper pot rattled against my long gun, Cricket's shoulders rippling with sweat and movement. I pressed my calves against his flank as we darted into a thicket of blackjack oaks. Brambles clawed my hair, and sunbeams got tangled up in the canopy. Below, a luster rippled in the taupe water of the stream. I was so thirsty, but first I must stake claim. Cricket's hooves crunched over a layer of walnuts, and deep in the forest was the blur of scarlet hawthorn apples, the silver bark of a hackberry, the gnarled twist of a mock orange. This land could sustain me during winter. Most nesters would starve, freeze, or just plain wither under the tumult of the prairie wind. Without time to plant crops before winter, my horses and I needed access to food and water if we'd survive until spring.

Beyond the woodland, the earth swayed in slopes and rises. Eastward, the prairie lifted to a hillock perfect for a few cows. I glimpsed no one—this prairie could become my home. Most claims were a stretch of sandstone red dirt. The meadow here was cider and fawn, ivory and the deep emerald of evergreen. There were scrubby wild grape bushes and holly berries, and under the glow of Oklahoma sunshine, all imaginable shades of gold.

I withdrew my claim flag: the linen coarse in my palms, ends thrashing in the wind. A surveyor's cornerstone marker sat between a ragged thistle and some wild oats. I charged forward, flag thrust high. At the stone, I vaulted off Cricket, pulled my stake from its rope fastenings, and jammed the pole into the ground. It didn't budge a fingernail into the hard, dry earth. I yanked off my iron skillet and pounded and pounded and pounded until the rod finally sank into the soil.

My hands shook as I tied my flag to the stake. The russet lettering rippled in the wind, a proclamation stamped into the fabric:

This claim is taken by
Minnie Hoopes

My heart thumped, my breath expanded. The weight of time along my forearms, the tug of legacy at my back.

I spun. Strands of hair scattered across my cheekbones and stuck to my eyebrows. I pushed them away. I could build my house snuggled against that embankment. It'd be warm, the blackjacks barring the torrent of wind. And there, in that patch of sunglow, my horses' barn. A southern orchard, perhaps a glossy orange sapling sprouting toward the sky. From horizon to horizon, an expanse of my own. I'd done it. I'd braved this brutal race and claimed my future.

Beside my flag, I dug into the soil with my shovel, the ricochet against dry earth reverberating up my arms. All the women of my heritage, none had owned land. I thought of my ma, in the dawn light a month earlier, as I'd tightened my last saddlebag onto Cricket. She'd placed her pocket-size Methodist hymnal in my palms, the embossed leather worn, her hands cupping mine. *Ma, you sure?* She carried that hymnal in her apron every day, humming low in her throat as she worked, sometimes cracking open the spine, lips pursed as she flipped the pages to her song, her timbre a crisp prayer resounding through the sagebrush. *Take a breath every now and then,* she'd said and drawn me into a hug. *Write home when you can. And make sure you tell the Lord about your adventures every day.* She'd squeezed me round the shoulders, then let go, her black boots stepping back a pace, beyond the shadow of my silhouette.

After digging a couple of feet into the earth, I untied a few boards from my saddle and tossed them cross the hole, fashioning a makeshift cellar, some evidence I'd improved upon this quarter section. Battles over land ownership could be overlong and brutal. I jogged to Cricket and brought my nose to his soft, soot-black muzzle. "We did it, old buddy." I mounted, and with one last glance at my flag snapping in the wind, we galloped to check the other three corners of the claim, to make sure no one else had beat me. But I knew this was my land. I'd gotten here first. A gleam of afternoon gold brushed over the field as we checked the markers—none had been claimed.

Down in the creek bottoms, I drank and filled my canteens. I lay in the water, submerging beneath the surface, cleansing, reviving, and then we rode back through the gilded land, and I swear, the power of the earth pulsed below Cricket's hooves.

The ground shuddered and groaned as if awakening. Perhaps a norther blustered through the meadowflowers. Maybe a stampede approached from afar. Or perhaps my land had come alive to welcome me.

I swung down and walked through fiery red grass, drenched skirts dragging behind. I pushed aside the braided layers of stiff, pale groundcover until I found the dirt. Pressing into the soil, my finger pads felt the warmth of the earth. "Hello," I whispered.

It was quiet. The rush of the wind, the faint song of a meadowlark, some guttural gunfire faroff, but no brothers, fathers, neighbors. I'd heard of the isolation, of the deep loneliness of homesteading life. But I hungered boundlessly for space. To be rid of remembrances and begin anew. I pushed up, wiped my palms on my skirts.

Time to hurry onward to the land office. This was still a race, after all. I jogged back to Cricket and grasped my saddle pommel—then hesitated. An all-overish quiver of disquiet shot up the back of my neck.

Something had changed.

I lowered my boots back to the dirt. Unease spread across the expanse, like ink in water. I swiped a palm across my forehead, unsure.

And then I smelt it. Warm and deep, the scent of winter's end.

Fire was coming.

CHAPTER FOUR

Beyond my rolling hills, along the edge of the horizon, spread a line of orange. The blaze careened forward; two cowboys silhouetted the glow. They must've set the fire, supposing it'd chase me off. I squinted—was that brawny one the Lawman?

Cricket reared, tendons contracting on his neck. I grasped his bridle. White sclera was visible below his amber irises, wrinkles tented above his eyelids. "We're fine." I rubbed his nose. "Hold on to your boots."

I must start a backfire. With my hunting knife, I sliced off a branch from a hazel shrub, then dug in my satchel for matches.

The box was damp. I cursed and struck the lucifer. Nothing. Struck again. Nothing. The wind pummeled southeast, which would draw the wildfire straight to us. During a drought, with a strong wind, a prairie fire could flare past in minutes, devouring everything in its path.

I struck the lucifer on the box, struck again. And—finally, the match burst. After lighting my hazel branch, I raced to the hilltop and studied the bearing of the wind, the oat-colored grasses tossing about in discord. I lit the grass before me.

A feathery plume of fountain grass caught. The red-orange ember glowed, and then the flame expanded, blackened waves unfurling, ready to ravage. I gauged the direction of my backburn. The blaze burnt true, upwind and straight toward the oncoming fire. I swept my hazel brush in a strip before me, igniting the grasses and honey mesquite bushes along the cusp of the hill. Fire tumbled down my branch, the entire stalk almost ablaze. Heat singed the hair on my forearms. I moved along my line, creating a burnt refuge, my backfire creeping down the hill with crackling flame, wind roaring across the prairie. The springtime fires of years past had echoed with voices. Lark rushing up and down the line, jittery with enthusiasm; Magnolia poised below her bonnet, her gaze focused on the burn; Pa hollering instructions to Ezra; Willie cursing as he burnt himself.

I tossed my branch into the flames, yanked up a stalk of dried thistle, and sliced off the prickly edges. Around the stalk, I looped a nightgown and wetted the fabric with my canteen. I dumped my other canteen onto my necktie and pulled the doused cotton over my mouth. Then I squared my shoulders and battled flame. My fire behaved well, slithering down the slope, but here and there it burst backward. I stomped and swung. My shoulders ached; my hands throbbed. Smoke sank into my skin, clogged my breath, but my fire fell back. My fire would fight fire.

A few knolls away, the headfire loped across the plain at unbelievable speed, gobbling up all the colors and nutrients of my land. The flames rose as tall as a wood grove. Fingers of crimson reached outward, as if to grasp me, as if the hunger and greed of this race had infected the flame. I recognized the wildfire's frantic need to devour, its inability to harness control. But I hoped I never again was that destructive.

Once my fire had burnt a couple of feet of blackline, I grasped Cricket's reins and stepped onto the charred earth, the coals hot against the soles of my boots. I knelt at the hill's divot, tugged Cricket toward me. He jerked his head, eyes wide in terror and pain, but he didn't run.

The oncoming fire boomed like a thundering locomotive. I pressed my knees into our refuge, the ground searing the white cotton of my skirt, the embers blackening the tiny bluebonnets growing along the fabric. The fire a column of red and bronze, violet and cobalt shadows, wisps of ochre and mustard. We were surrounded by flame, the wildfire roaring and snapping, my hair sizzling, the swarm of heat suffocating.

And then, after a moment engulfed, the terror surged past, racing on to devour whatever next fell into its path, its hiss dimming and dimming until I could again breathe.

Flakes of gray drifted onto my shoulders: ashes floating in smoke. I tugged the damp fabric off my mouth, swept the cloth over my face. The white cotton coiled in my palms, covered in soot. Somehow I knew my life would never be free of ash again. I fingered the ends of my hair, walnut-brown strands dappled by smoke and chalk.

The wildfire had burnt roots and branches, scars and memory. The sky above transformed into gunmetal-tinged clouds of smoke, as if the earth had exhaled a puff of exhaustion, and then something murmured up from the deep. I felt whispers.

It was like the earth groaned.

I toppled backward into the debris. I needed air and water. The fire had stolen my senses and left me dreaming. I held my temples, inhaled, and stood. I must continue.

I strode to my saddlebag, my body full of smoke, my bones sluggish, and yanked out my Winchester. Trained the barrel on the horizon.

Like a ghastly mirage, through the haze, the cowboys perched atop a slight incline, slumped back in their saddles. I didn't have time to battle robbers—I must race to the land office before anyone else. After such a fire, they'd expect me to be weak.

But fire was a cleansing, an uncovered hope. I felt remade. Who knew what I was capable of after such an attack?

A grin cracked across my face—brittle, dark, dangerous.

CHAPTER FIVE

Through the cloud of dust and ember, the cowboys charged across the field. The butt of my rifle rested on my shoulder, the barrel trained bullseye on one rider. It wasn't the Lawman. The robber was gaunt, eyes cruel, skin taut across cheekbones, a garish red bandanna tugged up over his mouth. Fellers thought the colorful handkerchiefs added flourish. I thought of blood.

A pulse of rage banged in my palm, and my finger tremored on the trigger. I wanted to shoot. I wiped sweat from my brow with my forearm, smearing layers of gritty charcoal. I didn't know what other horrors they'd stoop to—but no one was taking this land from me. I steadied my rifle, widened my stance. But, damnation, I couldn't just pick them off. If I killed them, if I was convicted of any crime, I couldn't stake claim.

The other cowboy was that spiraling, wayward sort, as if his veins pumped whiskey instead of blood. His clothes rumpled, posture languid, expression carefree, as if he couldn't even care that he'd just attempted murder. They were close enough. I tipped my rifle skyward, fired a warning shot. I opened the breech and loaded another shell, then focused my Winchester on Red Bandanna. His nostrils flared, but he pulled up on his reins.

"You sons of bitches burn my land?" I hollered.

"Nah," came a graveled voice. He cantered closer and yanked down his bandanna, spit out some tobacco. "We want this claim."

"Get off my land."

"Now, now," said the drunk, "we just wanna chat."

I worked the lever on my rifle, chambering the round.

Their horses' flanks quivered; streaks of sweat dripped between the dust. Bandanna swung off his stallion, and before I could decide whether to shoot, I heard a notch. Well, damn.

"Gots ya down my barrel," the drunk drawled. "I'm a fair shot."

I'd been so focused on Bandanna, I'd forgotten to watch the other. If I picked off Bandanna, the drunk would shoot me.

"Sugar, just get gone." Bandanna sauntered closer. "You obviously can't survive uncivilized territory. Leave before the situation gets nasty."

"*Gets nasty?* You all-fired burnt my land." On my gun, my palms were slick. "I will shoot."

"Call it off, bitch. You know you're beat."

I swallowed smoke, my hands shook.

Bandanna darted forward and grabbed me. I jerked back, threw a hook. He yanked my arm, knocked my rifle away.

"No one's taught you how to be a woman yet?" His breath was damp and acrid, like spoiled potatoes. "You bend."

Horror smeared in my gut. This man was everything reprehensible about the frontier.

Clamping my arms, he yanked my revolver from my holster, tossed my gun away. I elbowed his gut, stomped his boots. But he shoved me to the ground, the earth smoldering with ashes. His body pressed over mine—I spit, kneed him. I smelt the burnt, the hollow, the ripeness of endings. His hands were everywhere. Bile squeezed up my throat. I couldn't get free, couldn't grab my push dagger from my boot. I slammed my head against his chin. A punch cracked across my face.

The drunk laughed. He'd unbuckled his pants. I gagged. Humanity was an awful, all-nature tragedy. My hands were crammed atop my belly. I edged my fingers toward my skirt pocket. The cowboy pulled down his britches, tugged at my skirts, the bluebonnet-dotted linsey-woolsey tangling between my legs. "Dratted riding skirts," he muttered.

I unfolded the spice packet, slipped my fingers inside.

His palm spread across my face and shoved my skull into the ground. As he pulled back, to get at my waistband, his vapid sneer showed between his sprawled fingers. I yanked out my hand and gouged cayenne pepper into his eyeballs, smothering the spice.

He yowled and fell backward.

I yanked his Peacemaker from his holster, shot the drunk clean between the brows. Bandanna slumped off me, clawing at his eyes. I cocked the hammer, pressed the pistol to his rib cage, and pulled the trigger, the gun smacking back against my chest.

He shuddered forward—the horrid weight of his body toppled onto mine. His blood soaked me. Something like a sob scattered through my body, oozed beyond my throat. I couldn't breathe. I tried to yank my legs free, press out from under him. My head slumped back against the earth; hot tears seared my eyes. I could do this. I shoved him off with a grunt and scrambled back, away from his body.

I pressed my hand to my mouth, felt the stickiness of blood. I'd killed. I stood and walked to the drunk, my steps slow and surreal, my leather boots somehow shiny against the dull coal of the land. The horses stamped and whinnied, antsy from the gunshots and the still-scorching ground. The white stripe down a thoroughbred's trembling nose was flecked with ashes, his nostrils puffing. The drunk had tumbled down a mound, his face smashed into soot. I kicked him over. His face was slack and numb. Dead.

Red seeped from the bullet hole; the haunting coil of crimson trailed along his forehead and plopped onto the dirt.

This land was gutted of its history. It had felt like everything was beginning again. Now anguish and death sank into the soil. Now I had more secrets to bury below ashes.

Cayenne pepper smeared around the eyes of the man who'd tried to rape me, into his hairline, down his cheeks. His face had lost its tension. Wobbly lines, the tracks of tears, streaked through the red smudge. How could someone force their evil on others? Greed, desire, want—those compulsions permeated this race. But there was something distinct between my ambition and theirs. I wanted something of my own, while these men wanted to steal and destroy. Already the battles over land were more brutal than I'd imagined. And yet I still longed to continue, to build a life on the frontier, to remake this world into my own.

I stepped forward and shot the rapist in the head for good measure. The black hole was stark against the chalky smear of cayenne.

My legs wobbled. My ankles spasmed. I threw his gun aside.

I wanted to crumple into the cinders, take comfort from the earth, from anywhere, but I must dispose of the bodies. I could burn them, as smoke wouldn't be conspicuous today, or I could bury them in that woodland. Across my land, the wind stirred up dust: White and black flecks fizzled in the rolling fog. A wave rumbled underfoot. I bent and dug through the coals to check for an oncoming stampede. The ground was warm and soft. A thump, like a pulse pumping blood through the land, struck my finger pads. The beat felt ancient. Something hidden under groundcover and soil, sunk deep in the memory of the earth.

I fell to the ground, gripped my forehead. I was woozy and shaken, my body stuck between turmoil and survival. The rhythm throbbed, a clattering like thunder. That wasn't a stampede, wasn't my land communicating—

Hoofbeats.

I clawed through the bluestem to clasp my pistol. I aimed my six-shooter northward, scrutinized the haze. This time I'd shoot. I'd already battled a wildfire and slain two men—I'd do whatever I must to protect this land.

The hoofbeats were just beyond the rise. I prayed that my bones would stay steady enough that I wouldn't spiral beyond my body.

CHAPTER SIX

A man charged over the rise, his shoulders leaning into the charcoal vapors. A shudder clawed up my body as I gazed down the barrel of my Peacemaker. My hands shook, palms slippery, calves tight and watery. I rubbed my handkerchief on my skin, wiping off ash and sweat and viscera. A dingy vermilion smear shadowed the hollow of my palm. It wouldn't erase. My throat felt stuffed, as if my body held back a scream. I didn't know how I'd ever move on, let alone face this next calamity. But I must. There was no other choice.

Wind shattered across the plain, saltgrass tossed in disarray, the cowboy dashing over the smoldering prairie, the world moving too fast, while I felt frozen in time. Soot clouded before me—I swatted away fragments and thought of a moment from long ago. I'd been perhaps nine, out in the south pasture, Magnolia off aways gathering dewberries, when a man had crept from between a strand of bitternut hickories. I'd reached for the rifle slung across my back, ill ease weaving up my neck. I'd screamed, the shrill rasp of my voice snapping across our farmland. The man had scrambled away, his stride tilted, his expression peculiar. In moments, Pa had swept up on his tobiano mare. *Sweetheart, what's wrong?* After I'd told him, he hadn't made me feel foolish, instead had reminded me to always trust my gut. Today Pa was faraway.

The gunslinger cut through the fog, only a few rods before me. He sharpened into focus, and I faltered backward. *The Lawman.*

"This is my land," I said, determined to sound strong and in control.

The Lawman glanced at the cowboys. The wind whipped, funneling onyx fragments around his form. His gaze slid to mine. "Clearly."

"I will kill you."

He swung from his mustang, boots echoing along the lowland. I cocked my gun, fingers wooden. The Lawman pressed his fingertips against the drunk's pallid wrist, his gaze snagging on the cowboy's loose britches. His scowl deepened. Unbothered by the pistol I trained on his body, the Lawman strode through the haze to check the other man. He didn't seem surprised or rattled by the carnage, his preternatural ease chilling.

I should shoot. Coal-black and fog-white remains dusted my hands; cardamom and ruby smeared across my fist. The Lawman hadn't threatened me. Killing him would be murder, plain as day.

He turned, palms raised, and slowly advanced toward me. "You okay?" His voice, low and thick, like clogged honey or sarsaparilla syrup.

I sank my teeth into my lip, kept the barrel trained on him. The Lawman took off his hat, scraped his fingers through his hair. It was a warm black, as if the sunlight had been only brave enough to barely brush the strands. His hair waved and tufted around the bones of his face.

"I'm not going to hurt you." He looked northward, squinted, the muscles on his neck taut. "I claimed the one-sixty just north."

The hell-fired gunfighter was my neighbor? Well, damn.

"I informed you this creek is mine," I said.

"Don't think you can claim the all of it."

"Maybe," I said, narrowing my eyes.

He flexed his fingers, as if trying to appear less intimidating. He didn't realize: I'd learned, long ago, to trust no one. Folks would either fail you—or betray you. That was just the way the world spun.

The Lawman pressed on his hat, adjusting its position by the crown. "Heard the shots."

All nature, of course others would've heard. Wouldn't be long until someone else galloped up. I scanned the smoky horizons. I must dispose of the bodies, straightaway.

"What will you do now?" the Lawman asked.

I wiped the back of my hand across my forehead. "Drag 'em into those north woods. There are wolves, right?"

He bent and grabbed a body. Was that an agreement to step beyond the law? He was a notorious bandit—surely he wouldn't snitch. But I didn't want to be indebted to anyone, let alone a renegade. "Wait." I lowered my Peacemaker. "No."

He gripped the drunk's shirt.

"I'm obliged to no one," I said.

He released the cowboy and crossed his arms, bootheels firm against the ground. He swept his gaze the length of my body. The attention of an outlaw should've made me uneasy, but his inspection felt scientific and well mannered. It was as if he cataloged me, recognized another lawless soul. For that was what I was now—an outlaw.

I crossed my arms, mirroring him. "I don't trust you."

"No one said anything about trust, darling."

He bent, hefted up the drunk's body, tossed it cross a horse.

"I said no." I followed him. "Do you listen?"

His brows lifted—course outlaws didn't listen to a two-penny woman. I shoved my pistol in my holster and strode toward the other body, clasped my hand round his wrist, tugged. The Lawman didn't offer to help, just went about tying the cowboys' horses together and binding the drunk to a saddle. I yanked and dragged the lifeless form through layers of ash until I was before his horse. I hauled him up with a grunt, his back pressed to my chest, arms hanging limp. The Lawman took his feet and tossed the body across the horse.

I met the Lawman's gaze. Then a wolf dog spit from the switchgrass—I jolted. The hound sat beside the Lawman and pawed at his muzzle.

"What is that thing?"

"My dog," he said, his tone implying an added *you imbecile*.

He looped rope around a body and tightened the knots. "Surviving the frontier will be brutal."

I shot forward, gripped his tie, the cotton flecked with silver ash. The hound leapt up and snarled, but the Lawman clicked low in his throat and the wolf dog eased.

"Preach to another choir, Lawman. No one hurts me."

"You actually think you'll survive winter?" he said. "You've tangled yourself in a few quagmires already."

"Don't belittle me. I will—" I scanned his bearing, the shape of his face. His irises were chips of peridot, vibrant in the brume. "I will slaughter you in your sleep."

"Alright, Minnie. Calm yourself a smidge."

He'd noted when Ezra said my name. And remembered. But he couldn't use my alias—in my new life, it was crucial that no one drew close.

"Amelia," I snapped. "No, wait. Miss Hoopes."

"Really?" He squinted at me, as if dumbfounded by my sudden grasp at propriety.

"And I'm calm." I let go of his knot and lowered my heels to the earth.

"You sure about that?"

"Well." I wrinkled my nose. "I'm not sure I value *calm*."

"Alright." He straightened his vest placket and swung onto his horse.

I took the rope lead from him, then led the cowboys' horses to Cricket. Like a charcoal sketch, scraggly bushes sprouted here and there, the plants now only a layering of ash. They'd crumple in the next gust of prairie wind. Cricket's eyes were glassy and fixed on the burning. A tremble quaked across his barrel. I grasped his bridle, looked into his eyes. "Hush now, old buddy," I murmured, then mounted.

I kicked my heels and pummeled toward the forest, the elms and sycamores and vines a black swarm of unknown. The wood looked haunted and alive, like it could swallow my secrets whole. The other horses jostled over the furrows, unsteady and creaky, the rope abrading my palm. Beside me, the Lawman leaned into the wind, atop his inky-black mustang, galloping fast enough to keep up with me, his wolf racing beside him. We pummeled through the trees, the branches clawing my skin through my overblouse, until we stumbled into a slight clearing. I swung off Cricket, tied the horses to a cedar, and yanked my shovel from its ties. I needed to rid myself of the bodies and dash to the land office—somehow the race went on.

A sumac tree winged before the glade, the leaves evolving from summer's green to autumn's flame red. I wobbled on a shard of shale, and a briar grasped my skirts. As my bootheel sank beneath the topsoil, an illusion soaked across the copse, of a woman burrowing through hawthorn briars, bramble snagging in her long dark hair, evergreen thorns slicing her thighs. The dappled sumac leaves melted backward in time to the scarlet flowers of springtime. The mirage flickered, then slipped away.

I heard a scrape and a rasp. The Lawman dug into the earth below the expansive roots of a water oak, his shirt rolled up over his forearms. I blinked, disoriented. Then I freed my sooty, floral skirt from the thorns and stepped deeper into the woods.

The ground appeared to wobble, as if the earth wanted to remind me that she was alive. I swiped my handkerchief across the back of my neck, the rhythm of the Lawman's shoveling unbroken. This day had depleted me of all sense. But as I slammed my blade into the parched dirt, I wondered what else was hidden in this wildwood, wondered who was buried deep in the earth. Linking back through time, others had lived on this land. Other lives, forgotten underground, their stories lost.

After tossing the cowboys' bodies into the chasms we'd dug, I removed their gear and slapped their horses' flanks, setting them free. From their bags, I looted some ammo and pots and a worn copy of *Ivanhoe*. I burnt the rest.

I thrust a pistol and a few saddle blankets against the Lawman's charcoal vest.

"You'll be alright?" he asked, straightening a cartridge bandolier across his chest.

"You do realize this is a race," I said, tossing his words back at him as I vaulted onto Cricket. "Ride quick."

And then I dashed westward toward the land office, the leftover blazes smoldering, a haunting sound calling out after me. A deep, primordial groan knotted in with the wind, the rhythm pulsing almost like words: *Settle in, I have stories to tell.*

CHAPTER SEVEN

The prairie grass before the land office swarmed with red-faced farmhands and thin, disheveled families. I wandered in search of my brothers, the crowd muttering of illegal deals and claim jumpers and the sooners who lurked in bushes. I just knew something would go wrong. I gripped my scattergun's handle and didn't flinch.

I found my brothers before a bonfire, Willie toasting the sunset. They'd staked claim to neighboring homesteads a thirty-minute gallop from my quarter section. Close enough to help build shacks or dig cellars, but far enough that they wouldn't interfere with everyday chores—I'd see them every few weeks or so. If they noticed my burnt clothes and all-overish disheveled appearance, they didn't comment. Ezra just scowled at the brume smeared along the side of my palm. Willie pulled me into a Virginia reel spin, our boots stomping a circle round the dusty ground. From the edge of the crowd, Ezra pressed his square thumb across his record book, crisping the paper flat.

Bonfires and disputes rose throughout the night, and then, at sunrise, I filed claim. Dipping the pen in an inkwell, looping my signature, the image of my scrawled name on paper visceral and sharp, the new memory rewriting over all those of my past. *Section 1, Township 26N, Range 8W*—that square quarter mile was mine.

In the afternoon, south of the new Enid townsite, my brothers and I rendezvoused with Pa and Lark's dad for the rest of our supplies. Sweat swamped in an arc across Pa's rough-spun shirt, and when he spotted me, a broad smile broke across his face. I swung from Cricket, and he tugged me into a hug, his gaze sweeping me, surely assessing if I was altogether unharmed.

"I got my own land, Pa," I said, the tension in my body easing a moment.

"God above, I'm so happy for you."

As I roped Cricket beside my other horses, Whiskey and Whistlejacket, my brothers and their buggy clattered up in a flurry. Pa congratulated them, heard tale of the pastures they'd found. Beside the buckboard I'd packed with my chest and other necessities, Pa tightened a knot rigging my Belgian draft horse Smallhopes to my buggy. After I finished loading up, I thanked Pa for hauling down my supplies. He clasped my shoulder. "You still got my push dagger in your boot, the one you stole when you were twelve?"

My fingers clenched the ledge of my wagon, as an image scrambled my thoughts. My palm slick on the Peacemaker's walnut grip, the chalky texture of cayenne pepper on my fingertips. The awful shape of the cowboy's face; the squeaky, guttural cadence of his voice; the splatter and gush of his blood. That faded red bandanna, misted with dust and wrinkling at the stitches. Pa considered my posture, tapping the tortoiseshell pocket watch clipped to his vest placket, the beat sounding with a ting. Pa never missed much. I shuttered away horrors of the rush, the texture of the cowboys' blood still a faint stickiness on my palms.

"Your brothers say you're off aways on your own." Pa's eyes pinched at the corners. "But that's what you wanted? You're sure-footed?"

"I've got your push dagger." I swallowed. Straightened the bridle across Smallhopes's jaw. "I also stole your buffalo-horn '73 Peacemaker."

He chuckled and squeezed my shoulder. "Proud of you, sweetheart. Be safe."

We bade each other Godspeed: Pa headed north to Kansas, I journeyed to my claim, and I hadn't seen hide of the lot of them since.

Six long, hot days of solitude.

I'd glimpsed the Lawman through the trees, thrashing across the fields on his mustang or slamming his shovel into the parched dirt. Reckoned I should have been frightened, having such a neighbor—but I didn't have room for worry. Supposed I'd lost that somewhere between the cannon boom and the prairie fire. I'd snuck through the wildwood a few times, studied the way the Lawman designed his camp, and the man wasn't a fool by any stretch. But other than those moments, my days were sky and horizon and distance.

Everyone told that life on the frontier would be desolate, with long winter nights stretching into oblivion. Most would fear the far-reaching stretches of quiet and this notion of isolation. And sure enough, No Man's Land was vicious and unexpected. My days had been filled with steamy, backbreaking work establishing camp, my nights long and musical under the sparkling black arch of an autumnal sky, a deep quiet with just the brush of my horses' tails against my tent and the ongoing prattle of crickets. But in all these moments, I didn't feel alone. There were so many voices on my land. The squeak of wind through branches, the clack of my horses' hooves on hard ground, the rustling in the grasses, as if the earth narrated something to me. I felt surrounded, comforted even, by what lived on my land.

Today a storm foamed along the southern horizon. Smallhopes and I galloped up a black hill, the wayward ash rising about her flanks, her powerful legs a burnt cinnamon that faded to alabaster below her knees. Dew wet my forearms, and mist singed my teeth. The air cold and wet, as if the rain was already here. We cantered over a rise, and in the lowland, my ramshackle camp came into view. I'd hung some waxed canvases between stakes, and there, with my horses and the unrelenting wind, I'd made a home.

I angled my thighs, guiding Smallhopes around the fiery scarlet sumac tree. I needed to run Whiskey and Whistlejacket as well before the rain. On my homestead, there was much to prepare, endless days of work. I'd foraged for berries and nuts and shot the prairie hens that wandered about. Tomorrow I'd plant potatoes and perhaps the following morn, if rain softened the earth, I could dig my cellar. And I must build a one-room shack, or dig one into the hillside, before snow dropped from the sky. I patted Smallhopes's withers to slow her down and vaulted off. Soon I would let her go—the bartered goods from selling my horses would be crucial to surviving winter. I rubbed Smallhopes's bare back and led her under the drooping canvas. Afternoon light seeped through a length of black fabric and glowed navy on my hands as I tied her to a stake. I threaded a simple rope bridle onto Whistlejacket, my blue roan mare. "Your turn, honey."

I wondered what my mother, my grandmother, all the women of my heritage would think of me creating a space of my own. I would have to spend five years proving up, establishing a homestead on this quarter-mile section, and then this land would be mine.

Faroff, rain clouds darkened toward midnight, inked shadows smudging the base of the clouds. I itched to grasp a piece of charcoal and sketch the storm, to capture that feeling of impending rain after a season of drought. I tilted my face skyward, and then, almost imperceptibly, a fizzle brushed across my cheeks.

Rain was coming.

I lifted my hands, and the damp shivered across my palms. I mounted Whistlejacket and plunged again into the great unknown.

~

Whistlejacket and I dashed along the ravine, a storm rumbling from beyond. After such frenzied days racing and establishing camp, the stillness was surprising. There was a deep sense of hush. An ease and a hope. A duality of satisfying isolation alongside a growing awareness of sound in the quiet. There was something alive in the silence.

Thunder boomed, and before me my barren landscape appeared sown with rosy prairie flowers, almost as if a translucent glazing of raspberry paint swept over the expanse. I heard a creak and grumble, and a shape spiraled up from the ether, like rose brambles bending before an unrelenting windstorm. Unease pricked my spine—that tangible recognition of pause before storm.

I felt as if I were slipping into someone else's dream. The atmosphere thickened and smelt of things longlost. Into the void between wind and hoofbeat, there was sound. *Once, the prairie was quiet and I was alone.* I rubbed Whistlejacket's neck, his legs blurring silver and smoke through the goldenrod. The mirage faded, the varnished gloss withering to muted tones. Into the quiet, buried deep within the earth, something clicked into place—a bullet guttered into the chamber.

Whistlejacket skidded on a deteriorating edge of the slope, and I jerked his reins, avoiding the bramble. I shook my head, irritated with my lack of focus. I was fatigued, just daydreaming old, forgotten tales. I shoved away fanciful notions and considered the autumn landscape before me—

Beyond the burn, tawny sideoats and yellow melilots trembled in the wind, and alongside the creek the blackjack oaks warmed toward autumn, brown crinkling the leaves, color and life seeping away. It seemed, all of a sudden, autumn had begun. And I knew, too swiftly, winter would be here. There was absolutely no time for nonsense and horsefeathers. I wiped mist from my cheeks and continued. We rounded the curve before my homestead, and within my tent, a long shadow moved.

I yanked my pistol from my holster, held it between both hands, cantered closer, the thud of Whistlejacket's hooves rattling and stormclouds gathering beyond the rise.

CHAPTER EIGHT

Within the stretched, gauzy light of my tent, the profile of a Native woman tilted skyward. Waist-length hair tucked behind her ears, her fingers brushing a copper pot I'd looped over a nail.

I slumped back in my saddle and lowered my Peacemaker, relief easing the tension knotted across my shoulders. Not a bandit but another woman. She wore a burgundy and ochre floral blouse with a navy skirt and ornately beaded moccasins, the cut of her shoes distinct from the Kiowa people I knew from home. The Kiowa lived a handful of miles westward from my parents. Through the years, I'd come to know the Kiowa tribe and learned they were curious about how we lived, just as we were curious about them.

The woman nickered low in her throat and caressed Cricket's nose. I vaulted from Whistlejacket and walked over. "Good morning," I said through the gap in my tent.

"I came to say hello," she said. "I thought you might be lonesome. It seems quiet out here on the prairie."

Though I knew it was common for Natives to wander onto homesteads, her curiosity seemed netted with compassion. "It is quiet," I said, "but I have the wind, the birds, the creaking trees."

She bit her lip and studied my face, surely assessing whether I was a threat. She must have attended one of the mission boarding schools, with her English diction and Western clothing. I relaxed my shoulders, adopting a welcoming posture. "My name is Minnie."

She considered the crates I'd stacked in a corner. "I'm curious about how you make your home."

I gestured toward my supplies. "You're welcome to look at anything."

She bent and riffled through the potatoes tossed in a wooden box, her brow furrowing at the cuts I'd made. Last night I'd flipped through Pa's *Old Farmer's Almanac* and supposed that was how to cut potatoes. I pushed up the flap of my tent and joined her below the canopy, the light dimming further. "I'm not practiced with planting," I said.

Her gaze sparked over my mud-splattered riding skirt and gun belt. Rain crackled against the tent. She said, "I don't enjoy household chores neither."

We grinned at each other, and I could tell this was a woman I'd once have chosen as a friend. There was a vitality to her that seemed plain fun. But, of course, with everything last spring, I shouldn't allow others close to me.

She shared that she was Osage but visiting her sister, who'd married into the Kanza tribe, just east over the rise several miles. She gestured to the tree line, where I now noted a few women in the shadows, wringing their knuckles. One had the same thick eyelashes and softly rounded shoulders. That was surely her sister.

The woman stood, hands pressed against her thighs, the black rays of a tattoo peeking from her sleeve. She brushed the foxglove sprigs I'd hung from a rope slung across my tent. "You're a healer?"

"No." I knelt and opened a polished wooden box with tonics and salves. I held it out to her. "Just everyday remedies, things my ma makes."

A breeze squeaked through the doorway, thinning the humid air beneath the canopy. After a moment she came closer and crouched, brushing the collection of amber and turquoise bottles, the strips of gauze and crushed herbs. Ma mixed elixirs and visited neighbors afflicted with one fever or another. I'd stuffed a box with her supplies, expecting there would be plenty of blood and illness in the wildlands. I hadn't been wrong. On my scrapes from the last week, I'd smeared crystalized honey and one of Ma's homemade salves. The pot was almost depleted, and I didn't know how to make more.

The woman sifted through my bottles, the glass tinkling a melodic chime, and held a vial of Peruna, the amber oil slanting toward the cork stopper. She placed it back with the others, her thumb brushing the thread across the neck of the bottle.

"Would you like it?" I handed her the bottle of Peruna, wanting to share a simple gift. "It's an elixir. For women."

She scrunched her nose, her finger bumping over the ornate lettering. "It's supposed to invigorate your body," I explained, "soothe any particularly feminine ailments."

She nodded and slipped the bottle into her bag, curiosity reflected on her face. She closed the medicine box and stood, exiting out into the drizzling rain. I followed and thanked her for visiting. She said she was headed homeward to her family in the Osage Hills on the morrow, but that she would come round when she visited her sister in another month.

"My name is Niabi," she said and walked away.

~

I placed one seed potato into the clay, then another, moving down the trench. Wiping my palms on my apron, I studied the furrows. They seemed deep, just as the almanac suggested. Magnolia and Ma had planted the vegetables, as I had such an awful time with mundane tasks. Instead, Pa had taught me how to be silent in the woods, how to soothe a spooked filly, how to lead a team into town. But now every responsibility on the homestead was my own.

I slapped away a horsefly, kept planting. Last spring, with the horseflies buzzing and the redbud trees bleeding fuchsia along the valley, Magnolia and I had foraged for morels in the wildwoods. I'd dug at the base of a decaying elm, my palms caked in mud and wrists scratched up by briars. I pressed back my hair, furious that Magnolia wouldn't stake claim with me. "I just don't understand the issue," I said.

Magnolia linked her hands before her apron, a floral linsey with rosebud embroidery, her basket hanging off the crook of her arm. "I'm marrying and staying home." Her posture was still, as if she'd dissolve away into that wet, overturned-earth scent of early spring. "It's the life I choose."

I scoffed, yanked a mushroom from the undergrowth. "You've never been brave enough."

She flinched, as if I'd slapped her. I lifted my chin, resolute.

"No." She crossed her arms, her blond plait brushing the lace cuff of her overblouse. "I've never been you."

"What's that supposed to mean? We've always—"

"Minnie, stop." She lowered beside me in the bramble, her knee bumping my hip. "I don't want to argue with you."

I unwound my cape and looped the wool over a low branch, the bough arching above a cluster of snowdrops. Though one of the first flowers of springtime, snowdrops felt like an omen. Their delicate white bells bent earthward as if they wept. Magnolia was making a mistake, and I didn't know what to do. I took her upturned hand, and she folded forward, resting her forehead against my collarbone. I wrapped my arms around her, and she muttered against my blouse, "I don't want to go. I want to stay here, where it's comfortable."

As a child, she'd grasped my palm and followed me through faroff pastures, holding on while I discovered new worlds. But homesteading in outlaw country was beyond measure. I supposed I should forgive her fear, having lost both her parents so young, but goodness—why couldn't she ever take a risk?

She found a new safe harbor instead. "And that future husband of yours?" I asked.

She sat back, wrought her hands, her joints shiny and almost translucent where bone pressed against skin. "Well, this week he's talking of building a home on down by the millpond." She let loose an effervescent smile. "I like his ideas."

I blew at my hair. "It's fear-flooded and sluggish."

She grasped her knees, studied me with those dark-brown eyes that never quite stopped thinking. "Just because you want some grand adventure and I don't, doesn't make my dreams any less."

"That's not what I said."

"Well," she said, tucking a lock back into her braid, "you just said it was *fear-flooded.*"

"Fine. I do think it's living in fear. A foolish grasp at control." I unearthed another morel and tossed the mushroom into my basket. I sighed and thumped my back against the elm trunk. "I don't understand you anymore."

Magnolia brushed a thumb along her white boots, the leather clean, without even a smudge. She dug out a morel, her posture austere, as if she was containing her own shape. "You don't have to understand my choices to support me."

Her lips were pursed, that elegant curve of her brow, the rose hue smudged under her pale skin, her small, deft fingernails brushing the soil from a mushroom: I couldn't hold on to the rapidly shifting pieces of her anymore. We were changing: Magnolia, soon a wife; me, chasing after rush and exhilaration. I was losing her—my tether to who we'd been dissolving. I didn't know how to let go. But it seemed I had to let her make her own mistakes.

On my homestead, the horsefly zipped across my forehead, and I swatted him away. Though Magnolia and her husband now tilled their own farm, on a stretch of smooth brome down beside the old millpond, leaving her had felt like a death. Our lives forever apart, our relationship broken—irreparable as if she had died. I shoveled more rows until moisture poured beneath my shirtwaist and my hands ached. Sweat soaked between my toes, so I untied my boots and sank my bare feet into the mud. The burn had enriched my homestead, causing all the nutrients to seep into the clay. The soil was sandy and rich, wetted by rain and warmed by sunglow. With the hush of isolation, my hands in the dirt, I heard a groan. I sat back on my heels and scraped my wayward strands back into a plait. As I looped the length around my head like a coronet braid and shoved in hairpins, I scrutinized the prairie. It was almost as if someone were retelling a story I'd once known. I didn't suppose I was losing my grasp on sanity, just that in my solitude, I could hear the space between silence.

I gulped from my canteen and noticed movement near the windbreak. A flock of bobwhite quail freckled about the understory. After grabbing my Winchester and boots, I stalked across the meadow toward the birds, the soft whir of their calls quaking between the rye grass. A twig cracked—the pointed ears of a gray fox twitched, and the quail scattered. I pinged off a shot, missed. Sighing, I looped my rifle's strap across my body and turned away from the hunt, slipping instead into the forest.

The cool shade of the wildwood washed over me. I roamed deer trails, popping violet hackberries into my mouth and unearthing roots. After filling a pocket with chinkapin acorns, I stumbled upon a sapling with velvety, coral-colored persimmons. I plucked one off the branch and ate, the bitter tannins puckering the sides of my mouth. Once the first frost passed, I'd gather the ripened fruit to dry in the sun. Dried persimmons were a luxurious treat, almost like gingerbread. The brush thinned before me, an expansive prairie opening beyond. I crept closer, adjusting the angle of my Winchester across my back to avoid a low branch, and scanned the claim just beyond the wood.

I heard a thwack and reverberation before I saw him. The Lawman hammered a long beam, framing his shack. His sleeves were rolled up, unfiltered sunlight casting harsh shadows in the shirt's creases. The muscles of his forearms flexed as he adjusted the angle of a sill, the naked wood linked between two corner posts. He glanced toward the thicket. Ran a wrist across his brow, wiping away sweat. How in hellfire had he heard me? I hunkered down, bit my lip.

His camp was methodically organized, tarps angled from stakes, several rows of vegetables already planted—*and* he'd dug a hollow for rainwater. Blazes, that was a mighty clever notion. I itched to sneak onto his homestead, study how he'd constructed the shallow clay basin. By all accounts the Lawman was troublesome, but even I'd admit that was a good idea. I pushed off the slope and continued homeward. There was much to be done, winter whisking in soon. An ancient oak had fallen across the pathway, the log rotted and smushed in places. I stepped over and continued on.

Slipping my hand into my pocket, I rubbed the key talisman I carried with me every day. One dawn, aways away in the deep of our childhood, Magnolia and I had ravaged across meadows and woodlands, gathering early spring blackberries and looking for some mischief or another. A flicker of dappled forest light had shone on the brass hue of the key, its tines sprouting from the earth. I'd pulled the skeleton key from the soil. It was small, perhaps to unlock a cabinet or gate. I'd been young enough that it felt like finding treasure. I'd wiped off the dirt with my apron and slipped the key into my pocket. The next day, Magnolia had strung a silver chain through the oval bow and held the talisman out to me in her palm. I'd worn the key round my neck for years after, a hope for extraordinary futures.

That had been long ago.

CHAPTER NINE

I gathered potato tubers in my apron and stepped beyond my waxed canvas tarp into the sunlight. The sweet, earthy scent of an October day sketched out all the empty spaces. My skirt caught on a sandbur, the bluebonnet cloth wrapped around the spiky seed head—I tugged. The burrs knotted up in the weave and wouldn't release. Right there, where the fabric bunched, a maroon smudge puddled over the indigo flowers. No matter how hard I scrubbed, I couldn't cleanse the bloodstain.

The cowboys kept on haunting.

I gripped tight my apron, the cloth heavy with potatoes, and unwound the golden, barbed seedpod from a blue floret. From the east, a shrill sound scuttered beneath the wind, a rumble like many voices. Foreboding swelled within me.

But it was only a woman and two girls walking across the prairie. I dabbed a cloth on my collarbone, my fingertips raw from the prickly sandburs, and strode toward them. I checked my wristwatch—today's daylight was half used up. Sunbeams soaked the woman's face, her skin a luminous deep brown and her black hair swept up into a bonnet. One hand wrought her skirt, a linsey-woolsey hued sepia with dust and dotted with clovers, and her other hand fidgeted with the red-checked edge of cloth in a basket. I noted both fierceness and hesitancy—she seemed giddy to come calling but also worried about how she'd be received.

"Afternoon," she called.

I nodded, wiped a hand across my forehead.

"I'm Mrs. Olive Brown. Everyone just calls me Olive." She pointed over her shoulder. "We've claimed the quarter section just east over the hill."

"Ah." I returned her smile. It felt brittle, not having smiled in a season. "Welcome. Amelia. Miss Hoopes."

"A pleasure." She handed me something warm wrapped in cloth. "My county-prizewinning pie."

Carrot-red clay caked her feet, her heels cracked light brown with use. She'd walked barefoot all the way here, for companionship. With a pie scenting of vanilla and buttermilk—a kindness, a generous gift. She introduced her daughters, Sophia and Poppy, then started in about the sewing circle and literary society. She told of the sharpshooting contest and taffy pull organized for this Saturday and the ball game the following week. "Oh, we'll have such fun. You must come round on Sundays for supper." Olive untied her bonnet's white ribbons, her fingers long and deft as they loosened the knot. "What gatherings are you most excited about?"

"I'll attend barn raisings. Help when obliged," I said. "But I've no interest in socializing."

Olive's hands faltered as she reknotted her bow.

"Ma—" Her daughter Poppy tugged at her scratchy, wincey-wool collar. From the energy charging about her like a lightning storm, she looked just out of pinafores, perhaps nine or ten, not yet comfortable in tailored blouses. "She has *four* horses."

"Four, huh?" Olive straightened her daughter's braid. "Make sure you stand back a pace. Wouldn't want to spook 'em."

"Don't you worry about that," I said to Poppy. "Go on, say hello. They're friendly."

Olive nodded and Poppy dashed over to my horses. Olive shared she'd staked claim with her daughters; her husband, Asa; and a teenage son, Thaddaeus. Asa and Thad were back on their quarter section digging their dugout into the slope of a hill. There was much to do—I didn't have time for chitchat. I peeked at my trenches.

Sophia pressed her knees in the dirt, several rows down, planting my potatoes—she'd practically finished for me.

"Good Lord," I said. "She mustn't do my work."

"Sure enough, your tilling's lovely," Olive rubbed her hand over her mouth, "but there's nothing wrong with being neighborly."

I transferred my weight to my spade. Was she teasing me? "You saying something about my planting, Olive?"

Her eyebrow popped up. She was radiant, her honey eyes crackling. Amused, I drummed my fingers on the wooden handle, then strode over to Sophia and thanked her. "You don't need to plant for me."

Sophia glanced up, her lilac bonnet perched atop black ringlets. "Oh, I just adore planting potatoes," she said. Sophia was perhaps sixteen, her ethereal demeanor startling with its similarity to Magnolia's. "Gardening is so full of hope, don't you suppose?"

I wiped at my nose. "It's practically transcendent."

Olive snorted. She thanked her daughter for being thoughtful, then walked with me to the patch of shade cast by my tent. Olive considered my camp, black fabric snapping in the wind. "It's just you?"

"Come hell or high water." I leaned my spade against a wooden crate and offered Olive a basket of pawpaws I'd foraged.

"I admire that," Olive said, grabbing a fruit. "The gumption to build such a life, on your own."

Poppy squealed—Whistlejacket's velvety nose nibbled her hand. I nodded toward Poppy. "I remember days like that."

"That one, she's a hot pan of live fire." She watched Poppy with affection, wiping dirt from the pawpaw, the yellow rind blotched with brown. "All nature, she's bursting right outta her skin, and sometimes I cannot find my patience."

"I caused my ma an appalling amount of suffering, scurrying about as I did."

"Well, I suppose." Olive studied me. "You must have breakneck grit to venture alone."

I saluted with my pawpaw, took a bite. It tasted overwhelmingly sweet.

"Gawd, but she needs the structure of schooling." Olive tapped her thumb on the pawpaw, gently bruising the velvety skin. Beyond, Sophia carried another load of potatoes in her apron. Olive shared that there was no school until the following autumn, that it'd take time to bring a teacher down, but that they'd make do, as they always did.

"You've primers for her?"

"No. No books," Olive said. Poppy stroked Cricket's mane, kept up a stream of chatter. "I hear there'll be a book wagon, sometime."

I'd packed only essential supplies, but I wouldn't have dreamed of traveling without stories. I'd placed favorite chapbooks and literary monthlies into my trunk, along with Dickens and Thackeray, Wilkie Collins and Sir Walter Scott. What else would there be to do during the long, dark winter evenings? A thought crowded my mind, of the *Ivanhoe* hardback shoved deep into a crate. The emerald-green cover with the smoky black vines, the book a haunting reminder of bloodshed.

"I've no primers," I said. "But I've some dime novels that might be helpful."

"In truth?" Olive brushed her fingers round her ear, looked through an opening in my tent with longing.

I dug some chapbooks from a chest and handed them to Olive. She held the books with reverence, aligning the askew covers. "We couldn't."

"Take 'em," I said. "Borrow more anytime you like. Just send the girls on over."

"You're a schoolteacher?"

"Was." I'd schooled our county's one-room for a season—I'd found satisfaction discussing science and literature and devising unexpected disciplines for the children, but I'd missed that feeling of contentment within my muscles after a long day of farming.

Olive clasped my hands. I itched to pull away but didn't want to be unnecessarily rude. "Folks round here need a teacher," she said. "You shan't have to fuss with planning socials—just teach."

I stepped back, untangled my hands from hers. "I don't want to become involved. It's just me, alone with my horses."

Olive pressed flat the lace rounding her collar. "I'm not sure life is for living, alone." She paused. "But I suppose there are many ways to live."

"There are," I said. "And this is mine."

Olive nodded, but her eyes had a glint. If I read Olive right, this conversation wasn't over. She picked up her basket, looped it on her forearm. "How are you faring, in truth? This is a grum hard life. We're gonna need community some, to survive the winter."

"I'm fine." Besides the prairie fire and the assault, the murders and the apparitions. I coughed something like a laugh. "Course I'm not okay. It's a dratted nightmare out here."

"It's wretched." She smirked, almost wickedly. "But we'll endure."

"We will."

I squinted at the sun moving too swift across the sky, noted the rhythm of Sophia humming, the trill of a wood thrush.

"I've not seen many others about on bordering homesteads," Olive said. "No women."

With the thicket bordering the creek to my south and west, the forest northward, and the rises to the east, I'd spotted no other homesteaders except for a few glimpses of the Lawman thrashing across his land on his mustang. Shark, he'd called him. A ridiculous name. And that wolf beast that followed him about—One Eye, even though he had two.

Olive rubbed her basket, fingers bumping over the weave of white oak, the ligaments of her wrist tense. "You hear about those missing men?" she asked.

"What?" My spine tugged taut, my body suddenly breathless. Round the other side of my tent, something skidded across the terrain, perhaps a tumbleweed.

"At a gathering in Enid a couple days past, some folks planning social societies and deciding where to build the church, a Wild Bunch outlaw made the rounds, asking questions." Olive straightened the band of her apron. "Apparently two cowhands have been missing since the rush. They bragged about getting plots right here, nearby the curve in

Crooked Creek. And some farmer saw them over yonder our way, a few hours into the race, looking into flames."

Sweat pebbled on my chilled skin. I wiped the moisture with a rag. I'd thought it'd be months until enough order established for folks to pay attention to the countryside—and by then the cowboys I'd sent to their maker would've been lost in the disorder of the rush. But those cowboys just kept looming. Gossip needed to be buried, so no one looked my way.

"Suppose they wandered on." My voice came out too thin.

"Perhaps." Olive leaned forward, relishing the gossip. "But did you know that vicious outlaw, the one they call the Lawman, staked claim just north?"

"I met him."

I wasn't sure what to make of that meddlesome gunslinger. Sometimes I'd wake at night, thinking of him—wondering whether he'd keep my secrets. I sure as starfire hoped he didn't turn me in.

"Oh?" Olive looked eager and horrified at the same time.

I shuddered dramatically in response.

"That bad?"

"Oh, he's awful. Arrogant," I said. "But I think he'll keep to himself. I'm not scared of him one bit."

"Maybe you should be?" She kneaded her shoulders, scrunching the fabric's green flora. "Heard he slaughtered four of them Dalton bandits in some battle or another."

"Glad someone did."

Olive laughed and refolded the cloth in her basket. "Well now, don't be a stranger. I know how the days stretch long and quiet. You come find us when you're ready for more pie."

As Olive and her daughters walked home, the blaze of sunlight dampened, day falling into later afternoon. Time continued on and on, days on the frontier an endless trail winding forever into the distance. Those cowboys kept rising from the grave. Olive seemed to relish gossip—I hoped her eager chatter wouldn't remake my secrets into something sensational.

I'd seen it, many times before, how a story could gather and build into a cyclone.

Along my hem, I picked at the blotch of blood. Why wouldn't it dissolve? I tried to reshape my thoughts into something calm, to shake out worry and find quiet in my mind. But horrors kept spiraling. I scratched at the dry skin on my collarbone, thought through the incident, considered whether any evidence might've been left behind. I released my skirt, the white fabric swelling like a low cloud—and walked on into the autumn-gold sunshine.

CHAPTER TEN

Oklahoma Territory—November 27, 1893

six weeks later

My black boots crunched chestnut-brown leaves. "Damnation." I wouldn't flush out turkeys if I stomped through the forest. It was deranged to infiltrate the Wild Bunch's hunting grounds, but I hadn't found game by my stream in a moon.

The seasons were changing, autumn tipping into winter. These past months had been backbreaking work preparing for the cold: churning butter and washing laundry, digging a cellar and hammering together a tar paper shack. During long autumn nights, the wind slipped between my shack's wooden planks, the gusts whistling and groaning. So I'd stuffed newsprint and fabric scraps into the gaps.

This past age had been me with the wind and the meadows and my horses. I'd barely spoken to another. Quick, curt information exchanged with my brothers every few weeks while I did their laundry. Them, asking for fresh butter and promising to come back on the morrow to help dig my well. Olive and her girls had dropped by a handful of times, and I'd met her serious husband, Asa, and their son, Thad. Asa, hands resting in his trouser pockets, watching silvery vines of vetch tremble in the wind, not one muscle in his expression changing. He was still but not melancholic—more like he'd speak when he had something to say. Through the wildwood, I'd studied the Lawman. As a renegade, he must wander the territory causing havoc, but every time I glimpsed him, he'd been almost reverentially tending his land.

Once, I'd dutifully attended a barn raising, working silently. Folks were unsmiling. Desperate. Water and resources scarce, much of the grass burnt from the wildfires those first days. A mood of lawlessness snapped across the frontier, like an old rawhide lasso.

I stepped over a hollow and crouched, touched a V-shaped indentation in the leaves—a recent turkey scratch. I yelped and stalked toward the stream, Winchester raised. Turkeys were social varmints. If I was close, they'd come running straight for my gun. I pulled a branch aside and continued deeper into the woods.

With the back of my palm, I brushed away a strand of splitbeard bluestem. The silvered, feathery stalks spiky and soft, the white seed heads shadowing as winter approached. I glimpsed a longlost moment of standing beside Pa building a new barn. I wasn't sure whether it was one memory or many, the edges of the recollection smoky and tarnished. Silvered, like bluestem or an old daguerreotype image.

It had been summer, the air glistening with sunshine. "You gotta make sure you look before you swing," Pa said.

I lined up my nail on the beam, tongue pressed against my teeth, Pa holding the plank for me. I slammed the hammer against nail, the reverberation shaking down my narrow arm.

I glanced over my shoulder, brows raised. "Like that?"

He gnawed his lip below his black handlebar mustache, as if trying not to laugh. "Sure enough, sweetheart, that's how you build. Just one board after another until you're done."

There must've been a time when he'd pushed me back into the house, hoping I'd learn to darn hems or bake a cobbler with my ma, but I only remembered those long afternoons on the farm with him, learning how to survive—how to hunt and clean a gun, how to break a wild mustang, how to speak so that my ideas were clear.

In the thicket, with the cinnamony scent of cedar and the damp autumn leaves, the turkey returned my cry. This was it—the end of the hunt. I must head home soon or be stuck to freeze overnight on outlaw land. I chambered a round in my gun, steadied my arm, mimicked his yelps. Course it was foolhardy to hunt on outlaw land, but I needed these birds. And I was bored, desperate for something.

Once, with a rumble, the Wild Bunch had swept through my woods. An azure bandanna covering the pallid face of unhinged Bitter Creek. The square jaw of a handsome Black man, Quiet Bill; the thick, curved mustache of Tulsa Jack; and a few others cloaked in their leather dusters. There was the clamor of hoofbeats, the eerie silence of their wordlessness. An exhilarating moment, and then they were gone. After not recognizing the Lawman, I'd studied the outlaw posters something fierce when I'd rode to town for supplies. Though tales went that the outlaws' hideout was still in Payne County down south aways, rumor had it they'd also staked a new haunt mere miles from me by the Salt Flats, an uncanny stretch of colorless wasteland.

I held my breath, Winchester at the ready. But the birds didn't burst from the brush—so I continued on. The angle of filtered sunlight reminded me of another afternoon pressing through buckbrush. I'd led Smallhopes along the ravine, showing her how to step over bramble and thorn, a basket of hazelnuts looped over her saddle. The autumn air had been thick with summer's moisture, the wildwood humming with forest sounds—when I'd chanced upon Niabi.

She strode between some evergreens, a foraging basket of woven cattail rushes pressed to her side. "Minnie?"

I stepped deeper into the emerald and gold shadows and said hello.

Smallhopes nipped at her basket, and Niabi offered her a handful of blackberries. "You have a buckskin?" Niabi grinned as Smallhopes nosed her palm.

"I do." I crouched, pulled a twig from the white feathering around Smallhopes's fetlock. "Wondering why I'm towing a draft horse through the underbrush?"

She knelt, removed a dried seedpod from Smallhopes's fringe. Raised a brow at me. "It is an odd choice."

"Just training on various terrains," I said.

"Ah." Niabi lifted her basket, her hands graceful and tapered, a smudge of blackberry on her fingertips. She tapped the woven white oak, her expression good-natured. "Why?"

I unlooped my bonnet from the saddle horn, wiped sweat from my collarbone. Deep in the thicket, a few doves sang a quaint, mournful song. "Readying for whatever may come."

"Would you show me how you train horses?" Niabi asked.

We trekked back to my homestead, and I explained how I worked with my draft horses. I brought out Cricket and performed a few complicated maneuvers as Niabi sat in the grass, drinking sweet tea. "What's your fanciest trick?" she asked.

I resettled my Stetson above my loose braid. Cricket and I had been practicing a handless swing mount. In case I ever needed to flee in a hurry, pistol trained—my other arm indisposed. One thing I'd learned in outlaw country: Prepare for anything and everything.

"Watch this." I lifted a pail heavy with whortleberries, the steel bucket ungainly, berries rolling about.

I gave Cricket the mount's signal, and he rested his knees against the ground, held steady, his black mane fluttering in the breeze.

I swung up, my arms full of whortleberries.

Niabi let out a surprised laugh. "By thunder."

Cricket rose, my hips aligning in the saddle. I patted his withers. "Steady," I told him and dismounted.

I offered him an apple slice, then held the pail of inky-blue berries out toward Niabi. We ate a few handfuls, the tart flavor bursting, the air full of the crispness of autumn.

"Well, come on," I said, gesturing Niabi forward. "You try."

Her posture was unsure, but I glimpsed yearning plain on her face. She wanted to try. Like me, Niabi rustled with curiosity and passion.

I shared a few tips. "Just be confident," I told her. "If you're at ease, he'll be calm too."

I rubbed Cricket's fawn-brown jaw. "Easy."

Niabi gave Cricket the command, and he knelt, his barrel at a slope. She vaulted—and her stomach slammed into his saddle, forehead slapping against the pommel. She was sliding off, moccasins peeking from her plum-pink skirt.

"Can I?" I asked, my hands hovering over her hip.

"For all the sky above, please." Her voice was muffled, amusement threaded through her tone.

I shoved her into the saddle, her posture adjusting until she was stable. Cricket stood, and Niabi grinned, laugh lines wrinkled beside her eyes—and a longing for friendship clicked open in my chest. I remembered long ago, splayed in the high grass of a downward slope, the tawny color of the wheat the same sheen as my leather saddle—watching clouds hasten on by, my sister on one side, Lark on the other. How many seasons had we lain and watched the sky, how many moments planning our future, my heart thumping my chest, myself too full of wonder?

A while later, after Niabi and I ate turnips and deer jerky, she perused my weapons, her fingers brushing the glossy wooden handle of my scattergun. "I don't know much of your tribe." I handed her my father's 1873 Peacemaker. "Do Osage women learn about guns?"

Niabi rubbed the buffalo horn, spun open the chamber. "Yes, women know how to shoot." She wrinkled her nose. Knocked her head back and forth, as if working through how to explain. "My husband—" She tucked a lock of her hair behind her ear. A faint red line inked down her center part. "Did I tell you I'm married?"

I shook my head.

"We wed last spring," Niabi said. "It's something new but my husband: He's a good man. We are two halves. Moon and sun, night and day. But—" Fondness edged the corner of her mouth. "My husband doesn't like me wandering among the homesteaders. He worries."

I handed her some bullets. "So why do you?"

"Let me find the words." She loaded the bullets into the chamber, one after another. "Much change is forced upon the Osage. Pioneers have been vicious: stealing horses, harassing women, causing havoc. Last week, as my sisters and I foraged rose hips along a ridgeline, several cowboys burst from the thicket and stole three of our horses—before I could even unholster my gun." She spun the chamber closed, the movements of her fingers tense and jerky, as if terror still knotted into her joints. She looked in my eyes. "Do your people tell you this?"

I'd heard the lawlessness of No Man's Land spilled over into Native territory, with outlaws and renegades causing all manner of havoc. But there seemed a haze in my perception.

"There's much I do not know," I said.

"I'm not just curious about horses." Niabi frowned at my timberline, the wind lofting and dropping the heavy limbs. "I keep my eyes on the horizon. Watching the changes overcoming our land. Threats surge along the borderline, and I must learn," Niabi said. "Training my horse, sharpshooting—this is about protection."

I rubbed at the dirt smudged along my cuticles. I hadn't realized how monstrously white men plagued their border. I remembered the stories my grandmother told when I was a child. Harrowing accounts of how tribes were dragged from their homelands, of how land was stolen or tricked away. Of trails of tears and unspeakable violence, of a bitter agony thread through generations. But the papers told another story. I didn't know what was real. The tale went that the Cherokees sold their ranching land for the rush. Decades ago, they'd sold other land to the Osage. Then the Osage moved from Kansas to Oklahoma Territory.

An awareness grew that perhaps I'd glimpsed only a fraction of the truth. As is true with most stories, there seemed a distance between what the storyteller told for entertainment and what was truth. "I heard the Osage bought their land from the Cherokees," I said. "Did your people want to move?"

"Of course not." She lifted one of her necklaces, rubbed it between her fingers. "Why would we choose to leave the land of our ancestors?

We weep, having left them." She scratched her nails along the ridge of her pendant. Let it go. "White men always want, they continue to take and take. When my grandmother's grandmother was just a child, we were forced away from the wide river valley of our homeland. Twenty years ago, when we moved again, a leader named Wah Ti An Kah thought that the forested hills of Osage Nation would be safe. That white men couldn't put their iron into that ground—and so they wouldn't force us to move again. They would leave us alone."

I stared at her, not quite understanding. My heart stretched, a bleak, heavy sadness squirming. They had left their home so they might be undisturbed. And then my people had opened surrounding land for the runs.

Niabi raised my pistol, aimed at the heaps of clay I'd set up as targets. "I always hold my posture until the shot plinks," she said.

My fingers clutched at my chest, still untangling what Niabi had shared. "Don't lift your gaze till the smoke clears."

Niabi exhaled, and her bullet thunked. The clod of red clay splattered, soil rushing earthward. The dust thinned, and Niabi eased. "Like that?"

I nodded, fiddled with my top button. "Thank you for sharing of your people."

She shrugged and turned back to our targets. I didn't know how to make sense of such sorrow. But watching how the trauma of displacement haunted Niabi, I realized: I didn't understand her story at all. And I wondered, once again, how men could be so brutal. Niabi gathered her basket to head homeward, and I invited her back anytime. "Visit me too," she said. "I would welcome you."

She straightened her blanket cloak, pulling her long black hair free from the wool. And then she walked across my meadow and into the woodland. As she disappeared into the forest's shadows, an ache crept and bubbled across my back. I longed for her to return, but I also worried that she might. Niabi was vibrant and fresh—and in friendships, I only knew how to destroy.

And now, weeks later, I was out chasing that quickening of excitement in outlaw country. A twangy rattle sounded in the buckthorn, jarring me back to the present. I lifted my Winchester as something burst from the thicket.

The jake thrust through the bushes, head twisting about, a clutch of ten turkeys wobbling behind him. Being surrounded, while wandering the woodland, looked suffocating. The turkeys were almost in range when a bang ricocheted. The jake toppled.

I dropped to my stomach.

Shots rang out, my Winchester pressed beside me into the mud. By God and all high nation—the outlaws had sighted me.

A riot of shots, the squabble of birds, the silence of aftermath.

CHAPTER ELEVEN

Honey mesquite brush was all about me, my face smashed into the dirt, a rock cutting my cheek. If I survived this, if the bandits didn't assassinate me, I'd blaze with fury—I *needed* that roost.

A sunray flickered low through slim sycamore trunks. Boot steps crinkled in the wood nettle, and I glimpsed wavy black hair, golden jaw, black slicker hanging like a cape.

I sputtered—that scallywag, in my way again. I jumped up, pushed back my hair, cowboy hat toppling earthward, and trained my Winchester on the Lawman.

"Minnie?" His low, resonant voice was easy and unhurried.

"Sakes alive, I told ya—it's Amelia." I steadied my weapon and groaned loudly, exasperated. "Miss Hoopes."

The Lawman raced his gaze across my face, as if remembering my features. I didn't lower my gun.

Well, I *could* shoot him. He knew my secrets. His glare lowered to my gun barrel, one eyebrow lifting. Mocking me as I pointed a rifle at his face.

He was the only one who knew about the cowboys—I had no reason to trust him. We were miles from our homesteads. Folks would assume the Bunch had finally got him. No one would know. The Lawman's gaze was detached, unafraid as he faced death. I could shoot.

Well, of course I couldn't. But Lord have mercy, part of me wanted to. To be rid of the worry, to allow this haunting to dim. If he told my secret, vigilantes would rise against me—and I'd be jailed or buried six feet under, clean and simple.

"You just tug back the little trigger," he said, his voice without inflection. "That notch there on the bottom of the gun."

"Gah." I cursed. Flung the barrel earthward. He deserved to be shot for such audacity. For shooting my turkeys. "Those were my birds."

"Yours? I've been scouting them all afternoon."

"Like hell."

"And you know where their den is?"

I flicked my hand westward. "In the woods."

He settled his hands in his pockets, sable leather gun belt gleaming in the gloom of his oilcloth slicker. His silhouette diffused the light, sunrays filtering between the mustard-yellow leaves. Dark hair fell about his face in waves. It'd grown longer these months, long enough for him to tie back.

"I'm not a thief," he said, voice hard. "I don't like being accused of things I haven't done."

My eyebrows flung upward. The outlaw was miffed, not that I trained a long gun on him but that I accused him of stealing. Or was he alluding to the men I'd slain? A chill cinched around my forearms, a panic that he'd tell, a fear of what I'd do if threatened.

I stalked forward, heels scrunching fallen leaves. "Those birds," I gritted through clenched teeth, "ran toward *my* call."

"Those pathetic caws were yours?" His gaze on the hardwoods. "I assumed it some injured magpie."

"It worked, didn't it?"

His thumb brushed over his leather holster. "Did it, Minnie?"

"Amelia."

"Darling, it don't matter what your name is."

"Just admit you snatched my kill." I shoved his chest. His hands shot out, encircled my wrists. I gasped. His skin was hot and calloused, his linen shirt coarse below my palms. I tilted forward, wondered what this gunfighter would do if I sank my nails deeper into his muscles.

He released my wrists, stepped back, ran a hand down his face. "You're a wild one, huh?"

"What in all creation does that mean? I can't accuse you of theft, but you can name me?"

He unsheathed a bowie hunting knife and methodically cleaned the turkey. The brush rustled, and I damn near jumped outta my skin. But it was just One Eye, his wolf dog, not some bandit intent on slaughter.

I stepped forward. "This isn't over."

"Stop yammering and help already," he said. "I'll give you half."

"Yammering?"

"You do know, this is outlaw territory." He sawed at the birds. "They will not hesitate. They will shoot."

Course I knew this was outlaw land—I didn't fancy being treated as a simpleton. A flush of heat raced down my fingers. "I'm not a child."

He rubbed the heel of his palm against an eye. "What does that even mean?" He waved a hand at me. "Obviously you're not a child."

"I don't like being coddled."

"Not coddling you."

"Felt that way."

"Well"—his voice was harsh, a whip—"stop feeling."

Apparently the gunfighter was hardheaded and wouldn't admit the catch was mine. But I supposed I could take half. He probably needed food as well—it was actually magnanimous of me to share.

"You're mighty—" I yanked my hunting knife from my sheath and *screeched* when I sliced my palm.

"All nature, Amelia. Quiet."

I pressed against the deep line of red spilling from my hand. I hadn't cut myself since I was in pinafores.

The Lawman sprang up, his voice astonished. "You cut yourself?"

"Don't you dare say nothing." I clenched my teeth, inhaled. "You all-overish distracted me."

"Distracted you, huh?" He edged closer.

Gloaming glinted low through the scrub brush, fuzzed about the lime-green lichen, as if the forest tipped. I was dizzy.

"Aw, damn." He rubbed his jaw. "That's bad." He reached for me, and I jerked away. He rolled his eyes. "Let me see."

"You a doctor, Lawman?"

He nodded as he studied my cut.

"You are?"

He kneaded his shoulder beneath his duster and seemed so uncomfortable I believed him. "No," he said. "Not a doctor, but I have some skill."

On my palm, blood pooled, the color shocking in the muted browns of the groundcover. I wobbled, and he swept an arm behind my back, lowered me to the forest floor.

"Don't touch me." I nudged him away with my elbows, my hands still pressed together to stanch the blood.

He ripped some fabric, then wrapped a piece of his butter-colored shirt around my cut. His hands were wide, with defined veins and square nails, trimmed and clean. His shirt was unbuttoned at his throat below his white kerchief and black vest, his fingers warm on my wrist. I thought of Magnolia pressing salve and rosewood calico to my sliced thigh. Her gasps of laughter at catching ourselves amid honey locust thorns, her palm swiping her forehead, smearing a translucent stain of red blood. All autumn long, no one had touched me.

He tied off my bandage and pressed the back of his palm to my forehead. "Can you walk?"

"Course I can walk."

"Where's your buckskin? Cricket, right?"

I gestured behind us. Then folded forward over my crossed legs, pressed the pads of my palms to my eyes. It had been a long while since I'd felt so known. Here in the wildwood, with an outlaw, I felt authenticity. I glimpsed that vulnerable and rare pulse of friendship, in a way I hadn't since everything that had happened last spring.

"You're just lightheaded," he said. "Lost some blood."

"I know that," I snapped.

"I truly thought they were my catch," I added, my tone somewhere between a grumble and a sob. "I don't like sharing."

"I can tell. Me neither." The wind cracked through the dried leaves of a pin oak. "Perhaps we'll learn?"

His boots swept through the grass toward the turkeys. These past months, I'd felt rooted to the earth, steady and unwavering. But this man was a raging storm. He made me want to race into his winds and feel something. Get lost a moment. Abandon myself, make another shocking choice.

He wasn't good for me, just the sort of anarchy I should avoid. But Olive was right—I couldn't survive winter alone. Perhaps he was the safest, as I couldn't hurt him. "I won't promise outrageous things," I said. "I'll call you a cheat, when you cheat."

He tied together a couple of birds for each of us. Then stood, long body unfolding. "I won't treat you as weak neither."

"That's just an excuse so you can snarl whenever you like."

"Arguing with me is the most fun you've had in weeks," he said.

"You're dreaming."

He crouched beside me. Crinkles edged beside his eyes, his tan throat glistening with sweat. He was loathsome—but a smile tugged at the corner of my mouth. "You love it," he said.

"You—"

He cut me off. "Darling, I just don't have time for playing." He stood, hefted me upright. "Let's go."

I bit my lip, amused, off-kilter, then slung my Winchester cross my back and followed him through the brush. I couldn't remember anyone, ever, flinging fire back at me with such smoothness. I didn't know what to do with him.

Sound eased in that calm before nightfall. The softening of blackbird song in the overstory, the smush of leaves underfoot, the gawky yips of coyotes out yonder. We'd reach Cricket by candlelighting, and I knew the buffalo trails of this land well enough to ride by the glow of the full moon. Though lightheaded and unsettled, I hadn't lost that much blood—I'd be fine.

The Lawman whispered through the hardwoods, his broad shoulders turning to avoid a branch, his gaze roaming the timber: attentive, silent, lethal. The wind reverberated through creeper, and then a *thwupt* sliced through forest sounds.

I dove behind a stump, cocked my pistol.

A hatchet cleaved through my muslin sleeve, pinning my hand against the bark. The weapon jangled with hawkbells, and a golden eagle feather reverberated. I scanned the wood. No movement, no color, no sound, just the weight of the impending. The Lawman crouched beside me, hands raised, his gun dropped into the autumn-hued leaves.

All wrath—was this the borderline of Osage territory?

CHAPTER TWELVE

I didn't hear him, but in the twilight I saw him approach. An Osage man stalked soundlessly between the saplings, a multihued blanket cloak draped across his body, a pistol trained on the Lawman. He was the tallest man I'd ever seen.

"We mean no harm." I gestured toward the birds with my bandaged hand. "We're hungry—and I'm wounded."

The Osage's brows were drawn, fury knotted in the clench of his jaw, the deep divots along his cheeks shadowed. He pressed his gun against the Lawman's stomach. A few others came forward, moccasins silent in the shrub brush.

My breath hitched, held.

The Lawman didn't flinch. "Allow the woman to go." He spoke, the tone of his voice controlled. "Let us solve this matter."

The Osage man didn't respond, but I glimpsed comprehension in his expression. His posture was assured, shoulders pressed backward, an ease in the muscles of his hand as he gripped the pistol. His black hair was in a topknot, beadwork interwoven within the strands, sides shorn below the temples. One finger tremored, and I feared he'd shoot.

Two of the Osage had waistcoats and trousers beneath their cloaks and black cowboy hats settled over their long braids. Another wore traditional Osage clothing, a hair pipe breastplate visible below his blanket.

A turquoise lizard scuttled across a rock—I jolted. His yellow collar flamed before he disappeared into wavyleaf thistle. The Lawman hadn't moved, not even a suggestion of emotion across his face. The wind hesitated for a fraction of a second.

And then the tall Osage flicked his fingers, motioning for the Lawman to turn. The Lawman pivoted, palms skyward, and the Osage shoved the barrel in the middle of his slicker. To me, he gestured eastward with a riding whip, the braided leather snapping. I wouldn't resist—I'd trespassed. I didn't know where he was taking us, or why, but I hoped I survived this night.

The Osage strode into the thicket beneath the outstretched bough of a gilded cottonwood, his ivory bone pistol pressed against the Lawman's back. I followed, disappearing through woodland and into the mystery of night.

~

We arrived at their camp at sundown, a cluster of canvas lodges along a wooded river, spirals of ghost-white smoke lifting to the heavens. Beneath a bank of blackjacks, the tall Osage spoke his first word to us. "Stay."

He gestured for another to guard us, then stalked away. An Osage man in a tweed vest pulled out his pistol.

I lowered to the dirt, muscles weary, joints stiff. Beyond, a bonfire scratched at the navy sky, and a man played a rhythm on kettle drums, his chest tattooed with symbols and lines, a stack of four diamonds arrowing downward. The Lawman stood beside me, gripping his weapon belt. His shoulders knotted, his gaze roaming our surroundings—plotting. I feared he'd do something drastic. We had broken Osage laws. I supposed they'd be fair, but I didn't know what sort of punishment would meet my trespass.

I plopped onto my back, kicked wide my legs, and stared up at the stars striking between the branches. My palm throbbed, as it rested on a pile of damp leaves. The heavy drumbeat resounded, the pulse settling somewhere between my blood and bones; then a draught of wind passed across the night and hauled the deep sound away.

Folks always said I'd wind up jailed or slain or something else outrageous if I ran off to homestead. And they'd been right—I was an all-overish calamity, a danger to everyone. I rocked my shoulders in the dirt, annoyed by a rock beneath my spine. When I'd cut my palm, I'd hollered at the Lawman, signaling our presence to the Osage. My unruly passions and lack of control once again brought destruction upon someone else. If the Wild Bunch had caught us instead, this night surely would've devolved into a shoot-out. I felt shame with who I was, about my inability to moderate. Color swelled along the edge of my vision, an array of bright tones in the darkness. A man approached, the bells on his legs clattering and the garters tied below his knees smoldering like fire. I stood and wiped my skirt.

"I want you to know this thing," the man said. "Trespassers steal our horses and bother our women." He tucked his blanket cloak under his arm, his bearing undaunted. "Have you stolen our horses?"

"No," I said. "I thought I hunted on Wild Bunch territory, not Osage."

The moment stretched and bowed. My skin felt sweaty, as if coated in smoke and clay. There was a racket beyond, a baseball clattering into the thicket. "One moment," he said and went to grab the ball.

The Lawman flicked his gaze to the left. I squinted into shadow. Two iron spiders, with their three legs, were stacked beside a stump. He wanted to grab frying pans? And we'd what, fight off the Osage with holloware? Why wouldn't he just use his six-shooter? But we shouldn't attempt an escape. We were just mixed up in some misunderstanding or other about horses. Perhaps they'd drag us uphill to their agency and toss us in their jail for the night. But—there was no version in which I would fight these people.

I shook my head at the Lawman. A vein contracted on his jaw—but he didn't vault across the copse for the frying pans. The long trill of a nighthawk patterned across the silence; a shiver raced down my arms.

The Osage man dipped his hands within the blackberry bramble, pulled out the brown leather ball. I scraped my bootheels across the dirt, feeling this land of the Osage, these rolling hills and sweeping valleys. Niabi said that the Osage had been coerced from their home to a new land without their memories. Their children forced into white schools and clothing and language, yanked away from their culture and tugged onto the white man's road. I was forever indebted to the rush—my life began again when I'd saddled up Cricket and raced into the unknown. As a woman, I'd found safe harbor. I'd come to cherish my meadow as the dearest friend. To lose my land would demolish me. I couldn't imagine how the Natives must feel, if they'd lived on a parcel of earth for not a few months but a millennium—and then their home was taken.

I hadn't honored what little sanctuary they had. I'd trespassed.

The Osage elder strode back and sat on a stump. He crossed his arms, his forearms sharply muscled. "We are the Children of the Middle Waters," he said, "and my name is Wa-ah-zho."

He shared that he was one of the little old men, and chief of the Dwellers in the Upland Forest band. He seemed perhaps just thirty, but I'd heard that many of the warriors of the older generations had died in famine, war, and other atrocities.

"My name is Minnie," I shared. "My homestead's a forty-minute ride westward."

The Lawman muttered under his breath. "*He's* earned your alias?"

"Hush." I tucked a loosened edge of linen back into my bandage. "I am sorry that I entered your land, for any harm that I caused."

Crinkles pinched beside Wa-ah-zho's eyes as he gauged the Lawman. Firelight gleamed on the red fabric woven into his two long braids. "And you, cowboy?"

The Lawman hadn't stolen their horses, had he? It didn't seem like something he'd do. But, of course, I didn't know him.

"I did not steal from you," the Lawman said.

They measured each other. After a moment Wa-ah-zho pressed his shoulders back, hands resting on his knees. He had made a decision—one that ended with us, at the least, hauled to jail.

"I have friendship with an Osage woman," I blurted. "Niabi? Is she here?"

"Niabi?" Wa-ah-zho's brow furrowed. He drew his blanket together, the honey and red beadwork design arrowing toward the earth like lightning.

I wasn't sure where I'd stepped wrong, but it seemed I'd made another error. "She's about my age, early twenties. Long black hair. Lots of energy."

The keen of a mountain lion echoed back from the lowland, and I heard the rattle of tom-toms.

"She visited my homestead weeks back." I kept speaking. "I taught her a handless mount."

A stillness hardened over Wa-ah-zho's posture. He held my gaze. I didn't flinch. "That was you?"

"Yes, I taught her the swing mount," I said. "And how to hold until the smoke clears—when shooting a pistol."

The Lawman cursed, his pitch grumbly and muffled. Wa-ah-zho frowned at me. Perhaps I'd made our predicament worse—but what other choice was there?

My gaze scattered across the forested hills, the firelight glinting on the umber spikes of a bear claw necklace. "Do you know Niabi?" I asked.

"I know Niabi." Wa-ah-zho brushed his hand over his face. "She's my wife."

"Oh." I faltered. Well, damnation. I should've stopped speaking miles ago.

"I cautioned Niabi to stop visiting pioneers," Wa-ah-zho said. "It's treacherous out there." He called for someone to find Niabi. "With the full moon, she'll be in the wood gathering herbs."

Moments passed, long and brutal. Wa-ah-zho considered the Lawman. The Lawman's expression was barren, arms crossed. For all high creation, he could at least apologize. Then—a pound of footfalls. A woman raced up the path, Hudson's Bay blanket looped across her shoulders, hair liquid behind her.

Niabi halted before me, a wide grin across her face. "Oh, it is you."

She kissed Wa-ah-zho swiftly on the lips, his expression somewhere between exasperated and amused. Then she grabbed my arm, her gaze snagging on my wound, and dragged me downhill. "You must harvest the elm bark with me."

"Niabi," Wa-ah-zho called. "Could you please not race off to the woods with someone we don't know?"

"I know Minnie." She walked back, my hand held in hers. She wrinkled her nose at him. "Stop frowning and welcome them for the night."

Wa-ah-zho sighed and looked skyward.

"She's the one I told you about." Niabi released my hand and grabbed his wrist, rubbed her thumb across his skin. I looked away, uncomfortable seeing such an intimate moment. "There is much we can learn from homesteaders, of how to survive."

Wa-ah-zho scratched the back of his neck, jaw clenched, a tattoo of horizontal and vertical lines visible on his throat. "Dark has fallen. With the full moon this night, many won't slumber until grandfather sun arises." He frowned at his wife. Tucked his blanket up beneath his two braids. "But you are welcome, Minnie, to shelter with us this evening and ride on homeward in the daylight."

I exhaled a puff of air. "That is gracious of you," I said. "Thank you." Tension eased from my shoulders—it seemed I wouldn't be spending the nighttide locked up in a jail cell with the Lawman, but instead enjoying the full moon with Niabi and Wa-ah-zho.

Wa-ah-zho nodded. "You may share tales of the race and the changes overcoming this land."

Niabi tugged my arm, pulling me downhill. As we sped away, I glanced over my shoulder at the Lawman. He watched me, posture like stone, gaze tracking down my forearm to where my hand linked with Niabi's. "And what about you, cowboy?" I heard Wa-ah-zho say. "Convince me out of hauling you to our jail."

An expansive timberland spread beyond, the silvered light a'glow across the overstory. Niabi shared how she gathered bark and roots under the autumnal full moons. "My mother and my sisters and I adore the full moon's glimmer." She led me into the shadows of the thicket. "Do you have any sisters?"

"One." We slipped under the canopy, blackjack trunks reaching skyward, beginning starlight easing through the leaves.

"Well, go on, tell me about her."

And so I did, telling Niabi of childhood escapades with Magnolia. How we'd hide from our tasks and read, Magnolia riveted by the ideas in her *Popular Science Monthly* and me with my serialized novels. It ached to speak of her, but perhaps I needed to. Niabi shared some mayhem she'd instigated with her three sisters, when they'd been hauled off to school. "I couldn't stand being shut up behind walls—it was as if part of me died," she said. "But, oh, the pranks we played."

I knew of the boarding schools but hadn't known they were a spiritual death for the Osage. There was much I didn't understand.

Niabi crouched at the base of a slippery elm, the green and yellow, red and indigo stripes on her cloak mottled with twilight's shadows. She clicked open her knife and showed me how to harvest the bark without harming the tree. I knelt, pressed my unbandaged palm against the waving ridges of the elm's trunk, the bristles rasping my palm, this wide gap of moonlight full of something between haunting and effervescence.

"Niabi." I frowned, unsure what to say. "I didn't know—"

I trailed off. She waited. "I didn't know the horrors of the land rush," I said. "The ways my people have treated yours." I looked at my hands. My fingers blanched against the warm color of the bark. "I didn't know that in finding my own land, I stole from others."

She crouched beside me, held my gaze. "You know now."

I wasn't sure what to do with the truth. The land rushes had brought me such freedom. I thought of Olive, all the run had given her family. I didn't know how to untangle such a thing—how I could look upon my land with gratitude, when my opportunity had been built upon upending the lives of others? How could Niabi withstand my friendship, how could she even speak to me?

After harvesting roots and bark, we returned to camp. Niabi offered me a supper of fry bread, dried mulberries, and beans; wrapped a woven blanket round my shoulders; and settled me fireside beside the Lawman. Apparently he hadn't been jailed. I itched to have overheard that conversation—listened to the Lawman's tale, glimpsed why Wa-ah-zho chose to trust him. On a stump round the blaze, Wa-ah-zho's demeanor relaxed, but the Lawman remained tense and brooding.

"Wa-ah-zho," I said, tucking the striped wool up under my chin, "I do apologize, for hunting on your land."

"Let's speak of the matter no more," Wa-ah-zho said. "I see boldness in you. I reckon trespassing isn't your first misadventure."

"Well—" I rubbed the chapped edges of my hands. "I may have some stories."

The Lawman caught my eye, deliberately raised an eyebrow—and then Niabi challenged us to share of our most outrageous disasters. And so we spent the quiet hours sharing fragments of our pasts. Niabi snuggled beside her husband on a log, her tales of mishaps and debacles mimicking mine, her palm occasionally running across the hound curled at her feet. Wa-ah-zho refuted my anecdotes as hogwash, the Lawman tracked my every move below his Stetson, and we kept on telling stories until night was gossiping of morning.

CHAPTER THIRTEEN

The night passed full of color and sound. The Osage moved between bonfires, their clothes catching the flame's light. Several children chased each other silently, slinking in and out of shadow, sneaking round their white lodges, the domes a'glow in the dark. After hours fireside, Wa-ah-zho joined a game beside us, bone dice clattering as they slammed the wooden bowl onto blankets. Niabi roved the celebration with her hound, leaning forward as she chatted with a friend, squeezing another woman's arm, laughing without restraint. I was softly drunk on corn whiskey and relishing the weight of night's shadows.

Beside me, the Lawman leaned back into darkness, One Eye asleep at his boots. After the Osage had welcomed us, they'd sent someone to gather Cricket and Shark. The Lawman had clucked his tongue—and One Eye had bolted from the thicket, apparently shadowing us all night.

The Lawman stretched out his legs, heels sunk in the dirt, hat tipped over his face, body lengthened into something like a slouch, an impersonation of a carefree cowboy. Below the front dip of his broadbrim hat, his gaze darted around the crowd, sharp and analytical. He didn't entirely trust them. Well, a renegade probably trusted no one.

I sipped the whiskey, liquid burning the back of my throat. The Lawman leaned his shoulder close to mine. "You're naive."

I straightened the scratchy cuffs of my wincey blouse. "What are you scared of, Lawman?"

"Containment."

I snapped my gaze to his, my fingers moving to the buttons at my neck. "Just ride on home, if you're all affright."

His gaze roamed to my palm, the butter-yellow linen crusted brown with blood. "I won't leave you."

"I'm hardly dying here."

"I'll stay."

He leaned back again, his posture deliberate. Peeking from the woolen blanket over his body, a line of metal glinted, bullets organized down his bandolier. It was peculiar that he wouldn't leave me. If he didn't trust anyone, why would he form an alliance with me, a woman he knew had committed double murder?

Niabi bustled back, her arms full of bundles and pots, her shaggy hound trailing. "Let's mix a salve for your hand."

I joined her fireside.

The Lawman lifted his copper cup and sipped whiskey, watchful. Niabi poured something the shade of bruised rain clouds from a woven bag into a shallow bowl.

"Lavender?" I asked, the bonfire warm along the bridge of my nose.

Niabi nodded and held some grains out to me. They smelt like renewal. Niabi shared she was a healer, taught the ancient ways by her mother and grandmother. She did not hold her own memories of her ancestral land but had grown up among these hills, learning the remedies and gifts the earth offered here. She handed me the bowl and pestle, motioning for me to grind the lavender. I rotated the pestle across the grains, and Niabi laid her palm atop mine, a black spider tattooed on the back of her hand. She adjusted the angle of the pestle and modeled the right amount of pressure. My skin was dry, and I felt the texture of her palm across my knuckles. She showed me how to mix the ground lavender with some grease.

"You've all those books in your shack. Are skilled with horses and weapons." She stirred the salve with her forefinger. "What else can you do?"

No one had ever asked about my skills. She knew my strengths of bravery and boldness. That I could hunt, build, survive. And horses, I'd always understood horses. When I thought back, horses saturated my earliest memories, the moments blurry and imprecise: a coppery claybank flank; lifting a carrot toward an Appaloosa; Pa guiding my bootheel into a stirrup; hair snapping behind me as I rounded wayward cattle on my pony. After I'd heard the legend of Willie Matthews—a woman from nearby in Kansas who'd dressed as a man and drove longhorns up Old Chisholm Trail to Dodge City—I'd yearned to shuck my skirts, chop off my hair, and throw trouser legs over a mustang. But Niabi would expect a pioneer to establish a farmstead, train horses, withstand a harsh life. What other abilities of mine might be uncommon on the frontier? I tapped the pestle on the wooden bowl. "I can paint."

"Paint?" She tucked a slick strand of hair behind her ear, firelight striking on her sunset-hued beaded earrings. "Similar to how we make art with hand weaving—you paint?"

I scratched my ankle above my boot. "I could, once."

"You don't walk backward." She flicked her hand, swiping away my ambivalence.

Niabi bustled away, returning with charcoal paint and an earthenware pot. She explained the spider shape on her hand. Like *Ho e ka*, a name for Earth, the spider represented a snare that trapped all life. Niabi asked me to draw the patterns round the pot, and I explained some of my painting techniques. Later, she joined her husband on a stump, leaning her head against his shoulder. His energy was staid, while hers vibrated. She was vivacious in a way I'd once been, before these seasons of regret. I lost hold of those pieces of myself somewhere along the way. I painted for a time, the celebration muted beyond me, the Lawman ever present in the shadows, and then the night sky began to loosen, as it did close to sunrise, letting in the softer undertones of dawn. Wa-ah-zho spoke something to Niabi and tucked her blanket cloak across her lap, the navy ink of his tattoos climbing from his collar. He leaned across our circle toward me. "Will you come back? We'll share more stories."

"You can paint. Show me how to train my horse." Niabi held out her hand to me, her stack of bracelets jangling. "And I'll show you where to find herbs in the hills."

I clasped her hand between mine. "I'd be honored."

Wa-ah-zho nodded, then stood and drifted off into the edge of daybreak. Someway, unwanted, I'd made allies tonight.

The Lawman linked his hands behind his head and leaned back. "Who knew you could be civil?" His voice rasped in the dark. "It's almost as if you're used to being belle of the ball."

There was a time when I'd been the county darling. But I couldn't revive that part of myself, as I must hold tight to control. The last time Olive came calling, she'd brought buttermilk pie. Poppy had raced into my shack to swap out her dime novel, narrating an unbroken stream about her last borrowed pamphlet, the bell of her calico dress stirring up dirt. Sofia had settled on my porch to shuck partridge peas, and Olive had taken to sweeping, overfull of gossip. They'd stayed from midday to almost candlelighting, Olive desperate for companionship, the isolation of the frontier almost unbearable for her. While I'd misplaced space inside myself for friendship. They were too brittle, too messy. When I sifted through memories, it was hard to reconcile all the betrayals. Most of the time, it felt like some dream. Something that had happened to someone else.

I unbuttoned my blouse's cuffs. "Everyone has fun with me."

Our log rocked as he bent closer. The blanket parted to reveal his pressed black waistcoat and white shirt. "*Everyone*, huh?"

"Well, anyone not born of the devil himself."

Graphite-black scruff shaded his jaw, black hair curling behind his ears. In the distance, the amber and marmalade blur of the bonfire glowed. "So, what, you're jealous?" I asked. "You want my friendship?"

"I don't have friendships."

"Me either." Not anymore. My wind-whipped hands slipped below the blanket to press against my rib cage. "But sure, once I was the county's favored darling."

"I cannot envision you as a darling."

I crossed my legs atop our stump, turned toward him. "Oh, I broke every rule placed before me. But I can dance to sunup, carry on longer than anyone else."

"Hmm."

"Don't tell, though," I said conspiratorially. "I'm starting afresh, crafting a new alias."

Light glinted on the chain of his pocket watch, and a willow trembled in the breeze. "I won't tell."

It was as if he meant more, as if he spoke of the confidences he kept for me. The air felt thick and soggy with all that was unsaid between us. "You won't tell of the cowboys?"

"No," he said. "It's your secret."

My inhale clogged my throat. "Thank you."

I'd felt on pause, wondering what sort of man he was. But perhaps he wouldn't hold my debt against me. I'd scrutinized how folks spoke of the Lawman, and the tales were atrocious: him roving No Man's Land with rival outlaw bands, maliciously pitting criminals against each other. But it was becoming hard to envision him as a bloodthirsty gunslinger. I couldn't untangle the story from the man before me. Of course he was unyielding and menacing, but there was an honor to him. A righteousness and appreciation of order. Those weren't qualities one expected of a renegade.

The breeze whipped past, fluttering the baby hairs on my nape. He watched me, firelight striking across his jaw, highlighting the strong angles, the rough stubble, his austere demeanor. I felt uneasy, as if I couldn't hide myself from him. I adjusted a hatpin in my bun.

"It's Stot," the Lawman said.

"Stot?"

"Umstott."

His name. "Oh." I rubbed my thumb over a deteriorating section of the wood stump. "You still have to call me Miss Hoopes."

He doffed his hat, then settled back into his relaxed pose, as if he slept. The evocative rhythm of voices and drums and stomps thrummed along my spine. The song ended, and a hush spread like scent through the crowd. Though I didn't want to rely on others, I'd enjoyed these hours with the Osage. I felt a part of myself sit up from the grave and remember.

I tilted my face skyward. The night had weakened from black to an oily gunmetal, like water poured across a canvas. The fire warmed me, but beyond, a norther rumbled and roared. Winter was almost here. I hoped I'd prepared enough to survive until spring. A faint warmth pulsed along my boots, beckoning me toward home.

Around camp, day rustled from night, the Osage rising from their timbers, blankets looped around bodies, the warm scent of black coffee seeping through the air. Niabi settled beside me on the log, the four stripes on her cloak arresting in the oncoming light. "Greet the new day with me?"

I followed Niabi to the edge of their camp, where grass became forest. Beyond, where sky met earth, a brightness loomed. Dawn was rising.

The Osage chanted. I was honored Niabi had invited me to observe their rite. I wrapped my blanket tight across my shoulders and waited. And then a sunray slashed over the horizon. As they sang, they crouched and lifted a piece of earth, swiping the soil across their foreheads in sacrament. Before fleeing Kansas, I'd rarely ever thought about this concept of land. The prairies of our farm had just been ours, something taken for granted. But after feeling cared for by my meadows and my creek, after hearing the Osage stories of honoring the land, after all I'd lived this past season, I felt such deep gratitude for the earth. I bent and scooped up a fragment of soil.

I studied the red dirt smudged on my fingertips. It was cold and silty. I rubbed the soil between my fingers and looked homeward.

WINTER

December 1893 and January 1894

Earth

the same land—springtime 1087
eight hundred years before

Let me tell you a new tale.

Through the eons, I become something new, re-forming and evolving, my plates jostling mountains and carving rivers, the stretch of a valley, the burst of a volcano, my body reconstructing again and again. Alteration is something I know. But now change comes suddenly. Once, my body was wide, sweeping prairies and lost forests. Now, they hammer metal veins into my forearms, the railroads fissuring like river and tributary across my chest. Once, the buffalo rubbed their backs on my grassland, their rolling creating rainwater wallows for birds. With their hooves, they aerated my soil for new growth. But the buffalo disappear. And I am thirsty. My skin crackles and withers, and faraway through time, dust storms blossom across my robe.

The cries are getting louder. They writhe and they ache.

Across my body, women are screaming. It's time.

Minnie, do you hear me? I see you pause, watch the scatter of shadows between the hickories, and I'm trying to tell you—I understand heartbreak, I understand lonesome. But you're not alone. There's a community of women waiting for you.

For you to know the ancestry of this land, we must start at the beginning. Once, longago before time, there was a woman named Prairie Rose. She's the woman in your mirage—burrowing through bramble, journeying somewhere unknown. Prairie Rose lived. But then, she was remade into folktale. She becomes a flower, made of petal and thorn. While a southern wind rages, she battles to bloom on my meadows. Whirlwinds, always blustering against wildflowers.

Have you heard the unearthly tales, of the violent removal of the Natives, the unfathomable horrors and brutality? I watched. An era full of anguish and terror. Haunting voices bled into my body, sorrow loop-stitched up my spine. The echoes of Prairie Rose's agony quakes through my fields and my woodlands, her wails tangle inside the void. But, she endured. She bloomed.

Prairie Rose is just one of my stories, there are many.

Winter comes again, and I shudder. Haze creeps like gossamer over my meadows; the midnight hours lengthen and swell; the wind whips. Crevasses gnaw between my bones, hot flashes swamp over my shoulder blades, my body weary with age and mistreatment.

Minnie, are you listening? I'm rewriting memory.

I chronicle a narrative of this land, of these rolling hills nestled up to Crooked Creek. Of the women who've walked here—and the history they left behind. Do you understand? Like a quilt draped across time, women patchwork across my body. Lives stitched together, the quilted pattern repeating.

The story, this folklore of women, is always beginning again.

Let's restart.

CHAPTER FOURTEEN

Oklahoma Territory—December 22, 1893

four weeks later

I bunched the withering wool of my shawl below my jawline, the wind surly as all wrath. Winter spiraled deeper and deeper until springtime felt like a misremembered past. I led Cricket through the broad doorway of my barn into the carriage room. Patches of glow patterned with the dark across the packed-dirt floor. I felt in my bones the transition from bleak, howling winter to the quiet shadows of my barn. At his stall, I hung Cricket's bridle and saddle blanket, then tugged off kidskin leather gloves, warming my palms against my red flannel petticoat. I exhaled tepid air on my hands and rubbed Cricket's flanks, his gaunt barrel expanding with heavy breaths. He nickered—and I jolted. I'd become used to hush. There was peace in the steady expectancy of quiet.

Grayed daylight streamed through the wooden planks into Smallhopes's empty stall. It was strange to not hear her stomping. I flexed and unflexed my frozen fingers, then grabbed Cricket's hairbrush off a nail. I missed Smallhopes—but I'd needed this barn. I'd traded her to the proprietor of Enid's general store for some furniture, a stove, and the materials to build my barn. I'd wavered. The wife had offered her five sons to build my barn, a flock of chickens, twenty dollars' credit for food over the winter, and packets of sunflower and wildflower seed. I'd been eyeing those frivolous seeds. "Add that sketch pad and charcoal set," I said. "And that's a trade."

And so they'd built my barn. With leftover wood, I'd hammered together tables and built a bed frame into the wall of my shack. By tugging a length of canvas across the grass, I'd dragged my stove inside. I'd scattered the seed, rigged a chicken coop, and scowled at the fresh paper. I didn't have time to paint: This age of my life was wind, soil, work. On another venture down ol' Chisholm Trail to Wakita, I'd traded one of the cowboys' shotguns for a milk cow, Mrs. Dawdle. My palms wet on the Winchester, thumb brushing the checkered walnut stock, anxiety knotted in my gut. There was risk that someone would recognize the long gun—but I was hungry.

"Alright," I spoke into the smoky shadows of my barn, my voice gritty in the silence. I brushed my knuckles along the bridge of Cricket's nose. "You'll be safe here, old buddy. Good night."

Outside, the wind spittled, and coyotes clamored from off faraway. Golden light spread along the horizon as another lonesome night rushed forward. My land was tawny brown and rounded in dusk, pocketed with shadows and mystery. I pulled up my shawl and leaned into the gale, pressing through the current like wading through muddy Kansas ponds. The stitches on my gloves had frayed, the leather wispy, my hands brittle in the cold. Something shifted along the ground, and I searched for a rattler. I'd smashed another snake the day before last. But there was no rattle, instead a squeak and whistle threaded along the wind, as if a draught spun through a keyhole of an elm.

I scoured the shadows smudged between the hickories. All evening I'd felt as if someone narrated fireside legends to me. Fragments of wide tales, glimpses of other lives lived. A disquiet, that inexplicable feeling of not being alone. My rifle was propped beside my bed, so I pointed my broom toward the sounds—in the gloom of dusk, that would do the trick if someone was out there. But there was no one.

Just a rattling, muffled and hoarse. As if voices called across a great distance. An impression appeared before me across the landscape. The vision was like an ambrotype photograph developing on a plate of glass, a transient image of ghostly, dimensional shadows and granular lines. Glass dipped into a puddle of silver nitrate, a form slowly emerging, a world taking shape. I glimpsed a woman astride a buckskin mustang, clothed in brown Levi's waist overalls, galloping along a distorted expanse as if silver liquid spilled across the illusion. Gold snapped across the phantasm, the gilt braid round the woman's cowboy hat, the stars on her spurs, details coming into focus, then fading away into mist. The apparition wasn't fully developed, as if it existed in that space between when the glass was set in the chemicals and when an image came to be.

I blinked, but the daydream didn't vanish. Warmth kneaded my boot soles, as if my land breathed hot fire, as if the earth was awakening. Distinct notes emerged from the chatter, sound collapsing into something resembling words. *Memories intertwine*, and then perhaps, *a new history of women arriving.*

I didn't understand what was happening. I must be filling up the quiet and the broken and the hidden places of myself with old tales. I must, for what other explanation was there? I'd heard of diseases of the mind, of women who heard voices or saw prophecies. Of women locked in asylums. But I didn't feel like I was unraveling. I held my shawl tight against my throat. "Is something there?" I yelled, air rushing into my mouth.

On a sudden, the mirage dissolved, saturated colors and graphite shadows disappearing last. It was quiet, and I was alone.

In my gut, I knew I'd just imagined legendary Willie Matthews, costumed as a boy, driving cattle up Chisholm Trail. She was one woman, a moment in time, who had re-created history. And the other woman, the one with the long black braids scrambling through briars, perhaps another forgotten legend from long ago.

I couldn't explain what sorts of magic existed out on the cold, dark plains. I turned from the stories and disappeared back into the gloom.

~

Before the crackle of the woodfire, with the moan of an oncoming storm, I dragged a quilt atop my knees. I raised my fingers before me, considered my reddened, knobby knuckles. Just cold, not frostbitten. I flung my head back and sighed, tales wandering inside my mind. Sakes alive, course I wasn't infected with hysteria. My ma always told of discernment, of her Holy Spirit, of how forces beyond our realm would speak—if you'd just quiet, just listen. Whatever was knotted in the wind didn't feel like my ma's religion but like something not yet named. I recognized that the world was more expansive than my belief.

In my rock fireplace, the flames writhed and stretched. Minutes evolved, time an everlasting swell. I read several chapters of *Vanity Fair*, then grabbed my pencil and the *Guthrie Daily Leader* crossword. I marked the squares, my handwriting precise and angled, as wax bubbled down my tallow candle. The wind rattled—paper scraps shivered on the walls. To fill holes between boards, I'd shoved in newsprint and ripped up a sky-blue skirt, mismatched materials jigsawing up my walls. Hand-braided rugs lay on my wood-planked floors, and crates with curtains slung across became cabinets. My shack was cozy, quiet. And mine. I'd expected foreboding and terror, during lonesome nights on the prairie. But even after the horrors I'd experienced, I felt at ease. The shadowed, muted parts of myself felt at home in the wide dark.

For Yuletide, I'd plopped a sage bush in a brass drum, looped on popcorn and dried berries. In a few days, I'd light beeswax candles in tin holders and open the lone package resting on the tree—something the size of my fist brought over by the Browns. I pressed the newspaper flat. Five across, eight letters, *King of the Wild Frontier. Crockett*, the legendary frontiersman my brother Willie had imitated for a season with his antique coonskin cap—until our relentless teasing had pushed him into lavish cattlemen fashion. Fringed chaps and bright-chroma bandannas. I unwound my plait and trailed my fingers through my hair, swept up in memories of terrifying Magnolia with tales from *Davy Crockett's Almanacks*: Katy Goodgrit wrestling wolves, Sally Ann Thunder Ann Whirlwind's double streaks of blue lightning, or the giant haunting Old Sally Cato's woods. That had been years after Magnolia had come to live with us, but before the haunted look left her eyes.

One dawn, light slanting through the barn's eaves, I'd handed her the milk pail to haul inside. "If you spill," I'd said, "Billy Bally Bully will stomp down outta the hills and eat you in one bite, lickety-split."

She swallowed, whites showing round her brown eyes. "But Old Sally Cato killed him."

"Right." I dried my hands on my apron. "But he's got buddies. That crashing during thunderstorms are giants as wide as twelve barns strolling on down to Kansas from the Missouri foothills." I crouched. "If ever you hear *squeakity whirr whirr whirr* on the wind, that's the sound of Old Sally Cato spinning thread on her porch."

Magnolia's knuckles pinked, tightening on the iron handle. I told her how Old Sally Cato's boys had roused Billy Bally Bully from his sleep and then raced on home, the monster on their heels, his mouth as broad as a valley, teeth as sharp as pitchforks. Magnolia blinked slow, and I continued, leaning against a post. "But, quick as lightning straight up sideaways, Old Sally Cato fought the monster, then sat back down at her spinning wheel. *Squeakity whirr whirr whirr.*"

A few nights later, during the midnight hours, with a norther whistling between loose boards, I'd felt Magnolia slip from beneath our quilt. She knelt on the floor, the wood planks faintly creaking, and peeked under the bed, her golden curls gathered under her puffy sleep bonnet, the blue hue of night shading her with otherworldly shadow.

"Magnolia," I said, "sweetheart, come back to bed."

Magnolia shrieked and lurched, bumping against the bed frame, her pale lashes translucent in the moon rays. The big owl stirred in the eaves and flew away, his wings flapping into the night. I gathered her in my arms and pulled her into bed. "It's me, it's me, I'm so sorry," I repeated. "*Squeakity whirr whirr whirr* is just wind songs."

As far back as I could remember, I had stirred up disorder and chaos. With one mindless tale, her body had tensed again, her worries returned.

"It's me." I rubbed her back. "It's always you and me."

As moonlight crept through the cracks between wallpaper and fabric, my candle guttering, firelight a'glow on the mounds of wax, I folded my hair into a long braid. On the newsprint, below *Crockett*, I added the last words to my crossword, *a haunting*, then folded the newspaper in fourths and sat awhile in the loud silence. Flame glowed through my Ball jar of potpourri, brightening the melon and fuchsia and rouge tones of last spring, the wildflowers I'd gathered and boiled. Rose vervain and fleabane, hedge parsley and sky-blue aster. Now the petals were just abandoned memory, isolated in their glass cage. I tugged my robe tight over my nightgown. I felt hazy, detached from reality, my thoughts spiraling round and round, aimlessly circling how the wind screeched out in my open plain. A cattle drive spread across my land, a downpour foaming over the herd, Willie Matthews wrangling steers on her mustang, yellow oilcloth slicker bright in the gloom. Flame stretched from my fireplace, and my candlewick scrawled long shadows across my walls. I pressed my thumb into the warm wax, felt something. Then I stood and tossed the newspaper, with all those words, into the fire.

CHAPTER FIFTEEN

I trimmed my lampwicks with my dagger, fresh kerosene ready for sundown. Wiping my blackened palms on my apron, I grabbed the sagebrush broom off its nail. Swept the floor and chimney, whisking the pile of ash from my home, thoughts tangled up with long-forgotten stories. With household chores almost complete, I could gallop through fields, training my horses.

I groaned—I'd forgotten to clean the dratted butter separator again. I hated the slow, precise disassembling of parts, the gentle scrubbing, the absolute tedium. If I ever dragged out my oil paints, I'd grasp gray and brown pigment, toss some dirt across canvas, capture the monotonous emptiness that was winter on my farm. As I removed the crank handle and disks from the separator, the swish of skirts through grass broke my solitude. I squinted through unbroken sunrays. Olive strode toward me with a basket rounded by a cheery gingham cloth. "Joyous tidings," she called.

I dropped the separator and wrung my hands on my apron. "Olive, happy Yule."

She smirked. "You've ash all about your face."

I dragged my rag across my skin, scraping off dirt and weariness.

"It's in your hair," she added.

"Of course it is. Shall you like to come back after I've had my wash?" I flung my hand westward. "In the frigid creek."

Her gaze swept the clutter of projects strewn across my porch. "Mmm."

"Everything's fine."

"I never said it wasn't." She transferred her weight, the plum velvet ribbon rimming her hem wavering, then settling. "Heard tomorrow was Christmas Eve."

"Huh. Heard that too."

"Coming to the dance?"

I sat beneath my wooden shake-shingles. "Not likely."

Olive grabbed my pail of walnuts and sat beside me, puffing her starchy skirts over her propped knees. One warm autumn day, I'd tossed the pail of lime-green walnut balls across a hard patch of earth, and without restraint I'd set to stomping the nuts from the soft outer hull. Though homesteading was lonesome and monotonous, some moments were full of lavish, private abandon.

Olive unfolded her knife. "Hear there's to be watermelon and gingersnaps."

"Someone has molasses?"

She pressed her blade into the seam of the walnut. "That's the story."

After we'd shucked the pail of walnuts, and Olive blessedly cleaned my butter separator, leaving the pieces to dry on a cloth, we reclined against the bleached oak planks of my shack, the long wild rye tossing in the wind. A red dust cloud toppled across the meadow, obscuring the tree line. Olive opened the folds of gingham to reveal popcorn balls, her demeanor tranquil but her eyes solemn.

"What's troubling you?" I asked.

She snapped her gaze to mine. "What do you mean?"

"You're upset about something."

She wiped beneath her eyes, sweat highlighting her cheekbones. "You hear talk of those missing cowboys?"

Warmth shot up my spine. No one had spoken of the cowboys in months—I'd hoped interest in the story had finally dwindled, that I was free of those awful men. If provoked, if this story started swarming, the

Lawman would surely offer me up to slaughter. Why had I assumed a renegade could be trustworthy? There was no loyalty between us.

I forced my hands to unclench. "What's in the wind?"

Olive fiddled with the ribbon ties of her ivy-patterned bonnet. "Seen you out riding with the Lawman. You're friendly with him?"

Course we weren't friends, but Stot was useful on a hunt. And he'd re-sided my shack. "He's helpful round my homestead," I said.

"Just plain reckless to run about with him."

I coughed a brittle laugh. Reckless was all I was, all I had left.

Olive scraped at mud caked on the arch of her foot. Was she insinuating that he was responsible for the missing cowboys? I liked her like this—not just the pristine, competent homesteader but someone with edge and dust. A woman full of her own opinions—even if she was wrong.

"I do appreciate your concern," I said, "but I left Kansas because I tired of folks bossing me about."

Olive scratched down her neck. "Right."

I could tell she was annoyed—but I'd fought for my independence. I didn't want others judging me. "And he's not all bad," I said.

"So you believe people are shades of gray?" She straightened the swoop of her ruffled collar.

I tended to sift humanity into two categories: full of shadows or full of light. As either a risk to me—or me, a risk to them. In my pocket, I gripped the curved bow of my key. "Actually, I see saints or sinners."

"We're not all one or the other, though, right?"

"No. I forget that."

She grabbed a popcorn ball, handed one to me. I tasted the luxurious sweetness of the treat, my land fading in the distance, my thoughts muddled up with worry.

"I've seen your ease with horses." Olive rubbed her thumb along an eyebrow. "Thad's talking tales of joining a cattle drive come summer."

"He can ride?" I asked. "Knows horses?"

"Fair enough." She knocked her head back and forth. "As children, Asa and I were enslaved on the same plantation. He labored in the stables. But after we escaped—we haven't had much notion to spend time round horses."

"You fled during the war?"

"Yes." She grasped the edges of her rounded collar, knuckles tight. "Now I'm looking to the future."

When I mourned, folks' condolences or questions made the suffering worse, so I just sat with her a moment, waited. Hanging from the rafters, bags of geese feathers, curing for pillows, warmed in the sunshine. She didn't say any more.

"Send Thad on over," I said. "I'll teach him some ranching skills, so he's not a tenderfoot."

She thanked me, and we crunched the popcorn balls in silence. After a time I brushed my hands along my apron and asked, "You were saying something, about the missing cowboys?"

She tucked a piece of hair back into her French braid, turned toward me. "Here's the thing: No one's seen hide of them since September. Their wives back in the Dakotas are pressing for answers, screeching about foul play."

I wrought my knuckles, unease anchored in my stomach. "Why does anyone even care?" I scratched at a dry patch on my wrist. I couldn't figure why folks didn't just let this story die. It was the Wild West: People disappeared. "Men roam, leave their wives all the time."

"Story goes," Olive said, "that they weren't just cattlehands but Wild Bunch outlaws."

"Well," I paused, "damn."

"Bitter Creek, that gangly, unnerving Wild Bunch outlaw, he's haunting social gatherings, questioning homesteaders—all a'fire about the mystery." Olive studied the sunshine striking from a low cloud. "I don't fancy folks impassioned about one cause or another."

I broke apart my popcorn ball, hands sweaty, the crumbles sticky in my palm. Out in the frontier it was vigilante rule—everyone creating their own order. It didn't matter what the law said, it mattered what folks decided about you. Sometimes a claim of self-defense would save you, other times you'd be hung before nightfall. "You think the county's moving toward vigilante law."

"They just haven't chosen their target yet," Olive said.

Sakes alive, we didn't need more trouble. It was enough, just surviving winter. Perhaps Olive was right, that folks sought someone to blame, but I couldn't turn myself in, as men never believed a woman's story. But—no one had found the bodies. My corner of the frontier should be safe from a witch hunt.

My translucent bags of geese feathers fluttered in the breeze, sunlight a'glow through the linen, the feathery silhouettes gray shadows. I realized her earlier implications about Stot: I'd killed the cowboys, yet he was under fire. Once again my choices heaped havoc onto someone else.

"And it reasons," I said, "that the Wild Bunch could target their enemy, the Lawman, and me being neighborly with him—"

"Just take care of yourself, Amelia. Be watchful."

"You as well." I gnawed my lip. "And you can call me Minnie."

She snorted. "You truly don't let folks in, do you?" She took my hand and squeezed. "Think about the dance, won't you?"

She stood, brushing her hands along her faded raspberry-pink calico dress, and crossed my pasture, her empty basket hanging off the crook of her arm. My posture was taut, sweat slipping down my back.

Olive turned, spoke from across the field. "You do know: There are folks who can handle your dark spaces."

She walked up the hillock again and, soon enough, disappeared into haze. The scraggly branches along my horizon blurred, and distantly cows groaned. The sun tripped across the sky, day quickening toward the coming darkness of night. I strode downhill. I had work to do.

At candlelighting, I propped a wooden panel against the raised bark of a blackjack oak, a few tubes of oil paint clutched in my palm. I'd salvaged the board from a broken crate, the surface already primed with gesso. I was determined to paint with color again. Across the sky, the lush sunset soaked upward while the laundry lingered on the line and a pile of logs hulked beside my axe. I stepped forward, held a flat sable-haired brush vertical—then I painted the expanse in rushed, impressionist strokes, drenching the board in thick smears of vermilion and cobalt and amber. After the sky darkened several shades, I dropped my brush into the wheatgrass, hefted my axe, and went to split firewood. A while later, with the sun fallen beyond the curve of the earth, in that ghostly luminescence of twilight, I walked on past. I spotted something within my painting. There seemed a shape moving among the grasses, a flick of a withered shawl, the elegant curve of a collarbone—an impression of a woman not wholly there.

Apprehension squirmed round my shoulders. I'd read a story last year in *New England Magazine* of a woman who'd lost hold of her reason, haunted by a figure crawling about her hideous yellow wallpaper. I couldn't remember what had become of her. There was risk if someone glimpsed my sanity fracturing. Even though old folktales just wandered my resting mind, if I seemed the slightest bit unmoored, I could end up trapped and caged, imprisoned in an asylum. I turned the board around and walked on, oil paint smearing like warmed wax across my thumb and along the swoop of my palm, the air pungent with the sharp scents of mineral and woodland.

CHAPTER SIXTEEN

The next day I slammed my shovel into the dirt, forcing the tool farther into the earth with my heel, the ground hard and unyielding, the air today watery and too thin. I tossed the load, the brittle red clay crumbling in oblong circles and squares. If only I'd finished digging my well before winter. But no, here I was, still burrowing, my shovel barely edged beneath the surface. The sun submerged below the tree line, and a butter-yellow light speared between the branches. Winter echoed with faint sounds, like a lingering of long-gone summer crickets. The periodic whinny of the wind or the rustle of an animal scampering through brush. My shovel hit a rock, and the ricochet reverberated up my forearms into my biceps. I huffed out some air and leaned over the handle.

It was Christmas Eve, and I was alone. The days and years and seasons of my life blurred, the colors of our farm oat and sable and Magnolia's favorite rose-pink dress. But Christmas, those moments stood at attention. Evergreen and white, cranberry and gold. Magnolia and Pa before the fire, caroling. Willie pulling Ma to her feet, candlelight flashing on the pine boughs, my hand grasping Magnolia's, and we'd whirl round the room. Ezra scowling from the corner, smoothing his wiry waves of hair into place. Pa muttering prophecies of spring: *Now, did you note them stripes across the catapillas? We're in for a long winter*; Ezra arguing about rings around the moon or low quantities of acorns. I'd lie about seeing the thick tail of a coon or woodpeckers sharing a tree, send Ezra into a tizzy. That had been my life. But I was here, right at present, creating my own story. Memory was a lost place—distorted with time, forever ungraspable.

A remembrance settled over me, of the Yuletide celebration the year before, when families from across the county had roamed over to celebrate on our farm. A scratchy wool throw blanket wrapped around my shoulders, racing downhill, winter grass brittle on my bare feet, cold air scraping down my throat in gasps, our laughter an echo across the lowland. Beside me, Willie bound through the prairie, lifting his legs high, trying to avoid the inevitable burrs from catching on his new slacks, his hands full of Lark's clothes. I couldn't believe Lark had fallen for the prank, Willie daring him to stand outside naked for ten minutes, but, of course, we'd stolen his clothes and headed off yonder to the millpond.

There was a holler, and I peeked over my shoulder, skidding downhill over gravel, grasping Willie's arm so I wouldn't fall, a laugh cracking from me. Lark sprinted after us, his skin a white glow in the dark, a cowboy hat held over his unmentionables, the golden bonfires of the celebration a blaze along the rise.

"I'll handle the clothes. You stall him." I caught the bundle from Willie, then rushed downhill, the garments smelling of horses and sweat. I reached the pond and jumped across stones, headed to the mossy outcrop in the middle. I slipped on some algae and grasped the wide-flung oak limb overhead to steady myself—dropping Lark's clothes in the wallows, his overalls a blue smudge sinking in mire. Willie and Lark ran up then. "Ah, hell," Lark said, scowling at his clothes in the shallows, and then he rushed me.

He swooped me round the waist and tossed me over his shoulder. I gasped and called for Willie, but he just grinned and let Lark haul me away, surely to toss me in the pond.

"Lark." I smacked his back. "Come now, this satin will pucker, and my ma will have my head."

"Well, you might as well take it off then. You're headed for the water."

He lowered me, my bodice sliding along his bare chest, my ankles and hemline dipping into the freezing water, the creek trickling on by. His usual grin pressed into his face, but it felt thin at the corners. "I reckon we should be careful," he said.

I looked at my fingers, narrow and tapered along his chest. "When have I ever wanted careful?"

We left the water, Willie tossing Lark a blanket, the group of us settling under the broad water oak along the bank. "Whiskey," someone yelled from the shadows, neighbor boys running downhill to join us, hauling a barrel of red eye. We talked the midnight hours away, the night sky clear of clouds, stars bright and crisp. Willie leaned against the trunk behind me, Lark now clothed in overalls from someone's cousin.

"So who's all headed to the Strip this summer?" I asked.

Willie pumped his fist and howled. The other boys were unsure. "You rushing, Minnie?" one of them asked.

"Absolutely." I knocked my head toward Lark. "This feller here, Magnolia, my brothers, and I plan to find plots alongside each other."

Growing up, everyone knew Lark and I would someday marry, but now that the Strip would open soon, I didn't suppose we needed to hurry. We could continue on as we always had, finding plots of land alongside each other, living as closest friends and neighbors, and then, after I'd proved up on my land, we could marry and have children.

"Willie," I said, "we're linking up with one of the big groups, right, maybe those founding the city of Woodward?"

"Mmm." Willie drank his whiskey and looked over his shoulder, scanning the distant party, surely wondering whether another gang was up to something more fun than us. Willie looked at you like he was searching for the next thing. I nudged his boot, brought his attention back. "Woodward?"

"Willie," someone hollered from uphill, "you down there?"

"I am alright." Willie pushed off the tree and straightened his waistcoat.

"We've got a baseball game rolling," a neighbor said, "need you as captain."

"On it," Willie hollered and hastened uphill. The others followed, leaving me at the creek with Lark. I lifted my brows. "Baseball?"

Lark kneaded the back of his neck. "I like the pond at night. We could stay?"

I clinked my glass against his. The moment stretched long, somehow heavy and awkward. I rubbed my shoulders, warming myself. "The quiet feels thick-full of thorns," I said. "Why does this feel odd?"

"Everything's changing." He brushed a lock of hair off my forehead, his gaze stuck on my lips, his features indistinct in the understory. "I'm okay with that."

And then he kissed me for the first time, his skin a bit colder than usual. A flush of surprise, of hunger—I wanted so much. His fingers gripped my hips, my hands caught in his hair, the strands stiff like fraying wheat. And then we stumbled into the deep shadows behind the cedars, his hands tugging at my skirts, me fumbling with an overall buckle. There was a click as the metal loop slipped free of the button shank, his breath hot and ragged against my neck, and then we were having sex, his eyes wide, my gasps erratic.

It had been fun, we always had fun. But then it ended. On my homestead, the air blustery, I tucked my shawl up tight under my chin. Being intimate with Lark had been inevitable, ever since the two of us had raced around as toddlers, tangling up in all manner of trouble. Of course we'd ended up unclothed down by the creek. I'd just thought at the end of our wildness, we'd marry and dash off somewhere together. But—he'd never intended to marry me. I edged the tip of my shovel against the rock, the scrape shrill in the quiet. The sky darkened. Lark was my oldest friend, and I'd lost part of myself when he'd stayed behind. But I didn't miss him, not truly. I didn't want to return to my life in Kansas, didn't want to socialize tonight with folks I didn't know at some dance, but tarnation, I was exhausted with digging and building and pressing through my days, a blur of maintenance and chores and sprawling across my couch when dark hit, etching out letters on my crosswords. There was a part of me, buried under these seasons of mourning, that desperately needed something more.

I yanked open my door and shoved my hands on my hips. My woolen corset dangled from a cupboard. I should probably wear that. I frowned down at my timeworn linsey-woolsey shirt and ripped the wincey over my head. I shimmied into my corset and buttoned it over my chemise. I reached behind and pulled the ties tight, jolting myself back into proper society. Then I dug about my chest for my fancy attire. Wool petticoat, pine-green satin skirt bordered with velvet, ivory overblouse, emerald bow knotted at my throat, smart damask jacket, barrettes nested in my hair, and muff warming my hands.

I spun to my mirror. A grin shocked wide at my wild hair and proper outfit. I looked ready to ruin adventure. Well, of course I was. But most surprising—I couldn't wait.

CHAPTER SEVENTEEN

The shack's walls shuddered from the rollicking piano and fiddles, the harmonicas and hollering. I leaned against the wallpaper next to Olive, gripping a decanter of applejack brandy. The one-room home was cheerful and scrubbed clean, kerosene lanterns and tallow candles lit, furniture dragged outside and rugs rolled up.

"And gawd," Olive was saying, "the rattler just went up into the eaves of our soddy. Sakes alive, the critter's just living up there."

I snorted. "I would've shot the ceiling out."

She leaned against Asa and sipped her brandy, the golden candlelight gleaming on the voluminous sapphire gigot sleeves of her gown. "You know, probably should've done such a thing," she said, "collapsed our mud ceiling down upon us."

"It sure was a sight," Asa added. "Olive screeching, snapping uselessly at the air with her apron, the children racing outta doors into the rain." He chuckled. "They came in after a spell, joined me back at the table to finish our turnips and venison."

A rapid-paced quadrille began, and Thad, their teenage son, grabbed Sophia's hand and led her bounding across the room, their elbows linked, bare toes pounding the wood-planked floor.

"Can't believe we're living such stories," I said. "Not sure how anyone will survive until spring."

"Oh, we will," Olive said and clinked her glass against mine.

That seemed the vibrant truth of Olive. She tenaciously sought a safe and hopeful future for her family. Tonight homesteaders gathered from throughout the territory, as far as horse and buggy could pass word of a dance. Willie gripped the shoulder of a farmer in a grain-sack shirt: my brother's cheeks red, leaning in too close, his voice just below a yell as he emphatically told some story or another. Ezra stood beside Willie, wiping a splotch from his mug, bushy eyebrows a dingy shadow color in the dark. Across the room, US Deputy Marshal Frank Canton slunk from one cluster of pioneers to the next, his hands grasping shoulders, long-stemmed pipe dangling from his mouth, golden star a glint in lamplight. His gait was languid but his eyes shrewd. My stomach felt scraped hollow, terrified of what it meant to have a lawman establishing control in our territory. Folks were curious about those missing cowboys, but hopefully the marshal had grander worries than two lost bandits.

Under the glow of a kerosene lamp, the Lawman leaned against a doorway, a tin of whiskey dangling from his hand. Stot had brooded there most of the evening, arms crossed, withdrawn and nefarious. Next to the farmers clothed in shades of dust, Stot was shockingly full of contrast: black hat, black vest, pressed white biled shirt, shined boots. Gun belt oiled and low across his hips. Though we lived our life in the dirt, in layers of earth the colors of murky and rust, his shirt was always clean, stiff with white paper collars and cuffs, spurs gleaming, black wool trousers faded but clean, as if working his land was a sacred act.

"The most reckless buchario in these hills," Olive read from a piece of newsprint shoved into a crack between the shack's boards, a page from a chapbook. An inked drawing of Calamity Jane wiggled from the crevice, her waterfall curls windblown beneath her cowboy hat, elegant throat contrasted beside her dark jacket, hands clasping her mare's reins. I knew the next words in the story, had read it so many times before: *She can drink whiskey, shoot, play cards, or swear, if it comes to it, but 'twixt you and me, I reckon that's a gal who's got honor left with her grit.*

"Has Poppy read Calamity Jane's stories yet?" I asked. "Those tales will get her stuck in a tree, avoiding her duties."

Olive rubbed the ridge of her collarbone. "Suppose that's what I want—for any sort of learning before school next fall."

Poppy sprawled in the corner, playing jacks. Beside Sophia, a girl in taffy-pink ruffles and oversize bows vocalized opera scales. They spoke of putting together a play about Annie Oakley, the legendary sharpshooter who, myth told, had thwarted train robberies and slain beasts.

Willie hollered. "Minnie—you'll perform Buffalo Bill?"

I had a strong voice for leading a backyard spectacle, my male characters a crowd favorite back in Kansas. Sophia rushed over and grasped my hands, begging me to play Buffalo Bill. Once I would've been the center of the carryings-on, but I didn't want to perform tonight—I felt epochs removed from the carefree girl I'd left in Kansas. I shook my head and leaned against the wall between Olive and my brothers, haunted by the past. Even though Sophia was a handful of years younger than me, I felt comfortable beside her ma, the middle-aged homemaker. Willie furrowed his brow at me, then moved his attention elsewhere.

It was past midnight, the crowd frenzied as the party dragged on. A while before, we'd ate a second supper: The scent of warmth, of butter and popcorn, still lingered. Children slept—or whispered tales to one another—on coats in the barn. A bonfire raged outside, and the dance spilled from the crowded room into the starlight beyond. Willie wiped his forehead, his skin mottled with the flush of liquor.

I leaned closer. "You're coming day after next to dig my well, right?"

"Come again?" Willie drummed his hand on his thigh, watched the crowd.

"You promised after Christmas to help with some repairs and my well." I crossed my arms. Willie had been born lazy and never got over it. "Feel as if you'd be mighty distraught if I keep hauling dirt myself and that sandy soil caves in atop me, burying me alive."

"Oh, right." Behind him, ghostly hand-laced curtains framed a window. "We'll come round in a couple days, promise."

The marshal ambled toward my brothers, fingers thinning the curve of his mustache. Olive told me of her design for a new quilt, and I chewed my fingernail, straining to hear the marshal. As he'd heard tale of our family's skill with siring thoroughbreds, he asked after Ezra's opinion on breeding horses. For once, I was thankful Ezra took credit for my expertise instead of drawing me into the conversation. The marshal exchanged farming chatter for a span—I didn't overhear any questioning about the missing outlaws. But I didn't trust the marshal's friendly demeanor. He seemingly cataloged each pioneer who populated his corner of outlaw territory. Marshal Canton looked beyond my brothers to the Browns, flicking open his pocket watch and snapping it closed. I told Olive I wanted to wander outside, then slipped into darkness, away from the marshal and his questions.

I stalked through the switchgrass, scraggly winter-dead thistles snagging my skirt. I sat in the meadow, an elm bough framing the expanse. The night echoed of the dance. Wispy, silver-tinged clouds raced across the sky, tiny starblazes winking through the gauze. I hugged my knees, the velvet sleeves of my overbodice bunching. The thistles crackled as someone approached. A cowboy hat and broad shoulders silhouetted as a static shadow before the movement of the sky. Stot.

"Forget your cloak, duchess?"

I lifted my hand, waggled my wrist. "You'll share yours. You're a gentleman, after all."

He shrugged from his coat and dropped it unceremoniously on me, then sat beside me in the bluestem. I slipped my arms inside the long black slicker, its red flannel lining warm and cozy, smelling of smoke and wide meadows and linseed oil. We watched the sky, the calm of night shockingly still after the gathering. One Eye's shaggy fur and pointed ears peeked between the nettle, as he stalked a circle round us, guarding our perimeter.

"You smoke?" Stot removed a cigarette from a leather case embossed with interlocking circles, the knotwork medieval or perhaps Irish.

I held out my hand. "Course I do."

He reclined in the buffalo grass beside me, and I lay, too, lifting the cigarette to my mouth. I felt safe with him, and he seemed to view me as another comrade this long winter. Just two lost souls, taking a breath and watching the starlight. I dragged in the flavors of tar, my exhale fogging clouds in the cold air. I couldn't become friends with that kind preacher by the name of Poor a mile northward nor that banker who chatted with me last week at the county store. No, I'd become friends with the notorious outlaw. Stot rustled his shoulders about in the groundcover.

"You cold, outlaw?"

"You stole my slicker."

"So you're cold?"

"Of course I'm blasted cold, Minnie."

"Amelia." I bit my lip. "So the vicious Lawman is *cold*."

"You want me to act all tough or something?" His eyes were closed, his star-shadowed face softened by something resembling a smile. "You know I don't need to. I'm terrifying no matter."

"You don't seem so wicked." I unpinned my hat and laid it on the grass. "You're insufferable, but I'm not afraid."

"No," he said. "I suppose you wouldn't be."

I decided to take that as a compliment, an observation of my tenacity and grit. Above, oak leaves crackled, and from off yonder—the whine of a banjo, the grumble of wind, the squeal of voices. Warmth from Stot's shoulder brushed mine, as if I felt the borders of his body. One Eye stepped his thick paws between our legs. He turned and turned, then flopped, his body soft along my thighs. Stot petted One Eye, and I laid my hand across my mouth, warming my naked knuckles with my exhale. Stot yanked off his woolen gloves and handed them to me. I tugged them over my chapped fingers.

"I mined some coal last week from that shallow seam up north." Stot slid his hands under his thighs. "Reckon I could cart over a bucket for you tomorrow, if you'd like."

I thanked him—I hadn't had coal all winter. "I've some spare parsnips, if you'd want to get them in the ground before the first snow."

"I offered the coal to you. We don't have to keep a balanced scale."

Yet that was the way of life, especially on the frontier. Friendships were based on exchange, on what you could give and receive. "I'd feel more comfortable," I said, "if I repaid what was owed."

"That'll suit, if you prefer. But I'm not counting score."

I tucked his coat up round my throat and nodded. But I was keeping score. Approaching friendships any other way felt foolish. Stot's gaze roamed my face, seemingly untangling the contradictory pieces of me. His demeanor balanced between awareness of our perimeter and an uncanny ease, that liquid way he moved his body. His hat tipped forward, the crown's classic cattleman crease grabbing firelight and shadow, his profile indistinct in the starlight, thick brows anchoring his face. Perhaps he honestly saw me, as he knew some of my darkness. There was no need for acting, no need to become strong or weak or whatever anyone else expected. I was just Minnie.

CHAPTER EIGHTEEN

A bay mare lowered her head, swaying as she grazed. The clatter of footfalls broke the faint sound of her munching. I flopped onto my tummy, peered through the buffalo grass. Thad and Poppy rushed over, Poppy talking rapidly and gasping with laughter as she asked me for advice on a prank. Thad shoved his hands below his armpits, studied Stot. I told them about stealing my neighbor's clothes last Yuletide. Poppy clapped, and then they raced off to chase mischief. A year ago, I'd led the high jinks myself. Now I wanted to sit and watch shadows. How had I been so effervescent, so young, just seasons before?

"Thaddaeus, wait," Stot called.

Thad halted, and Poppy slammed into him. They walked back, Thad looking over his shoulder.

"Heard your pa say—" Stot said. "I can help you with roping and sharpshooting."

"What now?" Poppy said, flabbergasted.

Stot brushed off his trousers, made to stand. "Forget it. It was a poor notion."

Thad shook his head, eyes wide. "I'd be honored, Mr. Lawman. Honored."

Stot's face moved into something like an untried grin, a flash of teeth more feral than welcoming.

"Sure enough," Thad said. "Just come round whenever. Ma will bake pie."

Thad backed away, Poppy pulling him by the elbow. The moment stretched. Olive seemed wary of Stot, but when all sum was weighed, pioneers welcomed anyone into their home, renegade or not.

"What was that?"

"Heard of his notion to join a cattle drive," Stot said. "Know you offered to help him with riding, thought I could share some of my skills as well."

"You ranched before?" I asked. "Along with that mysterious doctoring."

A crinkle at his eyes. "Perhaps."

I rolled my tongue around in my mouth, the taste of watermelon lingering. "What else?"

"Surveyor. Railroads. Farmed," he said. "Everything, Minnie."

"And now cowboy trainer for farm boys," I said. "You're doing an awful job, keeping up that reputation of yours."

"I know your secrets, but you don't know what I've done." The undertone of his voice was gravelly and haunting.

A preternatural chill crept up my nape. If he spoke of his past in that tone, then it must be full of atrocities. I held his gaze. "You murder a woman and her baby, as folks say?"

He didn't seem to move, the night sky darkening beyond. "I'm wanted for the crime."

"That's not an answer."

"Answer don't matter—either way, I'm all-nation unsafe." He pocketed his matches and cigarette case. "I shouldn't be round you."

"Don't be ridiculous." I pinched his sleeve above his paper cuff. Distantly, the banjo twisted an elegiac melody, the string picks tiptoeing down my spine. "Don't go."

His shoulders tense, body tipped forward to stand. "It wasn't considerate of me to make a habit of publicly socializing with you."

"So just alone on our homesteads." I released his sleeve. "That seems proper."

"Minnie." He sighed, his tone somewhere between exasperated and resigned. "I didn't recognize that in befriending you, I entwined you with my reputation."

I tracked the bumpy texture of my linen blouse with my thumb. "I'm not worried."

I lay back down, nestled into the bluestem, and after a moment he joined me. It felt fragile and raw, those moments under the stars, the vulnerability of another becoming known to me. The tobacco sweetened the crisp scent of winter, and I closed my eyes, felt the flickering darkness upon my eyelids.

"So how'd you file anyway," I asked, "if you're an outlaw in truth?"

"Filed under my twin brother's name."

"Well, that's a convenient alias. So the Lawman has a brother."

"And six sisters."

"You close?"

Stot rubbed his fist, knuckles brittle with the dry winter air. "Yes."

One Eye shivered with some night terror, and I ran my palm along his back. "So why isn't he homesteading alongside you?"

"He's dead."

"Oh, damn." I reached out for him, let my hand drop. "I sure am sorry, Stot."

He took off his hat by the crown and held it to his chest. "Much obliged."

"And your sisters, where are they?"

"Home. I distanced myself after everything, to safeguard them."

I propped onto my elbows, bit my lip. That was something I understood. Laughter haunted the edge of the prairie, and a horse stomped dust with a muted thud. The Dipper tipped across the sky, the handle now almost horizontal, so it was well into the deep of night. Stot reached toward me and slipped his hand into the pocket of his cloak. I froze, his fingers brushing my stomach through the fabric of his slicker, my body buzzing, his gaze on my face, brow furrowed. He pulled out his flask and drank, the scent of whiskey tangy.

"I'm planning to call round on the Osage in a few days." He handed me the flask. "You coming along?"

The liquid coursed down my throat, abrasive and primal, tasting of wood spices and old books and all things worn. "We ain't taking a blasted buggy."

"Course not."

Our eyes met, held. Smolder from the distant bonfire haloed behind him, the rough shapes of his face black and gold and garnet in the tossed firelight. His hair, hat smudged and messy above his orderly clothes. His gaze roamed the length of my arm, the strip of my lace cuff, edging from the cavern of his slicker. He cleared his throat, pulled at his necktie. "Let's walk." He patted his vest pocket and pinched the divots of his hat, lifting it out of the shadows.

The prairie was vast and empty as we wandered through the switchgrasses and sideoats, space stretching forever away to the sky. The delicate winter clouds had fled, leaving glittering starlight. As we roamed, I heard the distant melody of a fiddle, the whoop and rumble of laughter, Stot's low whistle for One Eye. Several women hummed the rhythm of one of Ma's favorite hymns. *Tell me the old, old story, of unseen things above.*

Those few spare notes tugged me back in time, and I could almost smell those long ago summer weeks at the revival in Topeka: grass and sweat and musty Bible paper. Sunglow fizzling across my skin, the constant hum of hymns crooned round camp, the bluebirds nesting above our tent. Lark, Magnolia, and I roamed the edges of the grounds, slipping into the woods, down to the creek bottoms. We were no longer children, not quite teenagers. Sometimes we'd join Willie before a campfire, where he laughed with other boys and passed instruments round the circle. Ezra patrolled camp with a flock of older boys, chins lifted high, Bibles clutched in the crook of their elbows, a glint of righteousness in their eyes.

One evening my pa stood before a bonfire, hands on his hips, suspenders an X across his back. "There's nothing like this, Minnie," he said. "Nothing like the glory of our Lord."

Pa didn't often share musings, so I stepped beside him to listen, lifting my floral skirt above the mud. "You suppose so?"

"Course I do." He flicked a glance at me, bushy jet-black eyebrows flecked with gray.

Once a month, my family joined the other Methodists from miles round at our one-room schoolhouse—we sang hymns and listened to stories, but the zeal swarming this revival was altogether different. Across the grass, Ma and a few women sang as they scrubbed pots, Ma's dim brown hair twisted in a loose braid instead of her habitual bun. She had enlivened at the revival, befriending others involved in the Women's Christian Temperance Union. Between songs they planned a protest outside the saloons of our county.

Pa shifted his weight, studied me.

"I believe God's good." I scratched my wrist below my lace cuff. "I just reason folks will return to whomever they'd been before, when the tents pack up and they head on home to the everyday."

He rubbed his beard, his palms clean. At home his hands were always smudged with oil or dirt. *Tell me the story slowly*, the women sang, *that I may take it in.*

A cascade of laughter burst from the path: Magnolia beckoned me from a cluster of youths. She gripped Lark's arm, his body angled away as he hollered some nonsense or other across the crowd. The whites showed round Magnolia's brown eyes; she was always a bit lost without me.

"Settle your horses," I called to her and turned back to Pa. "You caution that men are fickle, that I should steer clear of the lot of them."

"Well now, I reckon that's truth too." A forlorn smile edged his mouth. "But you do realize man makes religion. What's being worshipped is something altogether elsewhile. Course men are wicked, darling—but that's precisely the point."

Tell me the old, old story. Ma's arm went round and round, scrubbing the pot, her wrist buried in the soapy water. *If you would really be, in any time of trouble, a comforter to me.* I nodded and walked away, my pa at the boundary of the revival, hands slipped into his pockets, in awe of the God of all things. I wonder what might have been if I'd stayed talking with my pa or had joined my ma cleaning, instead of joining the others in a game of chase.

In the stretched lantern light of the Yuletide celebration, the haunting tenor of the hymn lingered. As Stot and I roamed the prairie, youths chased each other round the hayricks in a game of scratch and gravel. The moon arose deep in the night, and then there was plenty of light to explore. We stood by the bonfire and warmed before drifting back out into the darkness. For a time Stot instructed Thad on dagger throwing, blades spiraling through shadow into a stump, Sophia, Poppy, and I huddled beneath saddle blankets. It was a night of watching one brutal, exhausting year slip into past and vanish away.

"Merry Christmas, Minnie," Stot said, as the bonfire roared toward the heavens.

I gripped my woolen mittens, the wind pressing me toward flames. "Happy Christmas."

At the end of the long dark, with smoke creeping up from the timberline to fog the inky-black expanse, the edges of the horizon turned purple and gray, like splotches of boysenberry jam smeared across the sky. Dawn had come, weightless and fragile.

I smelt daybreak as I walked the wood grove with Stot, the warmth of sausages and oatmeal. And across the meadow, the women sang, *Tell me the old, old story*. I stepped forward, ready to begin a new year.

CHAPTER NINETEEN

Osage Nation—January 2, 1894

a week later

"And so the fog stretched from one tree to another." Niabi adjusted her satchel on her shoulder as we wandered to the creek bottoms, harvesting the woodland for tonics and salves. "It was pitch-black but for moonglow," she continued her story, "and that disturbing noise kept echoing through the blackjacks, like the scream of a barn owl but more haunting."

A labyrinth of willow roots grasped ahold of the slope. Niabi's hound Drowsy darted through the canopy of frail brown boughs, and we climbed the crumbling dirt. After Stot and I had galloped over this morning, he'd gone off with Wa-ah-zho, handing him a farmer's almanac and seed catalog, flipping to a woodcut illustration of sweet peas. They would chat for hours about how to mark seasons and cycles, both intrigued by how the other approached crops. Niabi and I climbed to a bald on a high bluff, and I showed her how I breathed through a shot. *Don't shoot with your lungs dancing,* I told her. With her horse, I taught her a few simple commands that built trust with her mare. I was still reconciling all that she'd shown me.

Unsure what to do—what I could do. The past haunted, messy and full of violence. I didn't like the history, or my part in it.

We wandered the forest, Niabi sharing how she foraged for willow bark. "What happened?" I asked, about the haunting sounds.

Niabi crouched. "I suppose I'm about to stumble upon some mystical doorway to my future or past." She shook her head, her beaded earrings swaying. "And guess what I found? Right here, under this tree."

I lowered beside her. "Please tell me you found a doorway to someplace else?"

"I did not." She took a dagger from her satchel. "My nephews, the ones I'd tucked into bed *hours* before, slunk through the shadows and haze, blowing reeds, pretending to be ghosts."

I laughed. "No."

"Oh, for sure."

She ran her palm up the trunk, the fan of lines of her tattoo centered on her hand. "Right here," she said, "the willow is alive. See if you can feel her heart."

I rubbed my palms over the bark, the hollow caverns and bristly hairs scratching my skin.

"We do not take from the heart of the tree. You must honor the tree and do no harm." Niabi brushed the wispy twigs, daylight seeping in to glow on her raspberry-red blouse. "In the spring, scrape the branch here to the green."

Niabi told that the willow symbolized everlasting life, and the bark healed headaches, stomach pains, and the rambling pound of a wayward mind. I grazed the backs of my fingers along the wispy branches. I found rejuvenation in their swaying limbs. And hysteria, which had plagued women for ages past, could be eased by its bark.

Niabi tucked her chin into her blanket cloak and shivered dramatically. "Let's warm by the fire. You must update me on all the homesteader gossip."

Back inside her lodge, I scooped out a palmful of chopped willow from Niabi's turquoise and flax woven pouch, then tipped the bark in a mug. She poured hot water over the tea, the smell acrid in the winter air.

"You're quiet today," Niabi said.

"I'm mostly quiet."

A meadow of dried wildflowers hung from the hickory rafters. The once-vivid overtones now muted to the calmer hues of winter's rest.

"Nothing about you is quiet." Niabi untied a sprig and handed it to me, a bushy stem with a flat moon of white flowers. "Your essence is bold."

"Yours too."

"I know." She hopped onto a stool. "You do not speak of your sister. You quarreled?"

Niabi often bantered with her sisters, their teasing full of verve and laughter and that familiarity of a lifetime of loving each other. My relationship with Magnolia had none of that vitality now—it was something abandoned, something that haunted. Magnolia continued on back in Kansas, comfortable in her little safe haven, our betrayals forever mounting and hovering, dense shadows that just wouldn't flee.

"There's no possibility for reconciliation," I said.

"So now you're creating something new, here on the frontier."

I nodded and pressed a tiny petal in the cluster of many blooms. It was coarse and springy. "Oh." I tucked the stem in the crook of my arm and dug a package from my pocket. "I have a Yuletide present for you."

I laid the tile in Niabi's hands, the painting wrapped in an Irish linen handkerchief. Her thumb rubbed across the needlepoint: a field of violets embroidered by my grandmother.

I held my elbows against my side. "It's just our custom."

"What are we but our customs?" Niabi said.

She untied the bundle to reveal a ceramic square, the slippery material blasting with a multihued sunrise streaking above the soft curves of the earth. Niabi studied the tile, her fingers shivering over the wayward pigments.

I adjusted my hatpin. "It's just a splash of color on stone."

"Don't make it less." Niabi looked up, the tile held to her chest. "This painting seems to contain whispers."

I'd splattered flecks of golden paint throughout the grass. As if lightning bugs lit the prairie. It was as if the glow of sunshine had fallen onto my land and yet—was I now painting voices?

The afternoon smelt of distance and butter, of fry bread and black coffee. Niabi held out a hand. "Do you hear the voice of Earth Mother?"

I shook my head, felt as if all the blood within me drained out. Well, certainly not. That was absurd. "No, of course not."

I swallowed and gestured with the stem. "Yarrow?" I'd woven yarrow into crowns before, laid the circlets under pillows, a wish for health and happiness.

Niabi flicked her gaze back and forth between my eyes, then turned. She propped the tile on a shelf and grabbed an oval of paprika-hued dried flowers. "Some call this plant Thousand Starlight. We find them in sunglow, their thousands of tiny flowers open to the day." Niabi crushed the flower, the blooms like crumbled Yuletide velvet. "They're stronger fresh, in springtime." She moved her shoulders in something like a shrug, her long black hair swaying. "But dried, in winter, they're still powerful."

I snapped off my bloom, the white clusters like a foam of nighttime clouds. It smelt faintly of pepper and spice. Niabi told me to crush them. I smashed the blooms in my palm, then tipped the blossoms into a red oak bowl. She pulled a puff of eagle down from a rawhide container on the shelf. Niabi stirred the airy gray whirl in with the crushed petals, then lifted the mixture onto her fingers. "Smear this poultice onto a bleeding wound. The blood will stop."

I rubbed the chalky, brittle mixture between my fingers. "And if I don't have any eagle down?"

"Cotton. Sumac scrapings." She fiddled with the ends of her hair. "Fur."

I touched the blossom. To heal oneself, one needed flowers and trees, fragments of the earth. "But always Thousand Starlight?"

"You can also stab the stem into the gash." She fluttered her fingers. "Light it on fire."

"Light the flower. On fire."

Niabi grinned.

I motioned packing a wound. "And then press on ground petals and eagle down."

She nodded, and her smile turned wicked. "I like the fire."

I laughed. "You would."

She handed me the pot and pestle with the crushed white blossom, rubbed her nose. "Grind."

I ground, and Niabi placed her hands atop mine, adjusting the angle of the pestle. It was warm in her lodge, the sounds of others faraway. I mixed a pull of down into my bowl and held out my poultice. Niabi nodded and handed me my mug, the boiling water now frothy, lukewarm tea. I sat on the braided rug and curled my feet beneath my thighs. I stirred in some honeycomb and gulped the tea. The willow bark tasted sharp and harsh. It felt brutal to hope—that the marigold-hued liquid swirling round the cup could soothe my chipped and broken pieces.

Niabi grabbed a reed basket with some beads and ribbons for her finger weaving, tom-toms rattling beyond the fabric of her lodge. "Once there was a happy and peaceful tribe." She told of a tribe falling under the spell of a strange illness. Too weak to climb the hills, the medicine woman sent her granddaughter in search of a healing plant.

"Did the girl find the herb?" I asked.

She picked up a red bead, looked down at the weaving in her hands. This was the power of story: It broke through skin and bone. This story, like all stories, was alive.

"The girl was ill," Niabi said, as she flicked the red and yellow ribbons, "and very weak." In her tale, the girl struggled up the hills and came upon the habitat of the flower. But it was dark, and the girl could not see. She searched and searched, but the girl couldn't find the plant. She knelt and cried out in despair to Wah'Kon-Tah.

"Wah'Kon-Tah?"

"You don't know Wah'Kon-Tah?" She lowered her weaving, her straight black brows pulled together. "Wah'Kon-Tah brings everything into existence. The sky above, the earth below, the cosmos beyond. There are many opposites." Niabi gestured with her hands. "Earth, sky. Night, day. Sun, moon. Destruction, life. Birth, death. Woman, man. All things have meaning and purpose."

"Even destruction and death?"

"Of course." She cocked her head. "Your people find no meaning in destruction?"

"It just brings pain."

From beyond her lodge, I heard women singing. "And there's no purpose to pain?" Niabi laced a bead onto a ribbon.

I leaned against the pillows and sipped tea. Perhaps that was the question: Could someone grow stronger without having to endure trials?

"Life is but cycles and seasons," Niabi said. "Birth in spring, death in winter. Nothing is forever." She lifted the ribbon to her mouth, wet a fraying thread. "All will die. Survival depends on the blessing of Wah'Kon-Tah."

"So everything is meaningless?"

She tucked a length of hair behind her ear. "No, everything *has* meaning."

"What about chaos? Does that have meaning—"

"Stop." Niabi laughed, patted the air with her palms. "Just let me tell the story."

"So the girl was in agony, lost and in despair, calling out to Wah'Kon-Tah?" Niabi slipped back into the story. "In the sky, the stars seemed brighter and brighter." Niabi spread her hands. "Until the stars exploded.

"As the light fragments fell," Niabi told, "they landed on the ferny-leaved plant the girl searched for. The medicine woman was pleased that her granddaughter had found the right plant, but she was amazed at the thousands of tiny lights clinging to the blossoms."

"The tale of yarrow," I realized. "Of a thousand petals dripping with starlight."

Niabi leaned against a pillow, spun tea round in her mug. "From that time Thousand Starlight has had clusters of white blossoms."

How beautiful, to find creation in chaos. I didn't know what I thought of mystical, undefinable forces pulling and pulling on the world. The inexplicable voices on my land haunted me. Sometimes it was as if I'd stumbled into an old tale and chanced upon the sort of grand magic found in faerie stories. But then the sun rose, and I felt foolish. Unlike Niabi, I didn't see balance and order. I only saw those many blooms hanging from her rafters, blurry and browned in death.

CHAPTER TWENTY

The following week, Whistlejacket and I roamed the creek bed, her rope lead loose in my palm. Morning light cut through the canopy, rays falling in lines across the wooden planks I'd laid across the stream. At the bend in the rivulet, I rubbed her silvery blue withers. "How's that, sweetie?" I motioned toward the planks, introducing her to bridge crossings. She drank some water, and then we wandered closer. I asked whether she wanted to sniff the bridge, and she nosed the wood with her muzzle, her velvetlike black ears tipped backward. "That's brave, Whistlejacket," I said and offered her an apple slice.

The stream hissed on by, sound an unbroken simmer, and impressions of days training horses alongside Pa crackled past. Once, while practicing backing exercises with a mare, I'd tugged her bridle, frustrated. *Do not lose your temper around your mare,* Pa said, grabbing the lead. *Minnie, you've got a way with horses.* He crinkled his face into a smile, mustache wrinkling. *Just gotta learn a little control yourself, is all.* Memories folded together, images looping, but woven throughout them all was Pa alongside me, encouraging me to be a little bit stronger than the day before. In the thicket, a painted turtle plopped into the water, his dive fragmenting the steady rhythm of the rustling stream. Those days with my pa were long ago.

I encouraged Whistlejacket a while more, until she was comfortable placing her front hooves on the plank. When we returned home, I chopped firewood. As I worked, a norther screeched along the timberline and chapped my knuckles. The sky above seemed veiled, an indistinct pressure in the atmosphere. I placed an ash log upright on a stump and swung my axe straight on through. Then I gathered the pieces and piled them on my makeshift cart.

From the north, my brothers and their skewbald Thoroughbreds exited the forest and trotted across my prairie. I lodged my axe in the stump, then wheeled my cart to the barn, meeting my brothers in the carriage room.

"Boy howdy, have you sighted that Sunday hat Mrs. Fieldstone's taken to wearing, with the sharp black feathers like spikes," Willie said. We had an ongoing conversation about ridiculous fashions we'd seen round the county. I led Willie's white-and-sorrel horse into a stall, my palm rubbing the hitch in her hips. Willie followed, clapping his mittens together against the cold. Ezra unbuckled his saddlebag and drew out a canvas sack, the leather ties almost black in the gloom.

"That laundry?" I interrupted Willie's rambling about some farmer's hogs getting stuck in the wallows.

Ezra's herringbone waistcoat strained across the barrel of his chest. "And some trouser hems to darn."

"You reckon I wield a needle any better than you?" I said. "You know I can't sew. And I'm not washing nothing until you help dig my well."

Ezra kicked the stall door shut and shoved the sack against my chest, his ruddy complexion darkening to cherry.

"Ah now, calm your grumbling spells." Willie leaned against a post and snacked on an apple, his mustache oiled into an upward curve.

Willie usually stepped back when we fought. But lately, without Pa to moderate, Ezra and I snarled at each other like starved and beaten hounds. Thunder shook the oak boards of my barn, and Willie nodded outside. "A downpour is a'coming within the hour. We'll get mighty soaked." He plucked at his waistcoat, a slick jade brocade more appropriate for a Topeka drawing room than the farm.

"You're right up yonder from the creek." Willie offered the apple core to his mare and picked a piece of hay off his trousers. "You truly need a well?"

I breathed in through my nose. Yes, I needed a well. It was wearying, hauling water all the time. I'd spent days digging their wells in the sweltering heat of summer's end. Had helped hammer up their shacks, repaired one of Willie's guns when it hang-fired, worked with Ezra's mare when she'd spooked during storms. I was done. I held my arms out, dramatically dropped Ezra's bundle on the barn floor, and strode beyond the broad doorway. Outside, gun-metal-hued clouds foamed across the sky, a thundershaker rising from the south.

Ezra followed and grasped my arm. I tugged it back. "Don't handle me like that."

"You will wash my laundry," he said. "It's your role."

"I never agreed to that. Find yourself a wife."

His bushy eyebrows were straight lines across his brow. "It's nonsense, you off on your own."

I held my wrist where he'd grabbed me, his thumb imprinted on my skin. Ezra and I had fought the length of our childhood, but our arguments had always felt like sibling sparring, something on the edge of play. This didn't feel like play.

Disquiet clamored below my rib cage. Surely the feeling was misplaced, just unease from talk of the missing outlaws and the voices on my land. But watching the fury spike across Ezra's shoulders, the tautness of his spine, remembering all his righteous, anti-suffrage beliefs that threaded deeper and deeper, I wondered. And I felt fear.

"Darn my clothes," he said.

"Sure enough," I said. "You can come round and gather them—when you help dig my well."

"You will do as I say."

A forgotten moment flickered in and out, of another blistering fight with Ezra. I'd been maybe five, arguing that it was my turn to chop wood;

him, eleven and screaming to just get on inside. Ma swept out the door, drying her hands on a rag. *Stop hollering at your sister.* She reached for him, as if to draw him in for a hug, and he flinched. *Ezra?* He tossed the axe across the field, stomped away. From the switchgrass, I hefted the blade, wrapping my small hands around the wooden handle. Ma absently dried her hands, a deep wrinkle between her brows. I couldn't recall what happened next but after that, when Ezra rounded a corner, I'd learned to walk the other way.

I couldn't fathom his anger, as our parents had raised us in a happy home. I didn't suppose Ezra's cruelty was rooted in his zealotry, as he'd been tightly wound as far back as I could remember. Perhaps his fervent beliefs puffed up his need to dominate others, but they weren't the cause. Maybe someone had hurt him, somewhere I hadn't seen. Shown him a more ruthless way to live.

Near the windbreak, a few whitetail deer twitched their ears, sunset light flooding the hardwoods. The deer spooked—and ran away. Ezra smoothed wayward eyebrow strands, the veins on his palms bulging. He vibrated in his fury, waiting for me to relent.

Willie breezed outside, hands slid in his baggy, wide-legged trouser pockets, brows lifted. "It's fixing to gush a thunderclapper." He riffled through the coins in his pockets, the jangle bright in the terse silence. "We'll come round the next clear day, won't we, Ezra?"

I gripped my holster, didn't break Ezra's glare. "I don't trust you anymore."

Ezra scoffed. "Not sure you're qualified to judge anyone's character."

"What's that mean?"

"Hear that Lawman comes by, often enough."

"That's none of your business."

I stepped forward, but Willie looped his arm round my shoulder. "Two days, promise," Willie said.

"Fine," I snapped. "But I'm done with you today." I shrugged off Willie and strode through the high grass. I didn't look back. The uncomplicated days of our childhood felt long ago.

The following afternoon, the air fresh and crisp from a downpour the night before, I hung up the wash, a line stretching from the eaves of my shack to the quaking aspen uphill aways. I'd cleaned my brothers' wash but was determined to ransom their laundry with help round my homestead. I held a curtain between my fingers and clipped it to the line, sunbeams filtering through the lace pattern, sketching floral silhouettes on my hands. The week before I'd left for the Strip, this same curtain rumpled in my lap, Ma had leaned against the doorframe, quieter than usual. I crouched beside my travel chest, folding linens and shirtwaists. Ma's demeanor was fragile, unsteady as she navigated this season of change: Magnolia just married, her other three children venturing into the frontier.

"Lord have mercy," she said. "I'm proud of you—but you sure you want to go?"

I placed the lace curtain deep in my trunk. "Course I want to go."

She tipped her head back against the dark wood doorframe. "You running?"

"What?" I picked up a sheet, folded it lengthwise. "What would I be running from?"

She lifted her brows, pausing to let that thought hang, and then she held out her hands for the fabric. "Here, let me show you." She snapped out the sheet, cobalt lines vivid in the sunglow, and showed me again how to fold linens crisp.

"Ma, stop. You know I'll never be able to fold like you."

She sat beside me on the floor, sheet scrunched in her lap, blue lines coiled about directionless. "Well, and I'd never be able to shoot a rattler off a fence from fifty paces like you, so I think you're the one to venture off as a pioneer, not me."

I swallowed, the space inside myself not large enough to hold her hope.

She cupped my face between her palms. "Go." She blinked, her eyes wet and veined in red. "But remember, this will always be your home."

But it wasn't anymore. I'd lost hold of safe harbor.

On my homestead, the linens wandering in the breeze, the navy lines lifting and stretching, I wondered whether I'd answer her questions the same way now. I had run, but I'd always been going. I just hadn't thought I'd be fleeing heartbreak.

I missed my ma, missed the farm. But this space between the wild-woods and the creek was my home. At times my prairie was empty and lonesome, but then I listened. I clipped up Ezra's rough-spun shirt, my fingers raw and cold, and heard the edge of the wind, the chatter of finches in faraway trees, and then words. *It begins with the earth.* I faltered on the clothespin, the wood snapping shut on my forefinger.

One woman returned again and again, the tenor of her voice cavernous and archaic. She reverberated and she creaked, her timbre variable and throaty. Rippling through feathery wild rye, between the silences, her voice just kept on telling me stories.

CHAPTER TWENTY-ONE

A caustic thump rumbled into my dreamlife. I bolted awake and snatched the Winchester off my nightstand, knocking the novel *Waverley* to the floor.

My shack wobbled.

I aimed my rifle at the door. Something rubbed against my home.

It was dark. Quiet. No owls or crickets. The dead of night, the dead of winter. I slipped my feet from the covers onto the cold floor, chambered a round in my Winchester, kicked about for my boots. Keeping my barrel trained on the door, I bent and swept my palm along the oak planks beneath my bed, my fingers skipping over the cracks between the boards. Dust and crumbs but no shoes. I crept to the doorway, bare toes frigid.

A moan sounded through the fissures of my home, low and guttural, and woven into that hoarse scratch were ancient sounds. I couldn't quite grasp words. Couldn't fathom why she kept calling out to me. The walls of my shack rocked again, and yet no one knocked. If someone was here to rob or assault me, they would pound on my door. From the back of the sofa, I grabbed my woolen shawl and looped it across my shoulders. A ghost? Surely not, as I didn't believe in specters. I didn't, did I?

A whine crept into the stream of night. I placed my palm on the wall. A herd of cows must've wandered onto my quarter section. The uncanny light of a young moon streamed through my curtains, the lace flowers casting freckled shadows across the floor. It was mighty quiet for a herd of wayward cows. I stepped back and stumbled over my boots. I yanked them on, then kicked open the door. Flattened against the wall.

No one shot at me. No noise at all.

I heard the drift of the wind and a yapping dog, way off. I muttered a ditty under my breath, forcing myself to wait. A shadow burst low through the doorway. I aimed, and a slant of moonshine gleamed on an animal's smoky, tousled fur.

"One Eye?"

He padded over, pressed on my thigh, whined. I bent, scratched behind his ears, my gaze on the dark hollow of my doorway. "What is it, buddy?"

He nosed the back of my knee, pushing me into the night's shadows.

"Alright, alright." I swung my flannel-lined slicker over my white nightdress, grabbed my kerosene lantern and rifle, and followed One Eye out into the dark.

~

Starlight feathered through prairie grasses, the tottering oats casting a gnarled silhouette against the navy sky. The air smelt warm and burnt, the smoke from surrounding homesteads downwind. I followed One Eye on Cricket—he'd taken off westward from my home, away from Stot's quarter section. We splashed through the creek and continued on toward the salt plains and outlaw territory. One Eye panted, his gaze frantic, as if a thunderstorm loomed. A gale whipped against my chest and tangled my unbound hair. Surely One Eye was guiding me to Stot—I just hoped he wasn't dead.

Along the horizon, smoke coiled: a homestead, probably the hideout of the Wild Bunch. God Almighty, what was Stot doing out here? I wiped my handkerchief across the sweat bubbling along my collarbone. It frothed, then iced in the cold. At the slope toward Wagon Creek—the boundary of the outlaws' haunt—One

Eye yelped. I vaulted off Cricket and stumbled downhill. Aways off, fuzzy yellow, rectangular windows glowed. And in the tall river grasses, a body sprawled, rumpled and unmoving. Black Stetson above white kerchief. Stot.

Moon rays slashed across him, as if his skin was painted with soot and ash. I shook his shoulder, the fabric damp, but he didn't wake. I brushed my fingers across his neck, his skin slippery and warm. He had a pulse. One Eye pawed his stomach, licked his face. The metallic scent of blood prickled the thin winter atmosphere—he must be shot. Stot's saddlebag squashed in the mud, but I didn't spot Shark.

I jostled his shoulder again, slapped him across the face. Smelt his breath, my hair trailing into the silt. He wasn't drunk, just dying. My herbs and remedies were back home, but he was too large for me to heft onto Cricket. I held my slicker tight round my shoulders, the bitter winter breeze seeping through my cotton nightdress.

Tugging on his boots, I dragged him into the gooey mud of the bank, the creek a shadowed blue in the ethereal light. As One Eye paced the shoreline, I shoved Stot, and he rolled into the water. He flopped onto his back, his head above the stream. He lay there, passed out as the dead, liquid seeping round him, thankfully not sinking into quicksand. All wrath, he wasn't waking.

I untied my boots, swung off my slicker, and laid my clothes before the shore. Then I hefted up my gown in one fist and stepped into the creek. I pushed his head below the frigid water—and, on a sudden, he started flailing, kicking about exasperated and wrathy. I dropped him and scrambled away, but he slung an arm around my waist and flipped me onto my back, the air pounding from me as he crushed me into the bank, one hand holding my wrists against the mud, the other pressing a dagger to my throat.

"Stot!" I didn't breathe. "Stop."

He froze, eyes dazed, his drenched body smashing mine. "Minnie?" He withdrew the blade and ran a hand up my waist, his wide palm hot. He sank his hands into the mud beside my breasts.

He shivered. "Blazes, why am I wet?"

"You passed out. In the woods."

"What?" His gaze dropped to my lips, hung a long moment.

He was hard and rangy, a long thigh pushed into the ground between my legs. I shoved his chest. "Off."

He blinked. "Right." He rolled off, studied the tree line, his body shaking. "Why are we outside?"

"You drunk?"

"Don't think so."

"Shot?"

I stood, swept dirt off my gown, my bare feet freezing as they squished into the sludge along the bank. "Why're you out here—you up to some bandit nonsense?"

He touched his shoulder and lifted his hand away. Blood smeared his fingertips. One Eye nuzzled him, and Stot absently rubbed behind the wolf dog's ears. He was shot—my wrists trembled with cold, with fear. I felt around his body, the flush of adrenaline warming my face, my hands finding the slick, gooey place he was wounded. I ripped off a length of my gown, tied the cloth around his wound.

"Don't get mixed up in my mess." His voice a quiet rumble. He burrowed into the bank and closed his eyes. "Just leave me."

I finished lacing my boots and helped him into my slicker. "You're bleeding. You're on outlaw territory." I led him up the bank. "The size of it: You'll die if you don't whip yourself together."

With my grip looped around his waist, I tried to guide him onto Cricket. My hands slipped on his wet shirt, felt the shape of the muscles across his back. "Stop," he said. "I can mount a damn horse."

"Can you?" I taunted him, but my voice was threadbare.

Then he was up, and I swung behind him, his expansive body between my thighs. He looked over his shoulder, his gaze dark and heavy lidded, his palm holding the cloth against his wound.

"What?" I asked.

"I can ride. Climb before me."

"That's absurd."

"Can you even grasp the reins, around me?" he asked.

I shifted my hips forward in the saddle, my thighs fitting against his. "I don't need reins."

He swallowed. "Just climb in front."

I kept arguing, but he pulled me around, my body sliding along his. He settled me between his thighs. I shoved back against him, and he grunted. His hands smoothed along my legs to grab the reins, and his lips dropped to my ear. "Comfortable?"

"Just ride, you scallywag."

He chuckled, and I felt the rumble of his stomach muscles along my back. This was altogether unnecessary. He freed my loose hair bunched between us, then clicked for Cricket to ride. That sound, low in his throat, caused a spiderweb of nerves to burst across my side.

We galloped over our moon-shadowed land, his muscular body behind mine, thighs hot against my gauzy nightgown, arm looped tight across my stomach, our bodies surging in rhythm, and I lost the ability to breathe.

CHAPTER TWENTY-TWO

I hauled Stot inside and kicked my door shut, suffocating the howl of the wind.

"I got it." He swayed, held his arm against his chest.

He definitely did not have it. I maneuvered him onto the sofa, his chilled body shaking. One Eye padded over and curled up before the fireplace. After stoking the flames, heat searing my skin through my gossamer nightgown, I grabbed some supplies: calico scraps, gunpowder, a pouch of willow bark.

Stot watched, eyes wider than normal.

"Take off your shirt," I said, pressing my hair back at the temples, heartbeat pulsing against my palms. A tight shiver from the winter chill—and panic.

He dropped his head back against the sofa. "You're welcome to help, doll."

His eyes were closed with something like a smirk languid on his face, his wet hair curling all about. My slicker, which looped over his shoulders, fell back to pool across the cushions. He was drowsy and unbalanced.

"You been shot a lot, huh?" I lowered beside him and touched his necktie.

"I will undress myself."

"You just drawled for some *doll* to help." My voice light, my stomach all jumbled in knots. I couldn't let him die.

"Pestering you."

I rubbed my hands down my thighs. "Fine. Have at it." I sat back, crossed my arms.

One thing I'd learned from Ma doctoring folks all those years was to be calm and controlled. But—I needed to check his wound. Now. Not argue about nonsense.

My cabin was shadowed, and I squinted to see. He fumbled with the tie, fingers slipping at the knot. Blood soaked his white sleeve, a dirty black edged with carmine and bronze. I broke a match across the heel of my boot and lit a tallow candle, wax guttering over the brass chamberstick. He released his necktie, laid his head back.

I leaned forward and touched the button at his throat. "Just let me."

He was warm, his body still as I unbuttoned his shirt and vest. Beneath, he wore a tank, mostly white with cardinal-feather red blooming across his chest. I lifted his hem, but his hand paused mine, his palm calloused against my knuckles.

"I'm fine," he said.

"Dammit, Stot, you're dying."

"Nah." He raised the edge of his shirt, a glimpse of tan skin. "Stomach's not winged."

"Mmm." I wiped my forehead, my body clenched, fear corkscrewed all throughout. I helped him from his black waistcoat and edged the shirt over his shoulder muscles, the sleeve crunchy with bits of dried blood and sticking to his slick skin. I grabbed my scissors. "I'm cutting off your sleeve."

"Blazes, that's my favorite shirt."

"Not sure red's your color."

Crinkles fanned from his eyes. A frantic urgency heated my body—so I breathed, slowed the motion of my hands.

I removed the shreds of his button-down and tossed them on the floor. His wound was gnarled, but the bullet shallow. I could get it; he would be fine. In a mug of heated water, I stirred in a scoop of ground willow bark. Stot lounged on my sofa, one arm free, the other clothed, black tie still knotted, oilcloth slicker rumpled behind him, linens dirty and sticking to him. I handed him the steeped tea. He glowered at the shards of willow frothed in the water.

"Just drink it."

He lifted my dainty teacup to his lips. I pushed aside my cabinet curtains in search of supplies, glancing at him over my shoulder. He adjusted his grip on the cup and grimaced. I snatched some whiskey and poured a couple of fingers. "Better, princess?"

I tipped the bottle to my mouth, and the liquid scratched down my throat. I shivered, my damp nightgown chilling me. This was my only decent gown, my other threadbare, with a wide, loose neck. I banged about my shelves.

"What are you doing?" he asked.

"Looking for an all-fired needle."

"You're not stitching me up."

I lifted my brows. He tried to look at the wound on the back of his arm. "I can do it."

I leaned against my cedar-plank table. "Alright."

"I'm more worried about your sewing ability." He scrutinized an overdress tossed over a crate.

"There's nothing wrong with my garments," I said.

"Sure. Just the occasional holes and missing buttons." He closed his eyes. "You don't sew. Someone did it for you back home."

How in Sam Hill had he noticed that? I was careful to cover rips whenever I went into town. And furthermore: What had happened back in Kansas didn't matter anymore.

"This is my home."

"Then you'll need to learn."

"You offering to teach?"

He gestured to his satchel. "I have some thread and a needle."

His bag was organized and smelt faintly of oil and nutmeg. I opened a tin, assuming it held thread. Inside rested a jagged piece of ice-blue lace and a miniature of a delicate, blond woman. I flushed and snapped the tin shut.

"Stop nosing about." He studied me, his gaze on the bones of my wrists.

"Don't flatter yourself."

Though soaking wet and injured, he seemed comfortable sprawled about my cushions. I found the needle and a spool of white thread, then sat beside him and cleaned his wound with a strip of daisy-printed cotton. He didn't wince or grimace, but I glimpsed pain in his taut posture. Blood spilled across the fabric, soaking the flowers. My unbound hair fell forward in the gap between us, and candleflame lit the room's hollows. I bit my lip. I shouldn't ask. "Saw a portrait of a woman."

"Mmm."

I wrung out the cloth in a bowl of water. "You married?"

He frowned. "You think I've been hiding some wife in my cabin all this time?"

I braided my hair. His gaze followed my hands as they flicked down to the ends. "That's not really an answer," I said.

He closed his eyes. "Not now."

I poured whiskey over the needle and dug around the muscle of his shoulder. He clenched his fists but otherwise showed no reaction. So did he have some wife back in the Dakotas? A flock of children? Course it wasn't my business, but sakes alive, perhaps he could've mentioned them.

His skin was slick with sweat, his gaze curving along my temples, across my cheekbones. I wiped my neck above my gown with a cloth, tried to grasp the bullet. Finally, it plopped out and pinged in the dish. I sighed, fear seeping out, some relief easing back in. If I could stanch the blood, he'd probably be fine.

I cleaned his wound, threaded the needle, and pressed it through his ripped skin, rendering fairly uniform stitches. He said nothing of the gunfight or the woman. And I didn't mind overmuch. I was okay with secrets. After I sewed his wound, I crushed a palmful of dried Thousand Starlight into a tea saucer, smashed the blooms with the heel of my palm, then scanned my shelf for what to use instead of eagle's down. I knelt beside One Eye, scratched him about the neck and belly.

Stot's deep voice: "What are you doing?"

"Heaping together some rubbish."

"You know what you're doing?"

"Of course." Well, kind of. I sat beside him, folded my feet beneath my nightgown. Warmth from the fire brushed my bare collarbone and wintry air filled the empty spaces. I held out the yarrow-and-fur poultice. "I'm gonna press this on, alright?"

I leaned forward and smothered the mixture onto his skin. "The yarrow will stanch blood flow," I said. "Not sure about the fur."

Firelight cast oxblood and gold across his cheekbones, shadows sinking into the inky waves of his hair. I swallowed and dabbed salve on his wound. After I finished, I washed my hands in the basin and dried with a rag. A draught iced my damp forearms and slipped through my filmy gown. I swept a blanket round my shoulders, then ripped a length of freshly laundered linen, pressing one end to his biceps. He was bulky, but I hadn't thought he'd have such defined muscles. I tugged at my lace collar and kept wrapping his shoulder, aware of his hand resting on the cushion beside me, of the hot and elusive space between us.

"So," he said, once I'd tied off the bandage, "what do you do at night? Do you argue with the wallpaper or throw knives at the fire?"

I packed up my supplies, my one-room warm and cold and too dim. He uncapped a jar of sun-dried persimmons. I nodded, indicating he could have some.

He popped a piece in his mouth. "What do we do now?"

I grabbed a persimmon, the dusky-orange fruit tasting like gingerbread. "You go home."

He settled against my sofa, his hair drying in rough waves, its black color stark against the rose-and-mustard floral cushions. He gestured to the *Popular Science Monthly* periodical haphazard on the side table. "Read me an article?"

I coughed. I would not be *reading* to the man, especially from Magnolia's beloved periodical. My memories were clogged with Magnolia reading science journals or botanical texts, of her debating evolution or plant classification with Pa until dark hovered round the fire.

"You're not staying here," I said.

"All nature, I'm bleeding all over."

I rolled my eyes. "You're fine." A pause. "Go home."

"Nah." He bent and removed his boots. Candleflame wavered beside him, the scent of tallow heady. He settled his boots beside the sofa, polished toes pointed at the fire, spurs a dull glint in the shadows. His socks, undyed wool. "A blanket?"

I picked at the bodice of my nightgown, the newsprint and blue linen scraps papering my walls reflecting firelight. I should be terrified to have a renegade in my home. And yet I felt safe. Perhaps more comfortable than normal. I grasped the ratty afghan spread across my bed, shook it to check for centipedes or scorpions, then tossed the blanket at him. He caught it, looked me in the eyes, questioning. But—he wasn't that considerate, was he?

"How do you fill your nights?" I asked.

He pulled the blanket up round his shoulders. "Read. Clean weapons. Whittle."

"Of course you whittle."

Something like a smile settled on his face. "When I'm not shooting out the lanterns in saloons and threatening babies."

"Well, obviously." I couldn't imagine Stot wrangling up slapdash chaos about the county—but I'd *just* stitched up a battle wound. There were reasons for his reputation. I must heed caution, keep my walls up. I liked Stot, but I didn't truly know him.

I settled on the sofa beside him, scratching my collarbone. After such an adventure, I wouldn't be sleeping for a span. I picked my crossword puzzle up from the credenza, frowned at the riddle that'd eluded me all week. "At least help with my crossword puzzle," I said. "Six letters. Has a *B* in the middle. *To conceal, a refuge*."

The wind cracked against fissures in my walls, and the thick of night oozed about like molasses. He settled deeper beneath the bumpy loops of yarn. "Harbor."

CHAPTER TWENTY-THREE

Golden sunlight feathered through my curtains. I kicked at my sheets, bunched below the quilt. I needed to milk Mrs. Dawdle and feed the rest. I flopped onto my back, covers falling about my waist. Winter air speared the naked skin of my collarbone. That zing, the subtle pain of coldness, a reminder that I could feel something. It was calm, predawn light, the crackle of woodfire, the fluting song of winter chickadees. Another moment and I'd get at it. Then the rumble of a throat clearing.

I lurched up. *Stot.*

He sat at my table, coffee mug dangling from his hand, a few days' beard smoking his jaw. I gawked at him, surely with wide eyes. He peered beyond the curtains, peacefully studying the oncoming light. But there was no peace about the man. He was wild emotion, a whirlwind debate at a precipice. But hell if I didn't relish the thrill of standing at a cliff's edge.

He raised his mug in a salute. His shirt was tugged beneath his waistcoat, buttons askance. The fabric was wrinkled and stained, one arm missing, calico bandage roped round his biceps. So unlike the tidy Stot I'd come to know, instead the likeness of a gruff, sultry outlaw. I pulled at a mauve thread on my quilt.

"Made myself at home." He adjusted his necktie. Wool socks against my oak floor, the heel of one well darned with cobalt thread. "Hope that's alright."

The fire crackled. The scent of coffee and timberwood and other things deep and brown drifted across my shack. I swung to the edge of the bed, blankets pooling at my waist, my square collar falling off one shoulder. "How's your arm?"

"It'll keep."

I scrounged for my morning robe. Last night I'd thrown my muddy, high-necked nightdress in the corner and donned my gauzy nightgown, pearl-embroidered neck stretched, billowy cuffs sheer.

He stared into his mug, a flush about his skin. This whole affair had been outrageously improper, but of course neither of us cared overmuch about senseless rules anyhow. He flicked his hand, gesturing where my robe hung from a chair. I moved across my shack, wood planks creaking, and swung the fabric round my shoulders, tied the emerald ribbon at my waist. I poured some Arbuckle's and lifted my mug, watching him above the rim. He cleared his throat, gaze on the fire. Which he'd built up. And my water bucket was full—guess he'd already been to the creek. All with an injured arm. I bent to rub One Eye, who slept before the fire. "You've been to the creek," I said. "Thank you."

He sprawled in my chair, gun belt removed and hanging behind him from a hook. "Your brothers still not dig your godforsaken well?"

I grunted. They hadn't, weeks passing right on by. I gulped coffee, the coarse grinds breaking apart across my tongue. I chewed, swallowed.

"That's disgusting," he said.

Amused, I sipped from my cup. "What do you do?"

A smirk threaded from his eyes. "Spit them out."

I leaned my hip against the wall. "*That's* disgusting."

"A matter of debate."

"When's it not, with you?"

"Right," he said. "*I'm* the one always arguing."

I gasped. "You are."

He glanced out the window. "Mm-hmm."

I plopped in the chair beside him. "You are the most disagreeable man I've ever met."

He rested his forearms on the table and leaned forward, green eyes unnerving. "You ever wonder why?"

His scent of spices and weapon oil right there. I wouldn't become unsteady round this man, no matter how much space he took up in my home.

"Because you're disagreeable," I said, my voice wispier than I'd like. "I just said that."

"Nah. I think it's you."

I jabbed my finger at him. "That right there. You're being quarrelsome."

"You're the one judging my character. *Disagreeable.*"

I leaned forward, bit my lip. "Maybe try not being disagreeable then."

The flames moaned and snapped. My coffee warm and fragrant. He straightened the lapel of his vest. "You like crosswords?"

"What's this? Changing the subject?"

"You're doing it again," he said. "You like quarreling with me."

I rubbed my mouth. "What else is there to do?"

He scratched his jaw. "We could plan it."

"How's that?"

"Perhaps on Tuesdays we debate some text in our own literary society. Wednesdays it's your crossword. Maybe on Thursdays we torture each other in a shooting contest."

"You want a weekly schedule."

"I like routine, like what's predictable." He stood, riffled through the hardbacks on my shelf.

A laugh caught in my throat—when I realized he wasn't joking. There was so much performance and big walking with cowboys, but this was something real about him. He pulled out my *Vanity Fair* hardback with the green floral motif, flipped open the book, and frowned at the inscription from Magnolia. And then I saw him as something altogether different. Part of him was undomesticated, but another part of him, perhaps buried under long ago tragedies, was traditional. His classic black trousers, old-fashioned cowboy boots, shined with perfectly spaced laces, the monochrome biled shirts and simple tie. Most cowboys flashed jeweled spurs, beaded hatbands, and slick mustaches. He pulled out my ma's black hymnal, the book tiny in his hands, and sat back at the table. I tugged my sleeve over my wrist, feeling altogether too exposed. I'd thought his subdued guise clever, that it helped him blend in, when perhaps he just liked what was classic. If life had come another way, maybe he'd have been the sort of man to be happy with a simple life.

He flipped through the pages, brow slightly lifted, unspoken commentary on such a book in my home. What had happened in his past? There must be much desolation to have remade Stot into the Lawman. It was foolish, but I'd stopped believing in tall tales.

Perhaps Stot did prefer predictability in life, but I certainly didn't. "I don't want a schedule."

"Then how about now?"

"I can't thwart you in some shooting contest this morn—I've gotta keep digging my well while this spell of warmer weather holds."

He scanned a page. "I can help you with that." It felt violently familiar, his hands curved round Ma's hymnal—all those moments Ma had deftly turned the pages, her fingers rawboned and graceful.

"What about your claim?" I asked.

"It'll keep."

"What about your dratted shot shoulder?"

He turned the page, fingers calloused but clean. "I'll be fine."

"I know I said I'd prefer settling debts, but you don't have to stay and help—don't have to repay me."

"I like being here." He closed the hymnal, rested his arms on my table. "I want to be here, helping you. You can't build a homestead all by your lonesome, nor can I. Your brothers aren't helping; I've got no one. We get along well. Just let it be."

I stood and pulled on the ties of my robe, looked beyond my curtains, my gaze unfocused, just colors: taupe, ivory, evergreen, gold. "Okay."

"Yeah?"

"Calm your britches." I tossed back the last dregs of my Arbuckle's, chewed. "If you're foolhardy enough to work with that wound, I'll take advantage of you."

A leer grew across his face. That rogue, he knew what I meant.

"And, um." I scanned the corners of my one-room. "I'll bake you a pie."

He shuddered. "No, thanks."

He stood and strode toward me, the wood floors swaying with his movement.

I crossed my arms. "I can cook."

"Mmm."

His body before mine, gaze on my lips, cheeks, collarbone. He reached out, fingered the ends of my braid. I couldn't breathe.

"Thank you for taking care of me," he said.

I stepped back. "I need to change."

He released the strands. He held the pause a moment, then turned.

I tossed off my nightgown, tugged on my long underwear and flannel petticoat, all sorts of wind caught in my throat.

"But," he said, "if it suits, you could join me helping the Browns prepare for their barn bee."

"Deal." I straightened the band of my petticoat. "You're friendly with Asa now?"

He shrugged. "He's practical. I like him."

"Practical."

"Sakes alive, you want a sermon? He's got a good soul."

A good soul. What in tarnation was that? And that was what he sought in companionship? I buttoned up my shirtwaist, tucked the ends, and shrugged into my slicker. I pulled on my wool stockings, slipped into my boots.

"I'm decent."

He turned. "Are you now?"

I snorted and thrust my hands into my mittens. "And you're preparing to dig," I said, gesturing at his armless shirt, "like that?"

I stalked over to my brothers' laundry, grabbed one of Willie's gaudy red dress shirts, and tossed it at him. Stot scowled, looked up. I smothered a smirk. I'd never seen the man in anything but white, gray, black. "It'll camouflage your dripping blood."

He studied the fabric in his hands. "Your brother's?"

I faltered tying on my gun belt. "Whose else would it be?"

"I don't know."

Was he actually asking whether I'd had some random feller over? "It doesn't matter to you whose it is."

I whistled for One Eye to follow, yanked open the door, and stalked out into the bleached winter sunshine.

CHAPTER TWENTY-FOUR

I lifted the lid off my pot, tossed flour into the soup. The flour lay atop the broth in lumps. Though I'd followed Ma's recipe exactly, something was off.

The day had passed, Stot and I tunneling underground, the air a perfect winter warmth; I didn't need my cloak and could feel sunglow along my forearms. Stot burrowed deep into the earth, filling buckets with soil, and I'd turn the windlass, hauling the pail up to pour aboveground. Except for a jaunt to feed his animals and change out of Willie's ghastly shirt, Stot had tended my homestead. All day. With a bullet wound. I had to study him to even register change in how he moved. He mainly used his hale arm, adjusting his stance for balance. No matter how he'd gained his notorious reputation, he could work. It reminded me of Pa's tireless labor, of the steadfast nature of a lifetime of sweat and hardship. But Stot seemed to enjoy farming: There was an ease about him, a settled happiness as he worked my land.

Early in the morning, he'd studied the bees about the sweet clover, with that long-suffering patience of his. Then he'd followed a bee across the meadow, returning after a while with a comb of honey and the location of the hive. I'd gaped at him, wondering why I'd never been so intuitive. Now I heard scrapes and humming belowground as he filled my well bucket. As long as the earth didn't cave in and smother him, I'd have a well soon. My own well—water, here beside my shack. I ripped up wild onions and tossed them into the pot. Maybe I'd gotten this man all wrong. Instead of wreaking havoc across the frontier, it was almost as if life had fought him, hardened him. What in blasted tarnation had happened with the Wild Bunch? I wanted to argue that tales of the Lawman were just sensational storytelling round bonfires, and yet—hadn't I just nursed him after a gun battle?

I twisted the ladle about, the oil and rust tinge of the stew foaming with caramel brown. It smelt halfheartedly of winters in Kansas, a faint, faraway remembrance of the past. Sometimes life on my homestead seemed but a phantom of life before, but today felt vivid and present. I thought of another warm winter's day nearly a year ago, when Lark told me he wouldn't be homesteading.

Impressions of that afternoon rolled over me: crouching down, slicing fur from a rabbit's body, sunshine a gloss on my collarbone, Lark leaning against a maple sapling, listening for game. Light glinting inside ripples of creek water, a willow bobbing below the water's edge. Unbuttoning my shirt, readying for a swim. That moment, when I'd glanced over my shoulder, my overblouse undone and loosened from my skirt, wind on my bare skin, and I'd recognized Lark's discomfort. His palms pressing into his eyes, his bearing weighted. Saying that he was fond of his life in Kansas, that he didn't want to gallivant off to outlaw country in search of something, that he didn't want *me* after all. I'd held my blouse closed, the ivy-embroidered linsey falling off my shoulders, wintry air slicing up my neck.

On my homestead, I ran my hand up the back of my dress, felt the buttons and the dips. In the end, like Magnolia, Lark hadn't come along. I'd been discarded to venture off alone. My closest friendships, the ones I'd held on to the width of my life, had disintegrated with one brutal divide. I reimagined my life now as a long quiet, alone on the prairie. I dropped a pinch of my boiled salt into the pot, noted the melody of Stot's humming. This wasn't the life I'd dreamt nor the man I expected about my farm, but Stot sure as hell dug a better hole than Lark.

I tossed a clove of garlic into the pot. Blast, I was supposed to smash the garlic first. With my ladle, I raised some broth above the surface, studied the gummy texture. Beyond the black curve of trees, the sun dimmed behind the broad gray clouds of an Oklahoman sky. Nightfall was coming. The prairie seemed to tip backward into the darkness, and the horizon swayed. I shielded the glare of sunrays with my palm. The ground shuddered, as if the large hands of someone's god grasped the edges of my land and shook. A zip, zap.

I slammed down the lid of my pan, grasped my pistol, and stepped toward the forest-green shadows. There was a sound, like breath pushed through closed teeth, and a short buzz. Perhaps one of my horses sneezed, faroff.

Let me tell you a new tale.

I spun. A cluster of sugarberries swooped in the wind, their small green leaves shivering like ripples in water. Springtime colors. The leaves dissolved, juniper to chartreuse to sable, then gone. The branches returned once more to the forlorn limbs of winter. I felt off balance. I searched the meadow for movement, but the expanse was now static, as if attached once again to the core of the earth. I blinked, eyes dry in the winds. Boots pressed against soil, I adjusted my grip on my pistol's ivory handle, the etchings denting my skin. I watched my land, waited. But there was only silence. And yet I could smell summer flowers. Rose vervain and honeysuckle and fresh hedge parsley, as if time wasn't stable out in the vastness of my prairie.

Gusts whistled through the high grasses, and I tugged at a loose thread on my apron. The haze stuttered into focus: a woman in a rocking chair. Afghan pulled across her lap, newspaper held open, the scent of orange pekoe tea, and I felt swept into her story. She resembled every homesteader I'd known, and yet—she was a startling likeness of my mother. The newsprint fuzzed, letters coming in and out of focus. *Let the women stir about a bit.* I stepped forward. *Their freedom has been purchased by the tears and heartaches of generations of women to whom freedom was but a name.* I squinted, but the vision blurred into fog. My skirt snagged—a jumble of burrs gripped the fabric. I untangled my skirt from the oats and tugged the burrs off, the seeds piercing my fingers. I didn't understand this phenomenon, of glimpsing moments of another's life.

"Minnie."

I flinched and spun around.

"You alright?" Stot asked.

"Course I'm alright."

His gaze brushed across my posture, the grip on my revolver. I sheathed my gun.

Dirt edged his temple, the carmine shade vibrant beside his mossy-green eyes, black hair. He wiped a rag over the angles of his face. Then he sauntered forward, trousers slunk low on his hips, a cowboy swagger, as if he drew from the slow tide of the earth.

"Oh—" I wiped my hands on my apron, stepped forward. "Is that well water?"

He leaned against the wood siding of my shack, peeked in the soup pot, a mug dangling from his hand. "Your soup smells off."

"It does not."

He crouched beside a small board, an oil landscape awash with moody grays and blues. His fingers hovered over the raised texture of the wheat stalks I'd carved with a palette knife. He glanced over his shoulder. "Did you paint this?"

"I did."

He studied my painting for a long moment, sunlight glinting against the metal cup. "Who's the woman?"

"What woman?"

He pointed to a translucent vapor hovering at the dip of a hillock, like a funnel cloud sworling. I hadn't noticed how the highlights gathered. The brushstrokes did resemble a woman strolling in a pale Regency gown, loose hair trailing behind, lights an array round her frame. But I hadn't painted a woman. She wasn't there.

It was just a reflection off the glazing I'd mixed of paint and linseed oil, just a trick of texture and luminosity.

He watched me, brow furrowed. "I like it."

"Okay." I held my arms. "So did you find water?"

"I did."

I took the cup from him: clear liquid pooled inside the silver tin. A well, on my land. I sipped.

And spewed out rancid water.

I gasped.

Underground was the awful water from the Salt Fork River? I thought my homestead would have clean, fresh water. It was why I chose this land beside Crooked Creek.

"All wrath, that's terrible water," I said, my voice craggy.

He drummed his fingers on his thigh. He wasn't usually fidgety. Could he have salted the water, pranking me? I pressed my fingertips to my lips.

"You rake," I said.

He lifted a black brow.

"You salted my well."

A smile shocked across my face, and on a sudden I felt a hundred summers younger, as if I could just about glimpse the Minnie of long ago. He gripped his hat between his hands as I laughed until my eyes watered and my cheeks burnt with the streak of tears. I hadn't expected such a thing from him. He pressed back on his hat and slipped his hands in his pockets, crinkles like rivulets at his eyes.

"I like you like this," he said. "Laugh more."

"Well, if we could just *not die* this winter. Then sure, I'll laugh more."

"Life's hard, no matter. Suppose we could laugh anyway."

Beyond, in the fallen dusk, the golden glow of winter dark fireflies floated about the hardwoods. "Do you even know how?" I asked.

A smirk tugged at his lips, unhurried and unrefined. "Well, no. But I'm damn sure amused."

Then he strode off, his suspenders an X across his white shirt. Beyond, light flashed among the oaks and the hickories, longlost magic caught in shadow and bramble. I bit my lip as he climbed down the ladder. The edges of my cheeks felt tender with such movements. I'd barely smiled all winter.

I strode to the barn to feed my animals, the sun drifting down to ooze russet and ginger along the horizon. Whistlejacket's smoke-gray nose peeked out from her stable window. Beside the barn were rows of vegetables and my cellar hid belowground. Behind, my tar paper shack shivered in the wind. My homestead was simple, in progress, with a long way to go—but I'd battled and sweat for this home, for this space of my own. And now I had fresh water. My ma couldn't own land, or my grandma or her ancestors before her. And here I was, with my own homestead, looping a knot on this thread of legacy, embroidering myself into a history of women. A torrent of air rubbed my shoulder blades, as if pushing me back somewhere faraway. The norther roared, and once again I heard the women speaking among themselves.

I'd worked this soil for a season and knew this land as one knew a friend. I supposed the earth could be alive with the memories of those who'd come before. I might not understand it, but something was happening out in the wide distances. Down the hill, sunfall slanted through the feathery ends of wheat stalks and cast an effervescent form, like a rising mist or a woman walking toward me, her story forever lost in time.

CHAPTER TWENTY-FIVE

I pulled on Cricket's reins, slowing to a canter, my heart pounding with the rush of racing over the knolls. A curl of smoke smeared the blue sky—Olive's homestead just beyond. I rubbed Cricket's pale neck as we trotted over the crest. Below, the land stretched bleak gray and cashmere to the horizon. The Browns' sod house pressed into a hill, the mud cut in neat rectangles, flower boxes with colorful pansies settled before the windowsills, twin apple trees and a willow sprouted to the side. Olive, in a blue gingham gown and white apron, bustled about before the soddy. Asa, Thad, and Stot chatted beside the rock-hewn well amid a pile of lumber, their sheepdog Old Watch loped the perimeter, and Poppy sang a ditty, somewhere.

I wasn't practiced in quiet moments with others. I felt at ease in noise, in moments at the edge of control. I scrubbed my face, my kid-leather gloves velvety on my tight skin. To join the Browns and Stot today was settling into this land, acknowledging that I'd found a community.

I galloped downhill, tossing an upburst of red dust into the timid blue sky. As I dismounted, Olive greeted me, drying her hands on her apron. Asa took Cricket's reins with a welcoming nod, and Olive slid her arm round my shoulder, guiding me toward their outdoor kitchen.

"Tell me you saw that enormous orange moon the other night?" she asked. I told her that I'd watched the moonrise from my porch, and she settled me beside Sophia to cut fruit. I hefted a barrel of Arkansas Black apples and dumped them on the wood block. The deep, wine-red apples were cool, fresh from the cellar. Olive handed me a folding knife, hilt out, an eyebrow quirked.

"I know how to use a blasted knife."

"Never said you didn't," she said.

"However—" Sophia lowered herself onto a blanket. From a basket, she grabbed a pair of trousers to darn: Sophia had made a fine reputation as a seamstress. "One wonders if you've ever used a blade against such natural pursuits as baking a cobbler."

Olive snorted and snapped a cloth toward Sophia. "Oh, stop."

"Y'all are something awful to me," I said.

Mirth edged Olive's mouth. "You adore us."

Olive watched me cut the apple, her brows drawn, anxious about my lack of skill. She opened her mouth to speak, and I held up my hand. "You asked for my help. I'll bake pies however in smoky Sam Hill I want."

She shared an amused glance with Sophia, then kneaded the dough. Olive brushed her forehead with the back of her hand, smearing a dusting of flour. We spoke of what novels we'd read these past weeks, the crisp scent of apples a texture in the air. Sophia and I talked of *Little Women*, which I'd recently loaned her. She thought perhaps she was like faithful Meg and supposed I was like independent and adventurous Jo. Poppy wandered past, grumbling that Sophia had told her she resembled the youngest, Amy, but that she felt like Jo.

"Sometimes I feel like Amy too," I told her with a wink. Poppy wrinkled her nose and adjusted her bundle of wood. "But you get to choose who you want to be," I said.

"See? I'm Jo," Poppy said to Sophia, then stalked off down the slope.

Olive smiled at me as she scattered flour across the table and tossed down a ball of dough. I chopped my apple and brushed the pieces into a cornflower blue bowl. In the shade before a statuesque post oak, Thad split the wood Poppy carried over while Asa and Stot discussed plans for the barn. Asa adjusted the brim of his bowler hat, and Stot gripped a sheet of ledger paper, their design etched on it. Olive followed my gaze to the men. "They're two peas in a pod, huh?" she said.

My eyebrows flung skyward. No one would ever say those two were alike. Stot with his powerful strides. His wayward black hair and sharp cheekbones. Asa, on the other hand, was steady as a brook, predictable as Stot was stormy. And yet there was an earnestness, a sense of being firmly rooted, as if they'd both lost the world, only to find it again.

A woodpecker dove from the sugar maple and drummed against their home. Olive shooed him away and clicked her knife through the dough, cutting defined shapes. It was peculiar, Olive likening Stot to her husband, as she'd cautioned me away from a friendship with Stot. Now she glanced at Stot with affection.

"When'd you start softening toward Stot?" I asked, scraping a pile of cuttings into a bowl.

"Suppose about the time I knew him as Stot." Olive cocked her head and laid the dough over sugared apples. Sophia stood, carried her basket of linens inside, and Olive continued: "Once, when Thad spent the better part of two days cutting wood, then hauling the lumber and some quail off to Cross Station for sale, Stot ran into him along the way, and then stood by him as Thad sold the lumber. Nobody dared barter with an outlaw beside him—Thad made eighty cents. A fair amount, I'd think." Olive pinched the dough on her pie, sharpening a star shape. "Stot just started standing by us, I suppose. He's like that stallion of his—sleek and striking and fierce but altogether different once tamed."

"Stot is definitively not tamed."

"No?" Her mouth twisted into a smirk. "Not yet?"

"Gawd." My face flushed. "Not ever."

"Mmm."

Warmth pressed up my neck. I focused on clicking my blade through the apples. I should be frightened of him but—I just wasn't. Perhaps the darkness in me took comfort in the darkness in him. I shoved each tale of the Lawman aside, reasoned that there must be some explanation.

Their sheepdog Old Watch knocked the back of my knees, and I bent to pet him. Across the field, Stot caught my gaze. He adjusted the angle of his broadbrim, and I thought of all the times I'd watched Pa adjust his hat the same way. Memories of bygone farm gatherings flickered past: plunging into the creek from a high bough, a last warm summer's day; Lark fumbling a pumpkin, insides splattering the crops, us laughing uproariously; my ma singing, *There's a wideness in God's mercy, like the wideness of the sea,* her aria slipping between the oat grasses; Pa gesturing to fox tracks in groundcover; looping a gun belt cross my hips, Magnolia studying the sketches in a botany tome; too many remembrances to parse, each nuance varied and the same. I didn't know when I'd stopped enjoying the moments of my life, when each day felt like a trial.

"I also admire that notion with his brother's widow." Olive set her pie in the outdoor oven, then wrought her hands in her apron, wiping off dust and dough.

"What's that now?"

She gathered bowls and rags, tidying up. "Surely you've discussed that?"

"That his twin died?" I washed my hands and grabbed a few apples.

Olive cracked open a log cabin patchwork quilt and settled on the ground with a bowl of pecans for an apple crumble, her brows tugged together. Her palm smoothed a ripple between a grass-green floral square and a navy-checked rectangle.

"Oh, honey." She sighed, the lines beside her mouth drawn. "He should have told you. His twin left a widow and four daughters. Stot's moving them down come spring, marrying the widow, caring for the children."

My hands clenched, fingernails cutting into the flesh of the apples. "No," I said. A weight sank in my stomach, myself suddenly woozy and adrift. "I didn't know."

"I do like the man." Olive split a nut and brushed some residue from a shell, tension knotted across her shoulders. "But he's a wanted outlaw *and* betrothed."

I joined Olive on the quilt, gripping the ridge of my pleated ivory collar. I pulled the halves of a nut apart, the heft fragile and airless, like worn leather. It shouldn't hurt to hear such a thing. I hadn't lost anything. I didn't even know Stot, truly. He'd seemed untethered like me, and yet—he had a sweetheart back home. Supposed that was the portrait of the woman, the slip of lace. I tipped my palm, sifting the crumbles into the bucket.

Olive picked up a wayward fleck of pecan from the quilt. "You respect plain speaking?"

"Please."

"You don't seem to operate with boundaries, alike the rest of the world." Olive crunched nuts over apples and butter. "I don't know what happened in your past, and it don't matter, not to me. I'm just saying: I wonder how firmly you'll keep to your own rules."

I stood and poured well water from a pitcher into a jar. "What rules?"

She cracked a brittle laugh. "Exactly." She stood, pie dish balanced on her palm. "Just make sure you slather up those walls of yours between him too." Her gaze moved to Stot, his sleeves rolled up, tanned forearms slick with sweat. "Lord have mercy, he's handsome. But not for you."

I gnawed my lip, nodded. Course he wasn't for me.

"Any red-blooded woman would need boundaries with him," Olive added.

I coughed on my gulp of water.

"Ah, now." She wrinkled her nose and placed the cobbler in the oven. "Don't waste the water."

Stot strode over then, his gaze raking across my posture.

"Fancy an apple, Mr. Tharp?" Olive asked, gesturing to the sliced apples on the table. Stot nodded and picked up a piece.

I wrung my sticky hands in my apron. "Tharp?" That was his last name?

Olive sighed. "What are you two jabbering about all the time, and you don't even know about his betrothed or his full name?" Olive wiped flour off the wood plank. "Ain't proper to call him Stot, anyhow," she muttered.

Stot's eyes jolted to mine and his hand paused, his apple held static in the air.

"Well," I said, "this ain't the place for propriety." I lifted my jar in something like a salute. "It's the Wild West, darling."

~

After we finished the pies, Olive carried utensils inside and I washed my forearms in a bucket. Stot strode over, palms resting on his gun belt. I gazed at his hands, nicked skin gripping sable leather. I didn't know how to reconcile that he was an engaged man. He caught my gaze, his bearing almost tentative, and handed me the plans for the barn and a chunk of charcoal. "Wanted your thoughts on our design," he said, dipping his canteen in the water barrel.

I placed the sheet on the wood slab. The plan was for a small, practical barn. I sketched some parallel boards below the dormers, then added swoops, the curve of the Browns' land, a few flicks of sparse grasses, and lines for that unbreakable wind. I set the charcoal down, leaned back against the table. "It'll suit."

"The boards there, across the dormers, are a fine notion." He touched the scuffs of grasses with his forefinger, lifted a brow in something like amusement.

The breeze rattled through barren willow limbs and screeched through the tongs of a rake. A homemade wind chime of copper spoons, leftover metal pipes, and chunks of sapwood hung from the rafters, the copper twisting from a length of twine and clattering against a pipe. Olive came out the door, her heels scratching the dirt.

Stot spoke low. "About my brother's widow—"

"We don't have to talk about that."

"When you asked, in your cabin—"

"When you were shot?" I flicked my hand, sending his concern away, as my body numbed beneath my rib cage. The wind chime rattled. "You don't owe me an explanation."

A vein pulsed on his jaw, the hollows of his cheeks contracted. His gaze flicked between my eyes. "Alright."

I picked up Olive's folding knife, snapped it closed, then turned back to the table to brush leftover apple cores into a pile. After a pause, Stot strode off, down the hill, his spurs silver in the dust. I pressed my fist to my chest, something hollow blooming—as a lonesome murmur cracked across the landscape.

Time continues to turn, around and around I spin.

Within the clamor of sound—wind chime, birdsong, faraway laughter, heartbeat at my temples—the women spoke. Forgotten memories, lost stories. The coarse, winter-dead grass of the soddy prickled my forearms. I could almost, but not quite, catch fragments of conversation: the Native woman, the cattlehand, the ancient voice, and another woman, perhaps the homesteader, as if I'd slipped into a different story, someone else's memories. The timbre of their voices something I almost recognized. In the bright spray of day, my boots firm against the present timeline, surrounded by Stot and the Browns, I recognized the insanity of listening for voices lost in another era.

The bristles of grass stirred in the breeze, and I cupped my neck, off balance. Whatever it was that called out to me—I didn't feel threatened, almost as if the women hollered at me to hold on, just a little longer. I pressed off the wall, dirt creasing beneath my fingernails, and returned to the present moment. Down beside the woodpile, Stot hefted his axe, the sun slipping along his collarbone and glistening on the chain of his pocket watch. He caught my gaze from beneath the brim of his hat, the old-fashioned cattleman crease catching the deep shadows. My heart felt stretched and raw, distorted beyond its shape to rub against my chest.

Let alone his fiancée from back home, the notorious outlaw wouldn't be attracted to a mud-smudged homesteader. I'd seen the fancy ladies who trailed outlaws, Rose of Cimarron with her waterfall curls blowing in the wind, Belle Starr with her elaborate velvet gowns and revolvers strapped about her waist, or spunky Little Britches with her quirky leather chaps. The women round outlaws were glamorous and arresting—absolutely nothing like me with my faded linsey shirtwaists and practical buns.

I grabbed an apple core and tossed it in the bucket. Sure enough, he was the most handsome man this side of the Mississippi. But goodness, why did any of this matter? I didn't need to distance myself from him. He had unavailable written all over him like fire on dry prairie.

CHAPTER TWENTY-SIX

The twang of a banjo clipped a steady beat as I placed a pie on the sideboard. On the Browns' homestead, the gathering simmered with energy, families from round our county arriving, the barn bee readying to begin.

Down by the wallows, morning light striking through the hardwoods, Stot and Asa hitched a wagon to an ox, the windows they'd crafted loaded onto the bed. During the long, dark evenings on my homestead these past days, I'd gnawed on this notion of Stot being engaged. As I'd washed my hands in a bucket, oil smeared along my palms and wedged beneath my fingernails, and as I'd scooped out the seeds from an acorn squash for supper, I'd considered whatever to do with Stot. I'd concluded: Nothing had changed. He could still function as my closest companion—there was nothing untoward in friendship. The only adjustment was that, before, I'd *assumed* he wouldn't pursue a romance with me. Now I *knew* he wouldn't. He was too damn honorable. In a way, there was freedom in clear boundaries.

As the cart rumbled across the furrows, the windowpanes reflected sunglow. Stot led the ox, the distant sound of the creaking wagon wheels forlorn and aching. Twenty or so homesteaders swarmed the Browns' homestead, everyone preparing to raise the sides of the barn. Women gossiped and served food, hair ribbons of every color snapping in the breeze. Men speculated, rocking back on their bootheels, hands in trouser pockets or patting waistcoats for some chew. A farmer beside me tugged on his suspenders, retold a tall tale of Davy Crockett, of how he could charm a grizzly bear and outhunt, outrace, outbuild, outgrin the lot of them.

Willie reclined against a stack of lumber, legs crossed at the ankles, tin of whiskey tipped to his lips. He winked at me, then added some ludicrous exaggeration to the folktale. Though I was thankful he'd shown up to support the Browns, a part of me splintered, realizing that I'd never been worth the effort. I supposed he just came for the liquor and celebration. Beside Willie, Ezra chopped wood, sweat wetting his brown button-down, the fabric ironed and pristine. And Ezra, he came because he wouldn't dare lax on his duty.

Willie pressed his hands to his back, rocked on his bootheels, paisley shirt bunching under his waistcoat. "You hear about that stunning roan quarter horse from Enid?" Willie asked me. "Homesteader swapped the stallion for a hotel. Fine horse to breed with Whispering."

"It's Whistlejacket." I grabbed some nails from a pail, slipped them in my pocket. "And you never came to help dig my well."

"Aw now," he said, tugging on his mustache, "don't be cranky. We'll—"

I held up my hand. "It's been dug."

Ezra lodged his axe in the stump and wiped his palms on a piece of cloth. He scraped a lucifer across his matchbox, the flame a spark of orange. "Who helped?"

"The Lawman."

Ezra grimaced, cigarette between his teeth, and Willie seemed unsure what to say.

"Don't you dare give me any more promises." I shoved a hammer in the crook beneath my shoulder, anger flashing hot along my back.

Stot hollered then that it was time to raise the side and methodically explained everyone's roles. Some nodded, but not everyone wanted to listen to reason from the Lawman. I noticed Ezra's lip curling in judgment, others wide eyed with nerves, sweaty hands brushing their trousers. Stot played well the brigand: never smiling, boots heavy against the dusty ground, palm resting atop the wooden handle of his Peacemaker. I dug my woolen mittens from my pocket and tugged them on, my hands raw and knobby; then I gripped a plank, the raw oak the undertone of wheatgrass.

Stot directed everyone to lift—there was chatter and grunting and the cascade of music, strands of hair escaping my twist, unfiltered light slashing our hands. We pushed up the side, Stot guiding how to tug the ropes and pulleys, and soon enough we raised the wall. Some held it upright as others hammered. Stot crouched several paces away, a few nails in his mouth. He aligned a hammer, his biceps straining against flannel, and caught my gaze across the grid of wood.

"You alright over yonder, outlaw?" I asked.

The lady behind me sucked in a breath, and a couple of men nervously laughed. Stot stood, lined up another nail. His eyes crinkled, just slightly, at the corners. "Actually, can you hold the wall for me, right here?"

I bit my lip, tasting the salt of sweat, and stood before him, my hands pressing the wood upright, everyone watching him. Of course they did, he was so blustery and bold. Different from everyone else—a tale just waiting to happen. I understood then the tall tales of Paul Bunyan or Pecos Bill, those men larger than life, who spit lightning across the sky and dragged down the stars as a blanket. Such presences that made stories. I glanced over my shoulder. He pulled another nail from his mouth, his gaze sliding down my face. I gulped a bucketful of winter air.

After a time, I walked to the refreshments, straightening my skirt, altogether too hot. Lord have mercy, it was tricky as a thorny bramble to be near him. I flung fiery banter at everyone, but with him—my taunting became molten. I must figure a way to exist with him, for his sweetheart waited, somewhere.

I scooped the ladle into the water bucket, and Willie joined me. He bumped me with his shoulder. "You know I love you—told you about that stallion, didn't I?"

I hesitated, then bumped back his shoulder.

"But what are you going on about, anyhow," Willie said, "being so friendly with the Lawman? After months battling these plains, you still have that death wish?"

I lifted the well water to my mouth, sipped. "Naturally."

"You hear of that shoot-out by the township of Bison, day before yesterday? Couple cattlehands met a violent end." Willie gnawed tobacco, his mustache bobbing. His fussy cobalt and copper silk tie knotted loose. "Rumor goes it was Bitter Creek—but could've just been some hell-fired vigilantes. This vendetta between the Lawman and the bunch is a'brewing." His gaze roamed the crowd. I took a sip of water. "Folks say," Willie continued, "I reckon you've heard tell, that the Lawman murdered some woman and her baby."

"I don't believe that."

"Well, that's what many a feller declare."

"He's complicated," I said. "But he's not cruel."

I couldn't believe Stot would hurt a woman and her baby—there must be more to the story. Willie took off his hat, scraped back his flop of wheat-brown hair. "You sure about that notion?"

"When have I ever been sure of anything?" I dropped the ladle in the bucket. "And what's got you prying? Of everyone, you've always joined me in havoc."

He resettled his hat, a showy sunburst motif burnt round the brim. "This one's dark."

He strode away. I didn't know Stot's story. Had no idea why I'd found him by the water's edge the week before, shot up by bandits. But—did it matter? What were tales but one person's perspective? Dreams and phantoms. Even the stories I told myself of my own past, the stories I'd told myself the length of my life, all those stories had been delusions. If I could lie to myself, well then, surely everyone lied. Stot's past probably *was* full of depravity. I just wasn't sure it mattered anymore.

Who'd helped dig my well?

If not for Stot, I'd still be ladling out the piles of earth with my soup can. I didn't know Stot's secrets, but I knew he would be neighborly. At least for a little while. And a little while was all I needed anyhow.

After sweat and hollers and a thread of too-thin jokes, we finally had the sides raised. We'd done it, the barn lifted against the colorless winter sky. Willie picked up his banjo and charmed the crowd with his crooning. And we celebrated: cider and cellar-cold apples and pie. Ezra halted beside me, removing his gloves. He didn't say anything.

The last time we'd built a barn together, I'd painted the dormers white with a flat, bristly brush. Below our expansive live oak, Ma showed Magnolia how to cut dough for pie, Ma's red gingham apron the anchoring color of the memory. I leaned close to keep my paint strokes straight, Ezra correcting my every move from a pace away. Since he'd finished schooling that spring, his irritability shifted to downright cruelty.

"Don't need supervision," I told him.

His bowler hat shaded his eyes, the bottom half of his face reddened in the thick sunshine. "Girls need a man's direction."

"Wait a minute, now." Pa wiped sweat from his brow, his saw hanging at his side. "We don't talk to womenfolk like such in this house."

Ezra lifted his chin, his black mustache bushy. They argued, Pa shaking his head, saying he hadn't raised his children to be cruel. I should feel wretched that a wedge drove between the two of them on my behalf—but I felt safeguarded. I knew men could be vicious. I just hadn't realized that the men I should avoid might be my own kin.

On Olive's homestead, Ezra stood beside me, the same soot-colored bowler hat casting darkness on his scowl. I pressed back my hair. "What is it?"

He placed his hand on my shoulder; I bristled.

"Much obliged," he said, "for your resilience."

"Alright." I held my shoulders, my hammer pressed against my back, a handful of nails biting my palm, unsure what to say, uncomfortable with his hand on my body.

He gave a curt nod and walked away. Somewhere, buried beneath my walls and worry was the understanding that I longed for a genuine and decent relationship with my brothers. I never believed we'd have that in truth—Ezra cruel, Willie careless. Ezra helped a farmer in feed sack overalls hammer a plank, and I wondered whether homesteading would change him. Perhaps with the brutality of our last argument, with him failing in his duty to help round my homestead, perhaps he recognized the gap between who he was and who he wanted to be. Perhaps it was okay to hope.

"You gonna help or just gawk?" Stot's low voice brushed the back of my neck.

I considered the community before me, the barn we'd built. "Just proud, is all."

His chest bumped my shoulder blades as he shifted his weight. I leaned back, allowing myself a moment with him. He stilled, then draped an arm around me, his forearm along my collarbone. There was nothing unbecoming with such a position, I supposed. Willie often hugged me the same way. Our relationship was perhaps almost brotherly.

Stot's arm felt heavy across my body, flannel soft against the baby hairs of my neck. All we had left was hammering up the remaining pieces of the barn, and then there'd be dancing. I was sick and tired of pretending I didn't enjoy parties. I couldn't just choose to be happy again, could I? It wasn't right, after my past. I didn't deserve to be carefree.

I felt wedged between past and future. I'd created a version of myself here. But I might be finished with her. Maybe I'd let her fade with the winter. Maybe I could begin again.

Stot brushed his thumb along my collar. Heat pooled in my stomach, the fabric making a dim scratching sound. His fingertip went back again, the edge of his thumb falling off the ridge of my blouse, the rugged texture of his fingers brushing my skin. I heard the bluster of wind, the clamor of hammers, the noise of many voices. He murmured in my ear. "What color are you wearing tonight?"

I stepped aside and straightened my skirt. For tonight's game, the women laid a scrap of fabric from their dress on the table, and the men picked a piece, having to dance with the matching maiden for the evening. So I couldn't just admit the color of my gown—that'd be agreeing to let him court me or something absurd.

I chewed my lips. "Midnight-dark navy."

"Navy, huh?"

"Mm-hmm. Jetted lace, black needlepoint."

"Likely," he said.

He rattled a few nails in his pocket, propped his foot on a stack of wood. His chest was golden in the gap between his black cravat and white shirt. "I'll figure it out," he said.

Olive dashed up then, her calico skirt whisking behind her. She pulled me into a hug. "We did it."

Asa shook Stot's hand. I thought then of times long ago, on the sweeping limbs of a lone live oak, when Magnolia and I would hide from our chores. We'd sprawl across a branch, legs dangling, then hang upside down, ringlets trailing earthward, blood rushing to our heads, and read aloud from *Great Expectations* or *The Princess and the Goblin*. More than anything, I'd wanted to live a life full of the sorts of adventure found in stories. After leaving Magnolia, I'd misplaced my ease in hushed, vulnerable moments with others. I couldn't decide whether it was brave or foolish to hope. Asa rested his arm around Olive's shoulder, and together they admired their new barn.

Olive tipped her face up to her husband. "Remember the plantation?"

Asa's grip tightened on her shoulder, drawing her closer, and he nodded. I'd only ventured from my family's farm, a few counties away—I couldn't fathom the breadth between the lives they had once lived and their world now. Stot lifted his hammer and spun it. The banjo screeched, the song paused, and I tipped forward onto my toes, leaned into the stillness. I couldn't see into the distance, it just held the murky smear of winter, but the haunting memories of my past began to fade.

I stepped forward and bumped my shoulder against the wall next to Stot, nails resting in my open palm. He took the nails from me, placed them in his mouth, and began again.

CHAPTER TWENTY-SEVEN

I spun straight out sideways, my hand warm in Stot's clasp, the dance an oil canvas of black and gold and distant evergreen. The burn of scattered starlight, the stretch of shadows between bodies, the wide swoop of a midnight moon. The shades of midwinter were fawn brown, mist white, obsidian; the scents deep earth, oncoming ice, faraway promises. Tonight the air was soft and thick, just a crackling singe of cold across my wrists, the clouds of fog as we spoke, veiled reminders that spring was months to come.

Stot had yanked me about the packed dirt all evening. Somehow he'd guessed my cerulean satin dress, with the wide bertha collar swooped across my shoulders. Before the run, I'd packed my chest with necessary supplies, but my ma must've added my party gown. I could envision her bending down, tucking the glossy blue fabric between an afghan and a lantern, always hoping for things I couldn't see.

"How'd you know?" I'd asked Stot earlier this evening.

"You pretend you hate color. I know elsewise."

I'd scoffed, and Stot leaned close, brushed a corkscrew ringlet bouncing above my ostentatious bow. "You adore parties. Love dancing."

"Doesn't mean I want to dance with you."

He'd grasped my hand and dragged me to the patch of sparse buffalo grass that was the evening's ballroom. I recognized there was nothing unbecoming partnering with him: just celebration, companionship, a dash of merriment. I'd danced away plenty of nighttides with Willie or any number of farmer boys. And so we'd danced. He did so with that effortless ease, almost as if he were some prop for me to spin about. He dimmed, let me shine.

The moon had long ago risen, the music dwindling from a fierce fiddling to melancholy. The violin lingered like a keening, and nighthawks sang into the silences. Even the bonfire dampened—but still we danced. We spun through polkas and quadrilles, schottisches and one long, slow waltz. I adored the colors, the noise, the sharpness in my throat, my body ragged, as if I couldn't get enough air inside. Why couldn't life always be like this? Easy laughter, no one hiding or judging—just dancing. I didn't mind winding across the grass floor with Stot neither. I reveled in the raised brows and the reputation I crafted for myself. If everyone thought I was brazen enough to befriend a gunslinger, they'd leave me alone on my quarter section.

I brushed my cerulean sash tied about Stot's upper arm. Firelight gleamed on the sharp panes of his face, his jaw shadowed with stubble like smoke before a sunrise. Circling the dance, some farmers played a spirited game of horseshoes and others chatted, sharing ways to establish a homestead. Willie slumped on a wooden barrel, liquored up and flipping cards in a game of faro. I hadn't seen Ezra since sunset. Now it was just that stretch of dark before morning, a few fiddles and an accordion lending a bit of chaos to the midnight hours. Stot spun me out, and I tripped over my skirts and then a stick. He steadied me, hands on my shoulders, my chin knocking his chest.

I held on to his gun belt and laughed, my forehead against his collarbone. My head fit perfectly. It was glorious to loosen emotions, to feel like I needn't contain myself. Stot could handle a blustery rail of laughter from some homespun woman. His gaze slid to my lips, his exhale brushing the wisps of my hair. With the boys from Kansas, I could surmise their thoughts. They were tame, predictable—manageable.

Stot? He was one wild unknown.

I flicked my gaze to his lips, and he leaned down a breath. My heart stopped.

And I sucked down my laughter in one big gulp. He slid his palms over my shoulders, down to my wrists. From the edge of the meadow, I caught Olive's gaze, her thoughts plain as daylight: *Lord, but what are you doing?* But we were just dancing. Just two friends who'd found a likeness in each other, just two lonesome pioneers.

And then, in between the clamor of the fiddle and the groan of distant wind, from across time and space, a woman narrated an outlandish story, not unlike those exaggerated fables of Davy Crockett. *I ain't know much, but my pa says my soul's lightning.* The boundary of a vision shaped across the prairie: a gauzy white Regency gown, axe resting against collarbone, golden embers floating about her frame. She seemed an echo of the woman in my painting, and I supposed, with the shocks of lightning rising from within her, she must be folk legend Sally Ann Thunder Ann Whirlwind. I remembered her story, had read it many times: *Folks say I can blow out a moonbeam, outscream a coyote, and leap over my own shadow.* And yet—I glimpsed a real woman, not a caricature from a tall tale.

Sounds and scents returned me to the present. The screech of an accordion, the smoke of winter bonfire, Stot's hands, warm on my wrists. I blinked, refocused. He studied my posture, brows drawn. I untangled my hands, then walked to the edge of the party, slow and careful, the world hazy and tipping, my palm on the pleats of my bodice, atop my breastbone. I couldn't let the world spiral away, couldn't allow myself to unravel. The dancers were blurry shapes and flapping open jaws, loud and wobbly, and for a moment they didn't seem real.

Stot slid a hand beneath my elbow. "You're anxious again."

I stepped away and rubbed my shoulders, cold. Why couldn't we just keep on dancing, keep on having fun, without any worries.

He glanced at the tension in my hands. "It's not everyone's worry of making it to spring," he said, "nor is it anguish from the first day as I'd presumed—your worry is something elsewhile." He shifted his weight, hands in his trouser pockets, shirtsleeves rolled to expose his wrists. "I don't scare easy."

No, he wouldn't. He'd managed the cowboy bloodshed just fine. But the possibility that I heard the voices of other women, from throughout time? Stot was as lawless as winter was long, but he was also rooted to practicality, like a blasted post oak that'd been growing for an epoch. He wouldn't abide the whimsy that my land told me stories—and it was imperative to my safety that no one knew I might've caught hysteria.

Stot edged closer, shoulders right before my own. He studied me, as if he took me apart and rearranged me. "You can't just keep tossing up barricades," he said, "pushing everyone away, listening to wind sounds."

I faltered backward. "What?"

"I'm not some two-bit farmer from Kansas," he said. "I see you watching the tree line, listening for something, painting women you don't see. All your bravado, I don't buy it. I like your strength, but I also fancy your gentler parts." He lowered his voice; the bonfire reflected red in his black hair. "I'm asking you to let me know you some, let me see the truth."

"The truth?" I scoffed. "Well, that's rich, coming from the outlaw."

"You know that's not who I am."

I stepped closer, below his brim. "Do I?"

His hat tipped low, a broody haze hanging about him as if he were some ominous god of war from another age. "You're hiding something."

"Oh, I apologize," I said. "I forgot you adore transparency."

"What does that mean?"

I threw my hands out. "I know *nothing* of who you are. You're a wanted outlaw, for all manner of nefarious crimes, shot up by wayward bandits, presumably rambling about the countryside with bands of desperadoes—and *I'm* the one hiding something?"

"Mmm." Crinkles fanned at his temples. He clicked open his pocket watch, closed it. "The tales are more interesting, perhaps."

"To hell with tales, I'd rather the truth." I crossed my arms, the rim of my collar brushing my forearms. And he had some sweetheart back home, wherever in netherworld that was.

He ran his thumb across the gold engraving on his watch. "Would you?"

I tipped forward on my toes, spoke in a mock whisper. "I don't spook easy."

He laughed, low, guttural, and shook his head. He pulled his flask from his pocket and drank. The muscles bobbed on his throat.

Sophia spun past, her palm rested atop some dandy's hand, the bell of her petal-pink gown curving. Such youth, such innocence, somewhere perhaps I'd never been.

He regarded the crowd, which was sloppy and fraying at the ends. "Come on, let's dance."

I held my shoulders, fingers clenching satin. I released my grip, sighed. "Liquor first."

At the refreshments, I shoved a pastry in my mouth and grabbed some jars of blackstrap rum. Stot rested his forearms on the table, leaned toward me until I halted and looked at him. "You wonder about my past?" he asked.

"You don't notice how everyone watches you, whispers about your secrets?"

"I mean, sure," he said. "But you don't care a whit about gossip."

"It's a turbulent story, right?" I propped myself against a mound of hay, crossed my feet at the ankles. The blackstrap tasted of warm molasses and the deep of night. "Who doesn't love a scandalous tale?"

Stot pressed his shoulder against the haystack, turned toward me. I couldn't think with him this close. A gap opened inside me, dark starlight full of so much space.

With Stot, it seemed as if speed didn't matter. I wasn't sure what did matter to him, but it wasn't memory, time, ages rushing on past. It was as if ol' Wild Bill told his tales of Stot. *Take time,* Wild Bill had said. *Be sure and not shoot too quick. Many a feller slip up for shootin' in a hurry.*

On a sudden a noise punched, a ping ringing off a stump. I dropped to the ground, spilling my rum.

Gunshots.

Stot crouched behind the hayrick, gun pointed at shadows. The music vanished, replaced with shrieks and swishing clothes as everyone rushed for cover. I yanked my pistol from my ankle holster, bent behind Stot's shoulder, gun raised. More shots rang out. Whispers, cries, pounding boots.

"Outlaws?" I whispered, scrutinizing the black expanse.

A zip soared beside the hay and thunked into wood.

"There's a land," a voice twined into the night, belting a melody, "that is fairer than day."

Blazes, that was just Willie, drunk as all wrath on applejack, thinking he's in some sharpshooting tournament.

"Willie Sheridan Hoopes—" I yelled. "Stop."

I crept forward, gun trained. Backlit by the low moon, Willie ambled toward me, pistol loosely held, crooning his ridiculous song. "In the sweet, by and by."

Shooting at his feet would just spook him. I must get his gun. Willie stumbled over some craggy bluestem, his gaudy scarf catching the firelight. I crouched behind a barrel, my hands clammy on my Peacemaker. There was a blur from the side as Stot tackled him and wrenched the gun from his hand.

"The dickens?" Willie slurred.

Stot punched him square in the face, knocking him out.

I rushed to them, skirts held in one hand, six-shooter pointed at the ground. Stot glanced up, jaw tight. "He's unacceptable."

I flinched. Stot was furious. I leaned over my legs and gusted a delirious laugh.

"You're laughing."

I yelled over my shoulder. "Everything's fine—" I collapsed onto the ground, legs askew. Called out, "Just a half-wit. We got the gun."

Stot unmanned Willie's other weapons. "I don't find this funny, at all."

I wiped at my tears. "Ah, hell. No, it's god-awful."

I pressed against the grass, held myself steady. Stot checked Willie's breath, then hefted him up. "Countryside full of selfish, dangerous fools."

I followed, and Stot tossed Willie over his stallion, the gold chain of Willie's ornate pocket watch silvered in the moonlight. Stot wasn't wrong. The slapdash towns were rum-full of drunk cowboys shooting out the lights and galloping about with feral madness. This was still the Wild West.

"You coming along," Stot asked, "as I haul him home?"

"I just wanted to dance."

Stot paused tying Willie to his mustang, a lightness flooding his eyes. "You truly like dancing, huh?"

"Mmm."

The night air smelt of fire and sugar, apples and gun smoke. I stumbled backward a few paces, then raced over to the hayricks. The townsfolk murmured in fragile clusters, shaken.

"Welcome to the frontier," I hollered and grabbed some Ball jars of blackstrap.

Beside Stot, I checked that the lids were screwed tight, then shoved the rum into his saddlebag. "If I'm missing the carryings-on, I'm at least getting sloppy at home," I said.

"Alone?"

"You'll join me, right?"

His fist clenched on the swell of his saddle. "Drinking."

"Right." I mounted Cricket and clicked my tongue. "Come on. Let's go."

Stot swung up, and then we raced across the subtle hills, chasing that thin curve of moonlight, my insides all shaky and eager and spun up like a tightly coiled cyclone, the wind and the trees telling tales of long ago women, the primordial voice narrating a connected thread, myself haunted not only by this life but by all those that had come before.

CHAPTER TWENTY-EIGHT

I reclined in the sweetgrass and tipped back my flask of brandy. Stot lay beside me, smoking. A high cloud stretched across the sky with shards of light blazing beyond. It smelt of space and darkness, that empty, clean scent of night. I took the cigarette from Stot as he told me about Asa's plans for the barn, how everything had worked just as they'd hoped. They hadn't known whether those crossbeams would hold. They had. They'd speculated that a northeaster might bluster on down. It hadn't. I didn't know the man could ramble, and yet here he was, going on and on, his wandering anecdotes somehow soothing.

We'd hauled Willie to my homestead, tossed him passed out across my quilts, then ventured outside under the starlight. Shadows scuffed across the curves of my land, as if the great paws of a bear pressed into the earth, leaving behind a graphite scratch of lines and patterns. I passed the cigarette back to Stot. He still spoke of the barn. He must not feel this press between our bodies, how the terrain between us was vivid and warm, as if I could run my hand through the air and feel a thickness, for he just lay there, eyes closed, rattling on. That was good, that he didn't feel the vitality between us. He was a complication, all over. An outlaw and betrothed to another woman.

He scratched his beard, his typical scruff grown thicker. He sat up, legs wide, thigh muscles pressing against his charcoal trousers. "You hear about those brothers that were hung, out yonder by Waukomis?"

I nodded and took the cigarette from him.

"Rumor goes," Stot said as he drew his knife from his holster and picked up a stick, "Bitter Creek questioned them, and the encounter went south. I know Bitter Creek—there's a reason his earlier moniker was Slaughter Kid." The dagger slid along the sliver of wood. "He's unhinged. Ruthless. On some enraged quest about those missing outlaws."

Disquiet crept up my back—Bitter Creek sounded terrifying. A vast foreboding spread across the frontier. I scratched at the dry skin on my wrist and waited, knowing Stot had more to say. He glowered at the shadows, as if he could tell them to return to their master.

"This story ain't dying." His fist clenched on the ivory handle of his dagger, the blade silvery blue. "Soon enough, the outlaws will target someone. I don't reckon you turn yourself in, but what's your plan, if your safety falls off the rails?"

I wasn't telling folks what happened, setting myself up to be sent to kingdom come by unwritten law. If I told my story to the deputy marshal, our community could turn on me, call for my execution. Folks didn't tend to believe a woman. My boots scraped through the mud, crackling crisp leaves. It was nonsense that killing those vile men was a crime. At the minimum, if I was convicted of a crime, my homestead would be ripped from me. I'd likely end up dead, in jail, or in an asylum. I couldn't imagine life shut up behind bars. But—there were no bodies, no apparent crime. After time, folks would move on to the next rumor and this story would disappear.

"I'm not turning myself over to vigilante law." I blew at wayward strands of hair. "Folks will rustle up some story or another of where the cowboys went. Seems like every idiot these days is chasing old gold in those abandoned Spanish mines of the Wichita Mountains. Perhaps I could plant that notion about."

Stot's bearing was tense, emotion braided down his spine, his grip all bunched up as he whittled. His blade flinched, lopping off the end of his carving. He dropped the pitiful twig earthward, then shoved his knife back into his sheath. "That's one idea—but if you decide in some wild hair to confess to the marshal, you'll allow me to accompany you?" he asked. "I'll support you, no matter what you say."

Anguish thudded at my temples. I couldn't endure this man interweaving into my life, pressing closer and closer—when he could never be mine. His coiled body language, those shoulders turned toward me, the viscous, tangible possessiveness. He postured his protection as chivalry, but at the root, with him bound with another woman, his concern was cruel. To her and to me.

"All nature, why are you pushing me on this?" I asked.

He stood and flicked his slicker behind him, palms gripping his sable gun belt. "Chaos is rampant all across the damn county." He ripped off his hat, raked his fingers through his hair. It smelt of oncoming rain: layered, earthy, primal. "I don't know how to protect you in such a world," he said, his expression unbalanced, forthright. The timbre of his voice rough, the edges bristly.

I stood, stepped below his brim. "Remember, cowboy—I'm not yours to protect."

The hollows paralleling his cheekbones deepened, black hair curling away from his widow's peak. Fury and frustration and something like fear knotted the ridge of his biceps, faintly visible through his white shirt. "I won't allow you to get picked off by outlaws or vigilantes," he said.

"Well." I leaned in. He had freckles all about his nose. "I don't need you for that."

He gripped the knot of my wrap, yanking me forward. I yelped, stumbled over my boots, my eyes flashing to his lips. The moment stretched hot and undomesticated. I swallowed as he brushed his wide palm along the curve of my shoulder to cup the back of my neck. "No?" he said, his voice deceptively bland.

I lifted my chin, and his demeanor softened.

"I can't balance it all." His gaze roamed to my mouth, and I sucked in a gulp of air. A pause. Another beat. Then I slapped at his arms, shoved him off, disappeared a couple of steps backward.

"You're engaged!" I yelled, breath ragged.

He clenched his jaw, a muscle ticcing along the bone. I let that notion hang—he had another woman to care for.

I thought of all that I carried, of all that I ran from. And I fractured—I'd judged Stot a good man, yet he was just as wretched as everyone else. People betrayed; all were broken. I'd learned that lesson already. Night sounds shivered in the trees, and faroff a nicker scraped against the wind—my palomino Whiskey rustling in the barn. I dropped to the grass and tipped my profile to watch the threadbare white clouds scurry across the starlit sky. Let time pass on by. Stot moved forward, the black toes of his polished boots a glimmer in the dark, spurs glinting like omens. He lowered to the grass beside me. He didn't speak of his sweetheart, didn't say anything at all, and the earth continued on turning and turning, night stretching on and on.

I told myself I was off chasing some grand adventure, rewrote myself into someone brave, someone with grit. But those were just stories. I pulled my knees into my chest, blinked back tears. In truth, I was just running. There was a buzzing in the grasses, as if moments and memories of other lifetimes spoke. "Be quiet," I yelled and flung my decanter. It clattered on a wayward rock, the sound shrill in the vast, echoing space.

I held my knees, my satin skirt stiff and abrasive, daydreams quavering on past. An image of the Native woman pressing into evergreen brambles. The homesteading woman bending down to pluck cabbage leaves. Lightning spurting from another's mouth. Wolves howled across the expanse, from one end of darkness to the other.

Stot gripped the back of his neck, stood to grab my flask. He crouched beside me. "Whether you accept it or not, we're in this together," he said. "You might as well tell me what's troubling you."

I felt heavy, my forearms numb. My secrets suffocating. His engagement unbearable. Stot's bearing was patient, waiting for what it was that I'd buried, what it was I held back. The voices groaned. They writhed, and they ached. They wanted out.

In wilderness, one slips toward oblivion.

Was that it, then? If I kept enduring, isolated in the wild distances, my breath might squeeze right on out. And so I told him—

"I slept with my sister's husband."

He stilled, his eyes darting between mine. Seeing me, recognizing the wide space between what I disclosed and what I buried. My fingernails dug into my arms, my flask cool against my blouse, the crisp scent of whiskey and apples creeping into the frozen-water scent of winter. A memory slapped against my chest, as if flung down from Kansas by the raging southern wind. It was the end of April, a week before Magnolia's wedding, a winesap apple core sticky in my palms. She sat beside me in the clover, a spray of wild violets scattered alongside the creek, Lark leaning against a mossycup oak just beyond. We'd finished a picnic breakfast, and they'd told me they really, truly wouldn't be coming along to homestead.

"So this is goodbye," I'd said, unable to see my future anymore. The apple in my palm, the backs of my fingers on the moss, the groundcover damp with yesterday's rain.

"There's no need for dramatics." Magnolia picked a fleck of oat grass from her skirt, her posture and carriage precise. "What's altered, in truth? We'll come calling all the time."

She glanced over her shoulder at Lark. His hands shoved in his overall pockets, his attention elsewhere.

"Won't we?" she asked him.

"Course we'll visit," he said, the white around his irises stark in the thicket. But I knew he meant nothing of the sort—as he saw it, our friendship was over.

Ever since he'd dissolved our romance, that day hunting beside the creek, he'd stepped further away, until I couldn't even grasp a figment of him. Magnolia pursed her lips, analyzed his stance. She recognized something was wrong but hadn't discovered what it was.

Oak leaves crackled above, our farm indistinct in the valley below. Lark pushed off the mossycup trunk, swung his rifle over his shoulder. "Told my pa I'd help dry venison today."

Another lie. Our fathers repaired the fences down in the holler today. But good riddance, I wanted him to go. Lark muttered some joke, cloaking the awkwardness between us, his ease frighteningly believable—but he wouldn't look into my eyes. I'd had one portrait of Lark the stretch of our childhood—but I'd been wrong.

He walked over, leaned down, and kissed Magnolia.

Lark stood, and she smiled up at him, fiddling with the lilac ribbons of her sunbonnet. And then he was off down the path, his stride lanky, haphazard as the forest swallowed him whole. A white-tailed hawk squawked faroff, beyond the crackle of brittle oak leaves. "We'll visit," Magnolia said, her gauzy white overblouse opalescent in the sunglow. "You're my sister, my dearest friend—I won't have you living without me."

I rested the mottled red apple in my lap, against the pleats of my skirt, the fabric sunny yellow daisies. But I didn't believe platitudes anymore. I couldn't envision how we could live alongside each other much longer. Magnolia bit her lip, ran a thumb across the tines of a fork, and I gathered the floral plates, slipped them back in our basket. "I've noted, since our engagement, you and Lark haven't ventured off alone." She hesitated, splotches of rose streaking up her throat. "I reason that's an above-reproach notion."

I folded a gingham napkin, and a cloud passed overhead, muting the glossy light. I felt vacant, all the way inside. She was the cleverest of us, but somehow she hadn't put the pieces together about Lark and me. I couldn't tell her, not with her this happy, not with him choosing her. The past didn't matter, not even in the slightest. It was past. It'd stay there. I'd let her write her own version of our childhood.

"Sure." I rubbed my clavicle, the ridge of my skin chapped. "No reason for us to go off alone anyhow."

Magnolia held her embroidered ivory cape tight at her neck and studied me, apprehension rippling under her poise. A yellow jacket buzzed by, darting toward the stream. She sensed my evasion but chose to believe me, a smile budding across her face. My sister, the person who knew me best, didn't see me. And I broke—she'd never even asked whether I loved him. Just one evening she'd come racing into our home, startling everyone clustered before the woodfire, and announced they were engaged. She'd vaulted into my arms, giddy and blissful, and I'd held her, shocked. I hadn't been angry then, the disloyalty sharp and debilitating—but as the days sped past, I smoldered. She wasn't that clueless, was she? I waffled between rage and sorrow, capsized by the carelessness of the betrayal. How could she not even ask?

Out in the grove, I plopped an enamelware plate into the basket, the clang unnatural in the wood. Magnolia glanced up, a furrow between her brows. I dropped another plate, the whimsical cornflowers and cobalt forget-me-nots shivering as the plate steadied. She opened her mouth, and I cut her off. "He's lying, you know."

Her lips pinched, a familiar expression of disappointment, the one when she thought my behavior was lacking decorum or moderation. She deliberately straightened the plates, morning luminescence like dew along her cheekbones. "I presumed we wouldn't have to discuss this," she said, her fingers resting on the sapphire rim of the plate. She looked up, her expression closer to pity than I thought necessary. "But we do, don't we?"

I picked up the apple core, gestured for her to continue. She rested her clenched hands in her lap. "Can't you just be happy for me? For once, let me step out from your shadow."

I coughed a stunned laugh. "You cannot be serious," I said. "How about: *I apologize for stealing your beau.*"

Magnolia dropped a trio of forks, her eyes wide. It seemed she truly hadn't known Lark and I had been together. Varying emotions flickered over her face before something rigid settled, as if she were holding on to her shape. "He chose me."

I stood, tossed the apple into the basket. "And you betrayed me."

"Betrayed?" She wiped her hands along her waistband, stood. She shook her head, voice rising in pitch, lines fraught across her forehead. "Now just hold on a minute. Of all the things you could say to me—"

"And you're not even homesteading!" I screamed, everything inside me overflowing, an eruption.

Her posture motionless as she migrated a cascade of thoughts, seemingly understanding all that had been hidden. Then, within the breadth of a blink, the moment passed. I wondered whether I'd actually glimpsed her disarray or imagined it entirely. She stepped backward, straightened the draping of her bodice, as if putting herself away, as if she must, furiously, clutch onto control.

"Homesteading was a childhood fantasy," she said. "By God above, you must become less histrionic."

But it hadn't been a fantasy, not for me. All our years planning had felt like a promise. Underneath it all, that was the crux of my heartbreak. My dreams—lost. My belief in others, shattered.

"You've been moody and ill tempered for weeks," she continued, "since we announced our engagement." Her expression static, her ivory skin now shaded ghost white. "Can't you just move on, stop throwing this tantrum?" She gestured at me, at my heartbreak, like I was some overreacting toddler.

I didn't recognize this woman who'd replaced my kind, demure sister. When losing an argument, when afraid or defensive, Magnolia often lashed out with a small swipe, an underhand insult or a petty observation. But she'd never responded like this. I supposed, after losing her parents and home as a young child, she couldn't allow life to slip through her fingers, forever afraid of losing safe harbor. A squirrel clattered up the loblolly pine, the noises of the forest rising as dawn slipped away from the day. She adjusted her stance, and a greenbrier thorn caught on her cloak. She looked over her shoulder, unwound it from the white wool. Tranquil and unruffled, as if she wouldn't allow herself to recognize that everything between us had gone to ruin.

"You're clasping onto him," I said, "just as you've always clasped onto me. Do you even love him?" I gripped the yellow daisies at my shoulders, palms sticky with apple sap. "I'm leaving, and you've never been brave enough to do anything by yourself. Because you can't imagine living any way but boring, predictable, safe."

Dirt from the forest floor smudged the tiny bluebells embroidered on her hem. She bent and picked up her basket, her once-fragile profile hardened. She'd broken and re-formed into something stronger.

"You've never had any restraint. I wonder why I thought anything would change," she said. "Just make it through our wedding day without embarrassing me."

And then she turned and walked through the copse, shoulders tight, her ivory cape rippling behind her. The air scented tart and coarse, of winesap apples and faraway woodsmoke. The memory unraveled, and I was once again in Oklahoma Territory. Moisture from my flask seeped through my sleeve, the bitter scent of applejack, the woodland timberline faraway, as if the forest wasn't actually there. Stot stared at the sky, jaw loosened, as if he readied to speak. But unlike the other men I'd run across, he wouldn't fill silence with platitudes. A norther whooshed, freezing the heat along my arms.

He adjusted his legs, something like a wince carved beside his eyes. He scratched parallel lines down his neck. "It's dreadful to fancy someone you can't have."

My stomach dropped out below me. I picked at some wild rye stuck to the needlepoint on my bodice. "It is."

He cleared his throat and tugged at his collar. I studied the prairie's many shades of black, like different weights of charcoal pigment pressed across the landscape.

"So you fixing to tell the marshal about the bodies or not?" he asked.

"Are you kidding me? No questions, comments," I said. "Do you ever react to anything?"

"React?"

"Are you aghast?" I asked. He poured some whiskey in my decanter and handed it to me. "Don't you want to know why?"

"Your past is my business none," he said. "Unless you're itching to tell me more."

"Assuredly not."

He leaned over his lap toward me, wickedness edging his mouth. "Course you do."

"I won't give excuses, explain it away. It was appalling."

"So's everyone's past."

Was that it, then? Was he remaking himself as well?

"Yours?" I asked.

He thumbed his pocket watch, the ivory dial uncanny in the surrounding atmosphere of grays and browns. "You watch others fear me, you know my reputation: Of course my past is full of depravity."

"I confessed my betrayal of the person I love most," I said. "What's all this treachery you're lugging about?"

He gazed at the silhouette of the woodland, beyond my land, into time and distance. The hollows deepened beneath his cheekbones, his hat in repose on the grass, dull black crown pointing away. He glanced back—I held his gaze, dew crisp in the air.

"I killed my wife."

CHAPTER TWENTY-NINE

"You had a *wife*?"

My fingers fanned over my collarbone, my eyes surely wide. The moment tipped, lopsided, as if something nameless had swallowed up the meadow in one gulp.

"That's the surprising part?" Stot asked.

"I don't believe you killed a woman you married."

Starlight shimmered above like salt or dust in the bruised-purple sky. I smelt something soft, like pecan pie, and the grassy balm of boundless space.

Stot pressed his bootheel along the dirt. "In essence."

"You can't kill *in essence*."

"No, but it was my fault all the same."

The portrait of the woman and the ice-blue lace in his satchel, perhaps it was hers. "You gonna tell me?" I asked.

"Will you?" He gripped the creases of his Stetson.

I didn't want to speak of Lark and Magnolia, of the havoc I'd left back in Kansas. I didn't want to pull the past forward. I wanted to leave that whole lost universe there, away in time. And yet—I must know about his wife. I nodded. He leaned back on his forearms, tipped his head to the cloud-feathered sky. "You can't share this, you know. It keeps us safe, for folks to be fearing me."

I motioned for him to continue.

"Yes, I was married," he said. "I loved her, endlessly. She was delicate and gentle—the kindest woman I've known."

It was agonizing glimpsing how deep this man could love. I scraped a clump of dirt off my bootheel, my hands calloused, mud smudged. Nothing about me was soft. "So what happened?" I asked.

I felt his gaze and glanced up. His expression had a wash of misery and the weight of past, but also, a smirk edged his mouth. "Well, I was the county sheriff."

I gasped. "You were not."

He grinned. "I was."

A laugh caught in my throat. "Of course you were," I said. *"The Lawman."*

He adjusted his legs, spurs thumping the ground, forearm across his knees. An upland chorus frog chattered from the oat grass, its raspy call wrathy, reminding me of the incessant noise of a summer field full of cicadas and crickets. Stot told that the Dalton Brothers had come through his territory, and they'd tussled. He'd essentially vanquished them during the Coffeyville robbery.

"Well, damn." I shook my head. Those robberies had become immortalized, frontier legends. "Wait." I studied his bearing. "Are you one of the Guardsmen?"

"No," he said. "I mean yes, I ran with Heck Thomas and the Three Guardsmen for a few years. Taught them to track some." He resettled his Stetson, straightened the brim. "Better pals with Bass Reeves, though. He's a good man."

I considered the line of Stot's trousers, his crisp white paper collar. I'd known he was unflagging, tenacious, that he sought honor with ruthlessness. After all was summed up, I supposed I wasn't surprised to learn what his life had once been.

"A few in the Dalton Gang had been neighboring sheriffs and marshals. After their oldest brother's murder, they began to muddle, to ask questions of justice and order, of the nature of law." He removed a cigarette from his chestnut-brown leather case. "We were tossed on opposite sides of that discussion. I foiled some of their exploits, made myself an enemy."

He twisted the whiskey bottle in a slow circle, holding the decanter by the neck. It brushed the grasses in a soft swish. "She was pregnant." He rotated the bottle, the lit cigarette a broken curve of light along the glass. "We'd just found out."

The moon tumbled from the clouds and tossed erratic, ghostly tree-limb impressions across my pasture. It was monochrome and static and suddenly too cold.

"They came for me, but I wasn't home," Stot said. "I didn't protect her."

I pressed my hands over my breastbone.

"They murdered her," he said. "Left her for me on the doorstep."

"Oh God." I grasped his hand. "I'm so sorry."

He slid his palm along mine, let me hold on. His other fist gripped the neck of the decanter. "It's past."

"Past is an awful bitch."

"True." He stubbed out his cigarette in the dirt. "And yet I wouldn't erase what once was. I have remembrances of her, the belief that somewhere, sometimes, there's beauty in humanity."

I laid my head on my knees, turned my face to watch him. "Their deaths were not your fault."

A vein beat on his neck. "I should've protected her, protected my child."

I scooted across the dirt until my thigh pressed along his. He said, "I failed."

"There is no version in which you failed."

I adjusted until I settled between his legs. He tensed, but then eased so I could lean against his chest. He looped an arm around my shoulder, allowing comfort from me. He scrutinized the night sky, the wind through the forest canopy, all that he couldn't control.

This sorrow was where his grief began, when his life had been rewritten. To have propelled Stot away from his intrinsic honor and into crime, of course his torments must've been barbaric. And now the threats to our community mimicked his past—I was another woman he didn't know how to protect.

"You cannot be responsible for the world," I said into the silence.

"I can't leave it." His fingers absently ran along the hem of my blouse. "Pain and regret are such vicious hauntings."

"But also, there's a wideness in God's mercy."

He cocked his head. "Quoting old hymns now?"

I shrugged, my hip catching on the metal of his gun. He pulled back and unbuckled his weapon belt, set them behind. His thumb brushed across the bones of my wrist, the cleft in his chin defined in the murky light.

"You want to know what haunts me during the midnight hours?" His voice was low and resonant. "I understand the Daltons. Understand their rage and confusion, how they tried to remake the law. Emmett Dalton's not a bad man. Just angry and misguided. Somewhere in the mist where we try to find honor and order, where we define truth, he became lost."

"And that's what haunts you." I studied the line of his jaw. "Being unable to determine right or wrong. That's the cussed awful truth, isn't it—we can't always know what's just."

Wind whistled through the high grasses, and thunder boomed in the distance. He idly brushed my wrist, across vein and bone and skin.

"So after Coffeyville, the Dalton Brothers framed you for your family's deaths," I said. "That's the bloodshed from the rumors?"

"Yes." He rocked his neck. "Among other crimes, which came later."

We'd settled into a dreamlike gap between what was foregone and the present, a depthless gorge full of cold air and ghost-white steam. These vulnerable moments of honesty were a transient vapor. I fiddled with the button on his shirt's paper cuff, unbuttoned and rebuttoned, the material softening. I wanted to know the specific lawlessness he'd fallen into and why he'd had a bullet wound last week. But more than that, I must know about this woman he was set to marry come spring.

And so I asked.

CHAPTER THIRTY

The night was a gasping place full of shadow and wondering and all things deep and black. I pressed Stot's cuff link through the buttonhole, felt the weight of his arm round my shoulder, breathed in deep through my nose.

His brother's widow was Clara. She'd grown up with them, a portrait of refined Victorian propriety and charm. Stot had kept his kin at a distance these past years, as at any moment he could be thrown into jail or slaughtered by one outlaw band or another. "I snuck in to see my nieces before the race," he said, "and Clara was struggling something fierce." He removed his arm from my shoulder, scrubbed his face. "She's never handled discord well. She grew up on a tidy estate amongst abundant farmland, and now she's surviving on a decrepit homestead in the badlands of North Dakota, my brother long gone. I decided that establishing a safe space of my own down here, then marrying her and taking care of my nieces, was perhaps the more suitable option for them."

Clara was a gentler sort of woman, never up for much excitement—and she was far too proper to venture across the country with a feller who wasn't her husband. But, he supposed, as they had a fondness for each other, she would marry him and move down once he'd fashioned a house and a farm. Whenever the weather seemed fair, the first week of March or so, he planned to head on up north and propose. He asked if perhaps I'd watch over his farm while he was gone. Air caught beneath my rib cage, his body hot along my spine.

"So you're not engaged but fixing to be?" I shifted to better see his face, my curved, starched collar rasping against his softer shirt.

He nodded.

"You want to marry her?" I felt each press of his body molded along mine.

His gaze wandered down my face. "It's the proper thing to do."

I gripped my decanter, the raised motif on the glass a coarse dent against my fingers.

"It's unfair to my wife, marrying again." His jaw was tight. "But I don't love Clara. So perhaps it's not a betrayal. I want to be a man who graciously hauls his duty. Marrying Clara and caring for my brother's children is the honorable choice."

It was brutal to be tugged toward him when he wasn't for me. I felt adrift, unable to balance what felt inevitable and what would be.

"Sometimes," he said, his body pressing along my back with his exhale, "finding the less bad in all the awful choices is harder than catching a toad in the mud."

I scraped a lucifer across his matchbox, touched the spark to the tip of a cigarette. "Sometimes I'm buried too deep in the mud to even see a toad."

He scooted me closer. I smelt the bitter tang of whiskey and faraway wintergreen. "So you left home and raced." His exhale lifted the wayward strands off my neck. "So your sister could be happy?"

A deep gap stretched between the clouds: the sky empty and lonesome. I didn't know how to bring words to my memories, of who I was before. Stot's hand trailed up my back, and I started at the beginning.

"I loved Lark my whole life," I said. Stot's hand hitched. I rolled the cigarette between my fingers. "Growing up with Magnolia was the best part of childhood. I loved her, more than anything." I flicked off embers. "Or so I thought."

"You can still hurt those you love most," Stot said. "It doesn't eliminate your love for them."

I glanced at him. "Perhaps."

Could that be true? It seemed senseless. But loving her was one of the only real things I knew. A hazy image overcast my thoughts—of shaking salsifies as wide as cabbages with Magnolia, the white seed puffs loosening and detaching. The cloudlike seedpods taking off and floating away into golden sunshine. All those roomy, expansive afternoons, all those long seasons stretching back to when memory began—I was losing grip, my memories beginning to fade. To leave Magnolia had felt like a death. I couldn't fathom how I could betray her, if I truly loved her. Stot widened his legs so I could turn and see his face. I slipped a hand in my pocket, rubbed the blunt tines of my skeleton key. Told him how Lark and I had started sleeping together last winter, how I'd believed we'd marry someday.

"What happened?" Stot asked.

"He married her."

"And you left?"

"I ran away."

A plume of smoke coiled from my chimney, and the sound of the hearth's fire crackled through my shack's walls. "But why are you punishing yourself?" he asked. "She married your feller."

I picked at the winter-dead grass. Across the meadow a barred owl whooped his eight-beat call. "Now, I realize she's your baby sister," Stot said and threaded my palm into his, "but could you be romanticizing her in your memory?"

My memory, the past forever tumbling and churning. The morning after we'd quarreled in the forest, as dawn bled red-orange through my eyelet curtain, Magnolia crawled into bed with me, her arms slipping round my narrow shoulders, her chin pressed against the center of my back, her forehead smoothing wet tears against the wisps of hair at my nape. *It's always you and me,* she'd said. I'd murmured that phrase as a child, her afraid of barn owls and monsters, her ringlets tucked up in a puffy white bonnet, her lashes translucent. It'd always been us two—and Lark. I'd thought he was mine. But he was hers. In the rosy vapors of morning, her body warm and soft against my back, I considered how she'd always been sweet on Lark. I'd thought it youthful infatuation, but it seemed she loved him. Of course I wanted her to be happy, to step out from my shadow, of course I did—but why this choice? I supposed I should be proud. She'd the gumption to chase after the man she'd always wanted. I grabbed her forearms, held on, whispered back, *Marry him.*

On my prairie, the owl's call elusive and wilting, I untangled my hands from Stot's, settled them in my lap. Time stretched; the owl flapped his wings. "There's more."

Perhaps Stot was right, that I idealized Magnolia's memory. Memories shifted and changed, all that was past distorted, until I wasn't quite sure what was truth and what was the story I told myself. Under the starlight, Stot's hands on my back, I told him the rest.

"I slept with Lark, my sister's husband, the night before their wedding."

There were those moments I didn't want to remember, in my father's barn. It smelt of whiskey then, as it did right at present, but then the woodiness stale, the tannins sour. There were so many sounds, meadowlarks roosting in the eaves, laughter prowling the wind currents, my moans in the dark, and then there were no sounds. My fingertips pulsed as I swept my palms over Lark's damp shoulders. The hay prickled my scalp, all those translucent bluebells Magnolia and I had foraged and plaited into my hair—the blooms crushed and beginning to wilt. And Lark. His outbreaths stirred my wayward strands. He pushed up from the straw, his palms brushing the heavy sides of my breasts, and rolled off me. We stared at the ceiling, rectangular slats of alder wood nailed together with cracks obliging streaks of starlight and the air backlit with floating dust. A draught groaned along the barn, the squeak as air slipped inside. He rose and yanked on his trousers, moonlight grazing the muscles of his back, shadows edging out the hollows. Time thumped as he shoved his flannel into his waistband. A distant giggle drifted across the fields, the stomp of a horse. He didn't say anything. He drew up his suspenders and climbed down the ladder, his eyes raking my half-naked form one last time. He left.

I hadn't been thinking, when Lark had found me in the foggy shadows before the barn and kissed me. There'd been a thirst, a possibility that somehow we could go backward. *Everyone will fail you,* Pa often said. *It's better to trust none but your own self.* But I couldn't trust myself neither. I had no control. I was a madly spinning tornado, destroying all in my path. *You've never had any restraint,* Magnolia had said. I unclasped the chain around my neck and let my key talisman fall into the straw. Everything that we had been was past. I must find my own space, my own wide skies. Somewhere safe, where I could allow my tornadic winds to expand and evolve and someday, hopefully, dim. To love Magnolia was to leave.

On my homestead with Stot, the owl keened, the beats of his call thumping across my wrist like a pulse. I studied my blackened nails, the mud smudged along my forearm, the oil settled into my palm, my regret screeching along the broken spaces of the wind. I unbuttoned and rebuttoned Stot's cuff, the calluses on my finger pads snagging on the paper.

Stot took my hand and brushed his fingers along my palm, relaxing the tension I held in my hand. He didn't say he understood, didn't say anything at all. He just kept on holding me as we sat in the gap of what once was. It was quiet, the night full of haunting, the sky so dark.

MIDWINTER

February and March 1894

Earth

August 12, 1873
twenty-one years before

You're in the right story, I whisper, but I don't think you hear.

It's cold as the days fall into midwinter. Frost encrusts my fingertips, icicles cling to my hair. I tell you of Willie Matthews and Sally Ann Thunder Ann Whirlwind, of Prairie Rose and the everywoman homesteader. I rove my memory backward twenty years into the thick of the Wild West, the age of thundering cattle drives. The terrain you live on is the same landscape as Old Chisholm Trail, once the hunting lands of the Cherokee, and further back in time, the homeland of the Wichita people. I squint and see much that is forgotten. Women lost in the wind swarm of history, stories never told.

Willie Matthews dashes alongside a gorge, the fringes of her chaps snapping, summer heat fizzling across her shoulders. The range gleams red, the horizon endless. She carves between the blackjacks on her mustang, steering the longhorns downhill, the clamor of ten thousand hooves echoing about the lowland. A tapestry of ancestry, a community knit through the landscape of time.

But Willie Matthews becomes fable. Sally Ann is forgotten. Their voices diminish to a haunting, just myth whispered on the wind. Minnie, do you see? In isolation, one slips toward oblivion.

Seasons pass, years rush on by.

Time, unstable on the prairie. As the century turns, the press of advancement is heavy, wheels clawing at my bones, metal automobiles scraping across my veins, smoke puffing toward the sky. Women fought for and won rights, a war spread across my entire body, times changed. Once, my prairie was quiet. Now, everything moves faster, louder, grander. My throat congested, my breath tinged with soot.

Alongside Crooked Creek, a woman roams through amber bluestem and, at her garden, kneels against my moist soil. Her name is Gail. Holding her cloak against her neck, the homesteader presses through the gusts to her porch, tumbleweeds whipping up into the firmament. These tales of Crooked Creek evolve, just as my body is ever changing, just as stories are rewritten over and again, memories of these women resurface and re-form, until I'm not sure where my own memory slips into myth. I try to tell you about myself, about this particular patch of rolling hills, but I cannot quite grasp my essence. I wonder, what does it mean to *be* something or other? Which parts of one's story are truth and which are imagined? Which parts matter when cobbling together an identity?

I am so tired. I am so many fragments.

Stir about a bit, Minnie. Listen. Knit yourself into this patchwork quilt of memory. And hold on.

CHAPTER THIRTY-ONE

Oklahoma Territory—February 7, 1893

two weeks later

I whacked my hammer against a rusted nail. Beyond the fence's pale wood, colorless oat grasses and wild rye matted together. Their feathered ends still, unchanging as midwinter dragged on. All season long, my prairie had been moody and sworling. Almost as if she was caught somewhere between fury and heartbreak. Weather in Oklahoma lands was primal and brutal—that feral unpredictability of No Man's Land. One day soaked in sunshine, a blizzard whirling on in the next. The air could snap in a moment and remind us winter was long from over.

Today the sky was blanched. A daytime moon perched above the wooded hills. A haphazard, imperfect circle, that last off-centered oblong before tomorrow's full moon. Everything felt unfinished.

I'd removed a pocketful of nails and some boards from a bashed-up buggy I'd found in the wallows, the materials perfect for a fence. Fencing my quarter section was long, slow work, but I savored the weighted feel of swinging my arm through the air.

Willie was off yonder, his crooning echoing about the lowland. He'd brought over some laundry, but I hadn't minded overmuch, as he'd set to work oiling my plow. The morning after the barn raising, Stot had upbraided him something fierce. Bedraggled and terrified of the outlaw, Willie had sat quiet, for once without excuses, his lanky shoulders hunched over my breakfast table. I'd pushed out my door, milk pail in hand, and a while later the two of them had exited my shack, Stot's arm looped across Willie's shoulder, Willie promising to do better, them all a'sudden the best friends this side of the Mississippi. I wasn't ready to trust that Willie would change, but maybe he'd finally looked at the dark parts of himself.

I lined up a nail, my bootheels wobbling on overturned mud, struggling to find the earth below the crispy wild oat stalks. I'd been off balance these past weeks, overfull of wonderings and worry. I longed to talk with my steady, insightful sister. After these seasons away from her, I was no longer outraged—just heartbroken. There was a gap where she'd once been. I couldn't imagine how we could reconcile. As time stretched on, the ache didn't ease, but deepened, craggy and festering. I didn't know anymore how to piece my memories into order again. I wiped dust from a nailhead, pressed the point against wood.

And Lark. I missed what once was, the friendships I'd had the width of my life. I recognized now that I hadn't been in love with Lark. We'd had something simple and untested. We hadn't known how to walk through dark truths together. It was spring meadows and lanky summer ponds. Boundary walls and safe harbors. Not love in the rough hews of this broken world. Lark was from another age, different memories, from a Minnie who didn't exist anymore.

I slammed my hammer against a nail, a bullfrog rumbling off beyond and some starlings rustling in the brush. The day full of prairie sounds. Yesterday I'd visited Niabi. We'd studied the groundcover and wind currents to gauge how the surroundings would affect a bullet. She'd tucked her hair behind her ears, gripped her pistol, and loosed her shot—with both eyes open, practicing as I'd shown her. I aligned the next board, and it was then that I heard hoofbeats along the edge of my land. I studied the horizon, not recognizing the paint horse, a russet tobiano mare. A star was golden on the rider's vest placket.

Sakes alive, it was Frank Canton, the deputy marshal, come calling. I balanced the dangling board against my fence, then removed Pa's push dagger from my boot and slipped it in a pocket. I straightened my apron over my blade and walked toward the marshal through the high grass, my heart a'rattling against my bones.

"Afternoon," I hollered.

"Good day, ma'am." He pulled up on his reins and dismounted. "Is it Miss Hoopes?"

I nodded, and he introduced himself. "Care for an afternoon tea?" I gestured toward my homestead, Willie hidden on the other side of my shack.

"You needn't trouble yourself," he said, his wide black mustache rigid over his cheeks.

"Ain't no trouble." I pulled a thistle off my shirtwaist, my other hand gripping the square handle of my dagger. His gaze flicked about my yard, then my clothing, as if he could see a hidden stain of blood on my hands. "How may I help you, Marshal?"

He spun his pocket watch, eyes shrewd. "Been to town this week?"

"Can't say that I have."

"Suppose word hasn't roved down to you then, about them missing cowboys." His palm adjusted on his pistol's buffalo-horn grip.

"Those cowhands?" I cocked my head. "Who folks say headed off yonder, chasing gold?"

"I'd surmised that, too, but—" His gaze was tight on my face. "Their bodies were found."

I stepped back. "What's that now?"

"Uncovered the bodies of those missing outlaws in them north woods, just beyond your quarter section." He flipped open his pocket watch, closed it, tracked my hand clenched in my pocket. "Shot up by a Peacemaker. Buried quite a bit underground, but that preacher by the name of Poor, his hound found them. Guess the foxhound was digging in the roots of a water oak."

"Well, by nation." I shook my head, blinked, allowed myself to look shocked. "They surely have passed on?"

"As no one's seen hide of them since the race, I suppose that's when someone dropped them." He studied the hammer sticking out of my apron pocket. "Now, Miss Hoopes, your claim being just beyond, it would've been natural for you to have heard the shots, to have perhaps even witnessed their murders."

I fluttered my hands to my heart, widened my eyes. "Course that day was lawless and smoky and full of all sorts of sounds—but I did not witness any murders."

He shifted his weight from one boot to the other. The faint tenor of Willie's singing slipped between the wild rye. The marshal questioned me about the race, what time I supposed I staked claim, about the fire on my homestead. Then he looked eastward toward the Browns' homestead. "Hear tell that you're friendly with the Browns." His gaze curved along the creek, then northward toward Stot's claim. He grimaced. "You sure found yourself with grum pickings for neighbors. If you're fixing to survive winter, you'll have to rely on all and sundry, sure enough—I just wouldn't want you to get tangled up with some bad bugs."

I unclenched my fingers, swept my hand down my apron. "The Browns are my friends. They're honest, kind folk."

He flipped open his watch, closed it. "Now, I mustn't share information about the investigation, but—I'd be wary, Miss Hoopes. As I've traveled about the county, I've heard grumblings. Of course, I'd prefer this matter solved within the law." He shrugged, gave a hearty, good-natured laugh. "But, unfortunately, vigilante rule reigns out here in the Wild West." He slipped his watch into his waistcoat pocket. "So, I tell you truth, if you had witnessed anything, you wouldn't be in trouble, see. You needn't protect anybody."

"I'm not protecting anyone, Mr. Canton. I didn't witness any murders."

His mare stepped about in the bluestem and bumped his shoulder. "Alright then." The marshal patted his vest and flashed his teeth, cream beneath his dark mustache. "How about some of that tea then? Got any pie?"

We crossed the field and came round the shack. From his crouch beside my plow, Willie halted his whistling. He stood and wiped his hands on an oil rag. "Well howdy, Marshal."

The three of us walked inside, and in scant moments Willie had Marshal Canton wheezing for air, his guffaws blustering through one story or another. Willie's gaze stuttered across my posture, and he caught my eye, lifted a brow. He registered something was off. Of all the times, this wasn't the one for him to pay attention. But I supposed it was time my big brother saw the world beyond himself.

We suffered through the niceties of tea, my heart thumping my chest, my push dagger a weight in my pocket. But there was nothing to worry. The marshal seemingly believed my tale. Instead, it appeared he suspected my neighbors. I felt altogether sick. All winter, Olive and Stot had supposed someone would be framed for the murders, while I'd foolishly believed the story would stay buried. And now my closest friends were under investigation, with vigilante bloodlust brewing and vicious outlaws roaming the countryside. Confessing to the marshal seemed to be the swiftest way to get locked up or meet a violent end—but I also couldn't let another take the fall.

"You hear tale about that town of women, just east aways? Bethsheba?" Willie straightened the lapel of his raspberry jacquard, double-breasted waistcoat. "No men."

I pressed against the wooden spindles of my chair. "Only women?"

"That's the rumor." Willie sipped whiskey, offered his flask to Marshal Canton. "Heard this one account of a male reporter come calling, and the lady mayor and lady police chief fired off their Winchesters until he fled."

"Well, that's nonsense if I ever done heard it." The marshal dug at his teeth with a toothpick, other hand resting on his stomach. "Lord, women always making up stories. Well," Marshal Canton continued, "it won't last."

I wanted to snap at him—but he wasn't wrong. Out on the frontier, communities were fragile. Townsites evolved and vanished along the horizon: Just like mirages, an image sparking, then dissipating, leaving only that uncanny feeling of something misremembered. Settlements like Bethsheba just one poor choice from becoming ghost towns.

As afternoon crept on toward evening, Willie started in about other news spread across our county. And then the marshal was gone, along with Willie, the sun sliding down to simmer along the blackjacks, and I had no idea whatever to do.

CHAPTER THIRTY-TWO

When dawn broke, Cricket and I galloped toward Olive's homestead. I scented magnolia blossoms on the breeze, but it must be an illusion. An entire season must pass on by before the huge, waxy blooms would open. There was a luster in the wildwood, like a juniper-green gemstone lost amid the bramble. I tumbled back in my past, to crawling across the curve of a gnarled magnolia bough, deep within the haven of emerald leaves. Starlight soaked the sky, the perfume of the blooms seeping about the canopy. Hours before, I'd snuck from my bed to eavesdrop on Ma and her literary society. They met once a month and fervently debated women's rights, wandering the threads of suffrage and prohibition. *We should submit to the opinions of our husbands,* some of her friends would state. Ma's skin would get mottled and all a'flushed, red splotches along her neck, her eyes blinking faster. I cherished seeing my hardworking, gospel-singing ma passionate, fighting for something that mattered to her.

At nine, I was old enough to understand that life wasn't simple. Ma walked a line between what seemed two conflicting existences: fierce loyalty to her religion and unbounded passion for women's rights. That night, I crept round the corner and listened as they discussed Susan B. Anthony's recent speech. *There shall never be another season of silence,* my ma quoted, *until women have the same rights men have on this green earth.*

"It's not enough," Ma said to her friends. From my crouch in the hallway, an image of my ma reflected in the curve of a silver plate, her form distorted and awash with gray. "Something must be done."

One of her friends clapped with a sharp boom and said, "Well then, let's just take a hatchet to the bar tops, like Mrs. Carrie Nation threatens."

Ma laughed, but I wondered—why not? So I stepped on out and asked. Ma stood, straightening her skirts. "Minnie." She wiped her hands round the curve of her face, glanced at her friends. "You should be sleeping."

"Why not demolish the bar if you think it should be destroyed?" Midwinter cool prickled my ankles, my cotton nightgown all a'sudden this month too small, the lace frill trailing my calves.

Ma slipped her arm round my shoulder. "I'll walk you back to bed."

"I'm not a child anymore." I pulled from her. "Take Pa's hatchet and go. I'll distract Mr. Anders."

And that was how I came to be crawling 'cross a gnarled magnolia bough above Mr. Anders's saloon, in the middle of godforsaken night, preparing to distract him something fierce so Ma and her suffrage friends could slash up his saloon. I sat on the branch, ankles dangling from my white cotton nightgown, hair tied up in curl papers, and slipped my folding knife from my pocket. Like Ma, I supported women's rights but didn't understand why temperance mattered, how those two pieces were intertwined. I halted, my blade gleaming in the dark, unsure if I should attempt such a daring commotion. Folks always spoke that I trailed chaos behind me. But I thought my antics had reason. *I've a plan,* I had told my ma. *Oh honey, I know,* she'd said as she loaded a sack onto the buckboard, *you always do*.

Below the magnolia, Ma hunkered in the shadows with her friends, the wooden handle of Pa's hatchet gripped in her palms. Her ashen hair was parted severely down the middle, her bun tight at the nape of her neck—but her face wasn't hard. It was luminous. I wasn't sure about her mission, but I sure as starfire supported my ma.

I scooted to the edge of the magnolia bough and dragged in a deep inhale. Then I slashed my dagger across my shin. I smothered a yelp. Across the path, Ma's eyes widened. *"Go,"* I whispered and waved her on.

I jumped from the magnolia, slamming into the uneven soil, and started yowling something fierce. I rolled onto my side, tugged up my legs, my palm dripping blood, and just kept on screaming.

Mr. Anders shoved out the batwing saloon doors, his gray hair tufted out like a winged owl, his shotgun trained on the dark.

I howled, and Mr. Anders rushed on over, sighting me in the shadows.

"Ah, hell. Minnie Hoopes?" He cursed. "What have you got into now."

He gathered his wife, and I kept causing such a racket, blood smeared all over my palms and hemline, no one noticed my ma and her literary society friends slip into the saloon. Through the window, I saw Ma swing her hatchet, her dandelion-yellow dress fluttering, the arc of her bell sleeve distorted through the smoke-smudged glass. A flash of lightning in thunderclouds. That moment, witnessing Ma take axe to the bar top, watching her fight with abandon for what she believed, rooted in my memory. Ma tirelessly worked round our farm in her impeccably stitched homespun gowns. She resembled all the other mas, with perhaps a pinch more spunk, a bit more joy. But I watched her closer after that, and I realized: My ma walked through town different. She didn't let anyone tell her how a woman was supposed to be. A woman could be whomever she wanted. And now, here I was, homesteading on land that was to be my own. My ma and her ma and all the women before her would be so proud that I had carved out a space of my very own.

If I could only keep ahold of it.

Cricket and I dashed below glossy, emerald branches, the leaves' shapes blurring as we rushed on past. But they were holly leaves, not magnolias. I searched round the Browns' farm until I found Olive down by the creek, washing linens. The gilt of dawn spilt into the gorge, time stretching and pulling, heavy on my chest. I dismounted Cricket and climbed down to the bank, clumps of dirt loosening under my boots.

Olive called hello, her hands sunk in the water, white linens elegiacally floating in the creek. I glanced behind me, wiping my palms down the front of my skirt. She dropped the cloth and dried her hands on her apron. "What is it?"

"The bodies of the missing outlaws were found." I updated her that the marshal hadn't outright tossed blame at them. "But my gut is that he's looking at your family—and Stot."

Olive stumbled back, sat on the bank, red dirt drenching her lace skirt. "We can't have that."

"No." I dropped beside her. "Suppose we get him to look another way."

Her hands rested in her lap, her bearing still.

"Hey." I gripped her shoulder. "Perhaps I shouldn't have worried you. I don't think anything must be done yet—there's no evidence against your family."

She crossed her arms, a wet rag clenched in her fist, water soaking her sleeve. "How come you just know we ain't done it."

"It's not who you are."

She dropped the rag into a bucket with a plop, a spray of water misting my hands. "What if they attacked us, and it was self-defense?"

I gripped the lapel of my jacket, my fingernails brittle and too cold. She couldn't confess to my crime. "I know that ain't the tale."

She walked to the water's edge, bent to grab the linens. Light dappled along the current, the stream tugging ever onward.

"But I'm not finding another solution," she said.

"You can't claim self-defense," I said. "It makes you seem desperate."

"I *am* desperate," Olive said. "If the marshal frames us, and folks rile up about horsefeathers, as they do—I'll do whatever it takes to protect my family."

"I'm behind you." I joined her before the water.

I couldn't allow them to confess to my crime. I slipped my hands into the cold water, grasped the slippery, rectangular bar of homemade lye soap. Last night, before the waning flicker of my oil lantern, I'd considered different scenarios and strategies. I couldn't find a wiggle anywhere. So it seemed, if I didn't discover a solution soon, vigilantes would either come for the Browns or for me. That was law in the Wild West.

I grabbed a sodden length of gauzy linsey, rubbed the bar on the clothes, cleaning free the residue of earth. "Don't claim self-defense. We'll find a way."

And we would. I thought of what Stot had said a few weeks past, about finding the balance in a world without rules, of searching for the less bad among all the awful choices. The white cloth submerged in the foggy water, beneath the iridescent stretches of soapy clouds. Wriggling across the creek's mirrored surface, something almost seemed to take shape. A sweeping valley, someone else's barn, other women, a different community. I recognize the townsite as Bethsheba. Women walked the dirt pathways of Bethsheba's arms, the wind howled against the wooden boards of her bones, and Bethsheba shivered, her freckles of nails glinting in the morning glow. Just like the hazy women in my oil landscapes: something there, but not quite.

I'm not sure I'm in the right story anymore.

The words sank into the pit of my stomach: I felt distorted, the pathway through my life indistinct and warped. Other moments in time wavered in the water, nebulous and ghostly. I scrubbed at the sheen of red dust from Olive's laundry, my hands aching along the sides.

CHAPTER THIRTY-THREE

The following afternoon I brushed Ezra's mare Frailty, my fingers dipping in the hollows between her worn patches of chestnut hair. As I caressed Frailty's bulging stomach and sinewy muscles, her ears flattened. She needed a wash. "It's just the wind, sugar," I told her, then carried a bucket out to the well. Outside, a norther whipped furious and brutal across Ezra's homestead. I tied the rope around the handle and turned the windlass. There were sounds on the wind, breezes whistling through loose boards. I kept overhearing remnants of a faraway conversation, kept wondering about these stories rising from the silence. I hauled out the pail, the damp metal brittle. My fingers were red, my nails jagged.

The ancient voice narrated something longlost. As I untied the flaxen rope, fragments of a woman's tale broke apart from the crack of the wind. I pressed back through gusts, toward the barn. I was still cross with Ezra, but when he'd asked me to examine his pregnant mare, I couldn't say no. I hoped he'd continue the generosity I'd noticed at the Browns' barn bee. I thought through my past, wondered whether I should rewrite the version of Ezra I'd fashioned, if perhaps there was something about him I just hadn't recognized yet. I held my slicker tight at the throat and waded back to the barn. There was so much sky on my brothers' land. Smooth brome stretched to the edge of the earth, the sun already muted along the lower pastures. The dreary winter sky barely brushed with pigment, just a weak smudge of topaz and rose. I longed to grasp charcoal and show color with gray, to find something hidden between shadow and murky beige. Last week Stot had arrived with a gorgeous walnut-stained oak easel he'd carved. I'd finished my moody-blue and oatmeal-brown landscape, the one with Sally Ann Thunder Ann Whirlwind as an ephemeral vapor. Before dark fell, I'd gallop on home and perhaps sketch a new terrain.

Inside Ezra's barn, I dipped the sponge in the water bucket, hoping to provide comfort for Frailty, soothing her with a hushed monologue, gossiping about the handsome feller who lived just north aways. Perhaps Stot would stop over this evening, talk with me by the fire. Maybe he'd have a solution for the bodies. Something must be done: I just hadn't rustled up a strategy yet. These past weeks Stot and I had shared of our pasts, a little here and there—tales of our families, pranks of our youth. Unsurprisingly, he'd been an ungoverned little boy, not understanding arbitrary rules. He carried himself with unbreakable honor, but then he'd catch my eye as he sliced carrots beneath the kerosene lantern or as he fixed a molding board along my ceiling, and I'd glimpse such unbidden roguishness in him. He was just so much of one thing and then entirely another, and I couldn't quite untangle who he was.

He'd been helpful round my homestead, though. Framing my windows in pine, straightening a wobbly drawer. My hands stilled, overcome with memories of Stot's last visit, a couple of evenings past. He'd lounged on my sofa, his green eyes watching me. I ran the back of my hand across my forehead, smearing soapy water. Sometimes he was too unbearably magnetic. His stature, that scent of nutmeg and sunlight—he took up all the space inside my thoughts.

I squeezed the sponge over Frailty's flank, washing her brown and white patches. Though Stot had become a friend, I'd never uncovered why he'd been shot or what had happened with the outlaws. Although mystery seemed a part of him, I felt as if I knew him in truth more than I'd known Magnolia or Lark. But of course that was nonsense. I'd known them the width of my life.

The stable door slapped open, fracturing the slush of dripping water. At the doorway, Ezra straightened a brush on its peg. I dropped the sponge in the bucket with a plop and stepped around Ezra to grab my gun belt.

"You'll tidy this mess?" Ezra asked.

I turned slowly. "Were you to pay me for evaluating her?"

"You're not a veterinarian."

I buckled my belt across my hips. Along the sides of the barn, the wind moaned, uneasy. "And yet you asked me to come round."

"So she's fine?"

I sighed, grabbed a rag off a peg. "Frailty's fine." I dried my hands. "Wind's probably bothering her."

Ezra nodded, his coarse hair slicked back with pomade. "Not the foal?"

"Foal's fine. You know the signs to look for?"

An ugly frown tugged at his lips. "You'll come by every day."

I slipped on my cape, pressed the top button through the keyhole. "I can't ride over every day. I have my own claim." I explained again what to do, to give her space and watch for odd behavior. "Frailty's your mare. You can keep her safe."

He struck the wood slats of the barn, and the stall shivered. Surly energy buzzed from his shoulders. I led Cricket into the carriage room. Gloom drifted in wide puddles from the deep hollows of the barn, while glow seeped from cracks between boards.

"That outlaw of yours?" He ran his fingers over his mustache, the tone of his voice grating. "Stay away from him this week."

I yanked on my gloves and slid open the barn door. "He's not *my* outlaw."

Ezra straightened his bowler hat, the brim casting an ugly gloom on the rim of his cheekbones. "No?"

"Why would he be?"

"He's by, an awful lot."

"We're neighbors." I led Cricket beyond the doorway. "And it's not like you're going to help me improve my homestead."

Ezra grasped my wrist, yanked me back into the shadows. He leaned close, his spit spraying my face. "Do not say I don't provide for my own."

I lifted my brows. "Why, of course not."

His fingers bruised my wrist through the leather, the button on my glove incising my skin. I shook my hand free and walked outside. It was odd, him cautioning me away from Stot. "Why avoid him? Something stirring?"

"You don't need to know," Ezra said as he followed.

"Thought you protected your own."

His nostrils flared cavernous and oblong. "Ain't no matter: Nothing a lady can do about it anyhow. Them hooligan band just out west." He knocked his head toward the salt plains, the hideaway of the Wild Bunch. "They're taking care of him."

My blood iced, terror quick and visceral. I tugged at the high collar of my dress, my heartbeat a clear thump against my throat. "Why do you suppose such a thing?"

Ezra kicked at some gum balls strewn about the grass. "Other day, at the saloon, I'm drinking blackstrap, minding my own business. The Lawman's glowering from a shady corner, listening to talk about the murders like some emperor. Folks supposing the Browns must've slayed those outlaws. The Lawman clanks down his decanter, saunters over, demands the Browns be removed from speculation, that everyone get their heads out of the sand and suppose what's more sensible—that the Browns, amiable, middle-aged homesteaders, had killed two vicious outlaws? Or that perhaps it would've taken a faster draw to take them down. He glared at the crowd, hands gripped tight to his pistols, essentially confessing that *he'd* slaughtered the outlaws. He hulked there, glowering, until everyone closed back up their gaping mouths and aggressively nodded in agreement." Ezra grimaced, the barrel of his chest pressing at the seams of his tweed waistcoat.

My hands gripped the wooden slats of the fence. That foolhardy man. Sakes alive, I couldn't let him take my fall. I asked Ezra why he supposed the outlaws were coming for Stot, and he told that after the Lawman left the saloon, Bitter Creek had asked after his hideout. "I never approved of that criminal taking land from honest folk." Ezra pulled on a wiry eyebrow. "But either way, sure enough, one of your neighbors killed them."

"The Lawman didn't murder those outlaws, and the Browns would never hurt anyone. Ezra, tell me you don't support vigilante hogwash."

"There's only so much land."

"You weak-bellied bigot."

He struck me across the face. The landscape blurred a stripe of textures.

I held my jaw. The horizon wobbled, my boots unstable. Cricket stamped, uneasy, and I touched his wheat-brown withers, returning to myself.

"Come on now, women can't tend land on their own." Ezra smoothed the ends of his chambray under his waistband. "It's the dead of winter, our farms are struggling. It's high time you admit forfeit and move here. That's your role."

I clenched the lapel of my cloak; threadbare dusk light overlaid his pale skin. "I belong on my own land."

"Enough." He grabbed a tin can of chew off the fence and threw it across the yard, his knuckles red with sweat. The can clattered in the high grass. "I'm cross and done with your antics."

I gripped Cricket's saddle horn, my forearms shaking, and mounted. "I won't be back."

Ezra grasped my ankle and tugged me off. My shoulder bashed the ground, my arm knocking out of socket. I rolled onto my side, cheek pressed into the dirt, gasping for air. Cricket stamped, and Ezra yanked his reins. "Quiet, you ninny."

I drew my hunting knife from my boot sheath. "Don't tug at my horse."

He wiped his hands together. "You will forfeit your homestead to my control and come tend my home."

I pushed up to a seated position, left arm drooping across my belly, a creeper vine grasping my bootheel. "No."

"No?" His voice unnerving and low.

"I will not leave my home," I said. "Your farm is your problem. Figure it out yourself."

Ezra strode back, yanked me up by the collar, his rectangular face before mine, eyebrows askew. My blade slipped between my fingers, falling into the creeper. He spit in my face. "Disgusting, useless woman."

He dropped me and kicked, the wood of his boot sole shredding skin along my forearm. I coughed, mouth flooded with blood and dust, and found the knife in the bramble. He kicked again, clobbering my stomach, and I flung the blade, the eerie zip slicing the sound of eventide. The knife struck true, where his shoulder met his collarbone. He stumbled backward, ivory chambray disappearing into shadow.

I yanked out my Colt and stood. My body swayed.

"You won't shoot me." Ezra held his shoulder.

My gun trained on Ezra, I leaned against Cricket's mane and murmured *steady*, my command for the handless swing mount. "You know I don't miss." Blood pooled in my mouth, and my words came out slurred. "My blade would've been between your eyes if I wanted."

The color drained from his face.

Cricket lowered his head, kneeing down so I could mount. I swung my leg over and eased into the saddle, pistol trained on Ezra. "Try any of this again, and I'll kill you." The expanse of his homestead blurred, my grasp on reality hazy. Blood dripped from between Ezra's fingers and splattered the earth. "Unless the Lawman slaughters you first," I said, "when he hears you betrayed him."

"You have to be loyal to betray."

"He won't care." I anchored my boots in my stirrups. "I'd be scared, Ezra."

Cricket galloped away, the prairie vibrating as we tore across the earth. Night fell, opaque and thick. I shouldn't have been surprised, once again, by the vileness of humanity. This past year I'd observed depravity and baselessness. I expected folks to be unwholesome cowards who'd fail me. But then I'd let some hope in. Somewhere, deep inside myself, I'd a notion that perhaps I'd been wrong. That day we built the Browns' barn, I'd begun to wonder whether Ezra would change. To hope, that had been my weakness. For of course there was no space for hope on the frontier.

I tied a rope about my waist to keep in my saddle if I fainted. I tucked my limp arm against my stomach, sank my blood-slicked hand into Cricket's black mane, and laid my head upon him, held on. He'd bring me to safety, if such a place existed. But I needed someone, no matter how deep and dark their secrets went. I couldn't survive this alone. Before me, the horizon trembled, and the wind groaned, an agony etched in the curve of air. It was as if Cricket fell out from below me and I floated, as if I spiraled into the endless beyond, split in two, a Minnie who hoped and a Minnie who was honest. A woman arising, a woman half smoldering.

There was a whoosh, a crack of air, an uncanny awareness of the mutability of the here and now. A phantasm materialized over the landscape of a sky clogged with smoke, of strange, faraway scents, and of a gravelly rumbling I'd never heard before. I glimpsed the homesteading woman again—she walked through amber bluestem grass, wind snapping a sky-blue floral dress about her hips, dark hair loosely piled atop her head in voluminous Gibson waves, white oak basket looped over her forearm. The vision mimicked a quick, impressionist sketch—unsharpened charcoal, shifting baselines, the clouds a haphazard smudge, the woman a contour of lines.

The mirage slipped away as a mist; the woman vanished. Time wobbly out on the prairie. I lost hold of the thread, of my own story. *I am many fragments,* someone whispered. The endless horizon before me turned gauzy and indistinct, the atmosphere scenting of orange pekoe tea, Cricket a rhythm of galloping, and then I remembered no more.

CHAPTER THIRTY-FOUR

Osage Nation—February 11, 1894

two days later

Midmorning light warmed my eyelids, my dreams hazy with mirages. Of vast, barren spaces and a gilded, burning land, of breezes carving patterns through a wolf fur cloak, an oblong moon casting a silvered glow. The Native woman's profile tilted skyward, her feet planted against upturned soil, as if she bloomed. Of the homesteader clutching damp cloth against her mouth, the terrain behind her scorched, of a cattle drive foaming across my land, last sunglow glinting like fire in the oat grasses. Flame and smoke, ember and rainstorm and drought. I rolled from my bed these past days, a fur spread before the fire. Pulling a blanket coat over my shoulders, I shuffled about Niabi's lodge. My body ached and all-overish screamed, as if my bones and ligaments sucked in deep sighs and moans. I shimmied into my skirt and grabbed my overblouse from where it hung off a drawer. A cough racked my body as I threaded my hands through the sleeves.

I'd arrived after sunfall, bleary and disoriented, unable to communicate much to Niabi but the necessity of sending Wa-ah-zho to Stot, to warn of the impending vendetta against him. Niabi had set my arm back in its socket, rubbed salve on my scrapes, sat beside me as flame writhed across the ivory canvas.

Now light shattered in an array through the smoke hole and shadows patterned across the russet floor in lazy streaks. It'd been more than a day, and Wa-ah-zho had not returned. I held the pieces of my shirt together over my chemise, too worn to button. I folded onto the ground and laid my head in my hands. Though I knew disappointment was the way of the world, I still broke all over again. *Course men are wicked, darling,* my pa said, *but that's precisely the point.* I just hadn't realized how many times I could feel abandoned and betrayed in one year. I'd come so far, allowing myself to trust others again, and yet it seemed that failure, not resilience, was the constant in humanity.

I scooped out salve from a pot, a glob of mossy-river green. It smelt of dampness, of the deep of creeks and the wide of distances. I hissed as I smeared the salve on my brow, the cut burning. I prayed that Wa-ah-zho had gotten to Stot in time. I supposed Stot knew how to watch his back, but I couldn't stop worrying about him. What was this between us? It couldn't be love, could it? We were fire and lushness and delicious sparring. Sure, we helped each other round our homesteads, and we'd developed a vicious loyalty, and he listened to me about my longings and my fears, but that wasn't love. Love was—

Lord, but wasn't that the size of it—I didn't know what love was at all.

But we couldn't have a romance, him intended for another. I rubbed the salve on my forearm scrape and wound a piece of cloth round my arm. My fingers slipped. I couldn't tie the blasted cloth with one hand. Niabi strode in with a kettle. She set the pot down and took the cloth from me, tying the bandage. After pouring hot water over sassafras roots, she dribbled in some honey, just as I liked. I sat on the rug, and she handed me the warm mug.

"Your stomach?" She lowered beside me.

I shrugged. Stared at the pieces of tree wandering the deep, wine-red tea. The flavor was spicy, almost like root beer. Niabi had been gentle and patient as I healed. I envied her hope. She held on to her positivity without expecting me to join her. She waited and watched, like the sun knowing a flower will someday rise again from the darkness of the earth.

She grabbed a handful of bur oak acorns. "So the gossip of the morning—Stot's here."

"Oh—" I jostled my mug. "He's safe?"

Niabi told that Stot had not been at his homestead when Wa-ah-zho had arrived. Instead, Stot had been helping a neighbor deliver a breech cow—and it'd taken Wa-ah-zho a while to track him down. I inhaled, released a sigh. "But he's unhurt?"

"Safe and whole." Something like amusement tugged at her mouth. "But he's in a fury."

"Isn't he always?"

"Oh, this is worse," she said. "He's all churned up. Like there's warring tornadoes inside him."

"Where is he?" I needed to see him.

"Pacing outside. I wanted to check with you before he stormed on in, surprising you in your unmentionables."

I smiled weakly and told her I wanted to see him. She nodded and stood, then paused. "My Wa-ah-zho carries roiling weather within him too." She ran her thumb around the lip of her cup, glanced through the smoke hole. "The world heavy on him."

I nodded and rubbed my face, the scent of dried blood bitter. Stot was complicated, composed of stormcloud and lightning but also the steady drift of sunrays across aged oak floorboards, the sort of glow that returned day after day. "I need to see Stot," I said. "And then I need to go home."

"Good heavens, you should rest. At least a few more suns."

The pull homeward was dynamic. "I must go."

Niabi tucked her hair behind her ear and frowned. But she ducked through the doorway. Beyond the lodge, I heard raised voices. That low rumble was Stot. I set my cup down and stood, raking my fingers through my tattered hair.

Stot stormed in, his bulk taking up too much space in the lodge. I turned toward the fire.

"What in blasted burning thunder?"

I peeked over my shoulder. "Beg pardon?"

He strode forward, spun me around.

I yelped.

"Blazes." His fingers fussed about the bandage on my forearm.

I batted at his hands. "Stop it."

"I'm trying to help."

I grabbed his hands, stilled them.

His hat hung on his shoulder blades by a braided black cord round his neck. His hair was windblown and disheveled, his jaw singed with stubble—but he was whole and unharmed. He brushed his gaze down. I'd yet to close my blouse, my ivory silk chemise visible. I fumbled with the buttons, my fingers ungainly.

Stot's hand paused mine, his voice muffled and hoarse. "Allow me."

"Don't be ridiculous."

He flicked my fingers away and buttoned my blouse. A round of howls began, the dogs echoing throughout the camp. I lost the ability to breathe, the sweep of his thumb against my chemise. His jaw clenched, his body right before mine, his fingers on the button at my throat. He smelt of oil and of frozen water, salty and fresh.

He skimmed his fingertips above the gash at my temple. "I'll kill him."

"You will not." I stepped back. "This is my battle."

"No longer."

I shoved my shirt into my skirt. Exasperated that he kept grasping after pieces of my life. "And what are you about, confessing to my crimes."

"I didn't *confess*."

I inhaled, then tried to fling my cape round my shoulders.

"I couldn't allow folks to target the Browns," he said. "How about I go to town, after we get you settled, and I'll confess. Tell the marshal I dropped them in self-defense."

"You will do no such thing." I tugged on the hem of my cloak.

"I cannot fathom another solution. In my past, when everything went off the rails, I spiraled. For years. I didn't know how to hold on to control. Didn't know how to balance honor against vengeance." He stepped forward, pulled the fabric of my cloak around my body, held my shoulders a second longer than a heartbeat. "I don't know how to keep you safe."

"Then let go," I said, my voice threadbare.

He shook his head, mouth a firm line. "That's not the solution neither."

I leaned my forehead against his collarbone, closed my eyes, allowed him to slip his arms round my waist, myself completely unmoored.

"You won't allow me to take the blame?" he asked.

I stepped back. "No."

He stared at the floor. His hip cocked, one gun visible, bandolier strung across his chest. Somehow this outlaw had become my dearest friend. His jaw ticced, muscles flexing on his neck. I wanted to press my fingers there, feel his warmth.

"When he hurt you, Ezra became my concern." He transferred his weight. "Why did you come here? Why didn't you come to me?"

"Cricket came here. Niabi's closer to Ezra's—and she's a healer."

"So am I."

I swallowed, the air between us charged with questions and smoke. "What happened—with Bitter Creek and the outlaws?"

"Nothing yet," he said. "If there are intents on my life, Wa-ah-zho found me first. Thank you."

I nodded. I picked up Niabi's salve and screwed on the cap. The thread misaligned. "Is that why they shot you that day down in the holler, because they suspected you?" I sighed, tried again to screw on the lid. "What is it you aren't telling me?"

He reached for the salve. I held it back. He said, "You still don't trust me."

"Course I trust you," I whispered, quick and harsh. I finally capped Niabi's salve, tucked the pot into my satchel. Then I fussed with my gloves.

"No, actually." I loosed a weak, wet laugh. "I don't know you."

I jabbed at my gloves, trying to shove my fingers into the bunched wool. He walked up behind me. His heat pressed on my shoulders, the gust of his breath on my neck. I yanked off the gloves and threw them down, then lifted my hair, shoved some pins into a twist. My hand shook, my shoulder shattering with the movement.

He laid a palm on my lower back. "Just stop."

He took the hairpins from me and wound my strands into a bun, then pressed the pins through, his fingers slipping through the strands, brushing my neck, the texture of his calluses along my skin. A draught rattled the hide, his fingers in my hair. Then he took my bonnet and placed it on my head. His voice low, blowing the loose tendrils of hair at my nape. "What do you mean, you don't know me?"

I heard laughter, perhaps women down by the swamp. I'd fled Kansas determined to build a new life alone. But that hadn't been reasonable. That wasn't the way of life. We all yearned desperately, disastrously, for a place to call home.

Stot was interwoven with mystery and wonder. I wasn't sure what was truth and what was story. What made up the knowing of a person? Was it who he was, this moment, his hands all about my hair? Or those stories that stretched wide across the prairie? I turned, studied the white knot of his bandanna.

"There's just so much darkness in the world." I pressed my lips together, unsure how to share all that spun round me: gratitude for him, distrust of his secrets, disgust and horror at the world.

He nodded, as if he understood all that I couldn't speak.

He picked up my gloves, threaded them on my fingers. I swallowed, a lump stuck in my throat. "Come to me," he said, his voice a question, "if ever you need help again."

The lodge was cloudy with heat as he slid on my gloves. I nodded and untangled my hands from his. Then I flung up the doorway flap and stepped beyond.

~

The sky was forlorn, white and ash and bone. It was almost dusk. A time of pauses, a moment straddling possibilities. Niabi crouched before a fire, stirring a pot of lye soap. I lowered onto the log beside her, and she settled a blanket around my shoulders. I bent toward the flame as the Osage wordlessly moved about their tasks, unhurried and purposeful. Beyond, gusts rose in the blackjacks. "Have I told you the tale of Prairie Rose and Whirlwind?" Niabi asked.

I pulled my knees to my chest and shook my head no, the pound of music low against my back.

"Long, long ago, when time was young," Niabi said, sweeping her hand the length of their glade, her colorful bracelets clattering, "the prairie was quiet, and Earth Mother was alone. She longed for color and for sound. For blue flowers of a clear sky, pink ones of a spring dawn. Buried deep underground in her caverns, humming along her lost rivers, she yearned to be known."

Stot and Wa-ah-zho came round the lodge, bowls of broiled beef and vegetables in their hands. Wa-ah-zho tucked his blanket across his chest, over the ivory moon of a shell gorget pendant. As Niabi told her tale, a story of wildflowers and wind, of bravery and magic, Stot placed a bowl in my lap. "Once, long ago, there was a girl named Prairie Rose who believed she was ordinary." Niabi finished her tale, her hand brushing her hound. "But I reason, there is no such thing as an ordinary woman. So you see, memories are always intertwining, one reality blending with another."

I shivered, haunted by the legend of Prairie Rose and this idea of women connecting through time. Niabi handed me a bowl of water to wash, and I plunged my hands into the basin, the cold liquid biting. I scrubbed at blood crusted along the pad of my hand, then flicked off the water. The wet splotches darkened the dirt: spider-thin rivulets spreading like daddy longlegs. It was time to return home. There was much in our corner of the frontier left unresolved. Stot was unharmed, but I must make sure the Browns were safe as well. I thanked Niabi for the tale, her care, the food, then walked toward the stable yard.

Thin winter light spilled through leafless branches like watered yellow paint, and gusts roared across the meadow, speaking garbled words. A new memory replaced long ago moments, of when the apparition of Willie Matthews overcame me. Along the embankment, I looked for the legendary woman astride her mustang, but she didn't appear. I shivered, faraway from this moment, my mind elsewhere, clouded with smoke and wondering and worry. By the horses, One Eye prowling the clearing, Niabi brushed a lock of hair off my forehead. "I understand your need to go home—I've that same restlessness inside me too," she said. "But it's okay to need others, to ask for help."

I nodded. I felt like a woman beginning. The longer I lived in these wild spaces, the clearer it was I needed others.

She stepped back, tipped her gaze skyward, her black hair glistening almost blue with the overcast. "I sense a storm," she said. "The wind is wrathy. He rages, from the west."

Snowstorms here were rarely brutal, but I'd heard otherworldly tales of the ice storms of No Man's Land, of whorling blizzards that left trees draped in a canopy of ice and the frozen hills slick. Unlike Kansas's pillowy drifts of snow, the storms here could have a harsh, glassy coating that made journeys precarious and unwise. But ice storms were rare, one every handful of years, and my saddlebags had food and water, along with a tent and some dry firewood. I vaulted onto Cricket and winced, my body tender but surely able to withstand the ride home. I thanked Niabi again, and then Stot and I were off, dashing through the tall grass, fleeing into howling wind, the gusts blasting my cheeks raw, until I couldn't feel my nose. Our horses' hooves clattered across the hard ground, galloping into the broken colors of winter: black, white, gray, muddy mists. I pulled up my cloak and swallowed the brittle air, cold burning down my throat.

CHAPTER THIRTY-FIVE

We're lost," Stot said, the leather of his saddle creaking in the cold.

"Nah."

He sighed, pocketed his compass. "Will there ever be such a time when you'll listen to me?"

I brushed my hand across my brow, swiping off the snow that fell in round puffs from the sky. "Probably not."

Night raced on, graphite shadows roaming eastward and a gauzy, melon-orange hue smearing the dip of the valley. It smelt of darkness and rime and was altogether too cold.

Stot pinched his hat by the brim, held it crown down to shake off snow. "There's tree cover ahead, probably a creek. Make camp there?"

The light waned, details of the timbers becoming fuzzy and like smoke. The borders of individual trees lost, the shape of leaves. "I don't give up easy," I said.

"Damnation, I'm not giving up," he said. "Dark has fallen, and this snow could build. It's best to make shelter now."

I rolled my eyes. "We're not in the wastelands of the Dakotas."

"And you know where our homesteads are?"

I felt spun about directionless, but my land tugged at me from beyond. I gestured vaguely southeast, the snow searing the cuts on my hand. "Cowboys don't get lost."

"Mmm."

The distant terrain shimmered pearlescent in the snowfall. Stot's thighs angled Shark down the slope toward the forest canopy, the shape of his muscles in relief against the black cotton of his trousers. I followed, my body sore from riding, but I longed for home. It was almost as if I needed to be on my land to heal.

We clattered below the trees, the branches' scrawling black fingers reaching earthward, the low limbs dusting our slickers with snow. We skidded down the slope toward the creek.

"Wait." Stot held up his hand.

The land beyond was a haunting expanse of luminous ivory, like beginning starlight, all the way to the horizon. There were no trees or flowers. It was as if we'd stumbled upon another realm.

The salt plain.

Mist shimmered atop the white expanse, snow coiling skyward, as if spirits flew over the surface. The horror of the plain wasn't the eerie landscape, but that somewhere out beyond, the Wild Bunch stalked—under the ground, along the windbreak, in a lowland around the bend. This was their territory.

Stot slipped from his saddle and tied Shark to a tree, then headed southward, surely looking for the lake or another bearing so we could figure the direction home. Far into the distance, the long wings of a crane lifted into flight. The flaps thumped through the quiet as the bird soared overhead. I slid down and hushed Cricket, his pale ears relaxing back into his black hair. I hung his reins beside Shark, snow sworling down in looping currents. Stot and I whispered through the woodland, One Eye slipping in and out of shadow as we roamed this space between earth and sky.

Stot prowled forward, Colt revolver trained on the icy horizon, our boots sloshing through the slush, snow fizzling across my cheeks. Woven in with the wind's ebb and roar, Sally Ann Thunder Ann Whirlwind, with her twang, told cowboy Willie Matthews about one spectacle or another. *I'm a flash of lightning, straight up sideways, buttered with quicksilver.* The ancient voice muttered something indistinct, her cadence almost frantic. Alarm pulsed up my neck, and I halted, palm resting on snow-brushed poplar bark. Sakes alive, what on earth did she need me to know. Then beside me, a whir of cracked air—a bullet.

"Minnie, down." Stot yanked me into a snowdrift, his body pressed over mine.

This wasn't memory. The gunfire was in our timeline.

Blasts pinged, splattering the ground with wet thunks. What if I hadn't paused—

"We need cover," Stot said, withdrawing his body from mine. We scrambled up the rise, my hands sheltering my head, and tumbled into the brush behind a sycamore. I pressed back against the trunk, Stot beside me, and worked the action on my six-shooter.

A bullet zipped past.

Stot scanned the forest, a furrow trenched between his brows. He maneuvered me down, my knees sunk into the slush. "Get down," he said.

"The hell I will. You know I'm the best shot."

He muttered some curses but permitted me to stand. I couldn't spot the outlaws. Just the bent shadows of gnarled trees, the moonglow off the uncanny plains beyond, the zing of reverberating gunshots, the misty snowfall obscuring the woodland.

My exhale foamed against my revolver as I fired. "How many, you think?"

"Maybe five." He leaned around the bark. "At least three distinct guns. They're spread out some."

A cardinal aggressively squawked above, a scatter of leaves at the tree line, a thump twenty rods farther on. But no crimson-hued blanket cloaks or the blur of a body.

"Let her go," Stot yelled. "Your quarrel is with me."

"Boy, that's not even half the size of it, Lawman," a voice called, wispy and strident. "Your end is nigh."

"Well, come at me, Tulsa." Something like mirth glinted in Stot's eyes. "If you've even learned to shoot straight, with that dainty gold pistol of yours."

Tulsa Jack scoffed. Stot apparently knew him well enough to recognize him by voice. Stot leaned his shoulders into the shoot-out, his bearing at ease, cloak tight across his back. I watched him shift into a different version of himself. His brusque voice dropped lower, slowed to a drawl, a viciousness flooded his tone. Of course he was lawless as the day was long—but he could be so gentle with me. It was bewildering to see this darker side of him. I wanted to wedge closer, bind myself to the wildness of him.

The Wild Bunch continued their taunts, but I heard only fragments, Tulsa Jack's curses lost within the screech of blustery weather. A low branch with spiny twigs snagged my hood, and the storm tossed down handfuls of snow. The sky an ivory smear, an opaque wash of white before us. Shots plunked sporadically but with less regularity as the blizzard picked up.

"I can't see nothing."

"Neither can they," Stot said. "We could slip away."

"You've had worse notions," I said. "This one might just hold water."

Stot straightened my blanket cloak across my shoulders. "Now I'll get a big head with such praise."

I snorted. Then we snuck from tree trunk to tree trunk, zigzagging across the forest, from one cloud of whirled snow to the other, gunshots fading in the roar of the storm. Soon enough, we swung onto our horses and were off into the snowfall, disappeared with the fury of weather. *Thank you,* I spoke below my breath, assured that the ancient voice had protected me. I couldn't comprehend how she had such magic, but it was as if her hands had tossed down those clumps of snow, as if her apprehension had paused me. There was enchantment in the air.

We galloped along the ravine, the moonlit sky an unnerving shade of quiet mulberry. Balls of ice shattered from the clouds, battering my face and Cricket's flanks. I swung off and led him toward the gully. Beneath the overhang, a slick layer of ice hardened over the silt. My boots skidded, unable to find sure footing. Cricket stamped, hooves clacking on the rime. He wouldn't step down. A tightness spread over his hindquarters and thighs, the cold seeping into his joints. "Come on, old buddy."

Beside us, Shark reared his head, and a shiver racked One Eye's side. "They can't make it down," Stot hollered over the clattering hail. "We must make camp."

We were so close, perhaps a mile from home, but our horses couldn't cross the chasm, the nearest bridge a hundred miles away. I groaned and leaned my forehead against Cricket's mane. Ice slid beneath my collar as I unbuckled a saddlebag.

"Wait." Stot laid his glove atop mine. Snow clumped on the brown wool. "Let's head northward. They won't look for us north."

And so we journeyed over the slick ground, Cricket's eyes wide, icicles twirling the length of his mane. A layer of ice froze over my cloak, weighing me down. There must be shacks out yonder, some folks, somewhere. Any homesteader would offer shelter during a storm, even to the fearsome Lawman, but I couldn't see but a couple of rods before me, sleet falling in a thick blur. I searched for the boxy shadows of a home, for the glow of firelight, but saw only the eerie steel tones of ice and shadow, the pink of filtered moonglow. When the horses could travel no more, we stopped, hopefully far enough outaways that the bandits wouldn't find us. We'd heard no gunfire for a while through the storm's rumble, so the outlaws had either lost our trail or halted their pursuit. We slipped beneath an overhang of chinkapin oaks and made camp.

I untied my canvas and bundle of dry firewood, my fingers stiff and frozen, gloves clumpy with ice. A fire could bring the criminals right to us—but we needed flame, or we'd freeze. Above, the tree branches crackled like ominous chimes. Beyond, the sky was a weak and quiet slate blue, and underfoot the ground shivered, the earth buried somewhere below the layers of frost.

CHAPTER THIRTY-SIX

We'd burnt through our dry firewood a while ago and now fed the blaze damp kindling we'd warmed beside the fire. Smoke steamed from the logs and seared my eyes, but the blaze kept on. Beyond our haven, the world clattered and whirred. The chime of icicles, the groan of the storm, the forest the hues of ink and ghosts. It was peaceful, the whisk of cold draughts, the press of warm fire.

Beside me on a log, Stot whittled, his knife scraping a sliver of hickory sapwood.

"So, the Lawman?"

Stot rubbed his brow, dagger blade flashing in the firelight. "What?"

"I understand the summer name the Lawman, you being a sheriff and all, but—" I waved my hand, thinking perhaps he'd answer, in the sleepy, dreamlike atmosphere of the storm, like perhaps these intransient moments didn't quite count.

"How'd I get an alias to begin with?" His boots scraped toward the fire. "I spiraled for a few years, seeking revenge against the Dalton Gang, executed several of them, and folks began murmuring tales round fires."

I flexed my toes, frozen in my boots. "So you weren't ever an actual outlaw?"

He grinned, and lightning slid the length of my spine. "Well, I did ramble about with their rivals a bit, the Dunn Brothers and Belle Starr."

His blade rasped down his twig; breezes rattled the icicles above. "I lost myself. Lost my control, my need for order, my desire for goodness," he said. "Robbed some banks, transported liquor round the outlet." He straightened his collar beneath his ammunition bandolier. "But mostly I just came up with plans for Belle and the Dunn Brothers. I'm not wanted for those crimes, though, just rumors."

I saw him then, young and grieving, friendly with glamorous Belle Starr, Queen of the Bandits. He clicked his blade closed and open again. Our horses stamped their hooves on the other side of the fire, their shoes ringing against the ice. "I made a lot of vile choices," he said.

I pressed my hand along my thighs, leaned toward flame. He unbuckled his gun belt, turning at the waist to hang it off a limb behind him, his vest pulling across his chest in the cavern of his jacket. One Eye curled up by my feet, and I ran a hand along his fur. "The only warrants out for your arrest, they're for your family's murder?"

He nodded.

"So why don't you just tell the truth." I rubbed the tines of my key, the same question echoing about me.

"Reckon I allowed others to believe I was guilty, as I supposed I deserved it. Not sure how to shake the alias now." He straightened his hat, melted snow wetting the crown's creases. "What's that in your pocket, anyway?"

Of course he'd noticed my talisman. I hitched a shoulder. "A remembrance."

He watched me, brows lifted. Snow feathered between the sumacs and maples. I supposed it was high time I shared fragments of myself with another again. Stot knew me as resolute and brash, but there was part of me sentimental and soft. I told him of finding the key in the woods with Magnolia, of her hanging it on a chain for me. He clicked his knife shut, slid the blade in the pocket of his waistcoat. "Why don't you wear it?"

I pulled out the key, scraped at some dirt smudged on the hoop.

"I haul regret too," he said, gaze tracking my fingers. "Work daily to forgive myself."

"I've forgiven myself." Snow blew inside my slicker, icing the narrow line of bare skin at my nape. "I think."

"When?"

"I don't know, long ago," I said. "Someday. It's a process."

He slipped his hands into his pockets, pressed his heels against the ground. "I reckon so."

I rested my cheek against my hand, tipped my face to study him, his posture calm amid the shattering ice storm. "And what about that shoot-out in the woods last month?" I asked.

"Hmm." He crouched before the flames, adjusted the lay of the bonfire. In the firelight, a flush brushed up his neck. "I snuck up thataway, gathering salt from the plains. Tulsa Jack sighted me within the boundary of their land—and our taunts collapsed into a fire exchange." Stot swept away slush from a birch log, settled the piece crossways over the pile. Steam hissed, but the flame plumed higher, glow blooming in our grove. "I blasted Tulsa Jack up significantly, so he couldn't track me," Stot said. "Otherwise, sure enough, the Bunch would've dropped me."

The tendons in his forearms adjusted as he arranged the fire. As he stretched and crouched, he held his balance with such ease. "You just taunted him for rotten aim," I said.

"Tulsa Jack *is* a wretched shot." Stot rubbed his beard. "Cannot fathom that I let him wing me—not my finest moment."

I laughed and winced, my shirtwaist catching on dried blood.

He walked toward me. "Here, let me see to your wounds."

"I'm fine."

"Just allow me to reapply the salve."

I nodded. The scent of the bonfire warm and sweet, the snow crisp and mineral. Stot rummaged in my saddlebag for Niabi's salve, murmuring assurances to Cricket, the timbre of his voice muted and gruff, like something dusky and full of brambles. I unbuttoned my blouse, and he came toward me, the glow of fire patterning across his face. I removed my slicker and shirtwaist and handed them to him. He tossed my cloak over an icy cottonwood bough and tied my shirt to my gun belt. I pulled up my shift, the bruise purple and amber across my ivory skin.

He wiped my wound with a damp rag, his breath warming my collarbone, the air too cold. Dipping his fingers into the salve, his gaze flicked to mine a heated moment; then he smeared some across my stomach. I hissed, the mixture freezing. Stot rocked back on his heels, studied me. "I'm fine," I said. "Just hurry."

After he wiped his hands on the rag, he helped my shift over my belly. He stepped away to grab my blouse, and I swallowed a deep breath of dark, icy air. Stot slid sideaways on a patch of rime and dropped my shirt, steadying himself by grasping a sapling.

I gasped. My blouse sank in a puddle of fire-melted slush. Stot cursed. He bent and lifted my shirt: It was sopping.

"Damnation, Stot." I couldn't believe he'd dropped it.

"You can have mine." He shrugged from his slicker.

"I don't want yours. I want mine."

He tossed his slicker over a branch and unbuttoned his black waistcoat, his deft fingers striking down the center of his body.

"I said I don't want your dratted shirt." I shivered, my body hardened with too many emotions.

"Why do you always fight me about the dumbest stuff?" He held my pathetic, soggy blouse up between us, his vest gaping open. I battled between a ragged cry of exasperation and amusement. I yanked my shirt from him and looped it over a branch, the yellow blaze of fire roaring skyward.

Why couldn't I just take his flannel? Why did I have to push and push? Sometimes life got so muddled and sad, all a'sudden. Brawling my brother, gunfighting outlaws, racing home, all these wearying months building my homestead. With all of that, I was in control. I was fine. But my blouse slumping in the snowmelt: That toppled me. I didn't have the time or the energy to waste on nonsense. Fury and misery whisked about me. I felt consumed. I couldn't always keep strong, couldn't always control my rages, couldn't always react rationally—I was just so angry. About being stuck in the snow, about my brother, about Stot's soon *wife* moving down in mere weeks, about him hovering, expecting entirely too much but unable to give me anything.

"You don't have to be cruel," he said.

I stepped up to him, my shivering body right below his chin. "Why the hell not?"

His jaw clenched, the hollows of his cheeks deepened.

The wind howled, the icicles clinked, and snowfall melted across my back. I heard scratching along bark, perhaps some animal burrowing in a hollow. The moment pulled, an undefined battle of power. He broke my gaze, as if yielding. I nodded and stepped away.

He grabbed my wrist, spun me back. "Wait."

He edged closer and pressed me against the broad trunk of an oak, the raised bark craggy along my shoulders, his trousers fitted the length of my skirt. He slapped a hand against the tree, caging me, his body large and ragged and furious. He said, "You don't get to handle me like I'm nothing, like I'm a monster."

I dropped my gaze from his eyes to his lips, then back up. His eyes flashed, ivy green in the winter haze.

"That's not what I'm doing," I said.

Snow misted my arms, and I shivered. He settled a palm on my hip, steadying me. Warmth seeped from his hand.

"Then why are you always needling me?" he asked.

I ran my palm up his chest and lifted an eyebrow, my leg sliding between his thighs. His fingertips clenched on the bark; a vein pulsed in his jaw.

"Don't play with me," he said.

I didn't abide orders—I did what I willed, when I wished. He didn't get to tell me what to do. I scraped my fingers into his starless sky–black hair, and his hand clenched on my hip. I wasn't cold anymore: The fires from his body soaked me. He smelt of weapon oil and wide spaces and sweat.

"Don't," he said, voice rough, expression strained.

"Why not?"

His palm trailed up my back. "This is good. We shouldn't."

I lifted onto my toes, my words whisking against his mouth. "I don't like to be told *don't, can't, shouldn't.*"

I nipped my teeth on his bottom lip, and he groaned low in his throat. I brushed my lips against his, became liquid all the way to my toes. He tasted of ice. And then he unraveled, his mouth angled harshly across my own. His arms swept below me, hefting me up, my legs looped about his waist. It was hot and undomesticated and all I'd longed for.

He yanked his mouth from mine. "Damnation, Minnie," he muttered and kissed down my neck. I dropped my head back against the tree, gripped his hair, and my body lost a season of tension. His mouth along my throat, his hands skimming my sides. I dug into his handkerchief knot, and he stilled, his mouth hovering below the ridge of my jaw.

"Scared?" I murmured.

His palms trailed up toward my breasts, his eyes turbulent, and he lowered his mouth back to mine. I tugged at his tie, fumbled with his buttons, my hands scraped over the hard ridges of his muscles, and then his palm cupped my breast, and it was teeth and lips and the searing of ice along bare skin. It was so much and no pauses. We were lost in tumult, too gone to worry about the right choice.

"You're injured," he said.

I drew him back. "Stop talking."

He smirked, spoke against my lips, "This is what you want?"

I nodded, and he kissed me, his body against mine, until we were just heat and skin and blood, the air liquefied, snowfall hazed about, us just a hot pulse in an icy landscape. And then, somehow, we were beneath the draped canvas in the untamed wilderness, clothes tugged free, my body shivering in the freezing air, blazing where his hands touched. The fire dissolved, embers extinguished by snowfall, and it was just our bodies and moans and movements in the dark.

CHAPTER THIRTY-SEVEN

Crystals crackled and swayed in the breeze. Trees bowed, iced limbs arching earthward, creating ethereal corridors. The dawn sky clear and blue as if cleansed, the forest tranquil in the aftermath of storm. The cosmos before me a glittering marvel, as if I'd left my home and wandered the borderland of a new world. I could hear everything as my boots crunched through snow. Icicles encased the branches and dripped from crisp leaves. I tugged off my woolen gloves, touched a frozen oak leaf. The rime seared, melting against the warmth of my fingertip, a smear of liquid drizzling down to my wrist. With beauty always came destruction. The ice storm had crushed trees, heaped limbs across the ground, as if an overgrown god had thrown a fit in the woods.

Stot crouched beside the fire, packing our breakfast of oats. Afterward, when I'd rolled away and curled onto my side, he'd reached out to hold me. He'd cursed when I told him no, but he let me go. Through the night was the sound of his breathing and branches crashing against the earth. This morning we'd packed our gear and fed our horses in silence.

A rattle of finches, with their red napes and speckled bodies, swooped across the buffalo trail, flitting between branches, erratic in their exuberance. I couldn't believe I'd done such a thing. Sakes alive, he was marrying another woman. I'd lost control, again. Let myself be ruled by passion, impulsively done whatever I'd wanted, without a thought for his intended or for how sleeping with him would shatter the community we'd built. I rubbed my palms over my face, the wool scratching my raw skin.

Gleaming in the snowmelt before the campfire, a mirage of my land took shape, the meadow glistening shades of gold. The ground rippled, and with a zap my fertile grasses transformed to heaps of sand. The terrain shifted through mutating images, the feathered oat stalks and red paintbrush flowers shrinking, a gale thrashing the meadows, dirt replacing what had once been. The earth aged; the landscape transformed. There was a sense that I observed some horrifying future, my land a barren wasteland of dust.

I saw the homesteader then, in the midst of the prophetic terrain. The woman who seemed an echo of my mother. She waded through the billowing, red-speckled haze, her feet sinking below the layers of sandy loam, a peculiar metal shape roaring behind her, a wrap clenched at her neck, the yarn worn and dissolving away. The solitude, the sorrow, the exhaustion a mimic of my own days. I didn't know who she was, this woman I kept seeing. Perhaps she was my ancestor, somewhere in another age. Her land black ash, mine white ice. All of our stories, interwoven and repeating. It was the same story; it was something I'd never heard before.

I turned and walked through the woodland to the creek's edge. The water softly buzzed, and into the void the ancient voice spoke, *You're in the right story.*

A clump of snow fell from a branch and smashed into the stream. Other voices chatted, sharing the uncertainty and shame that spooled about me. Boots sounded behind—Stot moved down the slope. He placed his blanket cloak around me, his palms a weight on my shoulders, his breath puffs of steam across my neck. I turned, wrapped the blanket tighter. "I got it."

Snow crunched as he shifted. He took off his hat, ran his fingers through his hair. His face raw angles, his nose and cheeks pinked in the cold. He didn't say anything. Shirt tucked into dark trousers, ironed vest buttoned, not even a hemline cuffed up. He was stability in chaos.

I stepped around him and headed back fireside.

"Wait," he asked.

I halted, held myself steady.

He rubbed the band of his hat. "You're upset. I thought—" He studied my face. "Last night we seemed to want the same thing."

Course I'd wanted to be intimate with him—didn't mean I was proud of my choice. The finches kept chattering. "It's that feller from before?" he asked. "Your sister's husband. Lark."

Lark had nothing to do with right now—I hadn't thought about him in an age. Flurries drifted down, white dusting Stot's black hair.

"What do you want?" he asked.

"You think I actually know?" I lifted my skirts and rushed uphill.

I didn't know myself, my emotions foreign to me. And even if I'd known what I wanted, I'd just ruin my desires with want, with need, with my utter lack of control. I brushed my hands across my cheeks, swiping away freezing tears. Before the fire, I kicked at the snow, covering the flames as Stot hovered at the edge of the clearing. I tossed the cloak at him and mounted.

"Home," I spoke to Cricket.

As we slammed across the frozen white earth, black trees flickering past, all the days of my life stuttered by, stretching far back into memory. There was a sense that I'd stepped into a tale in the middle, the storyteller already speaking an age, me just catching up as they spoke. All the chaos and trauma and mistakes had brought me here, into the great quiet of the prairie, to this land that whispered and echoed with all the sorrow of timelessness.

CHAPTER THIRTY-EIGHT

Through my cedar-framed windows, white pillowed across the landscape and broken limbs scattered the forest understory. Ice crept inside, fractals freezing across my wood floor. A week before, I'd thought I'd scented spring, but winter held on, a fog I just couldn't escape. I kept slipping into other stories, glimpsing a realm of ash, a land of mist and smoke. The homesteader, her frail, dry knuckles grasping the disintegrating tangles of a rag, a black smudge brushing the underside of her jaw, a fraught yearning twined into her sorrow. I understood her. Our narratives spiraled together, until I couldn't quite disentangle the ice and embers of her tale from my own.

Crouched before my hearth, I scrubbed at soot that had scattered from the fireplace onto the walls. A charcoal stain marred the periwinkle linsey fabric that I'd shoved into a gap. I considered the baffling sounds wedged into the homesteader's vision, the metal shape hulking behind her. Magnolia had shown me sketches of horseless carriage prototypes; I knew there was talk of motor cars propelled by engines, but I'd never glimpsed one. I thought of the women as my ancestors—but the homesteader's carriage wasn't something from long ago. Now I wondered not only about who she was but about *when* she was.

I buffed my wall, and beside me, Olive placed the dime novels I'd gathered for Poppy in her satchel. Olive and I had spun the dilemma of the slain outlaws round and round, unable to find a solution. Rumors spread along the network of homestead gatherings, accusations flung at box socials and taffy pulls, anger and fear simmering, vigilante law coiling tighter and tighter, something terrible imminent.

Olive spoke with tentative hope of their springtime plans. Her resilience was astonishing. She told of the cattle drive Thad was set to join come the summer roundup: He felt prepared after a winter training with Stot and me. I swept away a layer of frost, clawed at the smoky grime. The stain wouldn't budge.

Olive buttoned her cape at her neck. "Have you thought more of teaching, come autumn?"

I picked at some burnt newsprint that wallpapered the corner. "What?" I swiped my forehead, squinted up at Olive. "I hardly think I'm the sort of woman to teach kids."

"You're the exact woman I want to educate my children."

I buffed the charred floor.

"Minnie. The floor is fine."

It wasn't; black smudge was everywhere. But I stood, wiped my hands on my apron, and said, "I slept with Stot."

Her eyes widened before she muted her expression. "And his brother's widow?"

"Heading on northward to propose to her in a week or so, I suppose," I said. "Stot's too duty bound for anything else."

Snow puffed in through cracks in the walls and floated to coat my table. "Anyway," I said, "I'm clearly not the sort to guide your children."

She pressed her hands along her skirt's waistband. She seemingly itched to ask questions. "I don't think the rest of us see you as you see yourself," she said. "No one's judging your choices as harshly as you judge yourself."

It was heartbreaking to have such grace when I didn't deserve it. She didn't know the secrets I kept from her about the outlaws. Of the guilt that racked me, that her family was being targeted and not me. I pushed open my door, spilled out into the thin sunshine of winter's end.

Warmth wandered the breezes, the snow oozing and melting, icicles stretching from the eaves. Olive placed a woolen shawl on my shoulders. She took my pot off the outdoor stove, the creek water boiled away to leave granules of salt settled in a long-handled spoon. My door rattled in the wind. I booted my craggy salt crystal doorstop over to hold my door shut, the stone the shade of white shadow, browned at the edges. I swept sepia-brown slush off my porch, my boots scratchy and strident on the wooden planks, and a woman said from somewhere beyond time, *Minnie, I'm rewriting memory.*

I paused, allowed such an idea to settle over me. She spoke again, words creaking between the crackle of ice. *Longago, when I was young.* Her voice faded, then returned. *The prairie was quiet and I was alone.*

I dropped my broom. It clattered against the slats, the handle smushing into a snowdrift. Olive glanced at me, and I lifted the handle from the snow, my arms trembling. Those words reminded me of the folktale Niabi had shared, of a woman named Prairie Rose. The Native woman I saw—burrowing through briars and collapsing beneath a whorling, shadow-stained windstorm—could she be Prairie Rose? Not only a legend but a historical woman, lost away in time. And the ancient voice was the earth.

I wrought my hands in my apron, knuckles raw and singed in the chill. I'd begun to recognize the different women who spoke, to glimpse fragments of their stories. Beside me, the impressionist landscape I'd been painting these past weeks waited on my oak easel. The foreground was rough smudges of yellow and green, grass tossing in the wind, the meadow dotted with wildflowers and shadowed with cobalt and periwinkle blue, the bowed outline of my barn in the distance. And now the form of a woman took shape, hair unbound, white gown snapping, the single black ribbon round her waist tugged on by some wind. I didn't know who she was, this woman I painted on my land. It wasn't me, wasn't Prairie Rose, wasn't the homesteader, wasn't the voice of the earth. Perhaps she was all my ancestors, all those woven into a communal narrative with me. In my loneliest moments, they had called out to me. In the deepest quiet of my homestead, I'd never been alone.

I brushed snow off the handle of my broom. I felt myself ease as I untangled mysteries of the wilderness. And yet—I wasn't finished. I was still exploring friendships, still searching for home, still lost and adrift. Not quite sure how to be a friend, a lover, a woman. The earth spoke of loneliness, of friendship, encouraging me once again to trust others. She was right: Community was survival in these lands. I needed friends who understood hard choices and deep pains. Friends who could know of my darknesses and not crumble. Olive bent to pick up a granule of salt, the atmosphere crisp with the briny scent of salt. Olive approached each day with hope. To hope, after encountering the bleakness of the world, I wasn't sure there was a greater bravery.

I was grateful for such a friend as Olive. After the snow melted, when the mud rivers rushed again, something must be done about the bodies. Gossip just wouldn't fade—someone would soon fall. I supposed it was high time I told Olive of the murders.

"Come inside a moment," I said into the hush.

Olive rubbed her eyebrow, then set down my salt pot and followed me inside. My feet sounded hollow on the planks. Gusts whipped through the doorway and tossed my cupboard curtain aside. My potpourri jar glowed pink and sapphire in the veil of winter-blue light. I took the potpourri from the shelf, uncapped the jar, and suddenly it smelt of sunshine. Of springtime and lilacs and the gentle sugar of rose vervain. I poured some meadowflower petals on a dish and placed it with a clack on the table. Olive touched the potpourri, her posture relaxed against my sofa.

I sat and kicked out my legs, boots squeaking across the floor. "I killed them missing cowboys."

CHAPTER THIRTY-NINE

Pardon?" Olive's satchel fell from her shoulder.

I told Olive that the outlaws had set fire to my quarter section, that I'd been the one to shoot them, to bury them in the wildwood. She fiddled with the silver barrette clasped over her bun, her expression perplexed.

"I don't understand." She stood, tugged her strap over her shoulder. "You're saying—" She shook her head. "*You* murdered them, Minnie? You've lied, this whole time?"

I reached for her hand. "I didn't mean to endanger your family."

She stepped back. "No." Her expression snapped from kindness into one I knew well: someone betrayed. But I hadn't meant, I hadn't—

Olive pushed out my door, her hand fussing with the chapbooks jumbled in her satchel. She stopped. Pulled the dime novels from her bag, pinched the covers between two fingers, and dropped them into the snowmelt.

I stood in the doorway, my fingers worrying a button on my blouse. "Olive—"

"We're done." She held my gaze. Her posture composed, her bearing decided, skin tight across her collarbone. "You hear?"

I opened my mouth. But I didn't know what to say.

"My family has been in danger because of your lies." Her eyes tightened at the corners, a vein spasming on her lower eyelid. "You risked our lives this week. It's like we don't matter."

"Olive, I—"

She lifted a hand, halting me. "That first day planting potatoes you told me you didn't want friendship, that you wanted an isolated life—well, that's what you got." She stepped off my porch and walked away.

I thought I'd built something rare out on the frontier. But I'd only been looking out for myself. All these seasons, and I hadn't learned much of anything. I'd failed, once again.

A discordant rattle thumped. A long, rectangular shadow eclipsed the pasture. Someone hollered, the words indistinct through my hazy thoughts. I hefted my Winchester, chambered a round, and ran after Olive.

A horse galloped across the prairie, rider bent low over a dark-brown mane, a white blaze striking down the horse's forehead. Olive dashed toward the uproar, gown snapping in the wind, clover-dotted hemline smudged with sodden, ashy dirt. I fixed the rider in my rifle's sights. But it was Olive's son Thad. He pulled up on his reins, his mare's hooves squelching in the slush.

"We need you now," Thad hollered. "Vigilantes set fire to our barn."

~

The Browns' homestead crackled with ember and coal and remnant flares. I sank the pointed toes of my black boots deep into the burn, heat rising from the earth, the land still exhaling devastation. All through the night we'd battled: stomping out cinders, shoveling snow onto the heat, passing buckets of water from well to blaze, smothering sparks with damp cloth, Stot hauling off enflamed boards to toss into the snowdrifts, the gleam an echo in the bleak of night. Somehow, at the edge of dawn, we'd thwarted the cataclysm from spreading and devouring the entire countryside, the snow-damp meadows soaking up flame. But the fire had obliterated half the Browns' barn.

Yesterday, Asa had heard a clamor of horses dissolving into the forest. Doubtlessly vigilantes or outlaws had started the blaze. Now, in the light of daybreak, we combed through the debris, searching for what could be salvaged. Burning scented the air, a reddish steam added dimension to the shadows, and I burrowed my shovel into the burn, tossing rubble aside. Stot hauled a charred board to the pile of refuse, smoke smeared across his wrist and up his forearms. Diaphanous ashen cloth floated beyond the cracked windows like ghosts dispersing, the edges of the fabric smoldering with embers. The air was brittle with winter but also swamped with lingering fever, a frenzied mixture of temperatures. At the edge of the burn, where cinders glinted beside a swoop of snow, Olive wiped her apron on a chunk of glass, her bearing weary. And yet her distinct strength hadn't faltered: her cheeks damp with sweat, the angle of her brow tilted skyward, the tension in her hands at ease.

We'd spoken in the middle of the night while passing buckets toward the blaze, the glow of flame soaking the curve of my face. "I am sorry, Olive."

She inhaled through her nose, handed me a pail.

"You matter to me. Of course you do." I grabbed the steel handle, passed the bucket to Poppy. "Your family matters to me. I see now, how my choices put your family's safety in harm's way."

"Honey, you gotta decide what friendship means to you." She ran a hand over her braid, soot wedged in the folds. "Because this? It's not working for me."

Now, in the fuzzy glow of morning, Olive hummed an old spiritual, one my ma often sang, *My Lord, He calls me, He calls me by the thunder.* Her voice was accompanied by the sizzle and snap of embers, the scrape and smush of wood dragged across earth. As I shoveled, I slid back into a long ago memory, one hazy and almost lost, that shifted between dreams and truth. As a child, I'd crushed an oil lantern and framed Magnolia, my ma humming *green trees are bending* off yonder. Pa crouched beside me, frustration in his eyes, but his voice calm. "Minnie, you've gotta choose." Pa rubbed his jaw, sending his beard into disarray. "When stuck between protecting yourself and the truth, the truth is always the brave choice. You understand that?"

I nodded, though I didn't understand. Distantly, my ma sang, *He calls me by the lightning, the trumpet sounds within my soul.* Pa lifted me up, rubbed my back. "Just keep on being brave, and you'll be alright."

"She bashed the lantern, promise," I argued. "Just threw it off the hayloft to watch it fly."

He chuckled, not believing my story in the slightest, and held me tight against his chest. "We always love you, sweetheart," he said, "no matter how muddled things become."

On the Browns' homestead, the resonance of Olive humming *green trees are bending* roamed through the burn. A breeze hurried across the meadow and tossed embers up round my hem. Whatever I was, I wasn't afraid. I wasn't weak. I wouldn't let someone else carry the consequences of my past.

After all was summed up, it didn't matter whether outlaws or vigilantes had struck the match—this chaos erupting across my community must cease. I'd been so lost, trying to find a wiggle out of my situation. When, in the end, there was no way out but the bare, vulnerable truth. Tonight, after all was settled, I'd dash across the countryside to Duke's Saloon, the known haunt of the Wild Bunch. I'd confront the outlaws, confess to the marshal—anything to keep my friends safe. I might lose my homestead. I might be assaulted by vigilantes. I might be shut up in some asylum or prison. I couldn't imagine being cloistered behind walls, isolated away from the wide spaces of my prairie—but I must take the risk. I would face the untamed judgment of this land with audacity.

Wild survived wild, here in No Man's Land.

CHAPTER FORTY

I strode across the saloon planks, wood creaking beneath my boots. Dusty farmers crowded the bar, hollering about who knows what, broken firelight catching on the jagged edges of shot-out lanterns. In the gloom, Marshal Canton held court, patting his double-breasted tweed vest. Beyond two quarreling cowboys, one grasping another's black suspenders, the Wild Bunch outlaws lounged in a shadowy alcove. Bitter Creek, Tulsa Jack, Quiet Bill, a few others, and their ladies. I thought that might be Rose of Cimarron perched behind Bitter Creek, one black glove resting on his wide, angular shoulders, her jade-green gown with black lace striking against her freckles. Marshal Canton sighted me—I angled toward the Wild Bunch, my pulse jackhammering my throat, hoping I wouldn't disintegrate right there.

Bitter Creek tracked me as I came closer, eyes narrowing when I touched the chairback across the table from him. I drug out the seat, wooden legs screeching. Every gaze in the saloon snapped to me. Noise was sucked outta the bar real quick.

"Mind if I join you fellers," I said and sat.

Quiet Bill's brows rose beneath his brim, and Bitter Creek's jaw paused its rhythmic chewing of tobacco. "Beg pardon?"

Tulsa Jack gripped his revolvers. Sure enough, each member of the Bunch was just about ready to shoot me for speaking. I could walk away. I could say I was mistaken.

And yet I must tell the truth. Though I couldn't ensure my future—myself probably picked off by gunshots by nightfall—I must exonerate Stot and the Browns. My stomach clenched as I leaned toward Bitter Creek. "I've information about your missing men."

Bitter Creek rubbed his black mustache, then spit tobacco on the floor. Someone in another room played a shuddery piano melody, and smoke filled the open spaces. No one spoke.

Marshal Frank Canton bustled across the room, the leather of his boots squeaking. He stopped at our table, gaze stuttering on the outlaws, and wiped a handkerchief across his sweaty forehead. "Alright now, Miss Hoopes." Marshal Canton straightened his wide, four-in-hand necktie. "Why don't we head on over to the office."

I kicked out a chair. "Sit down, Frank. Take a breath."

Quiet Bill snorted and slapped his thigh.

Marshal Canton smoothed a thumb along the border of his handkerchief, took a gander over his shoulder toward the batwing door. A decanter with lemon clicked before me. I flinched, but it was just the bartender. I slipped my hands round the glass, remnants of soot and flame a burnt texture across my palms. Bitter Creek leaned back against his chair's spindles, his expression almost hungry, as if he relished my terror.

"I've a story to tell." I cleared my throat, raised my voice. "Everyone has a right to hear."

"Alright." Bitter Creek stuck a cigarette between his teeth. "Let's have it." He kicked his feet onto the tabletop and spoke to the marshal. "Sit."

Marshal Canton sat in a hurry, his breathing fast and wet. I sipped the brandy, forced my posture to ease. My pulse thumped the undersides of my wrists. "Those missing men of yours? They set fire to my claim and attempted to assault me," I began.

Marshal Canton's elbows slipped off the table. Bitter Creek ran a coin over his knuckles, back and forth, the saloon a hollow echo. His gaze was frightening, feral and unhinged. I could understand why his summer name was once Slaughter Kid. I told of that first day of the rush, sweat soaking my spine, the entire saloon sidling as close as they dared. I chronicled the fire and the cayenne pepper, narrated a tale with enough detail to distinguish the missing cowboys. Marshal

Canton fiddled with his tie, and the bartender topped off my drink, his red-knuckled hand shaking. As I spoke, Bitter Creek evaluated me, coin racing across his joints, the Native headdress on the penny flashing and vanishing as the coin flipped.

"So I blasted them, sending them to kingdom come," I said, finishing my story.

A hush. A decanter fell to the floor and reverberated with an eerie twang as the glass spun. I knew then that I'd be shot by nightfall. I was as good as hanged. It was just the toss of a coin, a gamble that folks would be decent enough to treat a woman same as they'd treat a man. Why'd I expect folks to care about a woman's perspective? Why'd I think there was a possibility my story would be believed? This world was twisted upside down.

I squeezed my throat above the high neck of my lace overblouse. It smelt of burning, of red oak wood and history.

Tulsa Jack snorted, breaking the pause. "Sure enough, doll."

"You don't believe me?"

"No."

"Why would she come in here and make up stories?" Quiet Bill leaned against a post. "Saying notions that'll get her pushing up daisies?"

Tulsa Jack scratched his forearm, wiry hair beside large freckles. "I don't buy it." He leaned closer, his face windburnt along his cheekbones. "Sweetheart, in the Wild West we don't let little ladies make up stories," he drawled. "They were quick riders, surely got there before some woman—you must've slain them to get *their* land."

"Well now, Tulsa, I ride swift." I raised my glass in a toast, then sipped, the lemon peel bitter along the inner curve of my cheeks.

Marshal Canton kept shaking his head, the barrels of his arms crossed over his body. "Now, say this tale is truth?" He took off his hat, rested the brim on his stomach. "Why'd you hide the bodies?"

"Why do you think?" I crossed my arms, mirroring him. "Because I assumed none would believe me, that I'd lose my land and be hanged for murder."

"But did you *murder* them?" Marshal Canton asked.

"No. They tried to rape me: They would've slaughtered me for the land." I held Bitter Creek's gaze, then Quiet Bill's. "I decided I didn't want to die that day."

There was a long moment, the entire saloon steaming with the tension between the Wild Bunch and me, Bitter Creek's bronze penny glinting in the quavering lamplight, his skin pallid below his thick black mustache. I caught the gaze of the adventuress in the jade dress, her scarlet lips pursed. It was as if she wanted to say she believed me—but of course she couldn't. Women, even bold, renegade women, were trained to be silent.

Quiet Bill crossed his long legs at the ankles, herringbone trousers cuffed up above his golden alligator boots. "It ain't right to threaten a lady like that."

Tulsa Jack scoffed. Then Bitter Creek set his coin down with a loud clack, his light-blue eyes ghostly. "You're saying it was kill them or be killed."

"It was the only choice." I held his uncanny gaze. "I'm not sure about you, but when stuck between a bad choice and something awfuller, I'm choosing bad."

Bitter Creek stroked his mustache. He must know the predicament of balancing the black and the dark of a moral dilemma. In the smoke above, a lantern light winked out, and the grimy box of the saloon dimmed further. All a'sudden, Bitter Creek pushed off the table and lurched up. He snapped at the crowd, his gangly arms shaking out tension. "Every one of you—stop eavesdropping."

And quick as a punch, the swarm turned away and pretended to busy themselves with their own matters. Bitter Creek sat back down. His lady stepped forward and set her hands on his shoulders. He rearranged his spine about the chair, and her smile strained.

Marshal Canton tipped his decanter, the etched glass tossing refractions across the table's dark wood. He made slick, wet sounds as he chewed his tobacco. "You see," the marshal said, "what doesn't track for me—how'd you haul off them bodies?"

"Like I already said—tied 'em to my horse, dragged them away." I gripped my drink, black cinders an arc under my nails.

The marshal straightened his paisley tie. "I'm thinking you had help. The Browns, perhaps."

"Wasn't the Browns. They'd nothing to do with this. Honest folk." I lifted my brows, held Bitter Creek's gaze. "And we're all intelligent, sensible folks here. No one's stirring up any vigilante nonsense, right?" I shifted my scrutiny to a couple of sweaty, red-faced cowboys standing nearby.

I didn't waver, and after a span, there were a few grunts and nods. "Alright." Marshal Canton leaned back and spit out some chew. It splattered on the oak floor, beside my black lace-up boots. "But if you had help, you wouldn't be telling, would ya?"

Through the lone window, the light shifted from citrine to gold, sundown swiftly rushing forward. "Look here, are folks chattering that I'm a darling on Sunday afternoons? I'm solitary. I don't even keep with my brothers. Ask around," I said. "The Browns aren't mixed up in this. That's truth, so leave 'em be. This is my past alone."

Marshal Canton tapped his finger on his handkerchief, smashing an embroidered petal. I sipped my brandy, heat sweaty along my shoulders and up my neck.

"You're courting an outlaw, right?" Bitter Creek asked. "The Lawman."

I spit out my brandy sour, back into my glass. "Wherever you hear them horsefeathers?"

Bitter Creek sucked in a drag on his cigarette, exhaled.

"I myself," Marshal Canton cleared his throat, "overheard such notions from the Lawman himself."

Ah hell, they'd surely kill me now. I'd slain some of their own and was sparking with their enemy. I opened my mouth, didn't know what to say. The nesters who'd loitered about crowded closer, gazes flicking among themselves. I winced, realizing Bitter Creek probably recognized me from when I'd *shot* at them a few days past. "So was it you," I said, "that I picked off in the snowstorm?"

The marshal slumped back in his chair. "What now?"

"Nah." Bitter Creek smiled, teeth biting round his cigarette. He leaned forward, elbows resting on his thighs. "Your shots were wide enough."

Quiet Bill groaned. "Ah hell, I thought you looked familiar." He took off his hat and rubbed his short black hair. "I'd started to like you some."

"Well." I cleared my throat, my chest scratchy. "I'm not *courting* the Lawman."

"Darling." An adventuress a few stools over smirked, popped an olive in her mouth. She leaned forward, a curve of black lace luminous against her porcelain skin, her fluttering sleeves sweeping the wood paneling of the bar. "Maybe you should," she said.

I fanned my fingers across my breastbone. "Ain't no matter."

The moment stretched. A farmer just beyond spilled his whiskey, the scent piercing and sweet. "Fellers, I propose we believe her," Marshal Canton said. "I reckon that's truth, that she would've met a violent end. I say we let the law handle this matter here."

There was a rumble as the crowd discussed, deciding among themselves what they thought justice might mean in such a matter. Bitter Creek's lady caught my gaze, the feathers in her elaborate updo casting shadows across her cheeks. She nodded, as if saying she'd have done the same, as if she trusted me, as if she would've joined me in battle. I nodded back, one woman to another.

Bitter Creek rubbed his bronze coin between his fingers. He spoke, his voice carrying across the tavern. "If someone threatened to kill me, I know I'd shoot first."

Marshal Canton nodded, and these seasons of worry began to weaken, like oncoming dawn hazing beyond the rim of the earth. There seemed a possibility where I'd walk from this saloon tonight. I needed to jump on this moment and take control—and then get the hell out of Dodge. "We're sorted here?" I said to Bitter Creek.

Bitter Creek rubbed his eyebrows, sending the brittle strands wayward. The dark brows were heavy on his narrow, gaunt face. A beat, then he waved me away. "Just watch your back."

I stood and gripped the chair's oak spine, lifted my brows at the marshal. He fastened and unfastened his top vest button, still piecing together my story. "How 'bout you come by my office. You can sign a statement, and I'll take the investigation from there."

"Tomorrow."

After a long moment, he nodded—any fool would agree it was plain dumb recklessness to wander town after dark, after such a confession. I nodded at the Wild Bunch and their ladies, then strode to the door. My boots clacked, my legs wobbly, the entire saloon watching me depart, everyone holding their breath to see if I'd be shot.

But then I was beyond the door, the cool dark smudging up the sky, stars flashing in the black. I yanked out my six-shooter, trained it on the batwing doors, stumbled backward to the elm trunk where I'd looped Cricket's reins. I loosed a shuddery exhale—no one followed yet.

In the end, however this lawless frontier decided to hand out justice didn't matter, not really. Challenges would always come. I may go to jail; I may lose my land. Or perhaps the marshal would shuffle my report below all the other lost crimes. Telling my tale at the saloon felt like an end to this season of winter. Perhaps by confessing, I entered a new era. I'd done what I must and felt free in a way I hadn't been in a long while, perhaps freer than I'd ever been.

I vaulted onto Cricket and slipped sideaways, my bootheel missing the stirrup, my body all-overish fuzzy with drink. Come hell or highwater, drunk or not, I was riding straightaway to tell that renegade a thing or two about who I was and what we were and whyever would he say we're courting—the presumptuous bastard, himself intent on marrying another woman.

CHAPTER FORTY-ONE

Evening." Stot brushed Shark's flank. Light flickered gold and dotted from a kerosene lantern looped over a nail. "Heard you clatter on in."

I slammed open the stable door. "What the hell?"

"Mmm." He bent, brushed Shark's legs. "She won't bite," he muttered to Shark. "Well, not unpleasantly."

I faltered over my boots. "What in fiery Sam Hill, you arrogant sonofabitch, you're"—I touched my stomach, woozy, myself thoroughly soused—"telling folks we're *courting*."

His gaze flicked up. "You hear that?"

I knocked my shoulder against the wall beside the feed bucket, raised my brows. Stot brushed Shark's ankle, irritatingly calm. "From whom?"

"Who all are you telling?" I flicked my eyes to an open window. A northeaster whipped by, howling and wrathy, rattling the walls. "You tell about—"

"No. Not that."

I felt as if I'd been tossed from a racehorse, and not just because of the brandy sours, but because I had no idea what to do with this man. When I was wild, I chose it. But with him, I completely lost sight of direction, everything a'whirl, untethered to reason or topography.

Stot straightened his white paper collar and proceeded to brush Shark's other ankle. The air smelt of melting ice and weapon oil and perhaps fresh butter, drifting on over from his home. "Folks ask, you know," he said. "We're together often. Ain't no matter, is it?"

"Sakes alive, it absolutely does matter. You had no right."

"Then what's going on here?"

"Nothing now."

He paused. Stood, clicked the brush down on the ledge. Then he stepped forward, his broad shoulders just above mine. I swallowed. It was quiet in the barn, the scuffling feet of his animals and the wind now muted beyond the hickory boards. He fingered the ends of my hair, his voice gravelly, the texture grating my spine. "Nothing, huh?"

He ran a palm up my side, and a moan tumbled from my mouth. His eyes flashed as he slid his hand behind my back, pressing me closer.

I stepped away, slipped out beyond all the doors. Outside, I crossed my arms over my chest, swallowed a gulp of winter air, and blinked at the starlight pressing through the night. Stot stood behind me, his chest brushing my back. "You know there's something between us."

But there couldn't be. I couldn't be with him for a season, then let him go. We stood awhile, watching Cricket nip at the grass. Stot had put up fences, stained them a gorgeous mahogany. In the moonlight, they were blue tinged and otherworldly. I liked the way he did things. He stepped down the slight hill and stood before me. Air currents skidded through the fibers of my blouse and chilled my bones. His eyes were dark, shadows all over his face.

"We don't have to be some unbound mayhem." He straightened the brim of his Stetson—I even adored the way he moved his biceps, settled his hat on top of his black hair, the controlled way he held his body, everything purposeful, reverential. I didn't know you could relish every nuance of someone, and it ached to like him so much. "We can just see what it's like to be together, as such," he said.

His posture was relaxed, his face rugged with stubble. We hadn't kissed since the snowstorm, and it felt like a conversation forever unresolved. I didn't know how to keep living with this fire between us. Didn't know how to forget those moments in the dark, hadn't known intimacy could be like that. I brushed my fingers across his jaw, pressed my thumb into the cleft in his chin, as if claiming him. I'd already fallen, but he couldn't be mine.

He slid his arms around my waist, settling me closer. "Who you hear from anyway, that we're courting?"

I wiggled away, leaned against the hickory planks of the barn, exhaled. "Frank Canton." A beat. "The Wild Bunch."

"What?" His fist flexed above the walnut handle of his pistol. "Sakes alive, why did you speak with them?"

"Told them 'bout the murders."

"Come again?"

"You heard me."

"Well, damn." He grimaced and straightened the knot of his black cravat.

"What else was I to do? Vigilantes were rising against the Browns, outlaws coming for you," I said. "Told them at the saloon tonight. Loudly."

"Damnation, I requested you take me along."

"I didn't need you."

"Fine." Stot looked off, as if memorizing the horizon. He removed his hat, crown pointed at the loamy dirt.

The distant line of trees was a smudge of dark, like iron oxide pressed across parchment. I told him of the confrontation, of how I'd go on into town tomorrow, sign an official statement. His fingers wrought his gun belt, his black brows tugged together. "But they didn't shoot you, and the marshal didn't arrest you? And no one will go after the Browns?"

"I suppose."

"Of course you pulled off such an unhinged plan." He shook his head. "Not many would protect someone else over themselves." He grabbed my hand. "Come on, you can tell me the rest over supper."

I hesitated. "Oh, I should—"

"Just stay."

And so we cooked and ate, talking of what to plant this next week and his thoughts on how to take my fence before the wildwood. He updated me on plans for rebuilding the Browns' barn and had me tell the entire tale of the saloon, each and every facial tic of the marshal and the outlaws, and then, before I knew it, we'd spent all twilight before the fire, in his home, with such a natural ease and rhythm. Far into the night, he helped me into my slicker. Behind him, his saddle-brown leather bag slumped on the raw oak planks, a train ticket slipped in a side pocket. He'd already planned when to go pick up his new family. My inhale caught inside my chest. The air tinted golden brown, like a blur of linseed oil varnish swept across an oil landscape. That dusk after Magnolia's wedding the forest was sepia. Crispy, saddle-brown bur oak leaves clattered above, the sun too low to shine through the branches, the forest lifeless and dull. The delicate bones of Magnolia's wrist as she climbed onto the buckboard, her translucent white veil coiling in the air; the tiny, embroidered bluebells along her wool cape shivering above her spotless white boots. On the bench, Lark had snapped the reins, his lopsided grin tentative, and then they'd left, the buckboard off down the path, my two closest friends forever chasing a different sort of world. I blinked. Back in Stot's home my gaze fuzzed, his sable bag and train ticket blurry. I didn't know Magnolia anymore, besides a memory.

"Minnie?" Stot stood before me, straightening my slicker.

"I know how to put on a blasted jacket."

His hands rested on my top button. "Can you just leave it—it was a nice evening."

I closed my eyes and shook my head. I couldn't leave it easy and calm, this rhythm that postured as family. Couldn't let Stot traipse all over my heart, spurs and all. I couldn't lose another friendship, couldn't walk that line between destruction and ecstasy. Couldn't lose ahold of any more pieces of my heart. Before, my heart was playing with a boy. But Stot was a man from his Stetson to his black boots edged in mud. He had strength I'd never encountered before—he was brave and resilient and handsome as the dirt is deep. And I couldn't even conceive of the capacity at which he could destroy me.

"I can't do this," I said, unable to look at him.

He threaded his fingers into the hair at my nape. "What, exactly?"

"Any of it." I stepped back, hands pressed against the door.

His gaze ran over my face, his expression contemplative. "There's no hurry, for anything."

I crossed my arms, held myself together, an ache plummeting in my stomach. How could he say such things, when a train ticket to pick up his soon wife and children waited in his saddlebag? It wasn't fair to Clara and the children, or to me. I tugged open his door, fled into the atmosphere which just wouldn't shake free of winter. I strode to the barn, my life speeding forward, as stories do, spiraling into the deep of night like smoke.

Stot caught up with me before the barn, the oil lantern flooding the ground round his boots. He slipped an arm about my waist. "May I follow you on home, confirm no outlaws are waiting?"

I could feel his heat, smell his scent of nutmeg and evergreens. I pushed off his arm, stepped sideaways. "You've gotta stop touching me like that."

"I thought we were taking it slow?"

"That's what you said." I held my shoulders. "I said none of it."

He took off his hat by the crown, scraped his fingers through his hair, sending the black waves askew. "I don't understand."

I scoffed. I couldn't make sense of him toying with me. It wasn't like him. My heart withered and cracked.

"You're quick-witted enough to figure it out," I said. "I'm not fixing to be shucked."

He pressed his hat back on, closed the distance between us. "Now, you know I don't take to being spoken of as a scoundrel."

"Then don't mislead me."

He leaned down, the rim round his green eyes gray. "I feel as if I've been forthright, with what I want with you."

I gasped, clutched the barn's ring doorknob. "When are you marrying Clara?"

"What?" He squinted at me.

"I saw the train ticket, in your satchel."

He gasped something like a cruel laugh. He scanned the pasture, the faraway black distances. "You're jealous."

"You insufferable ass." I made to yank open the door, but he caught my waist and tucked me up against him. "I said, stop grasping at me all the time."

He gripped my chin, halting me. "You understand I'm not marrying her?"

Everything paused. "How would I know that?"

"We've been together. Far as I'm concerned, you're mine." His fingers ran along the line of buttons up my back, sweeping over skin then linsey cotton then skin.

I held his gaze. The wind shrieked through the switchgrass and shook the boundary fence. "I'm not something to be owned."

"Course not."

He angled his shoulders one pulse closer. "I do apologize that I wasn't clear." The vibrations of his deep voice rumbled against my bodice. "But I want to be with you."

He told me he'd bought the ticket a while ago, had planned to ride up at the first blush of spring to propose. All winter he'd felt conflicted, between his sense of duty to Clara and his growing feelings for me. Then, after the storm, he knew he couldn't let me go. He supposed, if another woman was about his claim, perhaps Clara wouldn't deem it improper to move down without nuptials, that perhaps we could create a haphazard family linked between our homesteads. He'd been mulling over how to pitch the notion to Clara when, the day before last, a letter arrived from her. She'd met someone. Clara, her four daughters, and her new husband inquired if they could journey south, if perhaps Stot would help them settle.

"After the ice storm, I assumed my intentions were straightforward." He bit his lip, his brows drawn. "I construed your discomfort as feeling unready to discuss a future with me. But I should've clarified that I no longer intend to propose to Clara. I reasoned they could make a home in my shack, and I—"

He trailed off. "You'd live where?" I asked.

"We can consider that, perhaps another time." He was flushed, his nose red. "But you know I welcome old traditions."

He untangled my curls from where they'd caught in my cape. "You've been pulling away because of Clara?"

I settled my hands on his hips, beside his gun belt. "Of course."

He shook his head, said he couldn't believe he hadn't recognized that.

"You're not marrying Clara this spring?"

"I am not." He drew me to him, and I felt on pause, rewriting all that had happened these past days.

"Can we stop talking about my brother's widow," he said, "so I can kiss you?"

I bit my lip, warmth foaming up. He wasn't beholden to another woman. I studied the way his waistcoat strained across his chest, and my heart took a wide breath. Then I leaned forward and kissed him.

It was gentle and curious, honest in a way our previous kisses had not been. And just as swift as my fury had raged, I quieted. I wrapped my arms behind his neck and pulled him closer. He tasted of salt and whiskey. His hands gripping my blouse, his mouth slow and thorough. As if he wanted to take the time to learn me. Then, all a'sudden, I was pressed against the barn wall, panting, his palms all over my body, my hands slipping beneath his shirt, leftover ice crackling above, hot in the swell of his cloak, the air scenting of all my favorite parts of the Wild West: warm leather, weapon oil, fresh grass. He kissed me until there was nothing left.

He spoke against my collarbone, his mouth roaming up my neck. "To be clear—are we still taking it slow?"

His mouth returned to mine, and I grazed my teeth along his lip. "Probably?"

I pulled away, straightened the knot of his bandanna. His hands brushed my sides, his expression thoughtful, cheekbones windburnt and dusted with cold. Knowing Stot, he'd want an orthodox relationship—marriage, children, forever. Growing up, I'd always assumed I'd wed, but I'd lost ahold of those notions a while ago. I didn't know what I wanted now and hadn't had a moment to consider a future with Stot. I always raced reckless and blustery, but for once I wanted to make a choice I was proud of. So it seemed wise to allow some time to let myself settle. I kissed him in the middle of his throat, somewhere vulnerable, and he clenched the fabric along my back.

"I want to be with you," I said, my mouth on his skin, "but perhaps—just grant me some time to envision it all."

Lamplight glinted on the gold-hued bullets in his bandolier; the barn's wood planks bruised a ridge up my spine. He kissed me, long and aching, savoring, then stepped back. "Well, permit me to follow you on home."

We led our horses outside and rushed on, the dark sky above a whorl of stars. Now that he wasn't intended for another, an immense gap opened inside. I felt on the edge of a precipice, just as adrift as I'd been a year earlier. But *marry* Stot? What lunacy, for two wild souls to try at making something traditional.

I teetered between hope and disquiet, feeling as if my story kept cycling, the narrative shuffling too fast between possibility and despair. I couldn't quite grasp ahold of all the pieces. Marriage seemed dizzying but, at the same time, the most natural thing. After staking claim, I assumed I'd just live out my days alone on my stretch of prairie. I hadn't expected to go falling for some cowboy.

CHAPTER FORTY-TWO

The midnight hours were swollen with shadowy dreams and screeching sounds. I slept fitfully, hot and then too cold, blankets tangled round my ankles, Winchester clutched to my chest—a habit since confessing at the saloon. I woke with a headache grating across my brow and a hunger for coffee: hot and black. I shoved out my door—and stumbled back, knocking my shins against a steel pail. Against my porch's wooden pillar an old bowie knife cleaved into a stack of papers. Terror shot across my shoulders and quaked up my neck. I yanked my pistol from my holster—scanned the timberline.

After a moment, I exhaled. I was alone.

But the size of it: Someone had been on my porch during the dark of night, and I'd heard nothing. I ripped the knife from the wood and unfolded the newsprint. Between all the words was a graphite sketch of a woman with features an exaggeration of my own, with elegant black eyebrows and menswear like Cattle Annie, the portrait labeled *The Famed Minnie L. Hoopes of Grant County.*

> Notice—Bloodshed solved. Word has reached here that the two slain cowboys of the Wild Bunch were sent to their maker in self-defense by Minnie L. Hoopes of Grant County. Col. Archibald Williams

> overheard the tale at Duke's Saloon in Wakita last night. "The lady held the entire saloon enthralled," Col. Williams recounts. "Them cowboys were god-awful bandits, preying on the chastity of our women. None in that room had a dry eye, everyone commending Miss Hoopes for her courage."

I didn't recall such an event, fearing that I'd be shot in the back. But folks apparently believed me, had reshaped my harrowing tale into something sensational. The story spreading across the territory wasn't quite truth, but it seemed my friends and I were safe from vigilante law. I slipped the newsprint into my pocket. A skein of geese lofted into the sky, their throaty sqwacks sharp in the hush. Who'd leave such a thing below my shake-shingles, with a knife whacked into my post?

I picked at a scab on my wrist, gaze unfocusing on the middle distance. On the oak slats underfoot, a scrap of rag paper curled in the breeze. The paper lifted, as if to blow away—but I caught it, gripped the note between both hands, black ink on buff-colored paper. *We won't stop watching you, Miss Hoopes. And lay off being so high and mighty. It's irritating.*

Terror sank into my bones. My wrists ached, clutching the letter. The message was clear: The outlaws retained power. The Wild Bunch could drop me anytime they wanted: in the dark of night, during the daylight hours, whenever I lowered my guard.

I wasn't safe.

But it seemed they wouldn't hurt me—yet. Perhaps they'd let past vendettas dim. The bowie knife's curved tip shone with faded morning light. I ran my thumb along the edge, wondered whose blade had been slammed into my porch. The polished maple handle was incised with "GN."

Rumors went that Bitter Creek's given name was George. I couldn't be sure—but when had I ever been sure of anything besides my own unbidden mayhem? I hauled up my skirts, dashed inside, and penned my own message.

I pressed my lavender stationery against the pillar, thwacked Bitter's bowie knife into the delicate embossed border. *Many thanks for the blade, George. But I don't fancy antiques. Next time, why don't you and Rose come on in for a fireside chat? Don't you worry—I only Slaughter those who threaten me or mine.—Minnie "Mayhem" Hoopes*

I frowned at the note, the embossed roses and ornamental filigree snapping in the wind's gusts. Wondered whether my audacity would get me shot quicker than gun smoke. The play on his alias "Slaughter Kid" felt particularly clever. I gnawed my lip, unsure what to do. My instinct was that Bitter Creek would chuckle and move right on along. That he'd respect a bit of pushback. I sure as starfire hoped my gut was right.

All day, I furtively minded the horizon, rifle slung across my back. The day before, Stot and I had ridden into town and signed a statement with the marshal. Maybe now I could just leave yesterday's worries and focus on my homestead.

I shaped dirt around the root ball of my new orange tree. The clay shone amber in the sunglow, the ground softened by snowmelt. Today the earth seemed ready for spring, for the smells and colors and sounds of awaking. I sat back on my heels. The narrow trunk lifted to a burst of small evergreen leaves. I'd dreamed of an orchard, with summer blossoms and fruit blooming throughout the year. And with this orange sapling, I'd begun.

I wiped my muddy hands on my apron and withdrew my flask, gulped some sweet tea. A puff of cottonwood floated on by. I needed to combine the boiling lye soap with some crushed lavender. Near the windbreak, under the stark midday sunlight, a stiff man loped forward on a thoroughbred. Alarm heated my spine. But I soon recognized that it wasn't an outlaw intent on revenge—it was Ezra.

I cocked my revolver but didn't yet withdraw my gun. I couldn't decide whether it was too much to greet my brother with a barrel lined up between his eyes.

Ezra halted before me, his stallion's hooves leaving a patchwork of indentions in the wet ground. He swung down, his gray-flecked brows combed upward. He handed me my hunting knife, carved-ivory hilt out. The blade rested in my palm, a visceral reminder of the length that now separated us. I flipped my knife and slid it into my boot.

"You cannot know how this has troubled me," Ezra said. He studied the soil, his expression pathetic and wavering, as if he placed upon himself some weak facade, as if he wanted me to pity him.

I nodded and walked past him toward the barn, my back bristling.

"Minnie, I—"

"No." I glanced over my shoulder. The afternoon sky was blank. "I won't listen to your rationalizations. Get off my land."

"Look, I'm sorry, hear." Fat tears smeared his face. He stepped closer, grasped my wrist.

I tightened my other hand on my pistol. "Let go."

His shiny pink fist, washed without a smudge, gripped my shirtwaist. I tugged my arm free and stepped back. There was a reverberation: A black mustang dashed across my land, its hooves sodden thunks against the rigid earth. Stot drew his pistol—hopefully he wouldn't send my brother to kingdom come. Ezra's hand clenched his vest placket. He seemed frightened but also confused, somehow not understanding the gravity of his abhorrent treatment of me. Shark pounded toward us with a clamor. Stot yanked on his reins, cocked his Peacemaker.

"Pause—" I patted at the air as Stot swung from the saddle. He strode forward, gun trained on Ezra, clouds of red dust pluming behind him.

Ezra swallowed and tread backward.

"You're just going to kill him?" I asked Stot.

A vein raised on Stot's neck. "Maybe."

Time moved slow, in the unfiltered sunshine, with a cowboy, but after a tight moment, Stot uncocked his gun and pointed the barrel earthward. He stomped forward, spurs clattering on loose rocks, and punched Ezra across the chin.

Ezra flew backward and smashed against the damp earth.

"Stop." I grabbed Stot's jaw, turned his gaze to mine.

His fingers flexed, unflexed above his six-shooter. Rage rippling beneath his control. I thought of what he'd shared, that long ago night under the stars, of how the search for truth, for righteousness in a brutal world, was vaporous and confusing. How easy it was to become lost. I saw Stot. Loyalty and honor, rage and revenge.

I spoke low. "This is not who you have to be."

A wasp buzzed past, and faroff my pot of lye soap bubbled. Stot rubbed his face. Hesitated a moment, as he chose what sort of man he wanted to be. I glimpsed the honor fundamental to him—and yet agony was stitched alongside goodness. He grappled with the dark parts of himself, those shadowed and hidden corridors. My palm looped his arm, and I felt the heat of his body, the fury taut and rumbling. I hoped to help him walk toward the lighter parts of himself.

"I'm okay," he said, voice hoarse. I let go.

He stalked to where Ezra sprawled in the mud, practically trembling with fear. Stot crouched, slowly, eerily. "You touch her again, and I will annihilate you," he said, voice resonant.

Ezra swallowed, his cheeks muddled and red, soil splattered up his jeans and starched chambray. I wiped my hands on my apron and walked away toward the barn. There was much work to be done, and I didn't have any more space for melodrama. I heard a scuttle and heavy breathing, my brother leaving. He didn't say anything, and I didn't watch him go.

After I'd poured the lye mixture, I moved across the meadow to Stot. He paced, shoulders tense, magnetic in his fury. But he stilled at my approach. I placed a hand on his hip, laid my cheek on his back.

His muscles were strained beneath flannel. Light glowed beyond the cottonwoods, the scent of sweetgrass from off yonder. Stot pinched his hat by its cattleman crease, straightened its angle against the falling sun. "I wanted to shoot him between the eyes."

"I know."

He turned, slipped his hands around my waist, his movements tender. He inhaled, his mouth right above my ear. I slid backward down the slope, pulling away, and he gripped me closer.

"Don't do that." He spoke into my hair. "Just be with me a moment. Don't analyze or worry." He laid his head on mine. "Let me hold you."

There was agony in the knowing, in being vulnerable enough to show someone your traumas, to allow them to see you. I felt the urge to disintegrate, or explode: An ache pressed and pressed against the walls of my chest. It was painful, surrendering.

But I let him hold me, his cheek on top of my coronet braid. And with time, air returned to my body. I allowed myself to feel safe, to calm. He was a stable rock amid fire and storm and the foreverness of weather. His lips pressed to my braid. "We're good together."

I nodded and pulled back. His throat gleamed golden with sweat, his bandolier bunching his shirt tight across his chest. I recognized that I was evolving, that I wasn't yet settled—and I wanted to be careful with his heart. I brushed my lips against his, then went to feed my animals supper.

While I tossed grain for the chickens and hauled a pail of well water inside, Stot fixed a popped board on the side of my home. A bluebird swooped by. A memory edged over my thoughts, time folding and layering. Dawn light, my ma's delicate wrists, the bluebird-colored lace of her cuff, her black embossed hymnal. *Make sure you tell the Lord about your adventures every day,* she'd said and placed her hymnal in my palms. I didn't know how to begin such a thing. I pushed open my shack door and walked to my bookshelf, oak floorboards creaking. I tipped out my ma's small leather hymnal, felt the weight of the book in my palm, then slipped the hymnal into my apron pocket, as she'd done every day of my childhood. Life on the frontier was clogged with hazards and escapades and tedium. I wasn't sure which moments were the sort you told to the God above, but I supposed I could just start talking.

I walked westward along the edge of my prairie, catching the last hour of sunlight, and Stot fell in step with me. It was primaveral, earliest spring, the cusp between one season and the next, when anything could happen. This space between seasons was my favorite time of year—there was such possibility after the long pause of winter. Colors pressed up from my ground, raw and gorgeous, a smear of lime along the groundcover, fuchsia edging the woodland. I imagined other wildflowers blooming: saltmarsh asters and milkweed, purple coneflowers and prairie roses. Stot strolled with me across the fields awhile, the scent of mauve vervain and dewy green leaves pressing through the damp. When the sun slipped down among the treetops, I wiped my hands on my apron and turned back home.

Beneath the porch awning, my oil painting dried on the easel, almost finished. The red of my barn shadowed with maroon, the atmosphere beyond a springtime sky, smudges of luminosity textured across the board. Around the woman, a ghostly blue haze shimmered, as if she wasn't quite a part of the landscape. I liked it that way, as if stories were forever unfinished.

About the wood nettle, I continued searching for those first textures of spring, for the snowy white feathering of dogwoods and for wild plum blossoms, for yellow sumac and magenta redbuds. Stot offered some oats to Shark, and I yanked up wild chives, the green stalks rising from the dead grass. A zip tinged up the stem, as if the ground zapped me. "I hear you," I said. "I'm not going anywhere."

And I wasn't. This was my land. This was my home. So be it wind or rain or wildfire or heartbreak, I'd be here. The voices rose in treble, speaking across time and distance. A feathering of ruby stems bent in the wind, and I waited. From deep underground, I heard the ancient voice of the earth.

Let's restart.

SPRING

March and April 1894

Earth

March 24, 1935
forty-one years after

Time spins, around and around.

In this age, raging dust storms plague your land, and my red dirt dims to ash. Once, wildflowers bloomed across my prairies, my soil rich and fertile. Now, this quarter-mile stitch of my robe alongside Crooked Creek has become a desolate wasteland. It's springtime, but I cannot find her.

I'm tired.

I'm congested and diseased, brittle and broken. Heartbroken, with the agony of being unheard. Dust chokes my throat, my skin grays, my ankles scab with itchy, dry skin. I age. But I must chronicle the heritage of this land. The women keep speaking, their voices coalescing into a roar. Their interwoven lives create a history. Not the sort you find in blundering history tomes of wars and political intrigue, but women who created something new with their remarkable bravery. Women who are stunning because of their unrelenting hope amid the everyday agony of life.

Under the midday sun, a woman tips forward into the windstorm, and like me, she's thirsty down to the marrow of her bones. Do you recognize her yet? Gail's skirt snaps against her calves, skin gritty with granules of dirt, boots sliding across the hot sands. A storm's coming.

She lowers her handkerchief shallowly in a water bucket, then layers the damp fabric over her mouth so she can breathe. My once green and fertile prairie is now black, smoke, fire. She doesn't remember when the grass vanished. It dissolved slowly under years of torrential dust and wind, so now she wonders which parts of her memory are real, which parts invented. Memory is such a thin, shifting thing.

There's a roar on the horizon.

Gail looks northwest, where the black blizzards typically attack. A cloud plumes, more expansive than the roomiest cumulonimbus this sky has ever seen, the black roller gobbling up loose soil as it rushes on forward. She picks up her skirts, and she runs.

Time continues.

The narrative of this land evolves and balloons, stretching on through wars and famine and change. Today, I'm still screaming, but most do not listen. Today, my throat's sore, my body's achy, and I'm so dizzy I feel a slosh about my middle, a throb in my side. Today, the storytellers speak of grand adventures. Of innovative technologies, a race into the future, journeys beyond myself into the stars.

Time continues to turn, around and around I spin, and I listen, as your legacy endures. Sometimes you notice me. You bend down, watch my soil simmer aboveground in a wind eddy or study the noises made in tree hollows. Sometimes you even say hello.

Minnie, keep listening. I will tell you such tales. I tell you so you see yourself, I tell you so you see me.

The legends are always beginning again. Let's restart.

This is my story. A handful of tales, from a single stitch of my robe. My stories are endless, endless.

CHAPTER FORTY-THREE

Osage Nation—March 21, 1894

a few weeks later

The drums pounded, the beat reverberating like a pulse beneath my rib cage. Smoke wandered through camp, shocks of color kaleidoscopic in the dark. Spring had come suddenly, with verdant colors and long-forgotten scents. We'd made it. We'd survived winter.

Sometimes the ancient voice of the earth rumbled from the underneath: *A storm's coming*. And I'd watch my horizon. But the Wild Bunch hadn't arrived for revenge. And so I began to hope that the outlaws would just let me be.

Stot came round regular now, and I let who I'd been this past winter fade away. After everything, with springtime's renewal, I felt as if I was allowed to become. I waded through visions of my future, considered what relationships were to me now. I'd been by Olive's homestead a few times these past weeks, helping with the remnants of their barn. Once, as I'd sorted through a pile of half-burnt shovels and pitchforks, Olive had wandered into the husk of her barn, the shadows long and gnarled. She wiped a hand across her forehead, her posture tight. *Well, come on in for supper, I suppose.* Her voice strong and clear, but without any stretchiness in her intonation for rapport. Olive had welcomed me. But the distance between us now was vast. I wasn't sure how to repair what I'd broken, but I'd keep trying.

Stot kissed me some on our homesteads, but mostly he allowed me space to reconcile all that was tangled in my life. I was comfortable in sensuous moments with him but still unsure in vulnerable ones. I found I liked to watch Stot work. I liked to laugh with him. I liked him nearby, and I started letting him see my hidden layers. And so we'd shifted into someplace comfortable and expansive. Well, not *comfortable*, as the man was too handsome, smelling of spices and adventure. Now I was aware of every accidental brush, every whisper of his skin against mine, and my body ached. We hadn't discussed where he'd live once Clara journeyed down, and I was thankful he was patient as I became accustomed to such an idea—of forever sharing all my wide quiet with another.

Before the bonfire, the log's bristles irritated my palm. I clapped debris from my skin. Niabi updated me on goings-on, occasionally taking a length of fabric and threading it into her finger weaving. Tomorrow we'd practice on a complicated mount with her horse—and challenge Stot and Wa-ah-zho to a sharpshooting contest. But tonight, we'd simply enjoy each other's company. The night smelt of honeysuckle and fresh grass and burning. There was the rhythm of the kettle drums, the warm brush of fire, the thoughts churning inside me. I remembered what Niabi had once shared, of how everything came from Wah'Kon-Tah, of how we just rearranged elements into something new, of how I'd been one woman long ago, and now I felt continually shuffled, as if I was becoming altogether rebuilt.

I scratched mud off my boots, dirt stuck beneath my laces. A girl rushed over, and Niabi leaned forward, listened to the fits and starts of the girl's story about a game of chase. Niabi wiggled her fingers and blew. "Now you're the wind—catch them." The girl ran off giggling, and I mulled over this idea of voices caught in the wind—of history calling out to me, ancestors speaking through time. I couldn't hold the stories inside much longer. The women wanted out.

"The story of the earth and Prairie Rose?" I asked Niabi.

Niabi peeked at me as she slid a red glass bead on a ribbon. I spoke in a low rush, telling her how I believed the earth, Prairie Rose, and other women throughout time were communicating with me. I tugged my legs in tight, my bootheels catching on the bark of the stump. "Sometimes I wonder if I suffer from hysteria."

Drowsy, Niabi's hound, sighed in his sleep, and she ran a hand along his back, firelight catching on the gentle curve of her shoulder. "And your people, they bind you inside an asylum if they think you've caught hysteria, if what you say doesn't have an easy explanation?"

"Yes."

"I know of white man's philosophy of reformation." Her brows pulled together, the weight of past horrors tight across her back.

"I'm so sorry." I was ashamed of my people. Niabi had shared glimpses of her time away at school with her sisters; I'd heard atrocious tales of other mission schools. They ripped away Native history and culture. The children couldn't speak their traditional languages, wear what honored their heritage, dance as they wanted. Asylums for women had that same cruelty, that same altering of minds.

Niabi set her weaving on her lap and tucked her hair behind her ears, her gold and red feather earrings reflecting the light's glow.

"Minds are as water," she said. "Full of ripples and waves, evolving, wavering. Rainstorms splatter the surface of your mind, your memories and passions and hopes. Winds whip and change the structure of the water as your opinions and beliefs change. Fires, always burning inside. So you see, like the body, sometimes minds need mending."

Niabi looped a yellow ribbon beneath a piece of black, the geometric design quaking as she wove. "You can heal, Earth Mother can heal, but neither can heal alone."

I nodded and scratched my nails into the fraying fibers of the log. I'd raced away from my past—had stubbornly tried to create an isolated life.

But I couldn't outrun the voices on my land. Earth called to me, connected me with the women who lived on my land before me, perhaps even lived on my land after me. All their voices braided into shared memory, a new sort of history arising. Women were never meant to live alone, to live quiet. I'd tried, but the voices of my ancestors broke through time and impossibility to speak to me.

"So you don't think I'm afflicted with hysteria?" I asked Niabi.

"I don't think I'm the one to answer that." She looked toward the forest, then grabbed a stalk of sweetgrass from a basket. "My people have always spoken with the land. Earth, she wants to be known. She will speak. You can hear her, if you listen."

Niabi braided the sweetgrass, layering the crisp lengths across each other, moss and olive-green pieces twining together. This land had a rich heritage of story. Beyond the Osage Hills, buried deep in the soil of my farm, were the histories of women past. Before, herds of buffalo roamed, these rolling hills and meadows the hunting grounds of the Cherokee. Perhaps beyond that history, lost deep in time, Prairie Rose had made her home among this same sweetgrass.

I brushed the sweetgrass stems, a texture women had known far back into the reaches of time. One of Niabi's sisters sat beside us. Niabi lifted her sister's hair and fixed a necklace's barrel clasp. They were amused about something, Niabi grinning and her sister's laugh full of hiccups, their ease with one another unsettling, my own sister long lost. I wasn't the only woman who'd broken and re-formed again, everyone a heartbeat from dissolving away. Memories of my parents' home faded and faded until my past seemed almost lost and my days on my homestead resurfaced as new memory. I decided to wander awhile and withdrew toward the edge of their camp, where starlight glimmered and the trees cast haunting shadows. I entered the forest, fireflies shimmering golden light among the understory, sound disappearing behind me. The Osage defined the spirit world as unknowable, as full of mystery and wonder. In the nebulous dark, with a blanket cloak around my shoulders, I supposed that I'd never suffered from hysteria.

I'd just been a woman, with questions. A woman enraged and aching and bursting with such smothered emotion that I cracked open to find past. Just a woman, desperately searching for home.

Faroff, a woman spoke, the timbre of her voice like the groan of wooden boards. I turned toward the voice, the cool of spring breezes rustling my braid. A veil of snowdrops bobbed, moonglow luminous through the translucent petals. After a time, I heard spurs dragging through the nettle. Stot stopped beside me, leaned against a blackjack. "You okay?"

I nodded. He jacked his boot back against a boulder behind him, and I felt his body like steam through air. The forest was too full, too loud, too hot with him near.

"Do you know I believe in faeries?" he asked.

I gusted out a surprised laugh. "What?"

"Honest to God." He lifted his hands, his expression earnest. "My ma's ma emigrated from Ireland, and she told me stories."

I opened my mouth, closed it, had no idea what to say.

"I'm just saying: Try me."

I bumped against a sapling. Stot pulled out his knife and whittled a sliver of sapwood, forever patient with me. Beyond the branches, dry lightning scratched across a foggy sky. The clouds were the colors of smoke and salt. I knew Stot could withstand honesty, but I didn't know how he'd manage something mystical. It was the brave choice to let him know me.

I exhaled, my body releasing seasons of worry. "So I've been hearing voices, on my land." I told him of my worries this past winter and what I believed now: that the flower from Niabi's folktale of Prairie Rose had been a real woman who'd lived beside Crooked Creek before me. That she spoke to me, along with the earth and other women who'd lived on my land throughout time.

"Is it comforting," he said, "to hear their voices, when it's dark and lonesome?"

I nodded. "Well now," he said, "I'm thankful you shared a story of such magic with me."

I watched him.

"Someday, I'm sure, something else will seem too dark. You'll think I can't handle it." His gaze resolute, thick black brows angled low. "I'll handle it."

He drew a gap in my blanket closed at my throat and tucked a curl back into my braid. I swallowed, my eyes surely wide. A burst of lightning gilt the wild scrawl of a branch.

"As you once reminded me—there's a wideness to mercy." He held his body with such enthralling ease, the straight line of his shoulders, the angle of his jaw, his crisp white collar and buttons visible below his waistcoat and slicker. "And when I run across something dark, something too heavy to carry alone, I know you're brave enough to help me heft it. You never step down. It's why I choose you."

My heart thumped against my chest, my gaze snagged on his lips. A blistering moment tugged, hot and alive; then he disappeared into the shadows, embers burning inside my stomach. *The fire is in me.* I watched the slope of his hat and his easy gait weave through the blackjack branches and exit once more before the bonfires.

CHAPTER FORTY-FOUR

Cricket and I dashed through the gnarled trees of the northern forest, looped vines and flowering creepers blocking the sunrays. A greenish haze slid across the atmosphere. Something was coming. I hadn't smelt a prairie fire or heard thunder, but ill ease hung in the air.

We surged out onto the open plains of my quarter section, headed toward the Browns' claim just over the hills. As we passed the orange and blue and yellow weave of milkweed, chicory, and dandelion, a memory burst full color of the first time I'd raced through these trees and seen my land. It seemed unfathomable that had been just a few seasons ago, not quite seven months. It felt an age, and the woman I'd been lost in time.

Memories layered, time collapsing, the weight of bygone days disintegrating as I became someone new out here on the Oklahoma frontier. Last week, the meadowflowers beginning to riot with their springtime colors, the fuzzy citrine-green sprouts of my sunflower seeds bursting from the undergrowth, I'd hammered up my fence along the eastern boundary with Willie. We chatted of the gossip round town, and I told him about the distance between the Browns and me.

"You know," Willie said, running his fingers along the curled ends of his mustache, "I'm just about as clever as two bronze pennies rubbed together—you've always been sharper than me."

"Fine excuse is what that is." I gestured to the fence. "You just prefer jabbering to working."

He grinned and lined up a nail, held his hammer at the ready. "But I know folks, understand what makes them tick." Willie tapped the nail, the golden buttons on his jacket gleaming. "Olive cares about you. Olive, she cares about everyone. Just give her some time, love. And find some way to show her how much she matters to you."

I propped my boot on the low rung, considered the wildflowers, the chicories glistening like flecks of sunlit sky fallen to earth. I could organize a box social to fund the schoolhouse, maybe write friends back in Kansas, ask whether they'd come teach, offer them board on my homestead. I rubbed the dull steel back and forth across my palm, the points abrading my skin. "You know, that's not the dumbest tripe I've ever heard."

"Yeah?" He twirled his hammer, then looped an arm around me. I leaned my head against his shoulder. Wind shivered through the flowers, the colorful overtones blurring with the green grass. "Homesteading's not what I'd expected," Willie said. "But I'm mighty fond of this vast, newfangled world we're building."

"It's home," I said.

He nodded, his expression half shadowed beneath the narrow ridge of his straw hat, the brim impractical but dashing. I squeezed his arm, then stepped forward, aligned the point against wood.

"What's in the wind, between you and Ezra?" Willie brushed at dirt on his trousers. "Y'all feuding or just practicing?"

I thwacked the nail. It wedged sideways.

"I'm with you, sure as rain." He tucked his tool under his arm and stepped forward, took my hammer from me. Wiggled out the nail. "But will you forgive him?" I crossed my arms; Willie tapped at the nail. "Anger'll eat you up, doll."

"I suppose I've forgiven him," I said. "I don't think of him at all. He's—released."

Willie rubbed the end of his mustache between two fingers. I took my hammer back, and he chewed on a wheat sprig, his gaze faroff, as if detached from our conversation. And I wondered, in a brutal flash, how many times I'd thought Willie wanted to be anywhere but beside me, his mind elsewhere, when perhaps he'd just been thinking.

Willie pressed the toe of his boot against some knotted grass, tapped down the gnarled and dry groundcover. He shoved his hands in the pockets of his trousers, jangled some coins. "Remember Mr. Becker?"

"I do." I lifted and aligned a board. I remembered the farmer, his ruddy skin shiny, his laugh a bit too loud, gaze a pinch narrowed. Though he'd charmed most of the county, I'd never liked him.

"You were young." Willie rolled nails in his palm, his grimace on the horizon. "But Becker beat him blue. Ezra came home once, skin blotched and bruised, like he'd tangled with a mule. It wasn't good."

Above, thunder cracked. The clouds plumes of charcoal and navy, as if they swallowed up the sky. Willie crouched, straightened a plank of unstained wood. I pinched my nail, hammered. Ezra had spent a couple of seasons helping Becker during harvest, but I couldn't remember much of that time.

"I suppose," Willie said into the silence as we worked, "darkness just festered inside him."

I thought of the anger knotted in Ezra, his fury at the world, his rabid, fanatical spirituality. I'd never viewed him as the one wounded, as he'd bullied those smaller than him, but I supposed pain was a cycle that never stopped turning.

"I don't understand," I said. Pa would never have tolerated a farmer abusing Ezra. "What'd Pa do? Why was Becker left standing?"

Willie's eyes pinched at the corners. He straightened his straw hat by the brim, sunlight a harsh slash across his jaw. "We didn't tell Pa."

Faroff a horse sneezed. Sound caught up and lost itself in the boundless space. There was much I hadn't glimpsed, of those who'd lived alongside me. "Thank you for telling me." I scratched my neck. "But it won't be me, watching for him to change." I placed my boot on a low rung, rocked my heel back and forth. I could let him go, allow forgiveness—but I still wouldn't welcome him in my life. "It's not for me to help him feel healed. He can do that elsewhere."

"Reckon that's a fine notion." Willie nodded and lifted his hammer. The air tasted young and sweet, the texture of honey and wildflowers. He added after a moment, his fingers positioning a nail, "I suppose it can be me."

Willie stayed with me, constructing my fence until sunset simmered down along the holler. Then he settled on into my shack for the night, us swapping stories, laughing at one shenanigan or another, falling asleep fireside, enjoying each other as we'd done once upon a time. Now, a week later, with the flaming milkweed and the sage sky, Cricket slowed to a canter. A swallow swooped by, her song high pitched, as if she'd detected something hidden in the clouds.

We came over the rise, and down in the valley I dismounted. Olive called hello, as she scraped butter into a bubbling pot on her outdoor stove. It smelt bright and tangy, the jelly mixture a deep crimson. Olive shared that Poppy had scouted some early-fruiting sand plums. She tapped the spoon on a wooden dish and wiped her hands on her apron. "You know how to make jam?"

I untied my bonnet and rubbed the navy gingham across my collarbone. "Will you show me?"

Olive explained how she'd prepared the plums and mixed the fruit, pectin, and butter. I poured in sugar and brought the jam to a boil. As I stirred, she tidied the wooden butcher block and laid out the canning jars. Across the meadow, beyond the scorched, black earth, the shredded ends of relics trembled in the breeze. We'd hastily partitioned the unburnt half of the Browns' barn with wide planks of raw-cut wood, the leftover shell lumpy and charred.

"Olive," I said, and she turned to me, a couple of jars in her palms. "I do apologize, for everything."

She nodded, lip tucked into her mouth.

"I've been considering our community, of what it means to be part of this family we've created." I whisked the jam. "Until someone opens a school, I'd enjoy reading with your daughters." From my satchel, I pulled out the *McGuffey's Second Eclectic Reader* I'd bartered for when last in town.

I handed Olive the book. "Perhaps I could assign readings," I said. "Spend some time tutoring the girls."

She dried her hands and brushed her fingers across the cobalt-blue filigree cover.

"I've sent word out to folks that I'm hunting for the *Sixth Reader* for Sophia," I said. "But until then we can discuss some of the novels or scientific journals I've in my home."

"Thank you. You know how much schooling matters to me." She held the book to her chest, the mustard and sapphire colors vibrant against her ivory blouse. "I'm still upset by your choices, but I don't need atonement." She reached for my hand. "We're your friends, Minnie. Friends keep at it, through all the tricky bits."

"You suppose that's what friendship is?" I said. "To commit to figuring everything out together, to not flee when life gets hard."

"Seems to me the make of it." She released my hand, brushed along her hairline. The jam gurgled in a rapid boil, scenting of frothy springtime.

"Here," Olive said, and showed me how to test the consistency, scooping out a spoonful, letting it cool. After a moment, she nodded that the jam had thickened enough.

"I'd like to help the girls," I said, removing the pot from the fire. "We already chat about what we're reading—I'd enjoy guiding them in lessons."

"Well then," Olive said, "you must permit me to make you supper at least once a week. How about you and Stot come round on Sundays?"

"I'd say that's a tip-top plan."

Though I'd fought against it, a community had built around me. These folks had wandered into my life and just settled. Olive and Niabi and Stot and the long ago, forgotten women. We worked for a time scooping jam into jars, with the soft, almond scent of the berries and the wind chimes clattering, the copper spoons clinking against metal pipes, the hollow thunking of the tree bark. Though I'd work to restore my friendship with Olive, my relationship with Magnolia was fractured, our life together forever unfinished. I supposed I'd always miss my sister—miss what might have been. Some days the ache deepened, other days it eased. But it wouldn't pass on away. I dipped my spoon into the warm, strawberry-red jam. A gust hastened across the meadow and tossed fragments of soil up round my hem. I'd thought I'd let Magnolia go, but regret and longing just kept on haunting. I didn't know how to release the past. My memory may still haunt me, but I wouldn't let shame control me.

I'd write Magnolia this evening. I'd tell her of my land, and perhaps she'd visit. I envisioned her back in Kansas, standing atop the western hill, sunrise lifting over the lowland, wind rustling her cotton skirt, sprigs of lavender brushing her ankles, her rose-embroidered cape across her shoulders. Lark would stroll up and thread his arm across her collarbone, nestle her against his chest, and they'd watch the world arise. Perhaps my memories of them were idealized, the version I created not the whole truth. But I hoped she was happy, that Lark would love her as deep as she loved him. I reached into my pocket and pulled out my key, linked the chain behind my neck, joined the clasp. Perhaps you didn't need to be finished to be a triumph.

After Olive and I filled the jars and plopped them into boiling water, we placed them on a towel to cool. The lids sealed with a soft ping, the delicate sound muted beneath the roar of distant wind, and on a sudden the afternoon darkened several shades. The sky dimmed with dull coppers and dusty beige, the heavens stormy and sick. A jagged line of dry lightning stitched through the sky, and faraway there was an elemental growl.

"I reckon a storm's blowing in," Olive said.

I nodded, noting the change in atmosphere. I said my goodbyes, with plans to drop by on the morrow to read with the girls, and then Cricket and I were off—I must rush home, call my animals down to the lowlands. As we dashed uphill, a southern wind snapped across the plain. *A storm's coming,* the land hissed at me. I turned my face toward the gale, but the wind abruptly dropped, the sudden stillness of the woodland unsettling. In the hush, voices rumbled underground. The women were rising.

There was an eerie roar in the distance. I jolted—but realized the storm wasn't in my own time. An apparition engulfed the terrain, a dark shadow swallowing fields, golden wheat melting into onyx-black sand. The homesteading woman studied the horizon, the line of her mouth taut, rawboned fingers rubbing her collarbone. Behind her, a charcoal cloud bulged, broader than a thousand barns, rising half the height of the sky. A moment of terror as she sighted the storm. Then she picked up her skirts, and she ran.

The vision vanished with a snap. Before me, an olive haze spilled from the heavens and blurred over the landscape like pickle-hued watercolors puddling across the sky. It smelt of earth, of centuries and stories and the deep of the underneath.

Tornado weather.

My land, and the women of generations past and future, must be cautioning me. There wasn't time to gallop home—Cricket and I needed inside, now. With a crack, stones fell from the sky and clattered against the ground. Icy hail battered my shoulders and glistened in the grass like globes of opalescent smoke. We fled the prairie into the wildwood the moment a downpour loosed across the earth. Rain swamped my eyes and sank into my mouth. It tasted of salt and frenzy. As we galloped over broken walnuts, voices lodged in a rumble of wind, the raspy tenor of the earth telling me again her story. *Seasons pass, years rush on by.*

We burst from the forest and pummeled downhill, Cricket's black ankles skidding in the surface water. Across the meadow, Stot's cheery cornflower blue shack waited, smoke coiling from the chimney. The barn door was open, a black cavern in the red arch of barn. Stot tugged a plow inside, his shirt slick with rainwater. His hat tipped skyward—he sighted me. And then he raced forward, mud splashing up to ink his gray trousers.

CHAPTER FORTY-FIVE

I crouched before the woodfire. Stot placed a blanket on my shoulders, his hands resting one breath. His shack was cozy, colorful afghans tossed all over, One Eye lounging before the blaze, a knotted rug the hues of sunset warming his oak floor. I ran a hand along One Eye's back and held off a shiver, the prophetic vision of the homesteader haunting the edge of my thoughts. It was fantastical, I couldn't explain it, but I recognized her. Not because she kept arriving on my land, but because I *remembered* her. The embers crackled; the air scented of smoke and storm.

I was much obliged that the voices urged me to take cover. As we led Cricket to a stall, Stot and I hollered over the wind about the cyclone. His cellar wasn't large enough for us both, so we'd wait out the thundershaker aboveground.

I rubbed my face, One Eye draping his body over my boots. "I could—" I wanted to check on my animals, but my horses should be safe in the barn and my cows should instinctively migrate to the lowland. Stot removed his pocket watch and placed it on the side table with a clack. Then he lowered beside me.

"Your animals ought to be fine." His hand swept my jawline, brushing back a loosed curl. "I'll ride on over, after the cyclone passes, check on them."

I nodded. A soup gurgled on the stovetop, scenting of spice and potatoes. I went to the window, pulling aside the starchy lace curtain to check the sky. Just the swell of rain clouds and the shatter of storm. I fidgeted with the hoop of my key, the necklace now resting below my collarbone. As he moved about making tea, Stot glanced at my fingers, a faint gentling beside his eyes. He handed me a cobalt flow-blue teacup. I sipped, chamomile sweetened with honey, and looked out the window, the ink of night pouring over his land, a scrawl of lightning to the south. Stot stood behind me, his chest warm against my back. He threaded an arm across my shoulders and tucked me against him, his shirt smelling of evergreens. Thunder rattled the walls. I turned, the bristly blanket snagging on his soft flannel, the firelight turning his eyes hazel.

He was nothing like anyone I'd met before. Others seemed a gesso haze when Stot was full color and texture. I scraped my nails up his nape and touched my lips to the underside of his jaw. He slid his palm along my neck and kissed me, slow and deep. A moment, warmth from the fire flushing my cheeks, then I tugged up his shirt, reached for his trouser button. He stepped back, the hollows of his cheeks deepening. "Are you sure you want this?"

"I think?"

"You know I want you." Under my blanket, he ran a hand over my hip, brushed the side of my breast. "But I want us to be a choice you can't walk away from. One that you choose because it's all the options."

There were unending options in life, unending people and places and possibilities. I could have stayed in Kansas, I could have fled. That first day in the creek, I could have been kind to him, I could have argued. I could have done so many things. How could the future be just one option? The possibilities seemed endless. But he hadn't said one option, he'd said all the options.

"All the options?"

"When I look forward," he said, "I see many likelihoods, but all of them include you beside me."

The rainstorm rumbled, wind roaring across the prairie. My pulse hammered my throat. His hair was damp, brushed back from his widow's peak. He asked, "Do you see me in any of your possibilities?"

"Yes." I spoke instinctively—of course I saw him in my future.

He held my hand, rubbed his thumb across my knuckle. "I want a romance with you, but I would like that to be when you've chosen it, not only something that happens in passion, in secret, in the dark."

I wanted his body on mine. I yearned for those hidden, unlit places—but there was nothing casual or haphazard about Stot. He was as traditional as he was turbulent. Honor and vows mattered to him. Of course I wanted a relationship with him—but marriage wasn't something decided in passion: It was something rational, something chosen. And watching my parents, I'd seen that marriage wasn't something chosen once, but daily.

"What about your wife?" I asked. "You never told me her name."

"Emily," he said. "My daughter would've been Elizabeth, like Emily's ma."

I swallowed. "Would you tell me about them?"

"Not now," he said. "Someday."

He sat on the couch, settled me across his lap, and wrapped the blanket around our shoulders. "But I reckon you're wondering, as I said marrying again would dishonor her."

"You did say that."

"I did, didn't I?" He rubbed his scruff. He shifted his weight, drawing me closer. "I don't think I understood what life could be. Now I can't figure how a relationship with you, something that feels as inevitable as breathing, would dishonor her. Emily's gone, and though I'll always miss her, the love I have for her memory doesn't brush up to what I feel for you."

I placed my hand on his jaw, tipped his gaze to mine. "I'm sorry you lost them."

He studied me, flames pattering across the hollows of his cheekbones. He folded my hand into his, pressed his lips to my knuckles. "Thank you."

We sat together before the fire, One Eye yelping in his sleep, a candle guttering over a brass chamberstick, and considered all that had come before. I supposed loss was never easy. He unwound the blanket, and his fingertips worked at my top button. "At least shuck these overclothes, let me hold you."

As he unbuttoned my blouse, rain plinked on his metal roof and heat from the fire slipped down my neck. I wasn't sure I'd ever felt a more sensual moment than him helping my worn body from my stiff clothes, shaking the blankets to check for critters, leading me in my chemise to bed. He tucked me below quilts, then slipped outside to check on the animals. With the windstorm howling outside, the air scenting of warm, sweet beeswax, I realized I could begin my life all over again.

After a time, Stot came back, scenting of rain, and changed into his nightclothes. He stoked the fire and joined me in bed, his long, hard body warm behind me. He held me, his inhales and exhales steady, storms roaring beyond. I rubbed the wiry hair on his arms and snuggled closer, his body a comfort on such a night—and I recognized I'd found something not yet nameable in the wide unknown.

~

In the morning, with sunlight flashing through his sheer curtains and the sparrows spiraling in their song, with the crackle of woodfire and the distant sound of cattle, in that ease of bright, honest, unhidden day, I reached for him. He woke, swept me below him. I wasn't sure of much, but I knew he wasn't just a reaction to my tragedies, he was something I chose.

CHAPTER FORTY-SIX

Hours later on my land, sunrays slashed through low clouds. White mist soaked golden prairie, moisture and haze distorting shape and distance. Though my homestead was mostly unharmed, the tornado had demolished a section of my fence and uprooted my new fruit tree. A robin landed on my orange tree, the severed trunk now just a gnarled arch. The branch snapped beneath the robin's rust belly, the bark crumbling toward the earth. I felt sorrow at the storm's destruction, but after the calamities I'd survived these seasons, I recognized my own resilience. I'd begun this race believing I was without control, but I now knew: I was unwavering and resolute. I would rebuild what was broken.

Stot grasped a fence post, tossed the smashed wood aside. He'd rolled up his sleeves, the veins and muscles of his forearms slick with sweat and dusted with debris. I lifted my orange tree, settled the mangled roots back into the underneath. And with a dim hope that my tree would revive, I shaped soil around the root ball. Home was more than the soil and the wood and the nails. Home was something alive, something intangible that you could just about touch.

I shaded the morning sun with my hand, the springtime air soft, scenting of sweet peas and burning. Across the pasture, Stot organized the broken planks of wood, muscles bunched against his cotton shirt, ash smudged on the brim of his hat. He was so handsome. His golden jaw, those piercing eyes, that languid, confident way he held his body. His black vest matching the shadows, sable gun belt settled over his hips, Stetson catching all the sunlight. I wanted to build a life with him, but no matter what I believed, no matter everything, I just couldn't shake my fear. I didn't know how to trust. Stot wouldn't hurt me on purpose—he wasn't cruel. But he wasn't a gentle man. He wasn't a safe man. I supposed nothing about love was *safe* anyhow. For someday, some way, he'd break me. Not because he had a pinch of wild in him, he'd fracture my heart because hearts weren't made to be whole all the days of one's life.

My bravest adventure wouldn't be fighting fires or battling bandits or navigating hysteria or building this homestead, the bravest choice would be to love him. I lifted my black boots from the soil and stepped forward. *It'll be messy*, a woman's voice said from beyond time, and I agreed. But I didn't want life any other way.

~

At twilight, I wandered to the creek to wash, then reclined on the bank, watching starlight ripple across the stream. Beyond the forest, I smelt distant fires. I tasted smoke and earth, the flavors bringing to mind the apparition from the evening before. A premonition of my land mutating into that desolate landscape should've been horrifying, but somehow it was hopeful to observe my land endure.

The history of women would continue on after me, stories forever enfolding together. Prairie Rose and Willie Matthews, Sally Ann Thunder Ann Whirlwind and my descendant, they were all legendary women, all immortalized inside grand tales, myself just one stitch on the elaborate patchwork quilt of time. Our interwoven lives creating a new sort of history. I gripped the soil along the bank, and I listened. Waited for the women of ages past or ages future to speak to me. It was the earth who spoke this time:

The story is always beginning again.

I closed my eyes, felt the weight of night's darkness, and began to tell the women my own tale, speaking aloud into the night. A while later I heard Stot approach, the rhythm of his spurs dragging through the groundcover. He lifted my plait and kissed the nape of my neck.

Then he slid his arms around me, settled me on his lap. I wrapped my blanket cloak across my chest, the springtime darkness cool. Above, the stars slipped round the firmament, those faraway sparks crisp, then fuzzy and indeterminate. Memories of Kansas dimmed and blurred, bygone reminiscences reshuffled beneath the weight of new moments. Memories of these past seasons flickered in and out: fire scrambling down my hazel branch, the blaze searing my palm; brushing Cricket's black ankles in the deep of winter, a southern wind howling outside, voices chattering in the grasses; Stot's white shirt rolled up over his tanned forearms; the sun slipping below the treetops, saturated watermelon-pink and orange; cracking open popcorn balls with Olive; yellow wildflowers sprouting the first warm morning of springtime; all the moments gathering, as I rewrote my history. The stars sharpened with many colors, and when I thought into my future, the landscape was hazy and faraway—but beautiful and arresting.

Stot rubbed his stubble, the sound a subdued rustle. I turned and he dipped his head, touched his lips to mine. He kissed me, soft and yielding—the moon roved across the sky, the night's glow filtering through the overstory, and in time we left the forest, Stot holding my hand and allowing me to lead him across the meadow, my shack and barn resembling oil pastel–sketched shapes in the dark. I wasn't sure when I'd begun to love him, perhaps that first moment in the swampy rivulet, but I knew now that I chose him. "I've decided," I said.

"Come again?"

"I'm done being scared."

He stopped, propped his foot on a stack of wood. "When have you ever been scared?"

"I've been *terrified*." I fiddled with the cuff of his shirt. "Terrified that if I lived, I'd ruin the world—"

His gaze roamed over my face, over lips, eyes, jawline. He waited. A scraggly juniper bush scented of citrus and tomorrow's rain. I said, "You're all my options."

"Yeah?" He folded my hand in his. "We can get married?"

"Marriage?" My bootheel caught in the juniper.

"I'd like to get married." He stepped forward, slipped his hands round my back. "You like what's boundless and exhilarating." Crinkles fanned beside his eyes. "But I like what's old fashioned, what's predictable. I like calm evenings and knowing that at nighttide you'll sit with me before our fire. There's nothing wrong with boring." His fingers brushed up my spine. "There's the person I am in all the tales, this man storytellers created, but I think you know what's true: I want a life where you'll be beside me on our porch, heckling the sunset."

I straightened his jacket lapel, lifted a brow. "Was that a proposal?" He shrugged. "James Solomon Umstott Tharp—try again."

He lowered, one hand holding mine, his grin upending me, and dropped a knee to my land. He dug his fingers into the groundcover, scooping up a handful of soil. "I've no ring yet." His voice was rough, that deep rumble of earth. "But I offer you all the possibilities of this home we'll build together. I cannot promise to protect you from the tragedies of life, but I will walk beside you through it all." He brushed his thumb across my knuckles. "I love you. Marry me?"

I dropped to the dirt and took his face between my palms, kissed him. I didn't know how we'd conquer the next obstacle, but I knew that with Stot beside me, my life would never be without hope.

He broke our kiss. "Damnation, are you marrying me or not? Stop being stubborn—I know you love me."

"Absolutely." I drew his mouth back to mine. "And yes, I love you."

We sat together and kissed a long while, with the rumble of the wind and the narrative of the trees and the thud of Stot's heart against mine. I'd delighted in the wide quiet of my homestead, but I didn't want to exist alone anymore.

After a time, with our horses pawing at the sideoats and the smell of springtime flowers crisp in the air, we made our way on toward my home. The haze had lifted, and in the starlight I could make out a graphite sketch of contours, the shape of the earth. The hollows, the secrets, the renewal buried underground. My land was alive. She would endure.

Today, I will tell you such tales, the earth said, reminding me again of the old, old story. *Let's begin.*

CHAPTER FORTY-SEVEN

Nash, Oklahoma—April 4, 1946

fifty-two years later

I rose before dawn, pulled aside the lace curtain, and looked through the windowpanes at my land. The night's rainstorm dappled the glass, blurring the dimly lit golden expanse. I swung my morning robe round my shoulders and straightened the quilt over Stot's feet, the muted rose and clover squares wrapped round his ankles. I strode through the screen door, scooting the salt crystal over as a doorstop, then walked through my orchard and the gardens I'd planted with my children after the dust bowl, past the cedar bench Stot had carved for our fiftieth anniversary, beyond the barn and into the wild grasses of my prairie. I stood with the winds lashing my skirts about my ankles, the air filled with dew, and waited for sunrise.

The sun broke over the horizon, golden light slashing through the blackjacks, the navy sky weakening to mulberry. I bent and touched the soil, murmured good morning to the earth, to all the sisters who'd walked these grasses stretching back before history.

Deep, below the surface, a pulse responded along my feet. *My stories are endless, endless*. All those who told tales said humanity, with their uncontrollable hunger, would devour the earth. But they didn't know the earth as I did—she wasn't one to surrender. I stood and turned homeward. Time to work. On the morrow, Magnolia was driving down for a visit. While today, my daughter Gail and my grandchildren were coming over from their homestead on the other side of the wildwood. And Verla, she always wanted to sit with me below the orange trees and talk of flowers.

My life began again with this land. I'd come to Oklahoma broken and angry, plagued by regret and chased by memories. I'd fought the dust and the wind, the turmoil and the fires, and I had emerged anew. I tell my daughters and my granddaughters of my adventure into the great unknown—of the epic race and of those early days, and I hope they tell their daughters and their granddaughters, but mostly I tell the story to remind myself. Memory is such a thin, shifting thing. The memories of our ancestors a haze that bleeds—our stories and our pains stretch past our lives and into the next.

And so I tell my story so they will remember. I tell my story so I remember. And what I remember? The land returned me to myself.

The land was the story. The land was always the story.

Settle on in, she has many tales to tell.

Minnie Leveretta Hoopes and James Solomon Umstott Tharp were married for forty-five years. They had four children, whom they raised on their land in northwestern Oklahoma, and many descendants, including the author of this novel, who is their great-great-granddaughter.

Author's Note

It was in my grandmother's sitting room, a light-filled space of tall windows, her blue floral rocker, and an ivory fireplace, where I first heard of Minnie Hoopes. It was just us two. My grandma Verla is generous and whip-smart, but she's also delicate, orderly, polished. Not the sort you'd imagine racing off into the wilderness with a six-shooter strapped to her waist. I asked my grandma to repeat herself, as I'd never heard this family lore before.

Our ancestor did *what*?

She told me the story of her grandmother, and I immediately saw Minnie: a vivid, clear vision of a woman on a horse, red dust clouding, brown hair caught in the wind, expression full of such desire. I saw her. Glimpsed her motivation and personality—her yearning, her determination. And I just knew: I must tell this story. Her tale was inspiring and thrilling, but I wondered, why on earth would she race off into the Wild West, *alone*? What was she running from?

People often ask why I write certain stories, why the need for this one and not another. My stories are propelled by my characters—I'm struck by a visceral, almost tangible glimpse of a woman and a moment in time. My characters feel more real than even my closest friends. I also write out of vicious curiosity. I was so unbelievably curious as to why a woman would do such a thing: race off into the dangerous unknown of the Oklahoma frontier. Minnie's story called to me as it's based on my ancestor and set in Oklahoma, the place that I've always called home. But I didn't long to write *In the Great Quiet* just because Minnie is my ancestor: I found her circumstances arresting and compelling.

When my grandma first told me of Minnie, I was writing another novel. And so, Minnie sat inside my mind for around five years, until I could write her story. That's one of the wonderful truths about art. I have found that if a story calls out to you—but then must wait—when you return to the idea, it's not gone. I've heard that you must capture an idea or it'll disappear. But that has not been my experience. You may change, but if you return to a story, there is no *dimming* of the idea. And so, Minnie waited. She wouldn't dim. *In the Great Quiet* was just an image, a hope, a deepest yearning, a patient hunger. I longed to uncover more about this ancestor of mine, and then, in 2019, with a stack of books and a pile of notes: I began.

I relish historical research and will absolutely check out five ten-pound books from the library to answer one question about the nature of fabric or a specific mindset of the time. My background as a historian is in the history of mentalities, a specific approach to cultural history that uncovers how those of the past looked upon their world. But of course, a search for worldviews is not concrete or definable. We cannot help but impose our modern constructs on the past, and we can never fully uncover what it was like to live long ago. When we look at the past, especially the women of the nineteenth century, there's a tendency to imagine a proper, quiet, well-behaved woman. Well, this is not at all what I see. They weren't dimmed versions of women. People were just as alive, just as vibrant. I enjoy uncovering specific, odd historical details: a woman carrying cayenne pepper for safety, the fashion craze of wristwatches for "sporty" women, the oral folklore women told round fires. I adore digging into historical research—but *In the Great Quiet* is a work of *fiction*.

In crafting Minnie's story, I did make several historical changes. The first I should note is that my great-great-grandfather James Solomon Umstott Tharp was not, in fact, an outlaw with the alias the Lawman. Minnie and Stot did not marry until a decade after the land rush. This was common, for homesteading women to remain unmarried, as they forfeited their land once wed. I changed this as I wanted to capture Minnie's love story during the timeline of the rush. From there, I crafted Stot entirely from my imagination. Minnie's brothers were not, by all accounts, as I depicted them. Minnie was probably close with her brother Ezra, as they lived together often until she married, even opening a county store together around the turn of the century. Any unfavorable depictions of Minnie's brothers were to explore themes of the novel. The 1890s was a rough time for women, with many cruel and chauvinistic men, and I wanted to capture that nuance of culture. I drafted *In the Great Quiet* in 2020, during the first part of the Covid epidemic, and was personally interested in exploring that feeling of failure by those you should be able to trust. I write to know what I think, and I am absolutely exploring what I do not understand about human nature in the stories I write. A tale for another time, perhaps.

I tried to be historically accurate with clothing, food, home goods, farmwork, outlaws, cultural trends, and everything I could uncover through historical research. Any errors and misrepresentations are my own. I did consciously allow a few historical inaccuracies: Crosswords were not yet invented in 1893, but quiet evening activities were prevalent, such as needlepoint, dictionary games, and word games such as rebuses or acrostics. My grandma shared a memory of Minnie enjoying crosswords. The phrase "get the hell out of Dodge" was not used until the 1950s. This iconic phrase resonated in a certain moment of Minnie's story. Minnie did not grow up with a younger sister or cousin named Magnolia. I had already imagined *In the Great Quiet* as a story exploring sister relationships before I researched Minnie's historical life. Most of my close female relationships are with my cousins from my Hays family, Minnie's line, and the relationship between Minnie and Magnolia was a nice homage and nod to my own heritage.

If you would enjoy reading more from this time period, some of my favorite historical resources for women homesteaders were the first-person interviews found in the Works Projects Administration archive and the first-person narratives recorded in *The Last Run: Kay County, Oklahoma 1893.* I also particularly enjoyed H. Elaine Lindgren's *Land in Her Own Name: Women as Homesteaders in North Dakota*, which is inspiring and full of anecdotes and quotes from women homesteaders, and Linda Peavy's *Pioneer Women: The Lives of Women on the Frontier*, which has many photographs and is an accessible, engaging read. On Goodreads I have bookshelves with over a hundred books about this time period and the historically relevant themes of *In the Great Quiet*.

Popular tales of the 1890s are threaded through the narrative of *In the Great Quiet*—folktales, chapbooks, legends, hymns, literature. In reading the everyday stories and folklore of an age, you glimpse the pulse of the cultural consciousness, the trends of a certain time period. A story of the land of Oklahoma wouldn't be complete without Native tales. But—these are not my tales. I read many Native history books and consulted Native sensitivity readers—but I will always approach Native history and culture from the outside. For Osage history, I fell in love with Osage writer and historian John Joseph Mathew's work, my favorites being *Wah'Kon-Tah: The Osage and the White Man's Road* and *Talking to the Moon: Wildlife Adventures on the Plains and Prairies of Osage Country*. The tale of Prairie Rose told by Niabi and the earth is based on a traditional Lakota and Dakota story. My other favorite Native writers are Muskogee Nation poet Joy Harjo and Potawatomi nature writer Robin Wall Kimmerer.

Writing a historical novel is chasing after figments, a haze of what once was. I hope you enjoyed how I imagined the world of the 1890s and this possibility of how my ancestor navigated her circumstances and her time. Thank you for coming along on this journey with me—it's been an honor.

—Laura Vogt, July 2025

Acknowledgments

Thank you, to all who've carried me on this journey—I couldn't have written this novel without you.

First, to my agent, Catherine Cho. Thank you for believing in *In the Great Quiet*, for seeing its potential beauty from the beginning. This story wouldn't be the same without Catherine: She pushed me further than I thought I could go. Melissa Pimentel, editorial director at Paper Literary, for your keen observations, round after round.

My editor, Emily Freidenrich, for your enthusiasm, hard work, and unwavering hope for this story, from the very beginning. You took on *In the Great Quiet* with such passion and care—thank you. Carmen Johnson, thank you for your support, encouragement, and guidance. Chantelle Aimée Osman, for taking a chance on my novel. Laura Chasen, for your unbelievably astute editorial suggestions: You helped refine and polish this manuscript until it shone. Richard Ljoenes, for the most magical, evocative cover. To production managers Jen Bentham and Angela Elson; copyeditors James Gallagher, Heather Rodino, and Tara Whitaker; the marketing and art departments; my team at Brilliance Audio; and my entire, incredible Lake Union Publishing team. *In the Great Quiet* found the perfect home, and I thank each one of you for your work on this story. Truly, dreams coming true.

My brilliant writing critique group: Mary Maeve McGeorge, Andrea Miles, and Steve Mihalopoulos. You offered insightful, inspiring feedback week after week, year after year. My cousin Lisa

Redmon. She's who I call—for encouragement, ideas, perspective. I couldn't have done this without you. Jaime Vogt, thank you for loving me for decades, for cheering me on, and for caring for my children so I could write. My entire extended family, the Wieses and the Hays, a family full of storytellers and people generous with love; my Vogt family; every barista who said hello; the friends who never stopped asking; my children's teachers; Elizabeth Hays Turner, for your friendship and delusional hope for my writing since I shared my first story at fifteen; my teachers; the librarians and historians who helped with research; Clint and Paige Merritt, for expert medical advice; everyone who's read my work throughout the years and offered feedback; those in the writing community who cheered me on; and all the industry professionals who I've yet to meet on this journey. You are all appreciated.

To my Hays women, Minnie's descendants, for being my sisters, my mothers, my friends. Growing up with so many inspiring, tenacious, and kind women shaped me into who I am. *In the Great Quiet* is a love story to all the women, all the sisters, who've lived life alongside me. Verla and Connie, Cheryl and Cathy and Kelly, Elizabeth and Lisa, Georgia and Haley and Morgan. And to the new generation: my daughters and all your daughters.

In the Great Quiet is a story of ancestry. And so, I thank my grandparents. My grandmother Verla Hays for sharing the story of your grandmother Minnie. For your gentle yet brave ways. Grandma Wiese. You would've loved Minnie. You would've been so proud. Minnie has just your sort of tenacity and gumption—alongside such deep, courageous love. Grandpa Wiese—there is no one like you. You were grander than fiction. And Grandpa Hays. At eighteen, when I shared my dream of being a writer, you gifted me your grandmother's bluebonnet-blue typewriter and told me to head off to a Montana cabin and get at it. My grandparents never paused to consider whether they should encourage me to chase dreams—they just walked alongside me as I figured out who I wanted to become.

My parents, Jay and Connie Wiese. You always supported me, always encouraged me to dream a little bit bigger. Thank you, for your love and your hope. Mom, you're my biggest cheerleader. And, Dad, after one brunch, I'm always ready to keep going, with clarity and resolve.

My children. Hava, thank you for showing me, daily, a more authentic way to be. For loving me, having faith in me, and joyfully living life alongside me. Ariella, you always listen, always celebrate, always encourage. Thank you for your kindness, patience, and love. Michael, thank you for your patience, laughter, and big hugs. You three are my greatest joy.

To the God above. I am thankful for your greater mercies, for the wideness of your love.

And Dustin, my husband. You've loved me for two and a half decades. Thank you for supporting me, making me laugh, and always listening. I wasn't able to get the helicopter scene into this novel but perhaps the next. And sorry I couldn't dedicate this feminist novel to you—but I love you the most.

My readers. Someday, I knew I'd be able to meet you. And I wrote, for you. For me and for you. I hope you loved this story as much as I loved writing it.

Book Club Guide

Verla's Homemade Ice Cream

Verla is Minnie's granddaughter and Laura's grandmother

- 4 junket tablets
- 2 eggs
- 2 cups sugar
- 8 cups milk
- 1 (12-ounce) can Milnot evaporated milk
- 2 tablespoons vanilla
- ½ teaspoon salt

Dissolve the junket in 1 cup of cold water. In a large mixing bowl, beat the eggs, then add the sugar, milk, evaporated milk, vanilla, and salt. Pour into a pan and heat over medium heat to lukewarm. Stir in the junket. Remove from the heat and let sit until the mixture reaches room temperature. Add the mixture to your ice cream maker, then churn according to your maker's instructions. Makes 1 gallon.

Serve with your favorite pie.

Dress Code

Wear what makes you happy. But if you like, a floral or lace maxi dress echoes the world of *In the Great Quiet*. Bonus points if your skirt mimics the sunset hues of the cover.

Games

Literary societies trended on the 1890s frontier, with gatherings often beginning with a playful game.

Charades

Silently act out a phrase until someone guesses. There's a printout of the words available at www.lauravogt.com.

- battling a wildfire
- churning butter
- canteen of sun tea
- Stot glowering
- cayenne pepper
- vaulting onto a horse
- hairpin
- shaking out bedsheets, looking for a rattler
- a tall tale
- gun holster
- shivering during an ice storm
- buried bodies
- hammering up a barn
- Stot adjusting the brim of his Stetson

- voices in the wind
- wildflower
- red fleece petticoat

Once, I dashed across the Prairie, and . . .

This is an add-on memory game based on the 1800s game the Key of the King's Garden. Someone begins by saying, "Once, I dashed across the prairie, and . . ." The next person repeats the phrase and adds on to the story. Each player recites the entire story, including all additions from previous players, then adds their own. If a player forgets part of the sentence or doesn't repeat it exactly, they must perform a "forfeit." A forfeit is something mildly uncomfortable, such as acting out a moment in literature, performing a silly dance, or sharing a secret.

Connect

Please share images from your book club. Tag Laura! Would you like Laura to join your meeting? She adores book clubs and may be available to visit. If Laura is unable to attend, she has a short video on her website discussing a few of the questions below.

- website: www.lauravogt.com
- socials: @lauravogtbooks

Book Club Questions

1. *In the Great Quiet* explores themes of ancestry and belonging. What is Minnie's relationship to her heritage and her role as a woman in her family? Did the narrative encourage you to reflect on your own ancestry? What do you wonder about the women of your own heritage? Have you heard stories of your ancestors? How do you think they endured? What do you suppose they felt and thought?
2. The narrative illuminates the fleeting, transmutable nature of memory and time. How did Minnie's memories influence the plot? Memories are shown to haunt, morph, and alter. What do you think about the idea that memories are indefinite? Have you experienced memories haunting or changing?
3. What was your reaction to reading the earth as a narrator? Did you enjoy this pinch of magic in an otherwise grounded historical world? How would you have imagined earth's voice differently? Share your thoughts about the prose of *In the Great Quiet*. Feel free to read some of your favorite passages or lines.
4. Minnie lived in an age when women had little autonomy. She raced off into the Wild West in search of a place of her own. What is she seeking? What are her deepest desires? How do these yearnings intersect with notions of feminism? Have you felt similar desires in your own life? What might *In the Great Quiet* be suggesting about how women are portrayed in

history? In what ways is this story feminist revisionist history?

5. Let's talk about Stot. What did you think about him as a romantic lead? Did you like the way Stot loved Minnie?
6. The elemental longing for friendship, community, and belonging is a fundamental thread of *In the Great Quiet*. Why do you think Minnie experiences such agony when her relationship with her sister shatters? How have relationships with women, with sisters or grandmothers or friends, influenced your life? Have you had friendships similar to Minnie and Olive, where you commit to working through the "tricky bits"?
7. *In the Great Quiet* explores characters grappling with their humanity and struggling with the "dark parts" of themselves. How are integrity, honor, and corruption portrayed? Have you had moments where you struggled to hold on to your honor and integrity? Do you believe people can or should change? When friends struggle, when do you choose to walk beside them—and when do you walk away?
8. Are you similar to Minnie? How so? Would you have raced off into the Wild West alone? Why or why not?
9. In ways, *In the Great Quiet* is a love letter to the earth. What is climate fiction, and would you place this novel in that category? How do the structure, world-building, and nature descriptions explore the earth as a character and humanity's treatment of the earth?
10. Alone on the prairie, Minnie grapples with her sanity. How do her perceptions of time, memory, and folklore influence her thoughts? What is the function of the novel's themes about fantasies, storytelling, insanity, and reality? Have you experienced moments where you felt like your grip on reality had weakened or fractured?
11. How do you understand the title of *In the Great Quiet*? The narrative explores the interplay of isolation and community. What is the function of these themes? Share how you imagine

the phrase "in the great quiet." Does your life feel quiet or loud? In friendships, do you feel more comfortable in quiet moments or those of noise?

12. *In the Great Quiet* illuminates the religious culture of the 1890s, exploring how Minnie grapples with spirituality and personal honor. Did you relate to Minnie's fumbling to understand the cosmos, or are you more like her parents, assured in what they know about eternity and the world? How would you describe Minnie's understanding of realms beyond the visual world?
13. Aliases, distortions, and creating one's own identity are themes in *In the Great Quiet*. How do Minnie's questions about story versus truth relate to today? Can you see a parallel between the aliases of the 1890s and the trends on social media today? Are you concerned with authenticity and how you actively know and then share your "true self" with others?
14. Minnie encounters many different friendships: Magnolia and Lark, Olive and Niabi and Stot, her brothers and her parents. Share how these characters are distinct from one another. In what ways does each character impact Minnie's life, and what does she learn from her various relationships? How do the idyllic friendships of her youth impact the relationships she builds as an adult? Although Minnie races into the wilderness determined to build a life alone, she's always searching for home. Do you find it fundamental to human nature to always be searching for home?

About the Author

Photo © 2025 Laura Vogt

Laura Vogt is a historian, storyteller, and poet. She loves all things wild and beautiful. *In the Great Quiet* is her debut novel. Laura lives in Tulsa, Oklahoma, with her husband and three children. For more information, visit www.lauravogt.com.